The Quinn Moosebroker Mysteries

by

Michael Friedman

Mockingbird-Books Publisher

ISBN 978-0-9860114-3-6

Table of Contents

Introduction

By Maria Jordan

In 1971, when I was ten years old, I was inexplicably drawn to '*McMillan and Wife*' on television. For six seasons, San Francisco attorney Stuart McMillan (Rock Hudson), now Commissioner, solved some of the cities most baffling crimes with his sweet, but silly wife, Sally (Susan Saint James).

In my thirties, I began a love affair with movie classics. I discovered the detective couple Nick and Nora Charles, played on the screen by William Powell and Myrna Loy, for six charming '*Thin Man*' films from 1934 - 1947.

Both of these unforgettable couples had staying power. Week after week...movie after movie...I couldn't wait to see what madcap mystery and adventure the respective husband and wife team would find themselves embroiled in... and how it would all turn out. The stories were truly character driven and based on mutual trust and love, mixed with a splash of fun.

Enter Michael Friedman, an author who draws the reader directly into the scene, that is *the scene of the crime...* in The Quinn Moosebroker Detective Series. I formed an instant connection with retired detective, Quinn Moosebroker and his leading lady, Betty Atwood.

In the opening story, '*2nd Street Playhouse Mystery*', Quinn's daughter, Kate, plays matchmaker for her father with the charmingly intuitive Betty. An evening at the neighborhood theater performance turns into a night to remember... filled with murder, intrigue, blackmail and some rather candid photography. It did not, however, take a detective to see that Kate had cooked up a true *love connection...*! Stage right... stage left...and it was becoming clear that Quinn and Betty were partners in *crime...**solving*** that is!

Quinn and Betty are next called to investigate the missing manuscript of '*Night of the Falling*' by Henry Farley, the most coveted piece of writing in English literature, when murder came calling on Big Jim Brady, the richest man in Clearview Terrace. This mystery takes readers into the world of books....from the publishing to the selling of first edition rare books and valuable manuscripts. With plenty of suspense, adventure and even some danger tossed in, Quinn and Betty move in even closer... to close the book on this case!

'*He Dreamt of Murder*' is the next and perhaps most personal story for Betty. Quinn overhears a mysterious dream in a barber's shop that takes them on a miraculous journey involving Betty's past -- straight to the USMC in Camp Lejeune, Jacksonville, NC. In the end, a cold case is brought to the front burner, and the leading couple is sizzling - hotter than ever.

Going home was not in the plans from NC, as *'The Radio Players Club Mystery'* begins. Quinn takes Betty to Allentown on a very personal journey to visit past demons surrounding events leading to his early retirement with a medical discharge due to a gunshot wound from the line of duty. Along the way, the two adopt an adorable stray terrier they name Duncan - Waffles and a workable *proposal* is reached.

'The Case of The Chocolate Girl' starts off as Quinn and Betty find an unlikely treasure at a local thrift shop that takes them into the beautiful but murky world of art. Unaware that evil tendrils from Allentown are on their trail, this adventuresome couple leave Duncan - Waffles with Kate, as they journey from London to Paris to Lake Como to discover the rightful owner of this original work by Jean Etienne Liotard. The concluding chapter will have you reaching for your tissues - blame it on the romantic backdrop of Italy...!

All clues have led you to this point. What are you waiting for...? Stop by and meet Quinn and Betty for yourself at the *Frosty Mug* tavern...! It would be a *crime* if you didn't!

The Quinn Moosebroker Mysteries

A 2nd Street Playhouse Mystery

Thin, Red and Deadly (1)

Retired Detective Quinn Moosebroker set down his paint brush and palette as he noticed it was time to get ready for the play. His well-meaning daughter, Kate, had arranged for him to take the widow Mrs. Atwood to a play tonight. *She means well*, he thought. But felt very unsure if this was a good idea.

A knock at the door of his studio told him that he was pushing the hour too closely and he must hurry to get ready. He turned and walked away from his afternoon in Venice to see Kate in the doorway standing there with a perturbed look on her face. She had assumed the role of his protector, even though it was unclear to him what he needed protecting from.

Quinn stepped through the door patting his daughter on the shoulders with his thick hands and gave her a smile of appreciation. He was a large man and some labeled him dimwitted because he spoke so little.

In his room, his blue suit was waiting on the bed. Quinn scratched the back of his head. This was a local play at the 2nd Street Playhouse Mystery Theater. *Why the suit?* Then he remembered Mrs. Atwood. He frowned then pushed the thoughts aside.

He dressed quickly and as he was leaving he gave Kate a kiss on the cheek.

She called, "Have fun tonight. And don't solve the mystery of the play and tell Betty the ending before the end of the second act." She returned to her room to finish getting ready for her date.

He had heard that Blake Knightly the owner of the local bookshop was the playwright. Quinn had met Blake when he first moved to Clearview Terrace from the city. Quinn was pleased that there was a constant supply of new titles at Blake's shop. Quinn would visit because he was allowed to smoke his pipe and talk about books and writing and even art. Blake even kept a bottle in his lower desk drawer for such occasions if they occurred late in the evening.

The theater group was made up of a dozen or so locals. They were mostly older creative types filing in the boredom of their daily existence. The theater drew the attention of some of the younger crowd for exactly for the same reason. There were opportunities for tech types for sound and lighting. An apprentice carpenter could learn a great deal in a hurry putting together the demands of the stage settings. Millie and Brad would go on hunting trips into the city to scout thrift stores for items for costumes and were very good at finding unique items.

Millie ran the coffee shop and Brad was the local photographer who was known to take discrete boudoir photographs using the theater stage props for his clients

Detective Moosebroker swung open the double doors of his one car garage. His heart always skipped a beat when seeing his partially repaired 1946 Chrysler Town and Country, affectionately known as a

Woody. Kate's emergency dried up the restoration fund, but he was very pleased with the interior. The exterior received many compliments but he had plans and those plans were set aside. He put the key in the ignition and listened to the purr of the engine. He shifted the lever on the column into first gear and drove out of the garage, braked, turned off the ignition and closed the garage doors. He found pleasure in taking the car from the garage. *It's the little things* – he told himself.

He pulled out onto Maple Ave towards Mrs. Atwood. He reminded himself to address her as Betty rather than Mrs. Atwood. They had agreed to begin the evening early with coffee at Millie's Café a couple of blocks from the 2nd Street Playhouse Mystery Theater. They would look through the windows as they walked the Antique and Artist District from the Café.

His mind drifted to the Cobalt blue oil paint he was using for the canals of Venice and the pleasant afternoons spent there with his wife years ago. He pulled to the curb and listened for the curb finder. Climbing out he grabbed a rag from under the seat and ran it over the chrome of the side mirror, stooped, straightened his tie and tossed the rag back under the seat.

Mrs. Atwood, Betty was sitting on the edge of her sofa. Her new Shamrock green dress made her feel young. This is the first time she had been out with a man since her husband of twenty-five passed away. She had been ready for an anxious hour.

Quinn walked up the flower-lined walk. He thought that he needed to talk to his daughter Kate. He had let his arm be twisted but thought, *Just this once.*

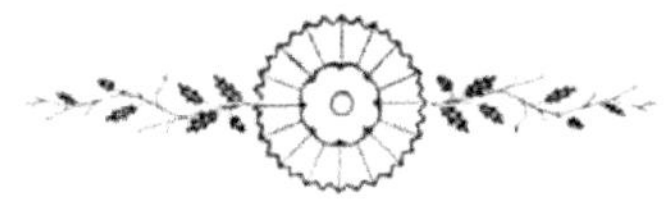

Quinn noted the cosmos that lined the walk were color matched on both sides of the brick walk. By the time, he made it to the door he had a warm feeling. Feeling like a fourteen year old, he knocked on the door. Betty took a quick deep breath and opened the front door.

"Hello Mrs. ah, Betty. Hello, Betty." Quinn managed.

"Hello," Betty said, extending her hand for a handshake.

So far so good; they both thought simultaneously.

"Oh, my word; would you look at that car." The words escaped her lips before she could properly formulate the thought. "My George liked old cars. Sometime let me show you his 1960 MG. He loved that car. He would reach over the door and strike a match on the asphalt to light his cigar. Man had burn holes in all his shirts. He was never happier than when driving that car."

Quinn immediately liked George. "Yes, I would like to see it." He opened the door to the passenger side and watched her sit and arrange her dress out of the way. Then he closed the door.

Quinn and Betty arrived and parked in the parking lot near the round-about where four gray haired men with ponytails had their band equipment arranged and were playing an old Seals and Croft tune to the crowd that was milling about at the evenings farmers market gathering.

As they approached the café Quinn witnessed a fierce right slap to the face of a middle-aged man from a young woman in the doorway. The man turned rubbing the side of his face and walked directly across the street toward the theater while the woman grabbed a hanky from her clutch purse and cried into it as she rushed away in the opposite direction.

Betty waited for Quinn to open the door for her as they entered the café. Quinn made note of the description of the young woman and the middle aged man. Quinn made note of lots of little details.

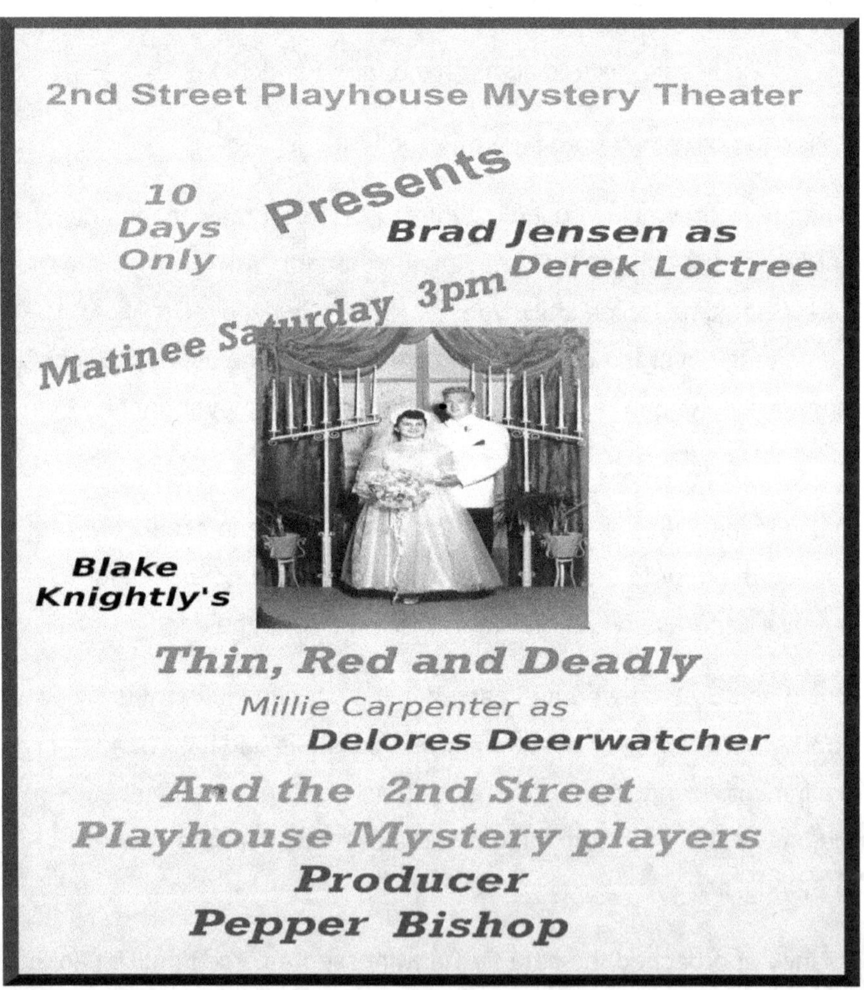

Mary Helen rushed through the cast entrance door and to the dressing room. She was thrilled to find one of the makeup tables free. She hurriedly slipped off her shirt and skirt and sat before the makeup mirror and began getting into the character of Morgan the Art Gallery owner. The imperceptible click of a hidden camera recorded her actions once every two minutes.

Gladys, a local hairdresser, rushed in, “Oh, hi Mary.” She quickly took off her shirt and hung it on a hook behind the door. She grabbed a full-length dress which served as her costume and slipped it over her head. She hiked up the skirt portion and shimmied out of her pants.

“Hi Gladys, I’ll be done in a minute.” She gave her ‘face’ a good look and then stood and walked away from the mirror.

“Can you zip me?” Gladys asked then sat quickly, and began her makeup. Once Millie arrived the chair would be taken until minutes before the performance began.

A 2nd Street Playhouse Mystery, Night at the Theater (2)

Jasmine a 23 year old climbed the wooden ladder that was attached directly to the wall with brackets and disappeared into the darkness. She pulled her 100 lb frame up over the top and into 'The Booth' where she overlooked the stage. The control panel consisted of six cassette players attached to a painted piece of plywood with big numbers painted next to them. A lectern was installed for the 'playbook' and had a convenient hole cut into it to hold a soda can. Once she climbed into that booth she was there for the evening. There was no getting out of it.

The play book not only had the script but every prompt throughout the play and where the sound effects were to come in. Jasmine sat on a stool in the dark with a small lamp whose light just illuminated the control panel and lectern.

Pepper Bishop was no longer a young man, but he still had a youthful demeanor. Tonight he wore black slacks and white pullover long sleeve shirt that flared out at the wrists and had a ruffled V neckline. Black patent leather shoes and a gold pinkie ring accompanied his ensemble. He walked to center stage and called, "Jassie? You set?"

"I'm set." Her melodic voice came from the recesses above the buildings restrooms. She had aspirations, and she had been made promises; tech was not always going to be her assignment.

Pepper mentally checked off 'Jassie is in The Booth' and walked to where a 3 n 1 can of oil was stashed and grabbed it to oil the casters on the reversible wall used in Act one and then again Act three. He noticed a squeak at last dress rehearsal and wanted everything to go right on opening night.

Jimmy and Annie, two Clearview Terrace High School seniors, arrived dressed head to toe in black that included black sneakers. They were the stage hands this evening. They also knew every line of the play and could feed them to anyone that had a moment lapse. They told their friends they both appeared on stage twice in tonight's performance. They did not tell their friends that no one could see them.

Pepper walked into the dressing room. Gladys, who played the unnamed flower shop girl outside the Mary Helen's Art Gallery, was finished with her makeup and just sat in a chair by the door waiting. "Hi Gladys, break a leg tonight."

"Thanks Pepper. Everyone here?"

"I am making the rounds now. Everyone is supposed to be here by now. They all know 5:00 pm on play nights."

Brad walked into the dressing room behind Pepper. "Hello guys. How is everyone doing tonight?" He began unbuttoning his shirt. He had a practiced smile placed on his face.

Gladys and Pepper left him to get ready. Brad reached back and flipped the lock on the door. He lifted and turned the mirror to the right, off its mount and set it on a chair. A recess held the camera with timer attachment. He lifted them out flipped the back of the camera open and exchanged film cartridges. This took under a minute. He returned the mirror to its place, unlocked the door and continued to change into costume.

The evening was beautiful. There were people browsing the shops as well as the Farmers Market. The temperatures from the heat of the day had broken. A very slight breeze rustled through the tree lined street. The city had changed out the globes to old style street lamps along this section of town. At dusk, the twinkle lights would automatically come on and the trees looked like they were filled with magic.

The figure dressed in dark slacks, bomber jacket, and a dark ball cap pulled down tight popped out the window glass of the door in the alley, reached through and let herself in. She walked down the corridor of suites until she reached, Brad Jensen Photography. She pulled the pry bar from the jacket and with more force than necessary broke the lock from the jam.

Inside she went to the desk and pried the top drawer open and retrieved the key to the locked file cabinet. Once unlocked she opened the drawer marked L-M-N and started reading tabs. She found what she wanted then another name jumped out at her. She stuffed both the files and the pry bar in her jacket and left the building.

She quickly walked to the end of the alley, took off the cap. Her hair fell around her shoulders. She tucked the cap into the waistline of her pants and walked to her green VW bug parked a block away. She opened the hood, glanced around and dropped the pry bar, two files, and ball cap into truck, took off the jacket and covered them and closed the trunk. *Mission accomplished.* She told herself and did a little dance to the car door.

Her adrenaline was up. She pulled from the curb and headed to her new favorite haunt the Frosty Mug a local beer and sandwich joint. In her mind, she repeated again and again: *No more blackmail payments.*

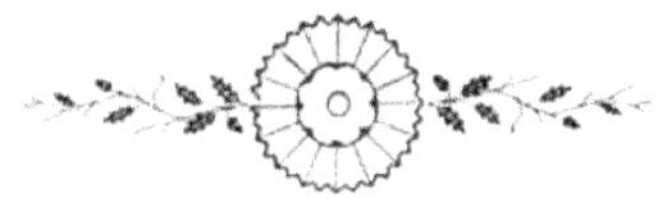

Quinn turned his head and looked west; he thought he heard the familiar sound of a VW bug. Quinn and Betty crossed the street and joined the people in a cluster waiting to enter the theater. Quinn noted the pullover knit sweaters and tweed sports coats on many of the older males in the group. And the blue jeans, loafers and sports coats on the younger males in the group. He thought they must all be from the college.

They entered the velvet colored lobby and looked at the billboards arranged around the room. There were billboards from past performances and for future performances. It appeared that the leading roles were rotated between three couples.

There was not assigned seating in the audience of the 100 seat auditorium. Betty went half way down the red carpeted walk and went to the center of the row followed by Quinn.

A 2nd Street Playhouse Mystery, The Artists (3)

The theater lights in the auditorium flickered representing something was about to happen. Pepper Bishop stepped out from behind the curtain and took center stage.

"Ladies and Gentleman, good evening. Thank you for joining us here tonight at the 2nd Street Mystery Theater. We have a play written by a local writer this evening; our own Blake Knightly the owner of our local bookshop." He put his hands together, as in prayer, "Please no eating in the auditorium and please do not take pictures. Again, thank you." And then he disappeared behind the curtain.

The lights in the auditorium went dark and the curtain opened to the sound of broken glass. The audience viewed a scene of an old kitchen in the background a broken pane of glass.

A hush fell over the audience as the fidgeting came to a stop.

Derek Locktree is sitting in front of an easel with his back to the audience. A partially blank canvas with a photograph pinned to it. Dolores, who was sitting at the kitchen table in a nightgown with a bottle in front of her, wears a wry smile.

Derek: "Why do you insist on throwing your drink though the window when you are angry? You know it takes me hours to get the window repaired."

Dolores: "Good, those are hours that you are not painting those pictures that no one buys."

Derek stands.

Derek: “Let me get a broom. Watch your feet; I don’t want you to hurt yourself. And your publisher called. She said you were late with your submission. Go grab up some of those wrinkled pages on the floor, smooth them out and send them along. She will publish anything you send to her. Your adoring fans await.”

Dolores: “At least I have fans. When is the last time you sold a painting? When is the last time someone lifted your painting and smiled in contemplation of buying? I am tired of paying all of your bills. If it weren’t for me, you would starve.”

Derek: “Yes perhaps, but I would starve in Paris or better yet Rome. Just because you scribble a few poems that people buy does not mean you are more an artist than I."

Dolores goes to the cupboard and bends to lift a dustpan then kneels as Derek sweeps the shards of glass into the pan. She empties the pan and returns to her chair after retrieving another glass.

Derek reaches on the floor and unwrinkled one of many pieces of paper there. He reads aloud the words scribbled in ink across the page:

Kiss me sweet

As the midnight hour chimes

Let me hear my name

brush across your lips

in a whisper

Hurry the time is near

my lips move slowly

there is breath for only

One last 'I love you.'

He turns to Dolores:

De: "You know there is a war going on inside your head. I don't know which way to bet. One minute you are berating me and now I see you have written a poem wishing for my last breath."

In the booth above Jasmine turns a page. She pushes the Play button on cassette number two and the sound of a phone fills the auditorium.

Dolores walks out of the scene into the bedroom stage right.

Derek reaches on the floor and scoops up the rest of the pages there. He smoothes them out and stacks them the best he can. He is reading another poem as Dolores returns.

Do: "That was my publisher. She is really mad that I missed the deadline. I have got to get her something and soon."

Derek flips through a stack of paper quickly glancing at them. He takes two and holds them out to Dolores.

De: "Include these two they are very good. People will be happy to pay you for such beautifully expressed thoughts like these."

Dolores takes them; then reaches for the rest of the stack.

Do: "My adoring fans will be happy to pay for all of these. Who do you think you are? You splash around a little paint on a canvas and call yourself an artist. I create. You smear oily colors."

As Dolores walks to the right Derek pours himself a drink. A spotlight is cast upon Dolores' figure, but her face is in shadows. Derek spots another piece of paper near her chair leg picks it up and reads it to the empty stage.

On the way to somewhere else

The red flag popped up

my time expired

our coins too few

to bring us to the end of time

My love short changed

meter reads expired

vacate the space

or pay for

unfilled emptiness

this place once dear

my carriage hauled from your curb

Derek faces the audience with a furrowed face. Dolores steps through the door into the bedroom and closes it behind her. The lights of the stage dim.

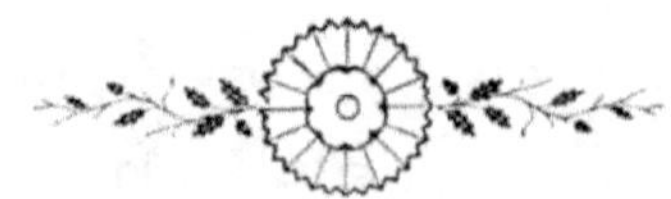

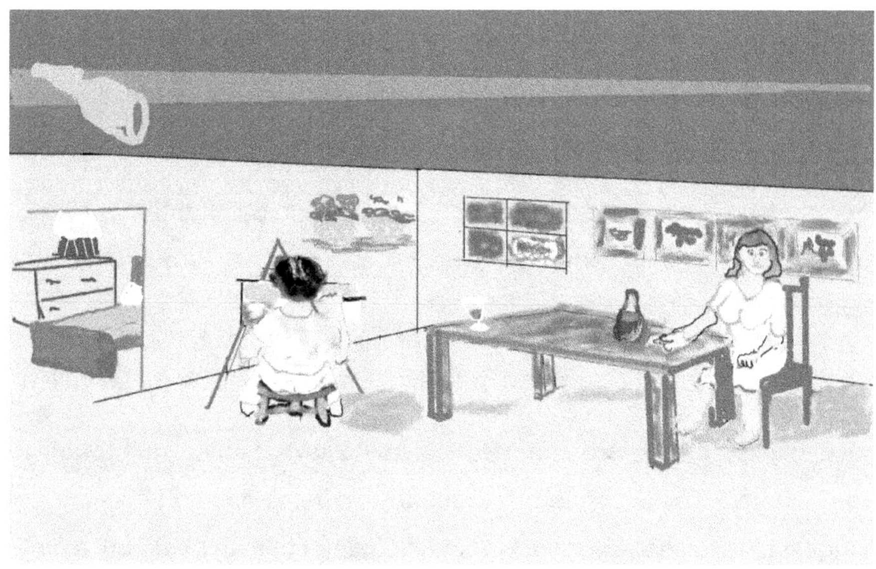

Betty shifted slightly in her seat. She moved her hand and placed in on top of Quinn's which rested on the armrest. Quinn did not turn his head, but a hint of a smile moved across his face. He was not enjoying the show. It was too melancholy for his taste. He shared a love of painting with Derek and wondered if Blake had somehow modeled this character after him in some small way. His mind drifted off wondering who Dolores would be modeled after.

The stage went dark and Jimmy and Annie unseen in black moved the wall built on casters a one hundred and eighty degree turn. When the lights returned, Derek was standing in front of Mary Helen's Art Gallery standing near a full figured woman in front of a flower cart near the entry. Her Calico dress was embroidered with lace and she framed it with an apron.

De: "Has anyone offered to paint you? I would most certainly like to paint you."

Flower girl: "No one has offered until now. I will always remember the offer….I"

She was interrupted as Mary Helen opened the door. He stepped through and the lights dimmed and the wall rolled out of the way by Jimmy and Annie. Flower girl moved her cart off stage through the back curtain.

Lights returned and Derek and Mary Helen were standing in the gallery.

MH: "Derek, get in here I need to talk to you. What have you brought me? You are empty handed. A client arrived yesterday and spent the longest time looking over your work. He did not buy anything but said he would be back. How are you? Listen to me go on?"

De: "He didn't buy one thing? I am getting a lot of pressure. It has been awhile since you sold anything I have brought you."

MH: "Darling these things take time. You are brilliant; you just need to be discovered. One patron can get the ball rolling then their friends will come in and also buy."

De: "I need an advance. What can you do?"

Jassie turned the page in her playbook. The lights faded and Mary Helen and Derek left the stage. Jimmy and Annie turned the Gallery wall around. On the back was a desk in an office building. Dolores was talking to a full figured woman in a business suit. Quinn noted with amusement that it was the flower girl from the last scene.

Pepper Bishop walking by the dressing home door grabbed his eye and blinked hard. He opened the door and made his way to the dressing table and mirror holding his eye. He sat and leaned close to the mirror to see what was in his eye. From behind with his black hair and white shirt, he looked a lot like Derek Locktree.

The door of the dressing room swung slowly open and an arm reached through……

A 2nd Street Playhouse Mystery, The Murder (4)

The sound seemed to reach Quinn's ears a full second before the rest of the audience reacted. Betty could tell he had heard it earlier than she had by the look on his face when she turned to him as her hand gripped the top of his hand.

The back row seemed to rise at once and made their way towards the exits, past the billboards in the lobby the double doors spread and the fast moving people spilled out onto the street and toward their cars. The audience emptied efficiently with the sounds of sirens in the distance.

Quinn sat; Betty by his side was unsure what to do. She knew he drove, there was no car waiting in the lot for her. Quinn noted the shuffling sounds behind the scenes. He rose and noted a flutter of dust drifting from overhead. The sirens were drawing closer.

"I'll meet you at the car." Quinn addressed Betty.

"Like hell," was her response as they made their way cautiously toward the four steps that led up to the stage. This was the first time Betty held a stage by herself. Quinn had made his way backstage. She was in awe.

The tires screeching to a halt in front of an almost empty parking lot and nearly empty theater made Betty turn and face the empty chairs. What the police officer saw as he entered was Betty standing in the middle of the stage. Betty turned and pointed backstage.

The young officer ordered her to stay put. Betty was having the time of her life.

Blake Knightly was too nervous to go to the premiere of Thin, Red, and Deadly. He sat in the back room of his shop. There was a bottle of scotch on his desk and a half empty glass sat next to it. He paced a bit then thought to do some work. He lifted a mixed case of Private Eye, Unrestricted Confessions and Detective Confidential that had arrived via mail from one of his New York contacts earlier in the day.

He tore open the lid and lifted the glossy covered magazine that some of his clients had been requesting that he stock. He read some of the titles: '**Where Does She Go at Night?**' and '**Is Your Wife Seeing another Woman?**' He dug down and grabbed a copy of Detective Confidential, took both magazines and went and sat at his desk.

He sat straight up in his chair when he reached page 34. There was Gladys from the cast with her shirt off applying some makeup to her face. Her arms seemed strategically placed, blocking full view of her, but two things were clear. It was Gladys and she had no shirt on. He set the magazine down slowly and thought, *What is Pepper Thinking?*

He hurriedly flipped through the second magazine. He recognized the theater backdrop in one of the pictures but the middle-aged unclad woman wearing only a plumed hat was unknown to him.

He rummaged around and located the invoice. He could not sell these items in his shop and had to see if he could return them. He grabbed his jacket and headed for the theater.

Katie ordered her second frosty mug of tap beer and was feeling very good about herself. In the morning, she would contact her friend Jassie and tell her the good news. *Not Good news*, she thought *Great news*. She stood and went over to the jukebox and dropped in a quarter for two songs. When the music started, she danced to 'Diamond Girl' on the parquet floor by herself.

Young Officer Harcourt called in the murder to the station. He gathered names and addresses of the cast who were still there. Before he had finished Detective DeLaMonte lumbered in. Quinn recognized him immediately. All he knew about DeLaMonte was he arrived in Clearview Terrace after a quick departure from the New Orleans Police Department and he had taken the job for less money than the city was prepared to offer.

“Get the names and addresses of all these people.” He shouted towards Harcourt. He saw Quinn and asked him, ‘What are you doing here? Get out of here.”

Quinn smiled to himself and walked out and collected Betty. They both left through the front door.

“We can’t go home yet,” Betty told him. “Do you feel like a beer? I am so excited. I hear there is a place just out on the highway called “The Frosty Mug.”

“I have heard of the place. Sure let’s go.” Quinn told her, while in he went over the crime scene in his mind. He noted the position of the body, the contents of the room, the hall leading to the room, the open ceilings, and the cracked mirror where the body fell against it. He noted everything.

When Officer Harcourt finished with the cast, he walked back out to the stage to get the last name of the people that were there but found the stage empty.

“Ain’t you done yet?” DeLaMonte fired at Harcourt.

“Yes, Detective, I am done. I am going to go get the crime scene tape.” He turned and left.

Brad Jensen’s heart was racing. Pepper was his silent partner or rather he was Pepper’s.

The ambulance arrived and Brad took the opportunity to slip away. He

went directly to Pepper’s mobile home in the Shady View Mobile Home Park. He drove right passed the Frosty Mug. When he arrived, he had to force a side window and climb through for entry.

He chanced flipping the lights on. He never did care for Pepper's taste. The lime shag rug and orange vinyl bean bag did not spell 'class' in his book. There were bottles of cheap booze on the kitchen table and Playboy magazines were mixed here and there with a variety of Detective magazines. On the wall behind an easy chair, there hung two paintings of nudes on black velvet and hanging from the ceiling next to them was a rain lamp.

Brad found what he was looking for in the bedroom. On the floor of the closet was a two drawer filing cabinet filled with his photography. He did not like this but had to chance it. He lifted the whole filing cabinet and walked out the front door and brought it to his car. He set it down and popped the trunk and stashed it there. He did not bother to go back in. He got into his car and drove away headed for his office.

Blakely arrived at the theater and saw a parking lot with a police cruiser an ambulance and Detective DeLaMonte's olive green Dodge Polara that belonged to the city. Without thinking he entered the side door in time to see Pepper's face being covered with a blanket and the curious gaze of Detective DeLaMonte.

The Frosty Mug

A 2nd Street Playhouse Mystery, The Date (5)

Quinn and Betty walked through the door of the Frosty Mug. "Grab us a seat." Quinn told her and walked to the payphone and slid the phone book from its tray. Bishop, Bishop, Pepper Bishop. He found the address and wrote it on a notepad he carried then returned to find Betty.

What he found was Betty sitting with Katie. He walked over and kissed his daughter on the cheek and sat down. Betty went on, "...it has been so exciting there was a gun shot backstage at the theater and the audience all ran for the exits; except your father and me of course."

The door of the Pub swung open and in walked Brad Jensen. Katie turned abruptly, let out a squeal and in doing so knocked over her beer. Quinn stood as a reaction to getting out of the way of the spilled beer and looked to see what had spooked Katie.

Brad looked in their direction and then continued to the bar. He needed a drink and he needed it badly.

Katie stood and apologized to her Dad and Betty. And used this excuse to excuse herself and hurriedly made her way to the door.

"Let's make this a quick beer," Quinn told Betty. "I have something I want to check on."

"We don't need to sit here and drink a beer. Let's go check on whatever you are going to check on."

"I should drop you home first."
"Oh, come on. Let's go detectiving!" Betty said good-naturedly and took his elbow.

Quinn glanced in the direction of Brad and let Betty guide him to the car.

Quinn found the Shady View Mobile Home Park with ease but had to circle the park twice to find the number. Driving a 1946 Chrysler Town and Country was anything but inconspicuous and in a local trailer court it stuck out like a sore thumb.

He found the unit and pulled as far to the back as possible. The lights were on in the trailer, but Quinn was confident the place was empty. They got out and Quinn saw the window. He walked to it and listened. "I am going in," he said over his shoulder.

"Wait, I am going to need a boost." She looked him straight in the eyes when he turned.

He clasped his hands together and she put her foot in and hiked herself half way through the window. Quinn heard her say, "Give me a little shove."

He planted both hands on her and gave a shove. Betty made an ungraceful landing then got to her feet happy that Quinn did not see her. She stood and lowered her dress from over her head as Quinn as pulling himself through the window.

"Careful not to touch anything," Quinn advised her.

"Plenty of me, touched plenty of that carpet when I came in," she quipped. "What are we looking for?"

"Clues. Look around and see if anything looks out of place. And don't touch anything. The police will be here with a fingerprint guy sometime soon."

Quinn noticed the Playboy Magazines and the Detective Confidential Magazines. The bad art, the bad taste, the bad booze and began to draw a picture of Pepper Bishop.

"In here," Betty called from the bedroom. She was sitting on Pepper's waterbed. "There," she pointed. "Look at the impression in the carpet. Something fairly heavy was sitting there recently and is gone. Nothing in this room would make those markings."

"Good eyes." He told her and spotted what might be just what he came for; an address book. An address book always revealed plenty about a suspect and a victim.

Quinn turned towards the door. He heard cars coming. "Quick the window." He tucked the address book in his pocket.

Betty dashed for the window and went through unceremoniously. Quinn followed. They were in his car and pulling around the back of a neighbor's doublewide when the two police cars arrived with lights flashing.

"A filing cabinet sat there. A short filing cabinet, based on the loud indigo paisley shirts hanging above the spot," Betty ventured.

Quinn glanced over and said, "We'll make a Detective out of you yet." At which they both laughed.

Brad sat nursing his cold brew. His mind was going a mile a minute. He sat and thought through the events of the night. He sat straight up, gulped down the rest of his beer and hurriedly left the Frosty Mug. He pulled out onto the highway and gunned it. He wanted to get that file cabinet out of his car and the only safe place he could think of was his office.

Twenty minutes later he pulled into his reserved parking place in front of the office building and let himself into the hall that led to his suite.

A sweat broke out on his forehead when he saw the door pried open. He pushed the door open and stepped inside and listened. He heard nothing and flipped on the switch.

Glancing around the room, he noticed a file cabinet drawer opened. He went to the desk and saw the drawer had also been pried open. He ran his fingers over the torn wood and knew it was going to be tough to fix.

He picked up the phone thinking to call the police. He laughed at himself and set the phone down.

He couldn't stay. He did not want to be caught with Pepper's files in is trunk. He walked back to his car with even more questions in his mind plus the anger that his office had been broken into. He emptied the files into boxes and returned them to his office. He left the filing cabinet and would dump it before the night was through.

Then it struck him. He had to go and recover his camera from the theater. The last thing he needed was the police to find that camera. The last thing he needed was the cops period.

He drove his yellow Chevelle with two five-inch wide green pin stripes running from the hood to trunk over to Millie's Café. He circled the block twice to get a parking space in front. He wore black slacks and a yellow shirt over a black tee shirt. He walked in and ordered coffee and a sandwich. Being back at Millie's reminded him of the slap he had received earlier in the evening. He had time to kill and Millie's closed in two hours.

Detective DeLaMonte and a police technician walked to the open door of Pepper's Mobile home and called inside. Hearing no one they entered and began their investigation. The technician dusted for prints while the detective walked around looking things over. A pint of Seagram Seven found its way into his suit pocket. He opened the refrigerator; grabbed a beer and opened it. He continued looking around. He flipped open a Playboy then closed it after checking the centerfold. He lifted a Detective Confidential then tossed it back on the table. He lit a cigarette then noticed another copy of the same issue of Detective Confidential.

He called to the technician, "When you are done dusting, gather up these magazines. Something fishy is going on here."
"Take a look at this," the technician called. When DeLaMonte arrived, he pointed to the impression in the carpet.

"Take a few photographs of the place then let's get out of here. I have somewhere I want to be."

Lt. DeLaMonte pulled his car into the shadows of the old train station with a view of the back of the theater. It was an old trick; tried and true. The suspect returns to the scene of the crime.

Brad Jansen stood and walked into the bathroom at Millie's Café. He washed his hands and then popped the window open and climbed through. He immediately took off his yellow shirt and left it on the ground. He crossed the street unseen and walked in the shadows along the side of the old Sunkist packing plant near the train station that ran behind the theater. He stopped short when he saw the green Dodge Polara sitting there ahead of him. Brad was not happy; he ducked down and continued passed the Polara and made his way to the side of the Bicycle Shop and used a dumpster to reach the fire escape ladder.

He made his way quickly over the rooftops that were all joined and let himself in through the maintenance access on the roof of the theater. He entered into what was costume storage and down to the dressing room. He ducked under the yellow police tape in the doorway and moved the mirror. He retrieved the camera, timer and most importantly the film.

He went the long way around behind the Barber Shop back to Millie's, deposited the camera in his car, then went back around, climbed through the bathroom window and put his yellow shirt back on. With any luck no one would know he was gone, he thought.

Sunkist Growe

A 2nd Street Playhouse Mystery, Shark Finn (6)

Quinn pulled to the curb in front of Betty's home.

"This was great." She leaned over and kissed him on the cheek. "Pick me up in the morning when you begin your investigation again. Please." She batted her eyes playfully.

Quinn smiled and told her he would be here about ten.

He left her and drove over to the theater. He pulled his Chrysler Town and Country in front of the barber shop and shut off the engine. He sat there for an uneventful hour watching the theater and then went home.

At 9 am Quinn pulled his car onto the lawn next to a 1967 Blue Javelin. He climbed out of his car and was met by Officer Harcourt on the front porch. Harcourt only wore a wrinkled pair of green fatigue pants. Quinn estimated the age of his daughter on his hip as two years old.

“They are a handful at that age.” Quinn offered.

“They sure are,” Harcourt told him. “Can I help you?”

Quinn looked at the Airborne Wings tattoo on his right arm and a nasty scar across his abdomen.

“Been out two years now.” He told Quinn when he saw him looking at the tattoo and scar.

“That had to be tough duty.” Then he went on. “There were not many people in the back of the theater when you got there.”

“Yes, and you were one of them.”

Quinn took out an ID that showed he was retired from the Police Force upstate.

“What can I do for you?” Harcourt asked.

“Were you in the theater in school?” Quinn inquired.

“ME?” Harcourt gave a laugh. “No, I went to a small school. So I was on the football team. Seems I was out of school for less than a year when me and two buddies joined the Army. You know patriotic duty and all that.”

“I was in the audience. Those walls did not move themselves around the stage. Did anyone mention any others who may have been backstage?"

"No, no they didn't." Just then a long haired brunette with green eyes, barefoot and wearing a sundress came through the door carrying a baby a few months old. "Millie would know, over at her Café. She is part of the cast at the theater; they must all know each other."

"Everything alright?" Harcourt's wife asked.

"This is Glenda, my wife. But she goes by Eden. I think it suits her."

Eden lifted her free arm and rubbed Harcourt across his bare back.

"Nice to meet you." He said to Eden. "Thanks, thanks for your help," he told Harcourt. "Enjoy the rest of your morning."

"Watch out for DeLaMonte, he is dangerous. He will want to wrap this up quick and there are so few names to pick from." Harcourt told Quinn as he walked away.

Quinn got into his car and headed off to meet Betty. For a moment, seeing this young family, he missed his youth.

Betty was waiting by the curb when Quinn arrived. She wore tan slacks today an emerald green blouse and comfortable shoes. After last night's adventure, she did not dare wear a skirt or dress. '*No telling how many windows I am going to climb through today,*' she told herself.

"Where to?" she asked as she climbed in.

"Breakfast," she was told and they headed for Millie's Café. "You look nice."

Betty beamed.

Betty and Quinn ordered blueberry pancakes and interviewed Millie between cups of coffee. She confirmed that there was a name that was not on Officer Harcourt's list, though she offered no explanation.

"Why Jimmy Glen's name isn't there. He is in high school. His daddy is a Police Officer over in Henley. His Momma comes in here after church on Sundays. Does that help you? She is so proud of her son. He's on the Gymnastics team, went to State Finals last season." She leaned down and patted Quinn on the hand. "I hope you catch whoever did it. I am still shaken up over Pepper."

Quinn paid the check and left a nice tip. They were out the door when Millie stood straight up and rushed after them. But they were gone. There was another name that was not on the list. She went back inside and poured a customer a cup of coffee.

Quinn turned to Betty, "Feel like taking a ride into the city?"

"Sure," she told him. "We paying a visit to the publishers?"

Quinn reached over and patted her on the knee. "That is exactly what we are going to do." An hour and a half later they pulled into a parking garage near the address he had from Pepper's address book for Private Eye, Unrestricted Confessions. Detective Confidential happen to have the same address.

He knocked on the glass door of the suite and let himself in. The air was so thick with stale smoke that both Quinn and Betty took an involuntary step back. Two men with gray hair sat at wooden desk at typewriter's typing away. Next to each typewriter was a glass ashtray with a mound of cigarette butts in them. They briefly stopped and one pointed to a second glass door that said Editor.

Betty glanced at the 'pin-ups' that were tacked to cork boards around the room. There were also many copies of previous magazine edition covers held with thumb tacks. Quinn and Betty just met the entire staff of the two magazines.

Quinn walked to the second door and tapped it with a knuckle just prior to opening it. The man at the desk had a phone in his hand. He held up one arm with his index finger pointed up indicating give him one minute. "Are the photos on the way or not?" He said into the phone. "This is the second time you screwed up my schedule. OK, ok, get them here." And he hung up. "I'm Felix Finn, they call me Shark. It's a carry over from college and it stuck." He stood and extended his hand. "And you are?"

"Here to ask a few questions about Pepper Bishop. I'm Quinn Moosebroker and this is a friend of mine Betty."

"Pepper? How is Pepper? We go way back. Pull those chairs over and sit." He pointed and waved his hand as the phone rang.

"Yes, the copy will be there this afternoon. Everything else on schedule?" He listened for the answer. "Great, we will be on time for once to the printers." Felix Finn set the phone down. "What can I do for you? Excuse me one minute." He stood walked to the door and opened it. "Ted, Jim called and is looking for your copy."

Quinn heard, "He'll have it right after lunch."

"Open a window in there," Felix said and closed the door and returned to his desk. "Sorry about that. For once we may be on time."

“Pepper is dead.” Quinn put it out there.

Felix plopped into his chair. “That’s too bad. He was my best supplier. The others bring me things that are staged. All their models look stiff as boards, like human manikins. Stiff yah know. Accident?“

“Murder.” Quinn watched closely for a reaction.

“Some jealous flaming lover?” Felix offered. “When did it happen? He owes me a little and one of his models always pumps up my circulation. The magazines I mean.” He added glancing at Betty. “For a guy in this racket he was ok. He will be hard to replace. “

“You don’t know anyone who would want to harm him?” Quinn ventured.

“Pepper, I don’t know anything about his day to day. Every two weeks he would mail me a packet of photographs on consignment and I would send him a small check. I did not have any other contact with him, unless he called asking to send more. He was always short on cash.”

“Can I see the last couple of packets?”

“The last? They may still be on the corkboards in the other room.” The three stood and left the room.

“Did you meet Ted and Martin? Or did they just grunt and point to my door? Monthly they turn in copy as Det. Donovan Strong, Det. Colt Baldwin, Det. Pierce Gunner, Lt. Rocco Cammon, Lt. Damon Harley, Lt. Sander Chance enough to fill two magazines. Not once in the twelve years I’ve known these guys have they used their real name on a story. They use Ghostwriter as an occupation on their IRS forms.”

Betty walked the wall staring at the corkboards while Felix and Quinn walked the other wall. Felix was explaining the art. Betty gulped hard reached up took a tack from a photo and tucked it in her purse while hoping the men were not watching her. No one reacted. She wiped some sweat from the side of her mouth with her thumb and kept walking along the corkboard display.

Quinn, Betty, and Felix ended the walk at the door they first came in. “Anything else?” Felix asked.

“No, that’s all. Thank you.” Quinn shook his hand.

Felix had stopped offering his hand to women years before. So few would reach out and take it.

“I would appreciate a call regarding the funeral if you can.”

Betty and Quinn left and Felix closed the door and shook his head all the way back to his office.

“Our eating schedule is all messed up today. Let’s eat before we head back. My treat, there’s a Deli right over there.” Betty offered.

“Ok,” Quinn said, “What did you find?”

“Let’s talk about that visit over Corn Beef on Rye” Betty took his arm.

Over lunch, Betty told Quinn about the photo she spotted of Katie but made no move to retrieve it. Prickly needles ran across the back of Quinn’s head. ‘*Kate’s emergency,*’ he thought. *‘First light I pay his office a visit.’*

Brad Jensen was in his office waiting for a locksmith. He decided while he was waiting go to his darkroom to develop his film from last night's midnight run.

The locksmith arrived and Brad asked him to take a look at the desk drawer lock also then went back to work in the lab.

'Money Shot' flashed through his mind. He lifted the photo from the chemical tray and hung it to dry. '$5,000.00 No, $10,000.00 kept scrolling across his mind."

All of a sudden he was anxious to get rid of the locksmith but knew he had to wait. He pulled out the phone book and found the number he was looking for. He paced.

With his connection gone it might just be time to leave town.

Detective DeLaMonte arrived at Blake Knightly's Bookstore at 10 a.m. "I have a warrant to search your store," Blake was told. "Go sit over there." DeLaMonte pointed to a chair.

In a matter of minutes DeLaMonte found the case of Private Eye, Unrestricted Confessions and Detective Confidential. This time he picked one up and flipped through the pages slowly. When he reached page 34, a big smile crossed his face.

"You are under arrest for the murder of Pepper Bishop and if you are not guilty of that then, there could be charges for you running a pornography ring. Stand up and turn around. Did he cheat you out of money?"

Blake was handcuffed and removed from his bookstore.

The locksmith finally finished and went on his way. Brad Jensen lifted the phone in his office and then thought better of it. He hung up left his office confirming the lock held and made his way to the phone on the corner of the building.

He dropped in his dime and waited for the dial tone. The phone rang and rang, just when Brad was going to hang up he heard "Hello."

Brad had to take a chance with the voice, "Listen carefully. Meet me at the Benson Avenue Bridge in two hours. Don't even think about not being there. I have a picture of you shooting Pepper Bishop in the back. Are we clear."

The voice said, "Yes, we are clear."

It was a grueling two hours for both parties. Brad sat in his yellow Chevelle in the shade of two Elm trees and watched. Just as the two-hour mark approached a blue Corvair Van with white stripe pulled to the end of the bridge and stopped.

Brad got out and cautiously approached, but he was full of confidence. "You don't have to talk. Just listen." He held the picture up. "This picture and the negative cost $10,000 and you have 72 hours to collect it. Meet me back here in three days at this time with the money or the picture gets mailed to the Police. Are we clear."

"Where am I going to get $10K."

"You'll get it. I have every confidence you will get it. It beats a lifetime in prison. Or you have three days of your life left. You cross me and the state will have you dancing on air." With that Brad turned and walked back to his car.

The Corvair Van pulled a U-turn and raced down the highway. The driver spotted a gas station with a pay phone on the corner and screeched to a stop. After dropping a dime the attendant heard from twenty-five feet away, "Pick-up, Pick-up, Pick-up damn it!"

The phone was slammed into its cradle and the driver got back into the Corvair and drove off.

A 2nd Street Playhouse Mystery, The Shadows (7)

Quinn spent the night fuming over the information Betty had gathered. He was thankful that she was along on that part of the investigation. At 7 a.m., the second Moosebroker in two days was breaking into Brad Jensen's Office. Someone in the building was in; the main entrance was open. Quinn walked to the office door, slid his Montgomery Ward credit card through the jam, between the strike plate and the face plate clearing the cylindrical dead latch. The door swung easily open. It took under a minute.

His ire brought him here. He was not sure exactly what he was looking for. What he did not expect was to wake Brad Jensen, who was asleep on the floor in a sleeping bag. There were boxes of camera equipment packed against the wall.

"Going somewhere?" Quinn began.

"What are you doing here? Who are you? I'm calling..." his voice trailed off. The threat did not even sound plausible to him. "Who are you?"

"I'm the cleaning man. At the moment, it appears I am cleaning up the mess you are in the middle of." He glanced around. He smelled danger. "Do you know a Katie Moosebroker? I want everything you have on her."

Brad swallowed hard and went to the desk and got the key, he opened the filing cabinet's drawer marked L-M-N and flipped through the folders. His face went white, "They are gone. Look there are only a few 'M's" folders there and Kate is not there.

Just then, the office door swung open. Det. DeLaMonte stepped through the door. He was hoping to find Brad for further questioning. He was not expecting to see Quinn. He was immediately angry. "I told you to get out. I meant the case."

DeLaMonte pointed his left index finger at Brad and said, "Stay put." He turned and with his right hand swung and hit Quinn on the side of his head slamming him into the filing cabinet almost toppling it. DeLaMonte's left made a cantaloupe sized indentation in the drywall right behind where Quinn's face was a split second before.

Quinn recovered, planted a foot under himself and planted a solid blow to DeLaMonte's ribs forcing him back two steps allowing Quinn to stand and balance.

DeLaMonte rushed him, arms wide like a crazed bull seeking blood. The arms clasped Quinn and the force of the two bodies left a bathtub sized depression in the drywall. Quinn's arms shot straight up underneath DeLaMonte's and his right elbow came down crushing DeLaMonte's nose sending him down on one knee.

Quinn took two steps back and gave DeLaMonte a mental five count. He watched the blood puddle on the carpet. He picked up his hat and walked towards the door. He turned, still breathing hard, "Brad got away," and left the office.

Jassie held her Genie phone to her ear. "Just because we slept together that one time does not make you a knight in shining armor." There was a pause. "Look, I don't know what to tell you. That's a lot of money. No, I don't have anything like that. No one asked you to do that. You should just run." After another long pause Jassie held the phone away and stared at it like it was a snake. She heard the loud click of the disconnect.

She glanced around her room above a private garage on El Morado Street. She reached under the bed and grabbed her brother's old duffle bag and started throwing her clothes into it. A boy she knew recently asked her to go to Matanchen Bay, in Mexico and just now that sounded like a good idea.

Then she sat on the bed and wondered if she could get her hands on that money. *Sunshine and money, now that is a nice combination*, she thought.

She picked up the phone and dialed. "You guys still going to Mexico?" She listened. "When is that set for?" After a pause she said, "That's perfect. Count me in." She hung up the phone and dialed another number.

"Meet me under the bleachers of the football field tonight at ten. I'll make it worth your while." She hung up, leaned back on her bed as a broad smile crossed her face.

Betty managed a bandage over the cut below Quinn's eye. There was nothing she could do about the eggplant colored bruise forming along the side of his face.

"When you are done let's take a little trip over to the high school. There is still a name we have not talked to yet."

When they got to the front door, Betty handed Quinn the keys to the 1962 MG convertible. "Let's take George's car. It will make you feel much better."

They arrived and made their way to the gymnasium. They found a coach and asked after James Glen.

"Jimmy, he is here every afternoon from three to five. Come back then you will find him on that balance beam." He pointed.

Quinn thanked him. As they walked away the coach said, "Witch Hazel will make that bruise heal faster. Just dab it around the wound."

"Thanks again," Quinn answered.

Let's see if we can find Annie Mackintosh." Quinn told Betty.

After a few inquires, they found Annie in the quad. They approached and introduced themselves. "Can we ask a couple of questions?"

"Sure she told them. I already talked to a Detective. I'll tell you what I told him and that is everything seemed to happen so fast. We moved the set wall when the curtain closed. Then I was to help Gladys and went around the back and that is when the shot was fired. I rushed to the exit then turned when everything got so quiet and went back. I was the first one to see Pepper. At first I thought it was Brad. Then Brad and Millie and Gladys all showed up." She took a breath, "The lights were out, there was a shot and Pepper was dead. That's all I know."

"And Jimmy, where was Jimmy?" Quinn asked.

"Man, no one asked me that. Last I saw Jimmy he was at the other end of the wall moving it out of sight. I did not see him again until school the next day. And even then we didn't talk."

"Thank you for your help," Quinn told her. Annie went back to eating her sandwich and watching the boys go by and thinking about Brad and the promises he made her.

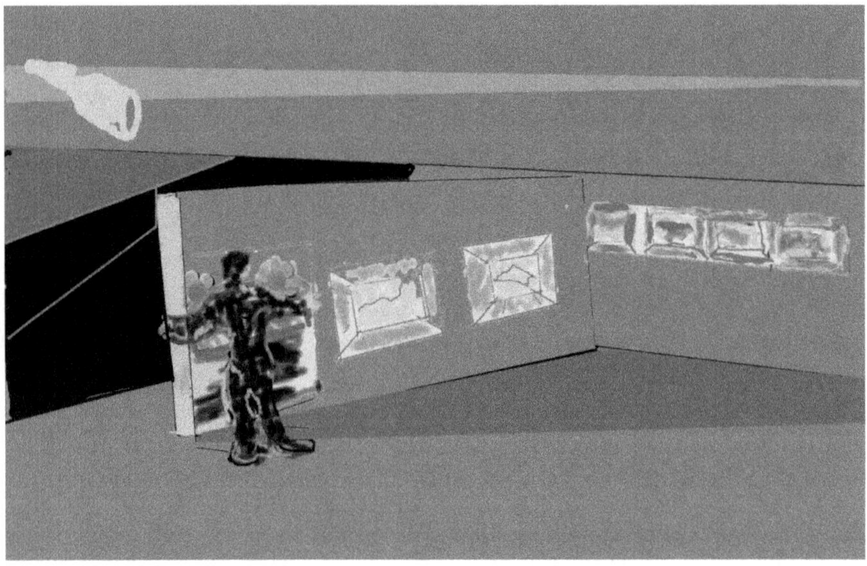

Betty took Quinn's arm as they walked back to the parking lot. She was talking to him when she realized that she did not have his attention. She felt a tremble in his arm as she held it. In a moment, she felt more like she was guiding him through the parking lot rather than walking with him. She looked up into his face to see that million-miles-away look she had seen from time to time throughout her life. A moment later she saw him return as he looked around the parking lot for his car.

"Quinn, here it is. We took George's car. Where did you go?" She asked as they climbed into the red convertible sports car. Quinn had forgotten that is what they used to drive to the school.

"Where to?" Quinn asked.

"Well, your car is parked in front of my house if that helps you at all." She reached over and rubbed him across his shoulder. "You good to drive?"

Blake Knightly stood in front of the police station with his lawyer. He stood there pensively; trying to listen and think at the same time.

"He is just an overly aggressive cop. You have nothing to worry about. Nothing ties you to the murder. And you operate a bookstore so the case of magazines is easily addressed. You'll see, the D.A. won't pursue this case at all. No bail is a very good sign." He put his hand out and Blake took it then the two men parted.

After receiving a phone call at the local hairdressers shop, Gladys got in her car and rushed over to Stu's News Booth across from the Clearview Terrace Credit Union. She bought the last four copies of Detective Confidential that he had. She flipped to the page that her Mother, who had received an anonymous copy, directed her. The blood boiled in her veins as the anger spread through her. She tore the picture of her out of each magazine and ripped them to pieces. The confetti was released from her car window as she headed to the Frosty Mug for her first beer ever before noon.

She hit the accelerator as she drove a dark thought from her mind. For the first time since that horrible day two years ago, she was glad that her Father had passed away. Tears rolled uncontrollably from her eyes.

A 2nd Street Playhouse Mystery, Into Darkness, Hours 72 (8)

Jassie sat in the shadows of the concession stand near the bleachers smoking a Virginia Slims. She had not been there long. She was going over in her mind what to say to get closer to a stack of cash. Her instincts were running hot; she would not go back to her room above the garage. She was sure some boy would let her crash at his place for a night and then she would crash at another spot until her friends were ready to head down to Mexico. Adrenaline raced through her for the second straight day. She was too close to murder and too close to a murderer. She thought she knew men, she thought she knew what they wanted and how to control them. The blackmail threats came as a surprise to her. She allowed herself to be photographed in Brad's studio. Just boudoir photographs to surprise a friend. When she was told, they were going to be published by a magazine in the city unless she paid a small price she freaked out.

Now here she sat, back against the wall. She was a little chilly wearing a short skirt and sleeveless blouse. Her mind scolded her for her poor planning. She fumbled with thoughts hoping to find the right moves to get her away from here without being bitten by what she now viewed as a dangerous animal. Yes, she had mentioned it to him; mentioned that she was being leaned on for both money and in lieu of money that sexual favors could be provided. But that is all, she mentioned it. That's all; she flicked the cigarette away, watching the illuminated arch drift through cool air a twirling tail of smoke chasing after. She watched the smoke dance and escape skyward and she enjoyed the splatter of sparks as the butt hit the ground.

She opened her bag and pushed things around until she found the pack of smokes. She lit another; then it occurred to her; she had to convince him that they could run away together. The thought of his clumsiness touching her sent a shiver all the way down to the tail of her spine. No way to avoid that; she would convince him tonight, underneath the bleachers. That's it, we can run away together. That would be the story. He could get the money and instead of paying they could run away. Her head leaned back against the cold block wall of the concession stand. She let out a long stream of smoke emptying her lungs. Two days ago she was just a normal girl, doing normal things but that was two days ago. She closed her eyes and took a deep drag and exhaled slowly. Yes, it was time she stopped being pushed around by life. Still with her eyes closed, she imagined herself on a Mexican beach in a tiny bathing suit, watching her friends carrying their surfboards into the tumbling azure sea. A smile spread across her face.

She thought the cold of the asphalt was running up through her, but the reality was it was the innocence in her escaping. She stood and brushed herself off. Her gaze caught a street light in the distance and she watched a couple walk by hand in hand. Her hands went to her face and rubbed her eyes. Walking hand in hand now seemed a far off distant vision. Her hand went to her heart; there was a hollow feeling like when she lost her only brother in the war. With Pepper gone the Theater would not open; her community was shattered. She was alone. The battle was over: darkness and light, right and wrong, good and evil, for her, as of now, these questions were answered.

Just then, two headlights turned into the parking lot and coasted to a stop behind the bleachers. She smoothed her skirt. Her bare legs moved forward, her hip movements swished; a strand of her web vibrated, she moved in the direction to survey what she had caught.

Her first feast, wearing the shroud of her new philosophy was waiting.

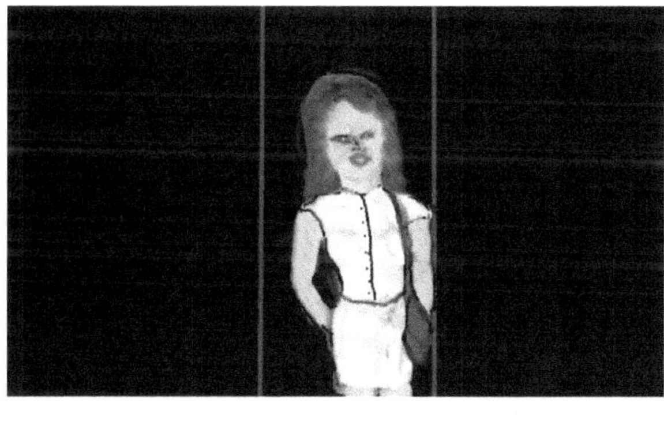

After finishing her beer Gladys had returned to a tough, tough day at the Beauty Saloon. She then went to her Mother's place and retrieved her copy of Detective Confidential.

"You are absolutely beautiful," her Mother told her.

Gladys knew her story of not knowing the picture was taken was not believed. She excused herself for a moment and went to her Father's garage and retrieved a baseball bat and put it in the truck of her car. She recognized the setting where the photo was taken and thought she just might pay Brad Jensen a visit first chance she got.

At 10 pm Quinn made his excuses to Betty and left her house. He headed back to Brad Jensen's office. He was not satisfied with this morning's incident or outcome. He knew if he was caught there by DeLaMonte he would be arrested. He thought rightly so.

When he arrived, he circled the block three times looking for a green Dodge Polara but did not find one. He parked in the alley, and let himself in the building and Brad's office using his credit card edge as a means of entry.

Once inside he took a flashlight and started searching. It did not appear Brad had been back. Quinn was sure he would return and debated staying and waiting him out.

He came to the four new cardboard file boxes and took the lid from the first one. Opening one folder after another he found pictures of women and a few men from the local community. He made a snap decision and carried the boxes to his waiting Chrysler Town and Country. He found the key to the filing cabinet still in the filing cabinet lock from this morning. He dumped the camera equipment and used those boxes to haul all the rest of the files to his car.

Once home he put his car in his garage and began the task of sorting through the work of Brad Jensen. It took over two hours to finish, but he had found what he was looking for and plenty that he was not looking for. He took all but five folders and began burning them in a metal barrel out behind the garage.

At 2 am a Police Car pulled into the drive leading to the garage. It was Officer Harcourt working his usual night shift.

When he found Quinn there were just a few envelopes left. As Harcourt approached Quinn tossed the remaining envelopes into the fire.

"Pretty early in the morning for burning leaves." Harcourt began.

"These are leaves that needed burning," Quinn replied. "I have something for you. Follow me." Quinn leads him inside the garage andover to a bench. The empty boxes lay on the floor where he had tossed them.

Quinn reached for one of the envelopes and handed it to Harcourt. It was marked, "Eden Harcourt."

Harcourt opened the clasp and partially pulled two photos up. He nodded his head and slid the photo's back inside. "They were a surprise birthday present. How do you happen to have them?"

"I think they were on their way to a publisher in the city. The publisher bought these kinds of photos from a couple of local boys."

Harcourt opened a button of his shirt and slid the envelope inside. "Put out that bonfire, your neighbors are complaining." He glanced at the four remaining envelopes on the shop bench then said his goodnight.

Brad Jensen lay on his bed in the 'Dance By The Light of the Moon' motel on Sandal Street in Henley behind the Piggly Wiggly. He was not happy with the events of the day. The second man through his door this morning was obviously Police he recognized him from the theater. That left no explanation to just who the first man was. He had never seen him and he referred to himself as the cleaning man. It was out of the question to go back to his office. He lay there bemoaning the loss of his camera equipment.

He would have to go and check out his apartment building. If no one was around he could pack some of his clothes and pick up the cameras that were there. The equipment took him years to acquire. He now needed the stash of cash that would be brought to him more than ever.

He lay there thinking he should not have given him 72 hours to gather the money; and thinking that the bullet in Pepper's back was meant for him. He went over the scenes that played out on stage two nights before. He was heading for that very spot for a change for the next scene. He had no idea why Pepper was sitting in that chair.

He reached over and set the alarm clock for 2 am. He needed to retrieve some clothes. He closed his eyes and thought about $10,000.

A 2nd Street Playhouse Mystery, James Glen, Hours 48 (9)

Jimmy Glen glanced at his watch, 'might as well get this over with' he told himself. He found his Mom and made it a point to give her a goodbye hug when she left for work. He drove to the Clearview Branch of the Bank of America. He stood in line and when it was his turn, he asked to cash in his U.S. Savings bonds.

"You'll have to talk to the manager," he was told and the teller pointed to the desks on the other side of the room.

"Hi," Jimmy said to the manager that greeted him. "I want to cash in the U.S. Savings Bonds that my grandmother left me. It's for college."

The manager looked around for a set of parents that usually were part of this transaction. "Ok, I can help you. I'll be right back." She walked across the room and retrieved the proper forms. When she returned, she handed the forms to Jimmy. "Fill these out and endorse the bonds. You will receive a U.S. Treasury check in about two to three weeks. Do you want to know their value today?"

"They add up to $10,000."

"They are not all mature. Would you like to know what you are cashing in?"

Jimmy swallowed hard and said, "I need the money today."

"The money's not here at the bank. The bonds were purchased from the U.S. Government. It may seem like a long time, two weeks, but college won't start until the Fall."

Jimmy's eyes became shiny. Again he swallowed hard and began filling out the necessary forms. Once complete he handed the forms and bonds back to the manager.

"Good luck in college. It'll be the time of your life and it will save you from military duty." The manager told him when he stood. They shook hands. The manager could tell he was shaken and made a mental note to call his parents. The phone on her desk rang and the thought was immediately erased.

Jimmy walked back to the line of the tellers. He had $67.00 in a savings account and thought to withdraw it.

He thought about what Jassie said under the bleachers. He thought about what Jassie let him do under the bleachers. And he knew that was all over. He could not expect her to run away with him with $67.00 in his pocket. He tried to shake the feeling that he was a piece of shattered glass.

The bank manager had given him an idea. Jimmy Glen returned home and sat under the shop light on the bench in his Father's garage looking at his Junior Yearbook. He flipped slowly through the pages looking at the pictures that now seemed to have been taken so long ago. He was about to turn another page when he spotted a picture of Clay Raybourne. He studied it closely.

He knew Clay casually and he hoped that would be enough to recognize him on campus. The look of decision crossed his face and he closed the yearbook.

For two days, he spent just enough time at school that his parents would not get a call. Today he skipped everything and watched the boy's locker room door waiting for Clay to arrive. It was fourth period when he saw Clay finally enter. He followed and watched to see what locker belonged to Clay. He stood close enough to see the numbers Clay used on the combination lock. He waited for the class to head out to the field then opened Clay's locker, grabbed his wallet and removed his driver's license and Social Security card and returned the wallet. He left the locker room and left his high school campus for the last time.

Jassie McClain had her back washed in the shower with an old friend from High School. She thought it was just the price to pay for a place to sleep for two nights. She enjoyed his touch but was lost in thought over the $10,000 that she would soon slip from under Jimmy's nose and be long gone before there was anything he could do about it. Everything was going just as planned she thought to herself. Yes, just as planned. "Wash my hair, will you?" The hot water was just right.

At 9 am retired Detective Quinn Moosebroker walked in the Clearview Terrace Police department and handed a sealed envelope to the desk sergeant and asked that it be placed on Detective DeLaMonte's desk. On the envelope was written DeLaMonte's name and the words, 'The Shadow.' He returned to his car. Betty was waiting. They had a date with Katie for breakfast at Millie's Café.

Katie was there when they arrived. She was happy that Betty and her Dad seemed to be getting along so well. She was quietly pleased that he was getting home so late these past few days.

She stood and gave her Dad and Betty a nice hug when they came to the table. "Hello, you two."

Quinn sighed, just then Millie came over and laid menus on the table and said hello and asked if they wanted coffee. "The other day I forgot there was another name."

"Jassie McClain?" Quinn interrupted.

"That's it. So you found out." Millie walked away to get coffee.

"What's that about?" Kate asked.

Betty began to answer, "Seems the recent murder has uncovered much unpleasantness here in our little Borough. Seems like what some of us consider, 'Our little sin' has been taken advantage of by some people who want to make an easy dollar."

Quinn sat quietly. In his pocket was the envelope with Kate Moosebroker's name on it. He took it out of his pocket and handed it over to Kate. He set down an envelope with Jasmine McClain's name on it and said, 'Give this to her when you see her. I am not making any judgments here. Human nature is what it is."

Betty reached into her purse and took out a photograph. "I took this off a corkboard in the seedy office of an upstate publishing house." She handed the photo to Katie. Katie's eyes began to tear up. She was also confused. She had paid Brad his money. She thought she just stole these very pictures. She was embarrassed not so much for herself but that her Dad had to know and she knew he would never say but this caused him pain.

"I am sure that this is that last of them," Quinn told her. "It's human nature. That's all. Let this go from your mind." He did not mention that there were many duplicate files that he had gone through the night before but could not find two files for Katie or Jassie.

As Millie came over to the table, Katie slipped the envelopes into her purse. Millie set down Quinn and Betty's coffee. She looked into three sad faces. Just a moment ago all three were smiling. "Ready to order?" She stood straight faced with her pad.

Officer Parker Glen returned home from his shift but was not tired. He poured himself a drink and went out to his garage and turned on the shop light above the bench. Jimmy's Junior Year Book lay there and he set it aside.

He pulled his gun cleaning kit from the shelf and popped the cylinder from his revolver and began to clean the barrel, cylinders, and hammer. When done he assembled the weapon and returned it to his holster.

He returned to the house and pulled his spare home protection weapon in a cigar box at the top of his closet. He brought the box to the shop bench and opened it. To his surprise when he emptied the chambers there was a spent round. He disassembled the gun and cleaned it. He set the spent round on top of the yearbook.

Jimmy's van was not parked next to the garage. He thought to wake his wife, then thought better of it. He would talk to Jimmy the first chance he got. He told his son a hundred times that this was not a toy. He picked up his diamond cut lowball glass and swallowed the rest of his drink. He tried to remember the last time he had seen his son.

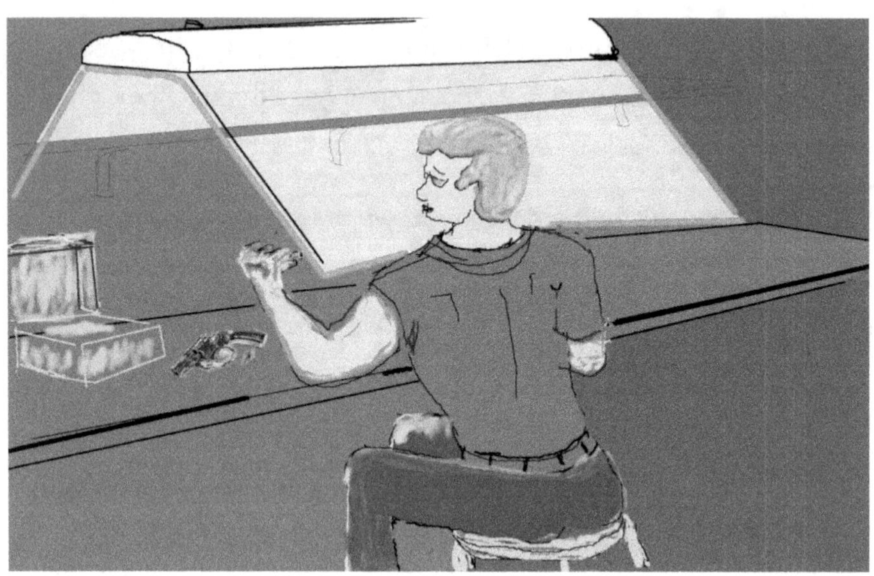

At 2 a.m. Parker Glen jolted awake. He left his wife who was sleeping by his side. He pulled on a pair of trousers over his boxers went to his closet and retrieved the cigar box. He slid his feet into his shoes and walked to the garage where he retrieved a shovel.

He walked to the old Elm near where he and Jimmy had buried the family dog. He dug a hole and buried his spare home protection weapon in the cigar box.

Returning to the house, he finished dressing. He left the house and began a search of Clearview Terrace for his son.

A 2nd Street Playhouse Mystery, The Bridge, Hours 24 (10)

Chief Petty Officer Mario Hendrickson liked to arrive early at his recruiting office in Henley. Monday through Friday there were one or two boys milling about the bus stop outside the Donut Shop waiting for him to arrive. This morning was no exception a muscular looking boy with short cropped blonde hair was pacing back and forth. Hendrickson turned the key in the lock and started a pot of coffee.

As the coffee was finished the blonde boy opened the door and entered. “I want to enlist. Is this the place?”

“It sure is son. Grab a seat. Can I get you some coffee?” Chief Petty Officer Hendrickson would make his quota for the month this morning. “Are you eighteen?”

Jimmy Glen had memorized the information on Clay Raybourne’s driver’s license. “Yes, sir,” and handed the drivers license to the recruiter.

“Don’t call me sir; I earned every one of these stripes.” He reached into the right side top drawer and pulled out some forms and handed them to Clay.

“When do you want to join, are you out of high school?”

“This morning.” Clay answered.

The Chief Petty Officer had learned not to ask a lot of questions. “Fill these out while we talk. There is a van scheduled to arrive here at 4:30 pm. Do you want to be on it? It will take you to The Great Lakes Naval Training Center for boot camp.”

“Yes sir, I mean yes, what do I call you?”

“Chief Petty Officer; that is what you call me.”

Clay filled out the forms. Name, address, social security number and a made up phone number. Height, weight, any known medical condition, the whole history but very few facts. When he was done, his hands were sweating. He handed the forms back and stood extending his hand to the Chief Petty Officer.

"Four-thirty. Don't be late. It is a long drive." He smiled and shook the boy's hand. "Welcome to the Navy. Pack light, toothbrush and toothpaste and a little cash." In twenty-two years in the Navy, this was the easiest duty Mario Hendrickson had ever had. He had made copies of all the necessary identification and forms for the Navy and for Clay. He tossed the packet into the 'Out Going' wire basket and sat back and drank some coffee keeping an eye out on the bus stop out front of the Donut Shop. 'He thought. *Just eight more years, I'll be fifty with a full pension.*

Jassie had not heard from Jimmy in twenty-four hours now and she was unable to reach him. As she waited for him at the time and place, she told him her blood began to stir. Over and over again she asked herself, *Where is she?* She was working herself up. She hoped to have the money by now. She sat and fumbled for another cigarette. She'd heard that the boys were heading out to Mexico later this afternoon. Her duffle bag was packed and there were no goodbyes to be said. She needed some music to fill her head, but she had to stay put waiting for Jimmy. She kept an eye for Jimmy and kept an eye out for the Chevy Van her and her friends would be traveling in for the next couple of months.

Gladys was on her way to one of her private clients when she spotted what she thought looked like Brad Jensen's car parked back beneath some Elms near the Benson Street Bridge. She slowed and pulled off the road then stopped.

She hung a u-turn and tried to get a closer look. She turned off onto a road that led past industrial buildings as she tried to get closer. She parked behind an empty building and walked through a field towards the car. She intently watched the car and surrounding area. No sign of Brad but it was his car.

She returned to her car opened the trunk and retrieved the baseball bat she had taken from her father's garage then pulled a pair of scissors from her purse, in case she needed them for additional protection. She returned to the car and first broke the windshield. Then it dawned on her. She broke out the driver's side window and unlocked the door. She took the scissors and started cutting the upholstery. She was now breathing hard but feeling much better. She took out a cigarette and lighter and inhaled smoke deep into her lungs. Then she tossed the cigarette into the cotton batting that was formerly the front seat.

She practically marched back to her car and drove away back to the main street over the Benson Street Bridge.

The fire started slowly, casually, in no hurry. An employee of Carson's Bearing called the police and reported a fire in a field behind the building. The contents of the glove box were completely destroyed. An envelope with the photo and the negative of Jimmy Glen holding a gun at the theater dressing room door were unidentifiable ash when the fire department extinguished the smoldering car.

Officer Harcourt was pulling a double shift covering for another Officer. He arrived on the scene along with a local fire department vehicle. When he got identification on the plate of the car, he radioed into the station to notify Detective DeLaMonte.

"Wait for me there," DeLaMonte told him. "I am going to approach from the South side of the bridge. You keep a close eye on the North side. Maybe we can catch this guy. He skipped out for questioning twice now on a murder case. And I have him on a lesser crime."

"Yes sir," Harcourt responded. He pulled his cruiser out of sight at the north side of the Benson Street Bridge and watched the speeders go by.

Four-thirty P.M.

A Chevy Van pulled to the curb where Jassie had told them to meet her. The driver had a 4-F draft card from the draft. The other two passengers, Brody, and Jude, were draft dodgers planning on relocating to Mexico. The tall driver got out and opened the back door and threw Jassie's duffel bag inside, "Climb on in." He told her. A joint was tucked behind his right ear. Jassie took one more look around, cursed under her breath and climbed into the upholstered interior of the van.

A faded white Chevy Van with 'Property of U.S. Navy' on the side panel pulled in front of the Navy recruiting office in Henley. A Seaman Apprentice climbed out and slid the side door open. "Welcome to the Navy boys," he told the four boys waiting. Over and over Jimmy told himself, 'you answer to Clay, you answer to Clay.' The four boys climbed aboard the Chevy Van on their way to see the world. They drove off; as the boys talked Clay began the lies that would become his background history. He thought about a time when the carnival came to town. He was ten years old his Dad took him on a Carousel. His Dad stood beside him, one hand on the pole; one hand on his shoulder. He told himself that is the image of his Dad he would carry with him from now on. Raindrops began to hit the windshield.

Brad Jensen looked at his watch and finished the last of his second beer. He had waited out the afternoon at a nearby bowling alley. He was ready to collect his money and make his way down the highway. He left the building and walked to the Benson Avenue Bridge for his appointment with Jimmy. He was set. He would verify the money then get the photograph and negative and be on his way to parts unknown. He walked to the middle of the bridge and waited. Then he paced.

Officer Harcourt got on the radio to DeLaMonte, "I think that is him, I recognize him from the theater. Over."

"I see him. Make sure he does not get by you." DeLaMonte pulled his green Dodge Polara to the middle of the bridge and got out. He walked over to Brad Jensen and pulled a photograph from his pocket and held it up.

Annie Mackintosh was on the bed, legs curled to the side facing the camera. She wore a sheer red Baby Doll nightgown with puffy sleeves and a red lace bow tied at the neck. Her thick black hair was freshly styled and the lighting made it look like silk. The bottoms of the Baby Doll ensemble were on the comforter by her knees.

"You are under arrest for possession with intent to distribute child pornography, " DeLaMonte told him.

“What are you talking about? Look at her.” Brad managed to get the words out.

“She’s seventeen,” DeLaMonte told him. He barely got the words out when Brad bolted.

Office Harcourt flipped on his cruiser's emergency lights and barreled down the length of the bridge. Brad thought if he could get to his car he could likely outrun the Polara. Harcourt caught up to him as he reached the end of the bridge while DeLaMonte made a show of chasing him.

Brad stopped short when he spotted a fire truck next to the burnt-out shell of his pride and joy. Harcourt grabbed a hand full of collar and threw Jensen down a little harder than necessary on the hood of the squad car. He leaned down and said, “That was for Eden.”

DeLaMonte arrived. Harcourt placed Jensen in cuffs and waited for DeLaMonte to make the arrest. “We were interrupted,” DeLaMonte began. “That picture buys you fifty-seven months in the penitentiary. Resisting arrest buys you another year.” He looked at Harcourt, “Officer Harcourt, did this man resist arrest?”

With just the slightest hesitation Officer Harcourt said, “Yes sir, he did.”

Officer Parker Glen, Jimmy’s Dad, received a call on his squad car radio informing him that a vehicle registered to him was sitting in a White Front parking lot in Henley. “Not many Corvair Vans with white stripes around,” his buddy told him. Officer Glen thanked his friend and worked his way over to the White Front.

U.S.

A 2nd Street Playhouse Mystery, Conclusion (11)

Betty woke to the sound of rain. It was Sunday morning. She glanced around and smiled as her eyes focused on where she was. There was a silk Kimono with cherry blossoms at the foot of the bed. She saw her clothes tossed on a chair in the corner of the room where she had left them. She threw her bare legs over the side of the bed and reached for the Kimono; slipping it on made her immediately feel spoiled. She followed the smell of bacon into the kitchen.

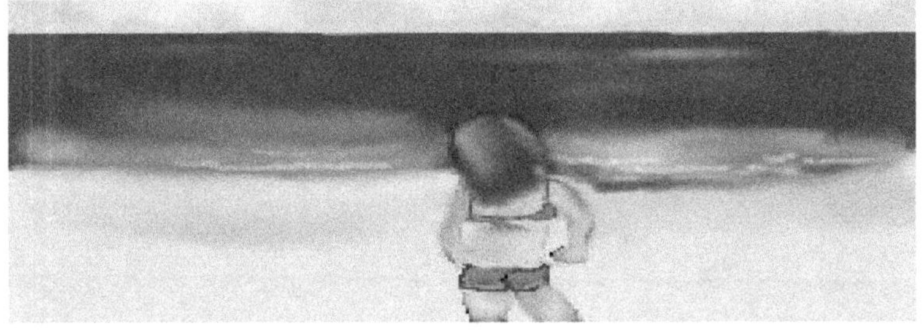

"Good morning, Beautiful." Quinn greeted her arrival. "Breakfast will be ready in a couple of minutes. I just guessed you liked your eggs scrambled." He sat down on the table a serving dish with slices of warm toast.

"Last time I talked to Officer Harcourt, he told me a missing person report was filed for Jimmy Glen. DeLaMonte suspects foul play. DeLaMonte has an all points bulletin out for Jasmine McClain. I doubt he is going to find her. She and Jimmy may be together, but that is not how I am seeing it."

Betty took a sip of very good coffee. "Can I do anything to help?" She asked Quinn. "Has anyone ever called you Moose?" Betty smiled at the glance Quinn gave her over his shoulder.

“This is how I think it happened,” Quinn told her while setting a plate of steaming eggs and bacon in front of her. He returned to the stove and put the remaining eggs and bacon strips on a plate for himself.

“One thing for sure; I don’t think Pepper Bishop was the target. From what we found out he did make a little money from selling photos to B Magazines, but as far as we know he was not blackmailing anyone. His life was the theater.” Quinn stood and got the coffee pot and filled Betty’s cup. “Most of the models signed releases for their photos.”

“From what Millie told me, Brad Jensen as Derek Locktree was heading for that very chair for a quick change and some makeup before the next act. Annie was due to be with Gladys helping her out of one costume and into another.”

Quinn watched Betty walk to the sink with her plate and return to begin clearing the table while Quinn finished up his eggs.

She turned on the hot water in the sink. “I am listening,” Betty told him.

“I think Jasmine somehow initiated all this. I think she tried to get the assistance of Jimmy to try to persuade Brad that it was not a good idea to keep pressuring her. She and Jimmy were likely sleeping together which made him feel protective of her. We know from Katie’s experience what Brad’s game was. I didn’t mention it but while you were lifting Kate’s picture at Shark Finn’s office, I saw a picture of Gladys on the other wall that Finn was showing me.” He stood and picked up his plate and sat it on the counter. He moved behind Betty and reached around her and loosened the belt of the Kimono and let it drape open. “Are you almost ready?”

“Ready?” Betty teased.

"The light in my study is perfect this time of day. We are going to start the painting you agreed to last night."

Quinn led her to the study. A chaise lounge chair was arranged near a window a few feet from an easel with a blank canvas. "Where do you want me?" Betty asked.

"Make yourself comfortable on the lounge."

Betty adjusted the Kimono and lay on the lounge.

Picking up a tube of pearl white and tan, Quinn mixed the two colors in a five to one ratio until he had a rich flesh tone prepared.

"The night of the murder, the lights had just gone out on the stage at the end of act one. The stage was dark and everyone had their assignments. I think Jimmy knowing Brad would be sitting at that makeup table just opened the door and fired one shot across the room." Quinn walked over and made some adjustments to the Kimono. The morning light had Betty glowing.

"Then with no effort at all for a gymnast he pulled himself up the opened ceiling wall and right into the rafters of the theater. He walked one of the support beams in the theater right over the top of the audience with the grace and agility of a cat. That would explain the drift of dust I saw as the audience was clearing. He dropped down into the booth, perhaps surprising Jassie, perhaps not."

Betty stirred a little; wondering if she was too close to the window.

"Jimmy must have changed in the booth. Being dressed head-to-toe in black may have attracted attention, and the last think he would have wanted is attention. Whether he was a surprise to Jassie or expected –

they both had to get out of there. The theater had emptied. There is a chance they saw you on the stage and they walked out the front door while the rest of us were in back. Perhaps just moments before Officer Harcourt arrived."

Quinn made a long, graceful slope with his brush as he began building the painting of Betty.

"DeLaMonte is going to make an arrest of Brad if he can locate him. I feel confident that he has enough evidence to bring him up on charges. Now, from what I can tell, there is no evidence of any of this. The list of people on the stage the night of the play is the prime suspect list, and as it turns out neither Jimmy's name nor Jasmine's name are on that list. Everyone was in shock the night of the murder, and no one thought to mention them.

"No doubt in my mind that Jimmy pulled the trigger. But there is no proof. It is sad really. His father is a police officer, and he has lost a son. Jimmy lost any chance of a future. He went from a promising athlete with college in front of him to who knows what."

Betty spoke up, "What are you going to do now?"

"It's not my case. All the damage has been done. We could track down Jimmy, but my heart would not be in that. He has given up his life already. Any peace of mind his parents had is gone forever." Quinn shook his head in disbelief at the pain and suffering caused by the bad seed known as Brad Jensen.

With that thought, Quinn walked to his desk and opened the top drawer. He pulled out an envelope stamped Brad Jensen Studio's on one side; on the other side was a name; Betty Atwood and handed it to

Betty.

Betty sat up and opened the envelope. A broad grin rose on her face. "Looks like I gained a couple of pounds since these were taken. These were a present for George; he wanted these tucked in his jacket breast pocket, 'to enjoy for eternity' he told me. I destroyed the negatives, but guess I didn't think of copies."The phone rang and Quinn reached over and picked it up. He said into the receiver, "Ok, we'll be right there." He hung up and looked at Betty and said, "Get dressed, we have another case."

Night
of
the
Falling
Henry Farley

The Night of the Falling, Quinn Moosebroker (1)

The body of Big Jim Brady lay in the bed of an upstairs bedroom, dead. His live-in 'significant other' had discovered his body when she returned from a shopping expedition to the city and called the police.

Officer Harcourt working the night shift heard the call from dispatch and arrived at the modest estate moments before the EMT's. It seemed routine, until he opened the doors to the library and the shelved books where now a disheveled pile and some stacked by the door. He had heard of Brady, they said he was the wealthiest man in Clearview Terrace. He heard in conversation with Blake Knightly that he had the largest collection of Henry Farley outside the Houghton collection at Harvard. Harcourt admired the array of old artwork on the dust jackets of the first edition titles lying on the floor of the mahogany lined room. He noted a toppled display case that was now empty, but had no way to determine if the contents now lay on the floor amongst all the other books.

Harcourt surveyed the house taking notes. He wondered if Detective DeLaMonte would be sent out to do a preliminary investigation or not. At the end of the hall on the second floor, a window seemed to have been forced open. Harcourt noted it and would add it to his report. He wondered if this could be a murder. 'Two murders in Clearview Terrace in a matter of weeks?' He asked himself. It was practically a crime wave.

The EMT's were ready. They had removed the body. Harcourt put some, 'Do Not Cross' tape across the doorway of the library, told Eleanor Pennyworth, a distant cousin to the Pennyworth publishing business to keep out until a detective cleared the room and then the two emergency vehicles made their way to the Clearview Terrace Memorial Hospital where Jim Brady was pronounced dead.

Officer Harcourt sat at a local donut shop in the early hours of Sunday morning and wrote out his report of his observations at the Brady house. He drank his coffee and enjoyed his crumb donut hoping he could avoid an early morning call from Detective DeLaMonte by filing his report on his way off duty.

By morning, all conversation at Millie's Café and the Frosty Mug were about Jim Brady and who got his money or his art collection or his books.

Phillip Berkeley was ecstatic with the news. Two years earlier he had been in negotiations with Jim Brady's lawyers for the Brady library. There were many first editions, but first editions were a dime a dozen in his circles. He coveted the Henry Farley manuscript of The Night of the Falling; that and two decades of correspondence between Farley and his publisher and between Farley and his Italian mistress. How Brady had beat out the major Universities for this prize is to this day a mystery to the universities. It meant Phillip Berkeley's name would be on the cover of at least two volumes likely three. The Correspondence of Henry Farley published in two volumes a year apart and The Catalogue of the Jim Brady Collection, which would make him comfortable in his retirement.

It was sheer good fortune for Phillip Berkeley that Jim Brady wanted the material to stay in Clearview Terrance where he had returned after his long distinguished career in publishing. He would wait the appropriate time and make inquiries to the estate about moving the material to Hourglass Trinity College where he was head of the English

Department and oversaw collections. He determined in his mind that Monday morning was the appropriate amount of time.

Blake Knightly owner of the local book shop heard about the news while having a quiet Sunday morning coffee at the Frosty Mug. He told the story of how he had long ago read in a tabloid that Ronald Colman and Clark Gable once had a fist fight in a bar over who would play, Read Fraser, the lead role, when The Night of the Falling was produced as a movie.

Blake Knightly sat and drank his coffee thinking he would not get his hands on one book from the Brady house. PITY, he thought. Every vulture within a thousand miles will be hovering over the Jim Brady Estate and there will be some very big vultures.

He turned to the classifieds and saw that the Clearview Terrace Library sale was happening this morning. He glanced at his watch and rushed off to search their offerings. It was a good place to acquire store stock and he was used to bumping elbows with the book scouts.

Eleanor Pennyworth called her long time friend Lars Bragdon the owner of Stacks, the largest bookstore in Boston and told him of Jim's passing. She told him the manuscript of The Night of the Falling was missing. She was aware of Jim's commitment to keeping the manuscript in Clearview Terrace even though she knew both Harvard and Notre Dame would go into a bidding war that could run the price near the $30,000 level.

They talked about the material promised to Hourglass Trinity College but Eleanor assured him that the ephemera would make him salivate. "You would be dealing with his sons, and there are books not on the HTC inventory list," she told him. He agreed to make the trip.

Eleanor Pennyworth flipped through the leather-bound address book in Jim Brady's study. By the name Moosebroker there was a word in Jim's writing that said, 'trusted.' She tapped her finger on her chin. It was just a matter of time before Jim's sons showed up and invited her to leave. This was the downside of being a significant other rather than a wife. Covington R. Brady was the oldest. He would show up with a lawyer and Matheson Brady would do what he always did when he was in the house and that is guess the price of the things around him.

Detective DeLaMonte of the Clearview Police Department pulled his green Dodge Polara into the drive of the Brady estate and climbed out of his car. He lumbered to the front door and knocked. Once inside and having Officer Harcourt's preliminary report in hand looked around while talking to Eleanor Pennyworth.

"You found the body?" He asked.

Eleanor was annoyed; she had just answered these questions from the police 'playbook'. "Yes." She told him.

"We are going to have to wait for the Coroner's Report to see if the death will be investigated as a crime. Is there anything missing?"

Eleanor led him to the library. "It is too early to tell, but there may be some books missing and a valuable manuscript is gone."

DeLaMonte grunted, and made a note, 'books' and underlined it. He would not be spending any time searching for any damn old books. He closed his notebook. "Thank you, Miss Pennyworth. We will get back to you very soon. Keep the department aware of your whereabouts."

She walked to the back of the house and grabbed two suitcases and brought them to the room-sized closet that held her clothes. She began to bring things to the suitcase then paused, grabbed the address book and dialed Quinn Moosebroker's number. When the phone was picked up Eleanor Pennyworth introduced herself; she mentioned Jim Brady and told Quinn that she needed his help.

He said into the receiver, "Ok, we'll be right there." He hung up and looked at Betty and said, "Get dressed, we have another case."

The Night of The Falling, The Book Scouts (2)

While she was waiting for the storm to come down on her, Eleanor Pennyworth loaded the two suitcases she had packed into the trunk of her powder blue Torino. When she returned, the phone was ringing. She picked up and listened, on a notepad she wrote Thomas Hoving, Director, Metropolitan Museum of Art, interested in Pissarro owned by the estate. *It begins;* she thought and left the note for Covington under a small Henry Moore on the mahogany desk, then thought better of it and carried the Moore to the Gran Torino and placed it in the glove compartment.

Blake Knightly returned to his shop after the library sale; he was the proud owner of two boxes filled with acceptable store stock. Nothing life changing, but he would be rewarded for his efforts. Once inside and the boxes stashed behind the counter he noticed a man wearing black pants, a black tee shirt and jacket, cross his doorway a couple of times.

The man finally made up his mind and entered. He struck Knightly as a bodybuilder, not his usual customer. This customer had the smell of licorice.

The man reached out his hand and said, "JJ" as an introduction. Then he reached beneath his jacket and produced a first edition Velden, The Obsidian Pear in a nice jacket.

Knightly did not think it odd, book scouts came in all shapes and sizes, and all times of day and night. The Velden was not really rare, but he knew of a collector that would pay $90.00 for a nice copy in very good jacket.

"I'll take $45.00," JJ told Knightly. "What do you say? I am short on gas money."

“It’s a deal.” Knightly had a few questions, but did not ask as he reached for a cigar box under the counter that served as his cash register and counted out nine fives. That left little in the cigar box. The exchange was made. Knightly thought this has been a good day. He took out a piece of paper and composed a note that included a detailed description to his collector. He noted the book was a Brady House Publication. He would mail the offer and wait for his check to arrive and post the book.

Quinn and Betty pulled into the drive of the Brady estate. Quinn felt his 1946 Chrysler Town and Country complimented the driveway. They were greeted by Eleanor Pennyworth and invited in.

“The reason I called you is that your name is in Jim’s address book. The word, ‘trusted’ is written by it. This house will be under siege for the next few weeks by every auction house, every major gallery, universities, collectors and the curious. I am also going to be under siege. I am afraid; I am the most likely suspect. I will be forced to move back to the dreary city now that Jim is gone. Luckily I thought it best to keep my apartment when Jim and I moved in together.”

She paused reflectively, “What am I telling you all this for? The reason I called you is that the centerpiece of Jim’s collection is gone. I want you to recover it before it goes underground in the vault of some collector. It is so rare that it can never be openly sold in public. But the rare book business, like the art world, has many connoisseurs who think nothing of possession at any cost.”

"I called a friend of mine, Lars Bragdon, from Boston. He will be here Tuesday. He will help you with ideas. He is very knowledgeable. I think you will like him."

Quinn cleared his throat, "Is there a number where I can reach him? Sometimes these things move pretty fast. A day and a half is a lot of time lost. Is there anyone local we might get some information that may prove helpful?"

Pennyworth took a sheet of linen letterhead and wrote, The Stacks, Lars Bragdon, and a phone number and handed it to Quinn.

Betty turned to Quinn, "Do you think Blake Knightly could shed any light on this?"

Quinn smiled, "Yes, that is something we can do while we try to reach Mr. Bragdon." He turned to Pennyworth, "If it can be found, Betty and I will find it."

Pennyworth knew this was going to take a great deal of strength. "Phillip Berkeley from Hourglass Trinity College will be on the phone Monday morning first thing to inquire about the transfer of Jim's bequest. The college types act prim and proper, but they are just as ruthless as the next guy."

She put her face in her hands a moment and then looked up, "It is going to be a circus here for the foreseeable future." She thought a moment and grabbed another sheet of letterhead and wrote a phone number on it. "If you cannot reach me here, I will be at this number. Oh and this might be worth mentioning, the thought just popped in my head. I found Jim laying in the bed of the first bedroom at the head of the stairs; for some reason you are the first person I told. He was not in his bed."

Quinn and Betty back in the driveway decided their best course of action was to go see Blake Knightly. “Let’s have a cup of coffee first at Millie’s Café, see what the rumor mill is saying. Then we can catch Blake at his shop.” Quinn offered.

About half the tables at Millie’s Café were empty. Quinn observed the room and made note of the strangers. Millie arrived to take their order. Quinn and Betty had had their breakfast and ordered coffee.

“I see a few strange faces here this morning.” He looked over at an older man with a long white ponytail flipping through a hard cover book while he drank his coffee.

“Book scouts,” Millie offered. Clearview Library is having their library sale this morning. These guys have been showing up here all morning. Then they headed off like a herd to stand in line for the sale. A few returned for breakfast after the sale.

Quinn thanked Millie. He told Betty he would be right back and got up and walked over to the man with the white ponytail.

“Hello,” Quinn stated.

The man looked up. His eyes were lost in thought and took a moment to focus on Quinn. “You a cop?” He asked.

“Ex-cop, but it does not have to be an issue. Millie tells me book scouts have been in here all morning. Does that include you?”

Nick did not like the police; he had spent some time in jail for stealing vellum incunabula from a library. “I guess that includes me, I just came into town at an invitation from the Friends of the Library,' I am on their list. I come to their sale every year."

"So, it is a circuit." Quinn was a bit puzzled.

"I guess you could say that. Yes, a circuit. That's right. I guess." Nick told him.

"Can you tell me some of the others?"

"Well, there is Sam, he's a funny guy. And Blum, eyeglasses so thick you wonder how he can see, but he can spot a find all the way across the room. And this morning the husband and wife team that call themselves, The Aristocrats, was there. Those two will take an aisle, one at each end and work towards the middle so no one can see any of the books in the aisle before they see them. They will talk all day about books but never say a word about who they are. Most everyone for miles around comes to the Clearview Terrace library sale. Between the local colleges and the chance of Brady House finds it usually puts some beans on everyone's table. There are others, and some are such hermits you can hardly get a word out of them. I hope that helps." He turned back and stared into his coffee, letting Quinn know the conversation was over.

"What do you know about The Night of the Falling?" Quinn asked with his eyes keen on seeing any reaction.

Nick stared into his coffee, lost in his mental, far away hideaway from the rest of the world. He did not even hear Quinn's question.

Returning to Betty, Quinn said, “This is going to take some doing. It is a whole world we know little about.” He sat and drank coffee talking to Betty, watching each of the strangers. In a moment, he said to Betty, "Let’s go see Blake.”

Blake Knightly was not sure he liked seeing Quinn Moosebroker at the door of his shop. Even with a woman at his side Quinn, this morning looked like trouble. Especially after the week he had had last week.

“I suppose you have heard?” Quinn began.” Big Jim Brady passed away last night. His partner Eleanor Pennyworth asked us to help her find out what happened and to recover some missing items.”

“Missing items?” Blake leaned forward against the counter. “What is missing?” He asked.

“Are you willing to teach me, ah, us something about where a missing manuscript would go?” Quinn watched Blake closely. “Where would you go or who would you see if a rare manuscript came your way?”

“A legitimate manuscript? Well, a legitimate manuscript would likely make its way up the food chain. Depending how much the person who has it knows; how hungry the person or persons is; and then a bit of luck would be needed.” Blake reached down and tore a piece of the grocery bag that he saved to wrap books and went to his rolodex addresses. He flipped through it writing down names of dealers. When he was finished, he handed the slip of brown paper to Quinn.

Lars Bragdon was the first name on the list.

The Night of the Falling, Blake Knightly (3)

Quinn read over the short list and memorized it. He handed the list to Betty, “Take a look at these,” he told her.

She read the list and repeated the names in her mind: Lars Bragdon, The Stacks, Boston; Fred Bass, The Strand, NY; Kroch & Brentano’s, Chicago; Moe’s Books, Berkeley; Moffet, Huntington Library, San Marino; Pierpont Morgan Library.

She looked at Blakely, “These are likely places the manuscript could go?”

“Likely? I don’t know about likely. Those names are book palaces who could afford to handle such a large transaction. Huntington and Morgan could absorb the manuscript and hold it for fifty years without a blink. Either would produce volume after volume: The Critique of Night of the Falling; The Meaning in…; The Metaphor in… get my meaning. The dealers could make a $5,000 to $6,000 commission for as little as a phone call to the right collector. No risk, no worry.”

Blake looked at his watch. It was too early to offer Quinn a drink. Blake loved talking about the trade. “If anybody had asked me I would have told them the big collectors are the ones that should be contacted. Just to let it be known that the authorities know who they are. That list is a little different. And, just a thought, if one of them hired someone to get the manuscript then you could hunt for years and never find a clue.”

He leaned forward against the counter. “If the manuscript leaves the country, Quaritch Ltd, London is one of the biggest dealers in rare book items in England.”

Quinn listened intently. Betty scanned the room looking at the books. What she saw were titles written mostly in the last twenty years, as far as she could tell. “You don’t deal in rare books. Do you?”

Blake stood up straight, offended, and no longer relaxed with the conversation. “This is a small community bookstore. I cater to my clientele. On occasion, something of literary interest passes through my shop. Not often, but I am aware of my business. I know what-is-what.”

Quinn interrupted, “No one is making any assumptions about your book knowledge. We are here to learn what you can tell us that might be of use.”

Betty said, “Yes, I was just looking over your stock and it appears to be current. Not old.”

“Old, does not mean valuable and valuable does not equate to old. Some of what goes on is just the current popularity of authors. But other works have a timelessness about them.”

Blakely reached under the counter and retrieved the first edition Velden, The Obsidian Pear. “This came in this morning.” He held it out for Quinn to take. “It is just thirty years old and one of Velden’s early works. The more popular Velden became, the more the price of his first editions escalated. The combination of low numbers of first editions of the early titles that were printed and his ever increasing readership drove the price up. I bought it this morning from a book scout.”

Quinn’s ears perked up. Betty noticed slight stiffening in Quinn and watched intently. “This morning?” Quinn asked.

“Yes, an odd fellow dressed in black. Black pants, tee shirt and black jacket. He was a muscular man. Not what you would expect from a book scout – said he needed gas money. I never saw him before. Maybe he was here for the library sale."

Quinn flipped from the title page to the copyright page. "This is a Brady House Publication." He looked at Blake, closing the book and handing it back.

"Brady House was in business a long time. They published hundreds of titles, both popular and unpopular. Jim Brady did not get that estate by being a bad publisher."

"Anything else you can tell me about the book scout? Height, eye color, hair color?"

Blake grimaced, he was sorry he brought the book out and sorry he mentioned the book scout. "Black hair combed straight back with lots of hair tonic to hold it in place. Dark coloration chiseled face, dark eyes, he was very intent. He looked like he could hurt you if he needed to."

"Did you see the car? Or did he say where he was going?"

"No and no," Blake said. "He just said he needed gas money. No, he said he was short of gas money. There is a difference. He knew what to ask for the book which was a pretty penny. So he may have needed a lot of gas money."

Quinn thanked Blake and he and Betty left the shop. Quinn stopped and led Betty back inside. Blake looked up, waiting for another question.

"If he is driving back to his own territory what kind of trail would he leave?" Quinn asked.

"Well, if he is living out of his car, then he will likely stop in every book shop he can find and scout them for errors by the owners. And he may need to sell more books from his stash to eat. A true scout cannot resist the hunt and like the fox they hunt to eat. I personally don't see a book scout with a manuscript like The Night of the Falling. If he has it, someone hired him."

Clifford Enders set down the receiver as a smile spread across his face. The caller told him the manuscript for Night of the Falling was in play. He leaned back in his overstuffed desk chair and let the feeling of euphoria sweep him away. To cover his bases he picked up his phone and called a book dealer in Miami with an exclusive clientele that he had done some business with, and let him know his interest. The word was spreading.

In a matter of hours, every notable book dealer and collector on the Eastern seaboard would have their eyes open for a chance at the manuscript.

Eleanor Pennyworth drove her Gran Torino to over to her friend Blanche to pick her up for lunch. While there she asked to store the two suitcases she had packed, explaining there would be many more to pack over the coming weeks and she did not want to be tripping over them.

Covington Brady had called and announced he would be there in the morning and would be accompanied by his lawyer. His position at Brady House Publishing would be put on hold while he coordinated an inventory of the estate and ousted Eleanor Pennyworth from the family estate. Then he and his lawyer would schedule a reading of his father's will. He had been advised that he might need to contest the will if it was skewed too heavily in someone else's favor.

Covington and his lawyer had discussed contesting the arrangement with Hourglass Trinity College. Jim Brady's lawyers had set the Trust up so they did not hold out much hope of succeeding.

Quinn and Betty stopped for gas on the way back to Quinn's place. While at the Texaco they picked up maps for areas that lead out of town, north, east, and south. Quinn assumed someone coming into the area from California would not drive into town. They sat at the kitchen table, where a few comfortable hours ago they ate breakfast and hoped to enjoy a Sunday afternoon at leisure in each other's company.

"This is worse than a needle in a haystack," Quinn told Betty. "The chance of finding a trail is so small. We are going to need some help. Tomorrow Kate will be back, we can set a route for her and you and I can decide which the best option for us is."

"You are sending Katie off by herself?" Betty inquired.

"We will take what we determine is the most likely route. She will look for tracks in another direction in case we are wrong. Tomorrow we can spend time at the Clearview Terrace Library to use their collection of phone books and locate the biggest bookstores leading toward Chicago, New York, and Atlanta. If Blake is right, our book scout may sell more items along the way." He reached over and patted the back of her hand which was resting on a map.

"While at the library we should decide where to spend the nights also. That way we can give Kate phone numbers where we can be reached and vice versa. What do you think?" Betty did not like the idea of Kate going alone.

Quinn's warm hand squeezed Betty's. "That is a great idea." He stood and walked over to a cupboard near the sink and pulled down the Quaker Oats. He opened the round lid and reached in and retrieved his service revolver and laid it on the kitchen table.

Detective DeLaMonte sat in the basement of the Clearview Terrace Hospital in the morgue watching Burt Collins perform an autopsy. He was anxious to know if he had a case of murder on his hands.

Collins wiped his hands. “Smothering to murder is difficult to detect. Where did you say the body was found? He died of asphyxia. Were there signs of struggle?”

“A room full of books was tossed in the house. But he was found upstairs laying across a bed.” DeLaMonte responded. “Something went on there, but what?”

“You’re sitting there thinking a crime has been committed. There are no bruises on his hands or face. No other signs of struggle. Collins frowned and took a deep breath. Let’s muddy the water; the Death Certificate is going to say suspicious circumstances. I have nothing to back up that accusation, but it allows you to investigate what the ‘something’ is.” Collin went to the sink and scrubbed. “He died about 7 a.m. Saturday morning and arrived here near midnight last night.”

“Thanks, Doc,” DeLaMonte said, reaching for a cigarette and walking towards the door thinking he had to pay a visit to Blake Knightly.

The Night of the Falling, Brady House Publications (4)

Katie was sitting in front of the television watching ALL IN THE FAMILY, when Quinn and Betty arrived home that Sunday evening. She recognized that worried look on her Dad's face and got up and turned the TV off. "What's wrong?" She asked.

"We need your help on a case. Are you interested?" Quinn asked.

"It might be fun," Betty added.

"What do you want me to do?" Katie was all ears.

Betty jumped in. "At first we thought you might follow a route to Chicago and interview at all the major bookstores along the way. Then we thought it would be safer if you did the interviews by phone. You could cover two major arteries and more of the bookstores by phone than driving."

"Interviewing? What would I be interviewing about? And where are you two going?" Kate was on the edge of her seat.

"There has been a burglary at the Brady estate, and possibly a murder. Eleanor Pennyworth has asked us to retrieve a manuscript that she reported missing. But there are also first editions missing from Brady's personal library. That is where you come in. If we can get a lead on someone selling Brady House Publications first editions, we may find a thread leading to the manuscript. Ahh…" Quinn looked at Betty, "And possible murderer."

Betty looked Quinn in the eyes and a light went on that Katie should not be sent on the trail of a murderer, even if there were a remote chance of putting her in danger.

He silently agreed. "Tomorrow we are going to spend some time at the library researching bookstores that advertize in the Yellow Pages. That should get us all the larger stores. We are searching for used bookstores rather than new stores. And we will make note of the Independents as well, they may sell both new and used books. We will focus on Brady House Publications and we want a description of the seller and a description of what he is driving. The license plate number would be ideal." He smiled at Katie. "Do you still want to help?"

Monday morning Eleanor Pennyworth was on the phone with Phillip Berkeley, explaining that an inventory would take place at the first opportunity against the checklist given to him as trustee of the Jim Brady trust to Hourglass Trinity College. The news was boiling Phillip's blood pressure. The manuscript was his guarantee of a comfortable future. Eleanor was listening to his concerns when two black Mercedes Benz pulled into the drive of the estate. Covington Brady climbed out of the first Mercedes wearing Tommy Hilfiger pants, calfskin shirt, and buckled loafers followed closely by what she assumed was his lawyer with two assistants in the second Mercedes.

She watched Covington walk to the steps of the entry full of what she thought of as 'Esquire assurance' and confidence. No question that he was in charge of every situation. She sighed BOYS.

The lawyer took the 'do not cross' tape from the library door and told the assistants to get the books picked up and handed them an alphabetized inventory list representing the Hourglass Trinity College bequest. "Start here he said, one of you read the title, the other check it off the list. I want to know what is here and what is not. There are 3,200 titles on the list. For now, just put them back on the shelf when done. There may be books in here not on the list. Stack those in the corner. We'll worry about boxing everything later."

Covington led Eleanor to a study at the other end of the house where he would tell her how much time she had to get out. The lawyer noted that Covington was doing all the talking. The lawyer armed with an inventory of the artwork at the estate began walking through the rooms checking off the names of listed artists and their paintings.

Eleanor had no chance to give the messages from the Metropolitan, or Christie's.

Kate, Betty, and Quinn were waiting at the door of Clearview Terrace Library when it opened on Monday morning. They took a table near where the library stacked the phone books for the three surrounding states and started their list of every bookstore listed in the yellow pages.

Quinn did not realize the quantity of stores on the list. The list included used bookstores and independent bookstores but not new bookstores. From what Blake had told them the new bookstores were run by corporate managers that would not recognize a valuable book. He knew he would miss some smaller neighborhood stores with the search limited to the yellow pages, but it was a chance he had to take. He reasoned the small retailers would not front the money for an expensive manuscript or scarce first editions.

When they were finished, they had a list of fifty-seven used bookstores and thirteen motels with phone numbers along six major highways leading away from Clearview Terrace. The concentration would be on the stores along the corridors leading to Chicago, New York, and Atlanta.

"I'll be right back," Betty said to Quinn and Kate. She walked over to the librarian's desk. "Eight-One-three-zero-eight-seven, ok got it. Thanks."

In a moment, Quinn watched the librarian pointing down toward an aisle.

A few minutes later Betty returned with her well worn and newly withdrawn copy of The Night of the Falling. "We should know what all the fuss is about," she announced holding up the book to Quinn.

"While we are here," Betty told Kate and Quinn, "we should make a list of questions to ask when we get a store owner on the line. Don't you agree?"

Kate and Quinn agreed.

Lars Bragdon arrived in Clearview Terrace in the wee early hours of Tuesday morning driving his light blue 1972 Montego. He checked into the Playa-Long Motel on the edge of town near the Shady View Mobile Home Park and planned to grab some sleep before contacting Eleanor Pennyworth.

Matheson Brady nursed his beer at the Frosty Mug. *My charm is wasted on the waitress. She sees through me. But what do I care. I will go make nice with Covington. My father's will is to be read in forty-eight hours and I will take a nice ski trip this winter. Covington will brow beat me relentlessly.* He took another sip of beer.

He took a room at the Playa-Long Motel rather than being too close to Covington and his lawyer and was sure he could find some company for the night.

The Frosty Mug

JJ after driving late into the night parked his beige '62 Ford Falcon wagon in front of a Ponderosa Steakhouse climbed out, stretched and lit A Tiparillo Cigar. He walked to the door and tried to open it but found it locked. Nick was asleep in the front seat. JJ pulled and tugged at the door, his eyes just slits, finally releasing the door handle and kicking the door. He turned red faced and walked back towards the car.

Nick stirred awake, looking around. "Where are we?" He asked as he climbed out and stretched. He looked in the back to make sure his boxes of books were there and safe.

"Highway 95 is just a few more miles. I'm hungry, and this damn place is closed. There was a Howard Johnson's a few miles back. Let's head back there. You drive." He handed the keys to Nick and kicked gravel.

They both climbed in. JJ yawning, picked up an old copy of American Book Prices Current, on the front seat, and started reading listings.

Cummings, Edward Estlin 1894-1962

-No Thanks, [NY, 1935]. Holograph Ed.

Mor. P May 6 (178) $425

He closed the book and thought IF I JUST COME ACROSS THE RIGHT BOOKS.

The Night of the Falling, Ephemera (5)

Tuesday Morning

Katie set the coffee pot on the stove and waited for it to percolate. She had her list of numbers and her presentation ready and she began to make calls.

"Hello. We are helping our detective lieutenant in Clearview Terrace, with the investigation of the death of Jim Brady. In connection with that we are asking you to give us a call if any Brady House Publication books of note, come your way over the next few days. The books are potentially stolen goods; so be warned that it could cause problems for you if you buy them. We especially want a description of the seller and the seller's car if possible. A license number would be very helpful. Yes, any information you can provide, call us, ask for Kate Moosebroker at 043-CV9-0100. Thank you."

Kate checked off one number and poured herself a cup of coffee then picked up the phone only 56 more calls to make.

The two law clerks finished the inventory just after 2 a.m. The list of missing titles began.....

An Arabesque Mystic, association copy, inscribed to the publisher. (Akil, Basim)

In the Middle of Murder, signed, review slip laid in. (Ashcroft, Arthur)

The Nuns of Saint Michael's, Errata tipped in. (Ashton, Marco)

The hand written list indicated a total of 102 titles missing from the Hourglass Trinity College bequest inventory. There just was no time to type the list out.

Quinn and Betty were running late. Eleanor Pennyworth had called to set an appointment with Lars Bragdon at the estate but had cut their time short to arrive. The Chrysler Town and Country pulled to a stop in the long curved drive and pulled behind a new 1972 Montego.

Eleanor opened the door to greet them, walked them past the library with the books back on the shelves and a wide pile of books in the corner. The mahogany bookcase had lost some of the luster. She led them to a large room where a tall man was holding in one hand a Revolutionary war parchment signed by Marquis de La Fayette and in the other a letter turning down a Brady House Publishing book offer signed Dick Nixon.

Lars put down the documents as Quinn approached. Eleanor introduced them. Quinn took Lars' right hand in both of his as he shook. Betty sat, and Quinn took a seat near her.

Lars began, "You may or may not know; Eleanor and I are old friends. She called me to make the estate an offer on the ephemera. So far, I have not gotten past the autographed material. The son has already brought in one of his lawyers and two assistants, not likely an offer of mine will be entertained at the auction houses in New York converging on the estate for the rest of the week. I am going to be here for hours then I'll make an offer on some items and see what Covington has to say."

Eleanor broke in, “Lars, I have an appointment to get to this morning. My car's blocked in; can I borrow yours for an hour?”

“Sure,” Lars said handing her his keys. “It will take me that long to fill Quinn and Betty in on the manuscript.”

Eleanor excused herself as Lars took the chair from behind the desk and moved it closer. “The word manuscript is being tossed around. But physically you are looking for a cardboard stationary box with typed pages. These pages are unlike any other. Henry Farley sat at a typewriter in a cabin in Colorado and typed out his epic story. Then he took the sheets and made notes and corrections in his own hand to the bestselling novel in seventy-five years. The work likely paid for this place all on its own.”

“Where is it likely to go?” Betty chimed in.

Lars rubbed the side of his mouth. “Likely. Now that is an interesting word.” He glanced back and forth between the two of them.

Quinn saw the same look in Lars’ eyes as he saw in the man with the gray ponytail at Millie’s Café. It was a transformation, an opium escape, a rabbit hole journey of the mind. A face, now blank left to its own device. Quinn recognized that look, a stare, a checking out, it was the one place where a man could be king. In a moment, Lars returned from that citadel of his mind; light and life returning to his eyes.

“I can’t address likely. There are so few possible destinations. There is not a good way to determine the length of the journey it will take to get there. There are a few institutions that would take it without the slightest thought of ethics or legalities. If it makes it into their hands, you do not have the resources to get it back. It could be sent across international borders for decades to maintain possession.”

Lars stood and paced. “It does not take a genius to know an inventory was just made in the library.” He tugged at his ear. “Seems to me….” He paused. “Do you know how many people took a public slap in the face when Big Jim Brady announced the manuscript was going in trust to Hourglass Trinity College? His one action pushed dozens and dozens of people at the likes of Yale and Harvard to the edge of madness.”

“Seems to me, you began then stopped,” Quinn spoke up. “What seems to you?”

“Ah, hmm, I have forgotten. How did Big Jim die?” Lars replied.

The door of the large room opened. Covington walked in and looked at the three of them, the female assistant was by his side. “Keep an eye on them,” Covington ordered the assistant.

Betty stood and walked toward Covington. “Where can I find the ladies room?”

Covington’s manners arrived. “The closest one is down that hall, um, third door on the left.” He left them.

Lars glanced at the assistant and began. “There is at least one major collector in every state. That creates a wild nest of speculation. They are all, in a way, in competition with each other. I guess I would contact the major book dealers in the country just to let them know you know who they are. I do not envy you the job of recovering that manuscript.”

Betty wandered around both floors of the estate. Looked in the room Eleanor said Big Jim’s body was found. She walked out the back kitchen door closest to the library and saw a drive for service deliveries bordered by a five-foot stone wall.

When she returned, Quinn was thanking Lars for his help and they both said their goodbyes. Quinn and Betty made their way out the front door. Quinn looked at the powder blue Torino near an arbor leading around to the four car garage.

Lars was again lost in the realm of books, autographs, and ephemera. A realm where time stopped or rather did not exist.

“He wasn’t much help was he?” Betty said to Quinn as he held the car door open for her.

“He did point out that we are not looking for a jewel encrusted tome with tooled Moroccan leather. We are looking for a box of typewriter paper worth upwards of thirty thousand dollars.”

Betty picked up her library copy of Night of the Falling and read a passage to Quinn that she had marked.

“A thousand stars reigned in the tanzanite sky forming a canopy over the veranda of the plantation house. The silhouette of the acacia tree longed for the eye’s attention as a leopard swept through the speargrass eyes glowing. Marguerite leaned against the rail, the lantern revealing her form beneath a flimsy nightgown. Her eyes glanced to Read’s. She hopped over the rail, pulled her nightgown over her head and ran naked across the lawn into the African night

.

Read grabbed his holster and ran off into the night after her; catching her in the grass they began to make love for the second time in under an hour; this time under the watchful eye of the black leopard.”

She closed the book. “It is no wonder that this became a popular read by so many.”

Quinn guided his Chrysler Town and Country out of the drive and back to reality. “Let’s stop and get some lunch at the Frosty Mug. Then we can bring some food to Kate and see how she made out this morning.

Quinn reached over and took Betty’s hand. “When this case is done, I know a secluded place upstate if you feel like running free in nature.”

Quinn’s grin spoke volumes to Betty.

The Night of the Falling, Montego, (6)

Tuesday Afternoon

Blake Knightly turned the key in his shop's front door and saw a green Dodge Polara driving up the street in his direction. He opened his door, walked to his counter reached under the counter and picked up his copy of Velden, The Obsidian Pear. He took the book's cover off and set it gently upright in an empty waste bin, then carried the book over to his gardening section and placed it on the shelf.

A moment later Detective DeLaMonte came in his front door. "You don't mind if I look around do you?" He had the look of a fox on his face that just came across a plump chicken.

"Do you have a warrant?" Blake asked.

"This is a bookshop isn't it? Do you ask everyone that walks through the door for a warrant?" The fox wanted to play with his food awhile. DeLaMonte walked around looking at the books. Lifting one and putting it back in the wrong place. "Did you know Jim Brady?"

"I knew of him. He wasn't a customer of mine. Why are you here?" Blakely said cautiously.

"Simple. A prominent book publisher is dead under suspicious circumstances. You are a bookseller. Don't you see the connection?"

"You mean because I own some books, and he owned some books that we are somehow connected? That's absurd." Knightly's mind swirled with the flatfooted thinking.

"Make sure your lawyer is paid up from last time. You may need him again, and soon." DeLaMonte fired back. "Can you shed any light on this case?"

“What case? What are you investigating?” Knightly would not be cooperating with DeLaMonte after his run in regarding Pepper Bishop.

A patrol car with Officer Harcourt at the wheel pulled up in front of Blake’s door. He got out and walked inside. “What are we looking for?” Officer Harcourt addressed DeLaMonte.

DeLaMonte’s face was blank, “A rare manuscript, of course. Look around.” The two police officers glanced at each other knowing the futility of their task this morning.

Eleanor Pennyworth pulled in front of her friend Blanche’s home and parked. She let herself in with the key Blanche had given her and lugged her two suitcases to the car and put them in the trunk.

She had a meeting with Phillip Berkeley. He needed reassurance that everything humanly possible was being done to secure the manuscript. She would relay that lawyers were taking an inventory and a list would be available very soon. Then he could arrange transportation of the rest of the library bequest into his care.

Quinn and Betty delivered lunch to Kate, threw two light suitcases in the back of the Town & Country and made their way to the Turnpike.

Kate had instructions and a list of places they would be staying each night along their route.

Betty assured Kate they would be careful and check in with her every evening.

It was late afternoon when Lars Bragdon wrote a check out to Covington R. Brady and walked out the front door with two boxes of ephemera and assorted autographs. He was met at the front door by Eleanor Pennyworth, who helped him carry one of the boxes and got them secure on the spacious floor of the back seat of the Montego. They gave each other a hug and Lars was on his way back to his bookshop The Stacks, in Boston. Covington took the thousand dollar check and placed it in his jacket pocket.

JJ parked his '62 Ford Falcon wagon in front of a bookshop he spotted while heading back to the highway after a break. He opened the back and pulled a nice copy of Dietrich's, Omen Hunters and a signed copy of Tomorrow in the Mirror and carried them through the front door of Midas Wellby Books. He extended his hand and said, "I'm Leandro. I have these two titles to offer. I'll take forty dollars for both." He laid the titles on the counter.

The elder man with crystal blue eyes picked up the Omen Hunters and opened it to the title page. It was a nice copy. He noted the Brady House Publisher logo and year printed. He flipped to the last page and saw the number one in parentheses denoting a first edition. Brady House Publishers later placed the words first edition on the copyright page to distinguish their first editions. He picked up Tomorrow in the Mirror, which upon inspection was found to also be a first edition. "I am afraid, I am not interested," the bookseller told Leandro.

"Not interested? This is an easy $40.00 profit for you. How can you not be interested?" JJ's eyes narrowed and his ears seemed to point backward.

"This is a small neighborhood bookstore. I recognize a book scout when they come into my shop to scrutinize every title. There is a larger shop on Grove and Fourth Street, you might try there."

JJ took his books and left the shop angry and confused as to why a man would walk away from two titles that would bring in a quick, easy profit.

The elderly man with crystal blue eyes walked to the door of his shop and made a mental note of the make and model of JJ's car. He walked back to his phone and lifted the receiver and dialed the number he jotted down an hour before. He set the note by the phone and listened to the ringing.

Just then, JJ walked back through the door, to the book seller's surprise. JJ walked briskly to the counter startling the old man. The phone continued to ring, as the phone fell from his hand. JJ picked up the receiver and the grabbed the note with a phone number.

Kate picked up her ringing line.

JJ looking at the bookseller's note said, "Kate Moosebroker, you're hunting me! No," in a loud voice, "I am hunting you." JJ slammed down the receiver and walked out of the shop carrying the slip of paper with the number.

JJ returned to his car, red faced. "I am going back to Clearview."

"Clearview? What are you talking about? I don't want to go back to Clearview." Nick told him.

“Fine!!” He opened his car door, walked behind his car lifted the top door, lowered the gate, grabbed the two boxes of books Nick had purchased at the Clearview Library sale and put them on the sidewalk. He returned to the driver’s seat, slammed the door and said, “GET OUT!”

He drove away leaving Nick and two boxes of books on the sidewalk a hundred miles from home.

The bookshop owner with crystal blue eyes picked up the phone and called his colleague at Mockingbird Books on Grove and Fourth Street. “Hi Mike, did you get a call this morning regarding Brady House Publisher titles? You did; good. Can I get that number, I seemed to have misplaced it. Thank you very much. There is a beefy looking guy that may stop in and try to sell you some Brady House Publisher titles. Yeah, he was just here. An unfriendly type if I ever met one. OK, thanks again.”

The owner of Midas Wellby Books picked up the phone and called Kate Moosebroker. “Hello, I am calling about your earlier call. Yes, the car he is driving is an older beige Ford Station wagon. The Falcon, I think they called it. Beats me why they called it that. Be careful. He seems like a young man with a quick temper. OK, you’re welcome.”

Just when he hung up Nick pushed open his front door pushing one box of books along with his foot. “What will you give me for these?”

The owner walked around the counter and bent over the books. What he saw was nice clean stock. “Forty dollars sound fair to you?”

Matheson Brady sat behind his father's desk in his father's chair and thought about the man who had such a low opinion of him. IT WAS ALWAYS COVINGTON THIS AND COVINGTON THAT. He was the only one that seemed to miss the old man now that he was gone.

Covington paced in front of the desk; waiting for an answer from Matheson about selling his portion of the business, 'since he didn't want to do any work'.

"You take a good salary for your time spent keeping the publishing house. I will keep my portion of the business and expect to be compensated for it. We both have shares that ensure we don't have to work. Covington, your offer is too low." Matheson let him know the being pushed around is over.

Covington left the library thinking, *It doesn't hurt to ask*. He returned to supervising the moving people from Sotheby's taking the L&JG Stickley furniture to auction in New York.

Night of the Falling - Covington & Matheson (7)

Wednesday

In the driveway of the estate sat a panel truck from Sotheby's with driver and helper waiting. Christy's sent an armored van painted a dull yellow with Stanley Steamer painted on the sides. Thomas Hoving, Director, Metropolitan Museum of Art, sat in his Cadillac waiting along with the rest of them; he wanted the Pissarro and would pay the right price to get it. They all waited, the funeral was this morning and Covington did not trust anyone to handle the details but himself.

Covington, Matheson, Eleanor Pennyworth, Phillip Berkeley and Detective DeLaMonte stood at the grave site of Big Jim Brady. The middle of the week funeral far from the city where Jim worked so many years ago made for a small gathering. Detective DeLaMonte was restless. He was hoping to glean something from the group. What he learned was the Jim Brady was not a popular man.

Jim Brady's lawyer was at the estate to read the will. Covington and Matheson were assured of wealth generated from the labor of Jim Brady. Phillip Berkeley was trying to remain grateful for the circumstance that put him in the right place at the right time. Eleanor Pennyworth had her clothes packed and some mementos of her years spent at Jim Brady's side. There were no tears to be seen.

Black suits and red roses where the color of the day. The cigarette smoke poured from the windows of the procession of cars heading back to the estate.

The simple headstone read:

James Brady

1900-1972

Letter Perfect

Only Eleanor Pennyworth got the joke.

Matheson arrived home first. He pulled into the driveway. The drive became crowded as the vehicles emptied and Covington began barking orders. He showed Thomas Hoving into the den, took his check made out to Covington Brady and watched Hoving leave with his coveted Pissarro. Hoving silently vowed to never have it leave the Metropolitan Museum of Art again.

Matheson made his way to the room with a television set and gathered the family albums of young days spent in the beauty of Colorado and stuffed them in the trunk of his car. He went back inside and emptied the liquor cabinet and carried the bottles back to his car.

The ousted Matheson left the estate for the last time. The exiled Eleanor returned to Blanches' apartment, picked up Blanche and headed off to The Frosty Mug for one last beer with her friend before she left town. Phillip Berkeley arranged to remove the completely boring collection of first editions that would bring him only the slightest bit of revenue and only brief, modest prestige to Hourglass Trinity College.

The egg on Phillip Berkeley's face from being the near curator of a literary prize to the compiler of <u>The Catalogue of the Jim Brady Collection</u>, left an acidic smell lingering in his nostrils. He knew deep pockets were converging upon the estate. He consoled himself with the fact that he would also find a publisher for <u>The Correspondence of Henry Farley.</u> His triumphant, coveted crown had been reduced to an ornamental headdress; he was now the academic equivalent of a man viewed as wearing an inverted birds nest on his head.

JJ pulled into Clearview. His eyes still two slits in a wild face. His instincts were hurt and his manhood provoked at the thought of a 'Kate' interfering with his feed bag. *He would show her.* He pulled into the parking lot of The Frosty Mug and went in. He found the payphone and looked up Moosebroker in the phonebook. He only found one K. Moosebroker on 321 Elm. He sat at a table and gave the once over EYE to Eleanor Pennyworth and her friend Blanche as they ate their lunch.

JJ ate his lunch and flirted with the waitress thinking of his next move. He asked the waitress if there was an antique district in Clearview Terrace. He had made money scouting Antique stores and finding underpriced books that these all-knowing dealers found for him. He often thought, "it was as good as stealing.'

What JJ found in the antique district was the 2nd Street Mystery Playhouse, which he judged shutdown, based on the peeling posters in the entry way and cobwebs above the double doors. He walked around and spotted the side door. This sleepy area with a closed down Sunkist plant and abandoned rail spur was quiet this mid-Wednesday afternoon. He went and brought his car around. He jimmied the side door and walked inside. *I guess I am checking into my room for the night,* he told himself. He unloaded the five boxes of books inside the theater. He reasoned stolen goods in the back of the Falcon might not be the best idea. Three-two-one Elm, three-two-one Elm ran through his mind. At sundown, he would prowl.

While JJ was roaming around the inside of the interior, Officer Harcourt in his Police cruiser happened to make his rounds of the antique district. He mentally noted a beige Ford Falcon wagon parked away from the shops.

Blanche and Eleanor said their goodbyes out in front of the Frosty Mug. They made their promises to keep in touch. Eleanor knew she would not be returning to Clearview Terrace. Her years with Jim Brady were filled with memories both bitter and sweet. The estate that was their home would be sold to the bare walls and then the property would be put on the market. It was just too far from everything to suit the Brady boys. She knew what Covington had yet to learn that he was not half the man that Big Jim Brady was and the publishing house fortunes were about to turn. She held out hope that Matheson found himself.

Eleanor Pennyworth climbed into the front seat of her roomy light blue Gran Torino and headed out of Clearview Terrace. On her way, she dropped a check into a blue curbside mailbox, made out to Quinn Moosebroker, for his services.

Her apartment in Boston waited her arrival; she would be there by morning if Hwy 93 remained clear. She thought she just might write a book or take a trip.

Quinn and Betty pulled into the parking lot of Time Tunnel Books. They got out and walked hand in hand to the front door. When they entered, Betty released Quinn's hand and began to survey the books. Quinn went to the counter and began his impossible task. What he was told is that the owner was not in. The clerk was unable to offer any help in their search as he was not the book buyer.

Returning to the Town and Country, Quinn sat for a long time before reaching for the keys. "This is a wild goose chase. He could be anywhere or nowhere."

Betty was learning Quinn's many faces. The face he was wearing now was new to her. She watched him stare a hole into the steering wheel, take a deep breath, let it out slowly and deliberately, and turn the ignition.

Quinn put the lever into reverse and let out the clutch. "What's next?"

"The plan was to head over to Hwy 81 and stay on it until it changed to Hwy 93. The first motel for the night is off the 93. What are you thinking?"

"I think wild goose chases are for geese. What is the next bookstore on our list?" Quinn pulled out heading toward the highway.

Betty picked up The Night of the Falling, saying, "This is where the title came from."

She read a passage:

"The electricity in the air prickled the hair of both man and beast. The temperature slowly dropped as the blanket of clouds rolled leisurely in; body and soul were lifted into incredible lightness. The bare natives, in their villages, would soon begin their rituals baths and their ceremonial dance of renewal.

Read and Marguerite, felt wild, they found it impossible to stay robed as their spirits were enveloped; their bodies sheathed in fingers of voltaic air; they moved in unison to the rhythmic sounds of their neighbor's drums pounding in their ears, announcing the night of the falling."

The Night of the Falling, The loss of $30,000 (8)

Wednesday Evening

JJ sat in front of the broken mirror in the dressing room at the closed down 2nd Street Playhouse Mystery Theater and combed his hair back with the comb he carried in his back pocket. He admired himself. He could understand why the ladies chased him.

He wore what he considered his trademark, black pants and black shirt that showed off his biceps. "You shouldn't let yourself get so worked up." He said aloud to his splintered reflection. Then staring into the glass, his eyes narrowed, he said, "Make it quick." He flipped the switch, walked out the door he had jimmied earlier and went out into the shadows of the night.

Covington Brady cursed Matheson when he found the liquor cabinets were emptied. He and his lawyer hopped into Cov's Mercedes and drove off in search of a bottle of Glenmorangie.

"You don't seem upset about the missing manuscript." The lawyer was making small talk.

"It doesn't belong to me. You said the Trust giving it to the college could not be broken. Besides, I have had everything that has left the estate since I arrived searched; including Eleanor's car and all her luggage. Do you think a local liquor store will have what we are looking for?"

"We might have to slum it with a Chivas Regal." The lawyer lit another Parliament cigarette with the recessed filter. He reached up and cracked the wind wing.

"It's not like you to take the loss of $30,000 so lightly," he said exhaling toward the window.

Covington glanced over at his lawyer. "Since when are you so free with your observations?"

"You have been behaving like 'The Godfather" for two days now; the pilgrims are practically kissing your ring. You have a pocket full of unreported checks and you began this liquor run complaining about Matheson. What gives?" He flicked his cigarette out the window. The lawyer knew from the sinister grin frozen on Covington's face that this conversation was over. "There's a liquor store," he pointed to a strip mall.

Lars Bragdon set down the phone and scratched his head at the caller. The caller insisted that he were contacted the moment the manuscript of The Night of The Falling reached him. Clifford Enders was being proactive. Clifford Enders made the same phone call to every major bookstore owner in the country.

Lars flipped through his current copies of American Book Price Current to see if any TLS by Mark Twain had recently sold at auction. This was just one of the items to research from the boxes brought back from the Brady Estate. He was behind schedule for preparing his Fall book catalogue: American Travels and Explorations, Life and Adventures on the Plains, Indian History, California, Oregon and the Northwest, Indian Portraits, Ephemera, Old Maps. Several James Brady items would be prominently offered. He slipped the letter into a mylar sleeve which would be its new home until a buyer would be found.

The words, "Now I am hunting you," rang in Kate's ear as she sat and nursed a beer at the Frosty Mug. She wondered when Quinn and Betty would get her message. At first there was a small amount of panic in her when the phone was slammed down in her ear. Then she thought to take her list of bookshops and go to Betty's. Betty had already thought to exchange extra house keys.

The owner of Midas Wellby Books told her on the phone what had happened and to be cautious that the guy seemed dangerous. Her nerves had been set on edge. She rummaged around in Betty's garage, admired the 1962 MG Midget and found what she was looking for in a circular bin that seemed perfect for this purpose. She pulled the wooden Spalding Little League Yogi Berra bat from its resting place and hefted it. She gave it an even swing and immediately felt better. She found a rag, gave the bat a dusting and carried it back into the house.

"Do not go gentle into that good night," she mumbled to herself. That's my new motto, she thought as she set the bat on the kitchen table and opened a bottle of Coke. She flipped on the radio near the kitchen counter and found it on an FM station playing music she liked. She sat and listened for the phone to ring.

Eleanor Pennyworth was very comfortable behind the wheel of her powder blue Gran Torino. The cruise control was set at 75 mph, and traffic was clear. She wanted to drive straight through, but she was getting tired. She kept her eyes open for a Travel Lodge and thought she would stop, grab dinner, a shower and get a good night's sleep. In the morning, she would make her way into the city and get there rested. She thought about the last time she and Jim had been in the city together. Jim had left her some money in his will, she would be ok for a while; a good long while. The chapter was closing on the Brady bunch.

Quinn pulled his 1946 Chrysler Town and Country into the drive of the Lucky Cuss Motel. They had made reservations; this was their stopping point for the night. Betty went to check in and Quinn got the car parked. He looked over and watched with interest a tall older man with a gray ponytail walk into the drive toward the lobby.

Quinn moved towards the man, "Nick, is that you?"

Nick was startled; then he recognized Quinn from Millie's Café on Sunday. "What are you doing here?" Nick asked.

"I was about to ask you the same thing?" Quinn told him and waited for a reply.

"Well, not that it is any of your business, but MY FORMER book partner kicked me out of his car. He came out of a bookstore angry as I have ever seen him and told me he is going back to Clearview Terrace. He threw my boxes of books on the sidewalk in front of Midas Wellby Books and drove off in a huff."

Nick walked passed Quinn toward the lobby. Quinn turned to go and find Betty. He reached her and told her what had just happened in the lot.

"Let's go. Get our stuff." Quinn told Betty. "He is likely our man."

"We haven't unloaded our stuff. Get a hold of yourself." Betty said smiling.

Quinn walked away from Betty, toward the lobby. He found Nick just as he finished checking in. "What is he driving? And about what time did he throw you out of the car?"

"Man, it was several hours ago, I have been walking and thumbing rides ever since. He's driving a rundown Ford Falcon wagon, beige in color." He fumbled with a pack of smokes. "What's all the fuss?"

Quinn looked sharply at Nick's weathered face. "Thanks for your help."

Nick turned to head toward his room, his gray hair obscured by Camel smoke.

"Wait, one more question. Where were you heading?" Quinn's mind was reeling.

"Boston," Nick said as he again turned to go; foremost on his mind was giving his feet a rest.

Quinn walked back to find Betty. She was holding a message from Kate and trying to reach her on the pay phone as he approached with a look of impatience on his face. "We should get going." He told her.

"I am trying to reach Kate to let her know we are headed back. But there is no answer." Betty hung up the phone. She handed Quinn the note. She extended her hand, "I'll drive; you have been driving all day." For a moment, they were frozen there.

Quinn noted the look of determination on her face and reluctantly handed her the keys.

The note said, 'Come home at once.'

Night of the Falling - 'Kate would be sorry' (9)

Thursday Morning

Betty pulled off the turnpike and eased her foot off the accelerator the needle dropped from the 80 mph hour mark as the Town and Country slowed. The hours had passed quickly.

"Why would he go back?" Quinn offered near the beginning of the drive home. "He would want his payday. He would want to get to where he was going. This guy is driven by something other than just money. Or he is not the guy at all."

Quinn got the slightest of responses. Betty's mind was not on the case. The note said, 'Come home at once.' Her mind could not get past that. It was her that planted the seed of an idea that Kate stay home to make calls. Now home seemed to be the target. She wanted to get home but did not dare push the old Town and Country further.

It was in the wee hours of the morning that she pulled into the drive of Quinn's place. She knew that Quinn would have never driven at such speed with her in the car for her safety sake. The Town and Country breathed a sigh of relief upon turning into the drive.

The house was dark, and they soon discovered that it was empty. Betty got on the phone and called to her own number, "Sorry to wake you. We are back. Go back to sleep we will see you nice and early. Oh, wait. Your Dad wants to talk to you." Betty handed the receiver to Quinn.

In a moment, Quinn put the receiver down. "We should get some sleep," he told Betty. "I am going to put the car into the garage. I'll be back in a moment." Quinn went out the back, down the two steps and around to the garage. He decided to take a quick look around the neighborhood. He climbed behind the wheel and patted the steering wheel.

JJ had made the rounds of Clearview Terrace. He pulled up behind the Brady estate to take a look to see if there were any pickings. Through a window, he watched two well-dressed men sitting drinking from an expensive bottle of scotch and hoped one day he would find himself in such rich surroundings. He went back on the prowl. He drove past 312 Elm three times. Each time the lights were off. It appeared that no one was home. This made him angry and made him wonder just what he was doing.

He parked his Ford Falcon on a cross street with a view of 312 Elm's front door. He quickly fell asleep on his stakeout. In the wee hours of the morning, the sound of a car starting woke him.

Light was on at 312 Elm and the silhouette of a woman in the side window made him sit straight up. He got out of his car and made his way in the shadows toward the house. He crossed in front of Mrs. Jones' front porch and ducked between the houses. He made his way to the window and peered inside just as Betty dropped her cornflower blue nightgown over her head. She turned out the light and walked over and crawled into bed. She had made sure the doors were unlocked for Quinn.

The hair on the back of her neck bristled and woke her. She threw her legs over the side of the bed noting that Quinn has not asleep at her side. She was disoriented, not realizing she was only asleep for a few minutes. As her eyes focused, she reached over and picked up a heavy bookend of a man on a stack of books overlooking a globe. Her bare feet moved quietly as a cat over the wooden floors.

The soft soled sneakers moved without sound on the hardwood floors. JJ an accomplished burglar by night was used to moving silently. He was self-assured and felt like a magnificent leopard. '*This Kate would be sorry she ever messed with him.*'

That was the last thought that went through his mind before Betty conked him on the head with the bookend. The thud of the body hitting the ground brought Betty an adrenaline rush. She flipped on the light to see this muscular man laid out cold. *Betty Atwood, in the cornflower blue nightie, by a knockout*, she told herself.

She turned in a quick panic as she heard the back kitchen door open and went quickly though cautiously to the kitchen. "Hi Moose – this way," Betty told him rising from her crouch. Quinn watched her go and followed. When he saw a man lying on the floor knocked out, he was speechless. "Call the police, will you? I have to go get dressed. I don't want to be seen in my nightie." Quinn watched her go, scratching the back of his head.

JJ stirred and moved to a sitting position. Quinn put the receiver down having completed his call. Quinn towered over JJ. "Get up. Please get up."

All the voices inside JJ's head told him to stay down. The sarcasm in Quinn's voice was clear, to all of them, even with a mild concussion.

Officer Harcourt arrived in his cruiser. He shook Quinn's hand as he entered. JJ who had remained sitting was glad to see a police officer after the treatment received by Betty and the intimidation of Quinn.

Harcourt drove JJ to the station for booking and gave Detective DeLaMonte a call. While he waited he wrote up his report along with information provided by Quinn and Betty.

Detective DeLaMonte arrived and was handed the report; he entered the interrogation room. His shadow cast a dominant pall across the table where JJ sat.

JJ squirmed in his seat; his confidence had already been shaken, and was about to be tested.

"It says here you got beat up by a girl," DeLaMonte said as he entered. He loved his games. "Says here you were caught in Quinn Moosebroker's place," he leaned forward, shaking his head, "the girl probably saved you from the-never-more. Just to be clear, we have you for those minor offenses. You are under arrest for the murder of James Brady," DeLaMonte eyed the transformation from resolve to cowering.

JJ rose from his seat. "Murder! Man what are you talking about?" His words slightly slurred from the lump on his head.

"SIT DOWN! If you stand again, I will make sure you cannot stand for a long time." Det. DeLaMonte was made for this part of the job.

JJ sat.

In the small hours, Phillip Berkeley shuffled with sagging shoulders around a stone storage hollow in the basement of the administration building of Hourglass Trinity College. There were fifty boxes of books to collate and catalogue. Under normal circumstances, he would dive into the work. But there was nothing normal about having a cherry topping presented to him, then snatched away from his vanilla life. He wondered how this happened and who the likely culprit was. He had made it this far without a ghost in his life. But this ghost seemed here to stay. He would call his sister soon and see if she still would allow him to have a small room built behind their home so he would have a place to live in his retirement. He sat the gun in his hand down and wept.

Covington stood in the drive of the estate, wearing gray slacks, Cordovan leather shoes a white wide knit pullover shirt and his Ray-Bans. His lawyer and two assistants just left in their black Mercedes. The two of them just signed a deal with Cohen Estate Sales, an operator to sell off the remaining furniture and household items to the bare walls. Everything of value had already been dispersed. Money would come in over the course of time from the sale of the art and collectible artifacts gathered by Jim Brady. He took a puff on a Havana cigar and climbed into his black Mercedes and drove off to the city.

Quinn sat on the edge of the bed and softly rubbed Betty's back. It was eleven a.m. and Kate's green VW Bug had just pulled in the drive.

Quinn was sure that Betty would want to tell the story of how she captured JJ.

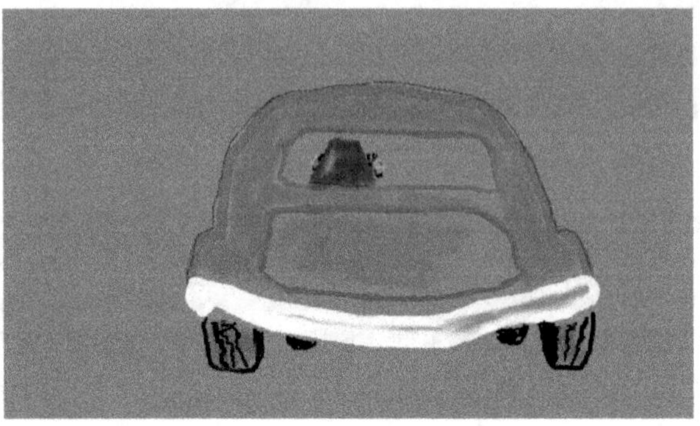

Kate walked in the back kitchen door, “What did I miss?” She called.

At 8 a.m. Eleanor Pennyworth received her wake up call. She took a leisurely shower; dressed casually in lime slacks and short sleeve white blouse; then went across the street to a diner for breakfast before checking out. She was three hours from Boston and it was a beautiful morning for a drive.

Night of the Falling, The Conclusion (10)

Friday

Kate heard the mailman deposit mail into the box installed near their front door and went and grabbed the mail. She was puzzled to see a letter from Eleanor Pennyworth addressed to Detective Quinn Moosebroker. She carried the envelope into her Dad who was sitting at the table with Betty.

He opened the envelope and Kate was pleased to see that he also had a look of surprise on his face.

"A check for services rendered." Quinn held up the check. Quinn leaned forward and said, "It appears we have been let go."

The bags under Detective DeLaMonte's eyes had taken on a dark haze. The side of JJ's face was bruised and he had a fresh cut over his eye. His night had passed in toothache minutes. But the confession to the murder of Jim Brady remained unsigned.

A lawyer from the city District Attorney's was standing listening to the report DeLaMonte was giving.

"Without a confession we don't even have enough to go to trial for murder. Write him up for the trespass. The judge will give him 8 to 10 months for that." The lawyer turned to walk away he then turned back, "Next time it's ribs and kidneys; we don't like them showing up in court with their faces bashed in. It looks bad for everyone."

Eleanor pulled into a parking space at her apartment building and felt lucky. She spotted two clean-cut teenage boys passing through the parking structure laughing. She summoned them and after some negotiation all her bags were brought to her front door. The boys went on their way laughing, richer by five dollars each for their trouble.

She got the bags inside with no trouble and walked over to see if a long time neighbor was home. She needed a phone. Her luck held and after hellos, she was able to reach Lars Bragdon.

"Lars, will you be at The Stacks all morning?" She asked. "I am going to stop by if that is alright with you."

She thanked her neighbor and left to drive across town.

When she arrived at The Stacks, she spotted Lars' 1972 light blue Montego and took the nearest space to it. She rushed in and was greeted by Lars, who thanked her again for the opportunity to get into the estate. He told her of his finds and was grateful. "There's a message for you." He handed her the note. It read, GREEN DRAGON TAVERN 2 PM.

"I left something in your car when I borrowed it. It's a gift for you. Let me borrow your keys and I will grab it – be back in a minute." Eleanor explained.

Lars took the moment to help a customer with her purchase.

Eleanor went to the Montego and popped the trunk. She lifted the two suitcases and closed the trunk. Her car was just a few spaces away and in just a minute she had both bags secured. She went around the side of her car and took the Henry Moore statue from the glove box and carried it inside.

“This is for all your help. It is a little something Jim got me a few years back.” She told Lars. “We will have to do lunch soon.” She made her excuses and left.

Covington arrived in the city in time to get his Mercedes’ hand waxed before getting to a late lunch at the Green Dragon Tavern. The timetable is working out so well. With the Mercedes gleaming, he pulled into a parking structure near the tavern.

Clifford Enders posted himself so that he could see the front entrance. He knew Covington by sight and watched him go in. He felt good; things were coming together. He looked at his watch and waited.

He did not pay attention to the powder blue Gran Tornio as it passed. He watched with keen interest as a smartly dressed woman approach the door of the Tavern. She paused and took a deep breath and went in.

Clifford Enders crossed the street and approached the brick building where his treasure awaited.

Covington and Eleanor stood as Enders approached. “Do you have it?” asked Enders as he extended his hand to Covington.

Covington flashed his golden smile. “Do you have the cash?” He waved his hand for the two to sit.

Enders tapped his suit breast pocket, indicating that he did indeed have the money.

Eleanor reached down and opened a sleek leather satchel that she had placed at her feet. She lifted a stationary box with tight fitting lid. Her fingers found the edge and with deft fingers exposed the contents and revealed their secrets.

The top sheet that had aged and acquired a tan border on it was typed "Night of the Falling" and below it was typed "Henry Farley and his signature." Enders gasped and reached for the box.

Eleanor smiled and pulled the box an inch or two closer to her.

"Of course; of course," Enders reached into his pocket and withdrew two envelopes. He handed one to Eleanor, who without ceremony opened it and flipped through the one hundred dollar bills. She nudged the box forward.

Covington did not count the money. He put the envelope in his breast pocket.

Clifford Enders flipped though the typed manuscript pages reveling in the handwritten notes, the lines crossed out, the margin exclamations, the 'x' out paragraphs; he did not notice when Eleanor and Covington walked out the front door. There was no hand shaking or goodbye exchanged. No shared smile for a job well done. There were just two envelopes of money.

Enders was lost in a magic hour of literary grace; he was transported to a South African adventure. He was, *Read and chasing the naked Marguerite* through the golden savannah. Years fell from his heart – he was again a young man; a young man for an hour.

Office Harcourt had finished his shift. He left the station as the impound tow truck turned in pulling a 1962 beige Ford Falcon. He recalled seeing that very car parked on the side of the 2nd Street Playhouse Mystery Theater and decided to swing by on the way home.

He arrived driving his dark blue Javelin and parked where the Falcon had been parked. He got out and looked up and down the street. He walked around the front and found the theater doors there locked. Going back towards his car, he pulled on the side door, which came open at the tug he had given it.

He pulled it open further and stepped inside. There by the door were five boxes of books. He promptly and triumphantly loaded the books into his car and drove them back to the station. He let Det. DeLaMonte know about the books.

"Books, books, books," DeLaMonte scoffed still angry from his night's work. "I don't want books clogging up the evidence room. They are not part of any case. Get rid of them."

Harcourt was sure where the books came from. He drove to the estate to find it empty and any warmth the home had was now gone. It was a cold structure, in need of a family.

Perplexed, and not wanting to drag the books home, he drove back to town, parked in front of Blake Knightly's bookstore and dragged the boxes one at a time through the front door. With the last box, he told Knightly, "A gift from Detective DeLaMonte."

He hurried off. Eden was waiting.

Quinn Moosebroker arrived at the Clearview Terrace Police station. He was given permission to speak with JJ.

"I don't understand what you were doing at my house last night." Quinn opened with.

JJ being reflective, "That makes two of us. I just went to Clearview to acquire some good books. That's all. I did not murder anyone and I will not sign a piece of paper that says I did."

Quinn sat back. "Go on."

"Me and Nick came into town for the library sale. With the Brady Estate close by it is always good and all the book scouts are hopeful. I knew of Brady, he is famous in book circles. You have to do your research. Ya know what I mean, man?" He paused, "Anyway, I went by the estate, just to check things out. I went up a trellised pathway to a window and slipped inside. The place was so quiet. I walked around this big place and there was no one. I slipped downstairs to what I discovered was the library and there he was clutching his chest. I peered around the corner. He did not see me. Then he stopped, just sitting there. Understand that this was a treasure trove for me. The room could have been filled with emeralds and pearls and I could not have been happier. I started stacking books by the library door. I couldn't stand it anymore. I mean the guy sitting there staring at me. So I carried him up the stairs and put him in the first room I came to. I began carrying boxes out the back door to the short wall where my car was parked. I had the thing almost done when some broad came in the front door. I wasn't done, there were books still stacked in plain view by the library door, but with a dead guy upstairs and now her…well I just got out of there."

"Then what?" asked Quinn.

“Then what…Well then, I went and joined Nick in line for the Clearview Terrace Library Sale. Then after that Nick was hungry again and went and had something at the local café. And now I am here.”

Quinn sighed, “And the manuscript, what did you do with the manuscript?”

JJ’s blank bruised face told Quinn that he did not know a thing about the manuscript. “Anything else yah wanna know?” asked JJ. His mind had wandered off trying to think of any bargaining chip he may have. He could not think of any.

Quinn, Betty, and Kate sat at the Frosty Mug. A plate with a steak sandwich and fries plus a mug of beer sat in front of each of them.

"As far as I can piece together, this is what happened. JJ claims to have been in the Brady house as a burglar. He has some history in his rap sheet to back that up. He told me 'A broad' came home referring to Eleanor. Her presence scared him off because he already had loaded several boxes of books into the back of his car. Eleanor spotted the books piled by the library door and empty space on the shelves. She cautiously searched the house and found Big Jim's body upstairs. She went back down to the library and a glass case with the Farley manuscript sitting there untouched. Her plan was put together on the spot. She removed the manuscript, tossed some books off the shelves and called the police." Quinn took a large bite from his sandwich and washed it down with beer.

"She then went and removed the manuscript from the estate and hid it somewhere and came back. She contacted the sons and let them know their father had passed. Both sons came running. Both had lived a Midas life from the publishing company. It is likely that the sons, one or both of them, who knew of the trust setup by their father had discussed at some point their disagreement with Big Jim Brady's decision with Eleanor. One of the sons or Eleanor may have already lined up a buyer or maybe a buyer phoned one or both of them."

"When we were talking to Lars, Covington sent an assistant to listen to the conversation. He was not taking any chance. Maybe he was trying to make sure the manuscript did not get too far out of sight." Betty offered.

"Covington was obviously distrustful from the beginning. I am sure he had everything that left the house searched. So, I am not sure how the manuscript was taken away from the estate. Unless, do you remember when Eleanor borrowed Lars' car when we were at the house? I wonder if somehow she got it into his car and then he just drove away with it. She told him her car was blocked in, but it was parked away from the entrance when we walked inside. And come to think of it, their cars the Torino and Montego look almost exactly alike. They both were light blue with a black top. No one would know which was which just by glancing in the driveway. Covington, who was checking everything, could have checked out the window over and over and seen her car parked there and would think she was in the house under his watchful eye. They seem to have all been stealing from each other." Quinn took another drink of beer. He looked at Kate, "JJ is the only one going to jail."

Kate spotted two of her friends at the bar. She leaned over and kissed her Dad on the cheek. "See you guys, I am going to go hang out with my friends."

Quinn and Betty smiled at one another. As they left The Frosty Mug a police cruiser with its lights flashing barreled down the highway. They reached home and got settled, Betty wore her favorite kimono; just as she sat down, the phone rang. Betty called out, "Don't answer it!"

A Quinn Moosebroker Mystery
He Dreamt of Murder – Man in a Green hat

Quinn sunk into the barber's chair. Luigi, his new barber in Clearview Terrace, leaned the chair back and applied the warm shaving lather to Quinn's neck and face. He opened the straight razor and pulled it back and forth a few times against the leather strop. As the blade was dragged along his throat, Quinn's mind focused on the conversation going on in the next chair.

"It was a dream?" the second barber, Mac asked.

The young man sighed, "Yes, I think it was a dream. Like I said, I sat straight up in bed like my back was fastened to a spring hinge. My scream 'No!' shook the window behind the bed. The scream at the top of my lungs echoed through the house. It was so real."

"When was that?" Mac expertly evened out the long sideburns with the clippers.

"Just the other night, scared the heck out of my wife. Yeah, it was so real. I was just a little kid sitting by a chain link fence with my hands tied behind my back and attached to the fence. There were three other boys and a little girl all tied to that fence." A bead of sweat appeared at the man's temple.

Quinn felt a slight tremor in Luigi's hand as he listened. A customer walked in and took a seat.

"A young couple was pacing back and forth in front of us. She wore a summer dress and he khaki pants, tee shirt, and garrison hat. The boys by the fence were all wearing summer shorts, striped tee shirts and had crew cuts. I heard him say, 'Where did all these kids come from? We can't fit them all in the car. One has to stay.' The young woman tried to push him away, but he was lean and strong. ‘Pick one,’ he screamed at her.

Luigi brought the razor down the side of Quinn’s face. The scratchy bristle of the severed hairs rang in Quinn’s ears and was accompanied by the ticking of a clock on the wall behind Mac.

“Is that it?” asked Mac.

“No, there is a little more to the dream. What woke me, and why I can’t get it out of my head is he took a step toward us. It was then I noticed the black baton in his hand. Well, he reared back and that baton struck the boy sitting next to me on the head. That’s when I woke up screaming. It was so real.”

The whole thing has made my wife so angry, she asked me in the morning, “Who is Nora?”

“Nora? I asked. That was ‘**NO.’** I yelled no. So, it actually happened, that dream? I was not sure.” The young man looked into the mirror that was being held in front of him. Mac grabbed the neck duster brush and swept it over the young man’s forehead, neck, and collar.

Luigi brought the razor up under Quinn’s chin a second time. Slivers of lather remained along Quinn’s cheek bones as Luigi wrapped a warm towel around his face.

The young man stood, dug into his pocket and handed Mac, $1.25 which included a $0.25 tip. He thanked him and left.

The man waiting his turn stood and took the seat that Mac had just brushed clean. “See those Cubs get beat last night? What is wrong with that Rick Monday, ya see him flub that line drive?”

Luigi sat Quinn up and wrapped a blue cape over him and ran a comb along the side of his naturally curly hair.

“What did you think of that?” Quinn asked. In the chair next to him, Mac listened to how the Cubs lost the game the night before.

Luigi was quiet for a moment. “Sounds like someone committed murder to me. Or that young man ate too much spicy food; one or the other.”

Luigi finished up and grabbed the bottle of Lucky Tiger and applied tonic to Quinn’s hair.

Quinn rose, handed over a $1.50 to Luigi and turned to Mac, “What is that young man’s name? Do you know?”

“Who, Anthony? He works over at the Texaco. He goes by Tony.” Mac went back to trimming his customer’s hair.

Quinn thanked him and left the shop. He stood in the doorway, hair neat and in place. He had a very close shave and he had that fresh from the chair talc and tonic smell. He headed toward his ’46 Town and Country and headed back over to Elm Street turning over and over the dream he just heard relayed by Anthony.

As he pulled into the driveway, his thoughts turned to his date with Betty. She had mentioned a little Italian place and they agreed they should give it a try tonight. Quinn and Betty had spent a great deal of time together over the last couple of weeks. Neither considered chasing cases the same as getting to know each other.

For the second time in a few weeks Retired Detective Quinn Moosebroker donned his blue suit, Kate Moosebroker adjusted his tie and kissed him on the cheek as he left the house and he made his way in his 1946 Town and Country toward Maple Avenue to pick up Betty Atwood.

Betty was sitting on the edge of her sofa wearing her, not quite new, Shamrock green dress which made her feel young. She had heard of an Italian restaurant named, THE LAMB BOR'S LINGUINI, near the edge of town and thought Quinn might enjoy a good meal.

He arrived, walked to her door and knocked. They gave each other a quick kiss before going to his car where he held the door for her. She got in and slid to the center of the bench seat and when Quinn got inside she was by his side and smiling.

Lamb Bor's Linguini

Arriving at, THE LAMB BOR'S LINGUINI, Quinn saw concrete Corinthian style planters with newly planted Italian Cypress aligning the entryway. Inside a wall mural done by a local artist of, The Basilica di Santa Maria del Fiore, adorned one wall. Quinn silently thought he hoped the food was better than the mural.

Betty seemed happy with the place and it was not his intention to compromise that feeling. Once they had been seated and wine and dinner were ordered Quinn began to tell the story he heard at the barber shop.

"Oh, that is such a terrible story." Betty began. "What do you think? Does it have any merit?"

"It has my curiosity piqued," Quinn replied. Their meals were placed in front of them. Quinn watched Betty pick at the plate. "I can at least go over to the Texaco and see if there are more details to gather. Maybe I can gather some family history to see if there really is a puzzle to solve."

Betty's mood changed, she pushed food around her plate but ate very little. When the waiter passed, she ordered another glass of wine.

Quinn stopped eating and talked to Betty as she finished her second glass. When done, she put the glass down, "Can you take me home?" she asked.

They arrived at the curb in front of Betty's house on Elm Street. Betty gave Quinn a quick kiss on the cheek, "Call me tomorrow." She pat Quinn on the chest and slid across the bench seat and let herself out before Quinn could get her door.

The 1946 Town and Country quietly pulled away from the curb through a murky darkness. Quinn rolled the window down and let the night air wash over him as he pondered the telling of death of a boy child. He estimated Anthony's age and guessed that if there was a homicide it took place in the early to mid-1950's. He cut across town and headed out on a lonely stretch of highway that went through rolling farmland. No street lights and wide open space was what he needed tonight.

Betty's house seemed cold to her this night. She straightened her kitchen and prepared for bed in eerie silence. Hours into her sleep the hair on the back of her neck bristled as she heard something drag across the wooden floor of her bedroom. The noise punctured her sleep and she sat straight up in the dark room. Through the fog of sleep, she saw, on the brass footboard rail two small hands. She struggled to bring into focus the ghost of a small boy.

He Dreamt of Murder – Texaco (2)

Quinn pulled his car into the drive at 3:30 a.m. and was surprised to see Betty sitting on his front stoop. She wore blue jeans a thick sweater and a baseball cap pulled snuggly down on her head. Quinn again noticed how beautiful she was.

Quinn did not put his car in the garage as he intended, but immediately came around the front and took a seat next to her. She laced her arm through his and said "I had a bad dream. In fact, it may have been the strangest dream ever."

Betty told her story while Quinn listened intently. When she was done, he stood and helped her to her feet. "Do you want some breakfast? Or do you want some sleep?" He asked heading for the front door.

"Sleep," she replied knowing she would be safe.

In the morning, she woke to the smell of bacon and raisin cinnamon toast. The fresh coffee aroma just added to the warmth that she felt when near Quinn.

"Is there anything we can do? Anything to investigate? What do you think?" Betty sat, her appetite returned as she ate scrambled eggs with green onion and a tablespoon of salsa. There was a stack of toast and a big mug of coffee.

"We can certainly ask some questions. Understand that we have nothing to go on and a dead end is a high probability. It is still early, later this morning we can pay a visit to the Texaco, maybe have the oil changed and we can talk to Anthony while he works on the car. Does that suit you?" Quinn took a quarter slice of toast in his mouth while he looked at Betty.

"My ghost had a striped tee-shirt on, I couldn't tell if he was wearing shorts, but on his left leg was a leather shoe and from the leather shoe were two shiny metal shafts that reached to a leather collar just below his knee. That shoe is what made the scraping noise against my floor. It still gives me chills to see that." Betty sighed and looked at Quinn hoping he did not think she had lost her mind.

When finished with their breakfast Quinn reached overturned on the radio on the drain board, it was set to WYSN 'Sunnie 101' and was just what Quinn thought was needed to help with the chill.

By ten, they had both showered and dressed. The morning was too nice for a sweater, so Betty borrowed one of Quinn's shirts that were too big for her. She tied the front tails in a knot around her waist which made her feel appealing.

They were the first to arrive at the Texaco. Anthony had just opened and was moving the oil stands next to the gasoline pumps.

Quinn parked in front of the first open bay got out and introduced himself with his customary two-fisted handshake and then turned and introduced Betty. "I happened to be sitting in the barber chair next to you yesterday afternoon and heard your story. Can we ask you a few questions?"

"Sure, I guess. I am at work so you will have to pardon me if I walk off." Anthony told them.

"I'll pump the gas for you if that helps." Betty offered still feeling young in her blue jeans, button down shirt and baseball hat.

Anthony laughed. "Sure, I guess. What is this about?"

“I am curious about that dream you told the barber. And I wondered about your family background.” Quinn had a smile pasted on his face so not to appear too stern or serious.

A car pulled to the pumps, Betty tipped her hat back and went with a smile and pumped gas for the customer. She returned with, ‘exact change’ and handed it to Anthony.

“The quick version,” he began then sighed.

“Oh wait, I forgot,” said Quinn. “Let’s get my car on the rack. As you change the oil, I can hear the story. I can listen to a slower version. That sound ok to you?”

“Sure Mr. I’ll guide you in.”

Betty attended the island when a customer happened to pull in.

Anthony relayed to Quinn that he preferred to be called Tony.

“The family I was raised in was a military family. Not real clear where my actual father went. Anyway all of us kids are confused about the ‘where and the why’ of things. We seemed to move a lot, never in one place too long, at a time. The Marine liked his liquor and the parents,” he said with a grimace, “loved to see who was the toughest and meanest. To this day, the kids cannot answer that question.”

“What year would you place that dream in? I mean if it had any relationship to reality, where would you put it in time?” Quinn was looking for more specifics.

“Oh, ah, let me – around 1955 maybe ’56 would be my guess. That would have been North Carolina. Camp Lejeune, ouch.” The wrench slipped on the oil pan nut and Tony whacked a knuckle. “Funny because that would have been about the time of our orders from North Carolina to California for our transport to Hawaii.”

“What do your brothers and sisters say about the dream?” Quinn inquired.

Tony lowered the wrench and watched the fairly clean oil, stream out from Quinn’s oil pan. He glanced at Betty, who was listening and also watching the island. “I haven’t told them about the dream. I was not even thinking of telling them. We don’t talk that much.”

“Can I get the names of your brothers and sisters?” Quinn asked, knowing it was a long shot and that Anthony might balk at the request.

“My brothers and sisters? Are you serious?” Anthony wiped his hands on a rag and then grabbed the oil filter wrench and loosened the filter. Holding up the oil filter, Tony said, “I may have to find a substitute for this. Do you mind?”

“Lower the car half way. I have a new one in the back.” Quinn told him.

Anthony’s mood lightened. “My sister is upstate. And I have a brother who now is ‘hanging ten’ out in California. I can get you my sister’s address and number. I don’t keep track of the surfer. Maybe Francesca knows his whereabouts.”

The island bell rang as a green Dodge Polara pulled over it. Betty turned to see Detective DeLaMonte pull into the island and went off to fill the customer’s tank.

DeLaMonte knew Betty by sight and saw Moosebroker standing under the Town and Country on the hoist talking to the attendant.

“Anything I should be aware of?” asked DeLaMonte.

“No, no,” Betty replied. “Just we are thinking of a career change. We thought maybe a gas station or a café.”

“A café; you are a funny woman.” He paid for his gas and pulled out into traffic.

Anthony finished up, lowered the Town and Country from the hoist so he could refill the pan.

Quinn backed it out of the stall and climbed out. He watched as Anthony fumbled around in his wallet for his sister’s address and number.

Anthony waited for Quinn to pay the $7.95 for an oil change.

“You ready for a trip upstate? The Town and Country is gassed up, oil changed, Tony checked the air in the tires and it’s a beautiful day for a drive?” Quinn told Betty, who had moved to the center of the bench seat of Quinn’s baby. He pulled out into morning traffic and headed for the highway.

Betty insisted that they stop once they were near their destination and call the number that Anthony gave them. “We just cannot knock on the door and expect her to talk to us,” Betty told him. “I’ll make the call.”

Returning to the car from the payphone, Betty told Quinn that Francesca had heard from her brother Anthony and to expect to hear from us. “She is just a few blocks from here.”

At the front door, Betty told Quinn to smile, “We are just friendly neighbors, not a retired detective and a crazy woman.” She patted Quinn on the chest. They both straightened as the door opened.

He Dreamt of Murder - Francesca

The door opened Francesca held the edge firmly as if to fight off an intruder. Her hand relaxed as she eyed Betty, she was still unsure of Quinn, even though he wore his broadest smile.

“Come in, please,” escaped from her lips, her politeness overcoming her good sense. Through the back glass sliding door, both Betty and Quinn saw three children playing on a swing set.

Betty held her hand out and said, “I’m Betty, nice to meet you.”

Quinn followed with his two-fisted grip on her small hand. His handshake made her feel safe with him.

“Here,” she waved them to the kitchen table. “Please sit down,” she walked over to the stove and turned on the gas under a tea kettle. “Tony called to tell me you were going to pay me a visit. What’s this about?” She leaned over and looked out the kitchen window.

“Did Tony tell you what we talked about?” Quinn asked.

“Not really, he said you eavesdropped on a conversation he had and that got your curiosity up. That’s what he said.” Fran replied her uneasy feeling was returning.

“Anything I can do to help you with the tea?” Betty chimed in.

“No, no, I’ve got it. Can you see little Cathy through the sliding glass door? I can’t see her from here.” Fran asked Betty.

“All three of them look OK. The little one is sitting at the bottom of the slide in the sand pit.”

Fran set a tray down on the table with three cups and a pot of hot water. She opened a package of cookies bought for the kids and emptied some onto a plate she had set in the center. After pouring hot water into the three cups, she pulled out a chair and took a seat facing the back window.

“Can you tell us a little about your family background? Tony said you moved a lot with your family; a military family.” Quinn said stirring his tea. He lifted an Oreo and told himself just to eat one.

“Yes, a military family.” Fran glanced off in a distant thought. “Marines, that was a long time ago,” she added as a point of clarifications.

“I did a tour with the Marines.” Quinn interrupted.

Betty glanced his way. She had just learned a new fact about the man sitting across from her.

“I was very young when we were discharged. We flew back early and then he followed. There was not much left of their marriage by that time. They soon drifted apart like two armies retreating from the field. It was tough on everyone.” She stood and walked to the window, then returned to her seat. “What is it you want to know?”

Betty began, “Quinn while getting his hair cut, listened to a story told by your brother and we were just wondering if you could shed any light on the likelihood the story has any merit.” She glanced at Quinn, trying to judge whether she was overstepping here.

“That is pretty much it,” Quinn added. “The story went like this. He dreamt that very young children were sitting with their hands tied behind them and latched to a chain link fence. There were two young adults pacing back and forth in front of them and then one of the children was murdered.”

Fran had lifted her teacup to her lips. Betty watched as her arm visibly shook spilling some of the hot tea onto her hand. The burn caused her to drop the cup. She hastily stood pulling the hot cloth of her dress away from her lap. Rushing toward the door, she shouted, “Keep an eye on the kids, please.”

Betty stood and found a dish cloth in the kitchen and cleaned the spilled tea, the cup was not chipped in the fall. Betty assumed it was an inherited tea set and was happy the cup was not broken.

Quinn stood and waited for Fran to return.

She came down the hall wearing blue jeans and a pullover shirt. “Sorry about that. I do not know what came over me.” She saw Betty with her eye on the kids and that the mess had been cleaned up. “Are we done? Did you get anything?”

“Where were you stationed before your orders to California?” Quinn asked.

“That would be Camp Lejeune in North Carolina,” Fran answered. “Look, this has upset me. I have to get back to my kids.” She showed Betty and Quinn to the front door. At the door, after shaking hands with Betty and Quinn she said, “I've had that very dream.”

“What was Devon's military rank?” Quinn asked.

“Devon? Oh, no, Devon is my maiden name. Wik was a staff sergeant, three up, one down, his last name is Violman. He is just Wik Violman now-a-days. He lives alone down South Florida now, last I heard.”

At the sound of a child crying Fran turned and closed the door leaving Betty and Quinn standing on the porch. They turned and walked toward the Town and Country. Quinn walked to her door and opened it for her. Betty climbed in and scooted toward the center of the bench seat, leaned and opened the door a crack for Quinn.

“What now?” Quinn asked as he pulled the door shut firmly.

“It does sound like there is more to the story. Doesn’t it?” Betty said as she adjusted the knob on the radio.

“Let’s head on back and think this over a bit. I have a few friends that are still in the Marines; maybe I can make some calls to see if I can get anymore information.”

“WAIT,” Betty called out.

Quinn hit the brakes. Betty slid to the door and opened it. She crossed the hundred feet to Fran’s front door and knocked.

Fran answered holding Cathy in one arm. She had a confused look on her face.

“Was there a child that wore a leg brace in your family?” Betty’s breathing a bit arrested.

“That was Michael. He stayed behind in North Carolina at a hospital for polio victims. We were later told he died.” She answered. A crash behind her drew her attention. She gave a weak smile, turned and closed the door. “Joey, get to your room,” was heard through the door.

Betty turned and rushed back to Quinn. She got in slid to the center of the bench seat and put her hand on Quinn’s arm as he drove off.

Quinn pulled onto the highway leading back down to Clearview Terrace. He brought the Town and Country up to speed and focused one eye on the highway.

Betty's left hand moved and rested on the back of his neck, "I did not know you were in the Marines. My George spent a tour of duty with the Marines. Where were you stationed?"

"One April on Okinawa sticks out in my mind." Quinn changed lanes to pull around a milk truck.

"My George was with the 8th Marines on Okinawa." Betty removed her hand from Quinn's neck at the thought.

Quinn glanced over at Betty. Her mind was much deeper than he was used to. He could sense a shift in her mood. "Your George is likely a hero then and is reaping his heavenly reward."

"Why would a man kill his own son?" Betty asked moving her hip closer to Quinn so their hips touched. She was seeking warmth to help ward off the implications of her question.

"If I heard Francesca correctly, she was Violman's step-daughter; which implies there may have been a step-son. So, neither would be his blood; there would be no bond, just mouths to feed."

Betty shifted to her left on the seat, bringing her knee up against the backrest facing him and braced herself for his reaction. "Michael is my ghost."

He Dreamt of Murder - On The Waterfront (4)

Betty pressed her index and middle finger on the side of Quinn's jaw and directed his eyes back to the road. She was glad to see there was not disdain in his eyes. She could not have stood that. "Fran's one-minute explanation is that there was a boy named Michael. He had polio and was sent off to the hospital and the children were told he passed. He wore a brace on his left leg to keep it straight."

Quinn spotted a café on the side of the highway. "Let's stop and grab some lunch. That cookie is not going to carry me all the way back to Clearview."

The Café

Quinn used the side of his toast to sop up some juice from the baked beans and put it into his mouth. The black pudding and fried mushrooms could wait a little longer. "I'll contact Colonel Remington. He is an old friend of mine from the Corps. Maybe he can pull some strings and get us some information about Wik Violman. But if that is a dead end, then I am out of ideas. We can't barge onto a Marine Corps camp and expect to get any answers."

Betty had ordered the soup of the day and toast and a cup of coffee. She lifted her cup and took a sip as she watched Quinn eat. The drive must have made him hungry she thought. "That is a good idea. There is an old friend I can also call . He may be kind enough to do some checking for us. Do we have enough information to make an inquiry?"

"We have a name and a rank. If we could get a serial number, we can trace his whole career." Quinn washed down a mouth full of sausage.

"I bet Tony or Francesca can supply that. They must have something in the old memory files. Do you remember either of them saying the name of the surfer? We need that also." Betty sipped her soup.

The two faced a mystery lost to time and it pulled at them. At the edge of the road in the drainage ditch, snowy egrets fed.

Three Weeks Later

"We have an entire list from Violman's company. I am wondering if the Marine Corps even knows." Quinn told Betty.

"My friend could not add anything. How can that be?" Betty sat in Quinn's kitchen drinking coffee.

Quinn shook his head. "We have called every number given to us. I contacted as many of their friends that I could locate. Every lead has turned up a dead Marine. That is just impossible. The whole company of men who served with Wik Violman is dead.

They all worked in supply and logistics. The odds are enormous that every member of his company has passed. It seems we have pulled a scab from a wound of unknown origin.

University of North Carolina 1970

Associate Professor Joe Pearson sat in his lab. It was after midnight. He had just heated water in a beaker with a Bunsen burner and made a cup of Sanka. It had been four months since he filed his report and tried to push the facts from his mind. Unbeknownst to Pearson was that his report was on the desks of Marine Brigadier General Miller at the

Pentagon and Marine Brigadier General Olson in Camp Lejeune, North Carolina.

Pervasive Ground Water Contamination: Elevated Carcinogens Camp Lejeune, North Carolina - University of North Carolina Associate Professor Joe Pearson

North Carolina 1956

"Wik! Back the truck up; you imbecile come on closer." The Staff Sergeant yelled while waving his arms.

"We'll get caught in the mud again," came the response yelled over his shoulder as he felt the wheels of the truck sliding.

In a remote forested area of the backwoods of Camp Lejeune, Sergeant Violman backed up a five-ton liquid waste truck, filled with aircraft cleaning solvents. They reported to the Motor Pool each morning and were assigned the truck. They made their way, hanger to hanger and pumped the truck full from catch pits. The daily routine was to haul the used solvents trichloroethylene and perchloroethylene as well as the fuel additive benzene, and dump it.

Violman jumped down and lit a cigarette and tossed the match on the ground.

SSgt. Carter who had an extra rocker on his sleeve jumped down his throat about the match.

“We all gotta go sometime,” Violman told him and puffed at the Winston cigarette while uncoiling the four inch hose from the side of the truck. “You worry too much.”

“Put it out!” SSgt. Carter ordered.

Violman field stripped the butt. Then fastened the hose to the outlet and turned the release valve. The smell was immediate; the vapors rose from the puddling fluid and bubbles rose as air escaped the murk.

“They should give us masks,” Carter voiced as the vapors chocked his airways. His nostrils burned as he walked upwind looking for air.

“Tomorrow let’s find another spot. All the trees here are dead. This stuff killed this whole area.” Carter choked out the words.

Wik looked at his Timex with illuminated hands. He watched the fluid recede and stop and dragged the hose from the pit. With ungloved hands, he coiled the hose and hung it on the side of the truck.

“Let’s go get a couple of beers to wash out this taste.”

Carter washed his hands and splashed water on his face from the five-gallon water can hanging from the side of the truck. He pushed some water into his nostrils with his finger to try to stop the stinging.

As Carter washed, Violman unlashed a bundle wrapped in the canvas of half a pup tent from the wheel well and carried it to the chemical pool and tossed it in. He then climbed into the cab and waited with a cigarette in his mouth. At eleven a.m., his five o’clock shadow was already apparent. He needed that beer and hoped that a Corporal would draw duty with him the next day. He’d had enough of Carter’s crap for one week.

“What was that you tossed into the pit?” SSgt Carter asked.

“Dog died. I am just too lazy to bury it,” came the answer.

Solvent was eating at the sole of his boots. He spit out the window; he pushed the gear into first and pressed down on the accelerator. His mind fogged as the vapors lingered in his system.

At 6 p.m. Wik Violman was back at the NCO Club smoking Winstons, drinking beers, ready for a fight, ready for a woman….plenty of time for another story.

He lifted his Pabst Blue Ribbon draft and downed the remainder.

Seven-year-old Francesca pulled the baking sheet from the oven. She carefully put one fish stick on each of four plates. She carefully cut the remaining two fish sticks in half and placed one-half on each plate. She served her brothers and herself. A glass of tap water sat in front of each child.

Marie Antoinette Violman sat at the bar of The Night Landing Club, on the waterfront with a Marine Corps Corporal by her side. She sat her draft down. “We got our orders. We’ll be leaving soon. This will be our last night together,” she told the corporal.

“Promise me. Look at me. Promise me that you will tell him about his father when he is older. Promise me.” There were tears in the Corporal’s eyes. He and Marie Antoinette had been together since Wik went off to Korea.

“He’d kill us if we were found out. Get yourself another girl.” She stood and downed her beer and walked out the door. All eyes were on Marie Antoinette Violman as she left.

He Dreamt of Murder – Road Trip (5)

A Saturday in 1970

Two platoons from the Army Corp of Engineers in the back country of the 246-square-mile Camp Lejeune in Onslow County, in Jacksonville, North Carolina were pulling soil samples at the request of the Camp Commandant.

Pervasive Ground Water Contamination: Elevated Carcinogens Camp Lejeune, North Carolina - University of North Carolina Associate Professor Joe Pearson sent a shiver through the entire Corps. The Camp Commandant wanted to investigate the findings and disprove them or keep them quiet.

Lt. Cooper was in charge of the team. It was a Saturday morning; the weather was warm on this spring day. The platoon members were wearing white Tyvek jumpsuits over their uniforms and respirators as they worked.

Private Hendrickson spotted a leather shoe laying face down. He reached down with his latex gloved hand and pulled at the shoe.

Anthony sat in a barber chair in Clearview Terrace. "A young couple was pacing back and forth in front of us. She wore a summer dress and he khaki pants, tee shirt, and garrison hat," he told Mac his barber.

The muck held tight to the shoe as Private Hendrickson struggled with it.

Anthony continued, "I was just a little kid sitting by a chain link fence with my hands tied behind my back and attached to the fence. There were three other boys and a little girl all tied to that fence."

A silver metal rod detached itself from one side of the shoe as it freed itself from the muck. Private Hendrickson stood erect quickly as the contents of the shoe were revealed.

Mac, the barber, asked, "Is that it?"

"No," Anthony said, "there is a little more to the dream. What woke me, and why I can't get it out of my head is the man in the green hat took a step toward us. It was then I noticed the black baton in his hand. Well, he reared back and that baton struck the boy sitting next to me on the head."

Private Hendrickson shivered at the sight of a pockmarked bone, of a child's leg that remained in the shoe held there by a thick corroded leather band hanging on a silver collar. Private Hendrickson brought his findings to Lt. Cooper. Cooper was not happy. He went to his supply truck, retrieved a plastic bag and put the leg bone and shoe into the bag.

Unseen by Lt. Cooper or Private Hendrickson was the ghost of a young boy standing next to the PVT. The boy wore shorts, striped tee-shirt, and leather shoes, one with a shiny new leg brace. He was finally freed from the muck by Hendrickson's kindness.

Lt. Cooper had two teams doing the survey of just how much damage to the area was done. He did not like being in the middle of the Marine Corps Camp; call it rivalry. There was very little growing in this portion of the otherwise overgrown backcountry of the Camp. The area was desolate, deserted and devastated.

The scene was surreal. There were tree trunks and thicket, devoid of all color, a grayish death had overtaken the area. It was charred from within, lifeless. The quiet weighed heavy; there were no birds, no insects – his men stood in a dead forest.

Once finished with the survey and the soil collection Lt. Cooper would turn over the remains to the Military Police on base. Private Hendrickson was ordered to red flag the spot and get back to work.

Clearview Terrace

The 1972 green Ford sedan with Marine markings pulled to the curb in front of Quinn Moosebroker's home. A young Marine Captain and an even younger Marine Lieutenant climbed out of the car and stretched then made their way to Quinn's door and knocked.

Quinn opened the door and was a little surprised at his guests.

The Captain said, "You have been making inquiries into Marine Corps business."

Quinn noted the holstered 45 on the Lieutenant's side. He asked, "Are you here to help with the inquiry? You two look a little tired, come in." He held the screen open.

Neither Marine moved toward the open door. The Captain held a stern look on his face, "We are here to tell you to drop your investigation. The Marines do their own investigation and we are not interested in your help."

Quinn stepped through the door letting the screen close behind him. He stepped right into the two Marine's space causing them to take a step back. "Just what are you investigating?" Quinn's look directed straight into the eyes of the Captain.

"How did you find out about the report?" Then the Captain hesitated, "You don't know about the report do you? Just what are you investigating?"

"I am investigating a suspected murder."

The Captain was just the messenger; he was finished, "Murder." He paused and turned a bit red faced. "Murder, is that all?" He brought his arm up and with the back of his hand tapped the Lt. on the chest to signal it was time to go. "You have been told." They turned and went back to their vehicle and drove away.

Lamb Bor's Linguini

The Lamb Bor's Linguini

Quinn picked up Betty and drove to The Lamb Bor's Linguini. Once seated Quinn ordered the Spaghetti alla Chamberlain and Betty the Manzo Brasato, they were giving the place another try. The wine arrived and Quinn began to relay the events of the day.

"Two Marine Officers arrived at my door this morning. They basically told me to stand down. Either your friend or my friend mentioned our inquiry and that news seems to have raced through channels. Something is going on, but we do not know what."

Betty took a mouth full of the braised beef and nodded her approval. "So now what? Are we done?" She sipped at her wine and tore a hunk of warm bread from the loaf sitting on the table.

"We can't do a head to head assault on the Marine Corps. Perhaps we can try a Blitz. In the morning, you call your friend; I'll contact my friend and see if we can get a name of someone at Lejeune that we can visit. We need to locate Violman. Maybe someone who knew him is still around." Quinn sopped up spaghetti sauce with the side of bread and popped it into his mouth.

“Francesca said he was down in South Florida.” Betty tossed in.

“Last she heard she said. An address would be nice.” Quinn said between sips of wine and thought he could grow to like this place. Betty was in much better spirits than their first visit.

“What is it they thought we were investigating? What’s bigger than murder?” Betty raised her arm to get a waiter’s attention. She wanted more wine.

Quinn tapped his glass to indicate he would like another glass also, “Let’s stop at Thrifty Drug Store on the way home and see if they have a map of North Carolina.”

Betty patted the back of his hand, “Let’s pick up a map in the morning.”

Road Trip

Three bags were secured in the back of the Town and Country. Two were Betty’s and a smaller one was Quinn’s. “It’s only a nine-hour drive,” Quinn said as he backed out of the driveway. It will do us both some good to get out on the open road.”

He guided his baby out to the highway heading for the connection to I-

95 South. Betty began to feel like she was on vacation. She even bought sunscreen.

She had called and made reservations at Bear Creek Lodge, in Jacksonville, NC on the east side. The two were exhausted when they arrived at 10 PM in the evening.

At seven AM two burly Staff Sergeants arrived at Quinn and Betty’s door at the request of Colonel Remington in Washington DC. The Colonel and two sergeants had recently rotated out of Vietnam together and were bonded for life.

SSgt Reilly drove the jeep through the Pinney Green Camp entrance; both Betty and Quinn's names were on the visitors list thanks to Colonel Remington as of twelve hours ago.

They had been on Old Bear Creek Road for a good half hour. The landscape changed from thick forest to what could have been the surface of the moon. Not much living on this wild land. "What happened here?" Betty asked. Before anyone could answer, a scream of terror escaped Betty. "Stop."

SSgt Reilly braked hard bringing the jeep to a stop. Betty leaped over the side of the jeep and ran toward the ghost of Michael Devon. The two sergeants followed close behind, followed by Quinn. The sight of Michael faded from Betty's vision as she was led to a small red flag stuck into the ground. Next to the flag lay a child's old black leather shoe.

He Dreamt of Murder – Provost Marshal's Office (6)

Three F4 Phantoms flew over at altitude leaving a vapor trail. The tree men watch them mark the sky. Betty stares at the child's shoe lying on the ground and looks around for her ghost that led them here.

"Will we be able to tell someone where this spot is once we leave?" Betty asked SSgt Reilly. She looked around at the gray once living world, which now stood as monuments to mankind's presence here. A shiver ran through her.

SSgt Godfrey who had been quiet up until now said, "We can leave a gas can where the jeep is parked. You ready to go?"

Betty nodded and they walked back to the jeep.

Quinn asked SSgt Reilly, "Can you deliver us to the Provost Marshal's Office and wait while we speak to the Desk Sgt?"

"Yes sir, Colonel Remington asked us to take care of you. That's what we will do." Reilly replied. They drove on; after about twenty minutes, Betty saw signs of green plants and breathing trees and heard the sound of a bird in a thicket. Her soul exhaled.

Captain Castillo and Lt. Cohen were on duty when Quinn Moosebroker and Betty Atwood arrived at the Provost Marshal's Office.

Quinn told his story to two uninterested faces while Betty remained silent in a chair next to him. The office was crisp and clean as were the Officers; this was a far cry from his memory of the Detective squad.

"You are here in regards something that may or may not have happened in 1955 or 1956." The Captain was unable to suppress his laugh.

"It's the death of a young boy wearing a leg brace possibly by the hands of a Marine. That is what we are investigating." Betty's face was red at the unwelcomed smile on the Captain's face.

Lt. Cohen excused himself. "Be right back, Captain." In a few moments, Lt. Cohen returned with two files. He handed the first file to the Captain.

The Captain glanced through the recent report left by the Army team from the Corp of Engineers regarding the old leg brace found while pulling soil samples from the lost zone.

The Captain placed both hands on the desk as if to raise himself. "Wait," said Cohen and handed Castillo the second folder. The Captain sat back down and flipped through the list.

No sign of a smile was on his face now. "How did you get into camp?"

Quinn explained his connection with the Corps and his old friend in Washington.

Captain Castillo stood and spoke to the Lt, "Have these two escorted off the camp by order of the Camp Commandant. He is on a No Entry list."

"We marked the spot at the point in the road where the red flag is placed if you are interested," Betty said as she was shown the door. She heeded Quinn's words about taking on the Marine Corps head on.

SSgt Godfrey and SSgt Reilly watched as two MP's escorted Quinn

and Betty to their jeep. The Lt. handed Quinn a card with his name and number on it. A Jeep marked M.P. pulled up next to them with instructions to escort them off Camp. "Call me in a week; I'll see if I can get him to move on this."

SSgt Godfrey, to break the tension began to talk as they drove through the Camp. “I am near the end of my tour here – twenty and out as they say. I did my first tour here at Lejeune; I knew an Atwood then; a big guy full of spit and vinegar. He loved cars and women. Any chance you are related?”

“My George was in the Marines. I don’t remember him talking about Camp Lejeune; he did not talk much about his time in service. We were married in 1958 after he was out. He passed ten years later.” Betty’s face was pale.

Quinn reached over and held her hand.

Criminal Investigation Team

Lt. Cohen returned to the Offices. Captain Castillo waved him over. “What do you make of that?”

Lt. replied, “The Army report was filed four weeks ago and the evidence went straight to a cold case file. With nothing to go on, there wasn’t much we could do. Now I think we were just delivered a connection. What do you think?”

“I don’t know what to think? He is on a No Entry list so he must have pissed someone off.” The Captain looked perplexed. “Pull Popovich and Gomez from whatever they are doing and send them into the lost zone and see what they find. Then report back.” The phone rang and ended the conversation.

Snead’s Ferry Diner

The sight of Quinn in a bib made Betty giggle. His order of lobster, crab, and clam lay before him, a feast at a roadside diner.

Betty picked at her clam chowder dabbing a hard bread roll into it and tearing at the bread. “I must be losing my mind,” she began. “I am afraid to tell you, but, I guess you did not see what I saw today as SSgt Reilly braked to a halt in that awful place.”

Quinn looked up from cracking a leg of crab. “I knew you would tell me in your way; when you felt it was time.” He pried the too small fork into the cavity of the leg excavating shards of crab meat.

“The ghost of Michael Devon was waiting by the roadside. When I leaped out he ran; he led me right to that red flag.” She lifted her schooner of beer and took a deep draw.

Quinn sat his too small fork down and wiped butter from his chin.

“Wait, there is more.” She took another sip. “While in Camp, I saw legions of dead. The parade field was full of them. Men, women, children.” She took a deep breath, “Oh, Quinn what in the world is going on. The entire history of the Camp is full of death. Everything is so neat and orderly and I must say friendly, but the ghosts are out in force.”

It was Quinn’s turn to lift his schooner of beer, “You are just tired. Ever since Michael’s first visit, after I told you Anthony’s dream you have been on edge. You seem to have some connection to Michael Devon.”

As he reached over to pat the back of her hand, his bib draped across his plate causing them both to laugh, relieving some of the tension.

“In the morning I will call Colonel Remington and let him know we were escorted out of Camp and to be prepared for some blow-back for helping me. Maybe he can help us more. I am not sure what to do now. It seems likely that an investigation will commence. It is also likely that we will never hear one word about it." Quinn stood and went to get two more schooners of beer.

Betty breathed a sigh of relief. Quinn had not looked at her like she was loony; though she was not so sure herself.

The sandpipers ran amongst the reeds of the estuary. The shimmering twilight displayed in the window showed dancing reflections on peaceful waters. Bullfrogs and crickets filled the seats of the orchestra while a pelican stood sentinel. A silhouette of a lone fisherman stood in the clay light of dusk with his line cast far out into the water. The night was warm, the food was good, the beer was cold and Betty was feeling very comfortable in the company of Quinn.

He Dreamt of Murder - The Cover Up (7)

Betty woke early. She felt like getting out and she dressed quietly and closed the door softly as not to disturb Quinn.

Stepping through the door, she faced the glory of the gift of morning. The dancing reflection of moonlight had been replaced with rippling sunlight on the water, clouds like crowns lifting spirits were accompanied by a chorus of birds and distant chugs of fishing trawlers. MORNING ON THE WATER she thought, I COULD GET USED TO THIS.

She got a cup of coffee from the lobby and headed for the Town and Country. She wanted to take a drive and clear her head. She went to the highway and picked up Snead's Ferry Road. A few miles down the tree lined covered road she hit the brakes hard. The car pulled hard to the right and the right front wheel went into a ditch.

A chill gripped her as she climbed out of the car. Across the highway she saw the wooden painted sign, THE SEA LANDING CLUB. She shook off the shivers and walked to the front of the car.

She was furious. "You have to stop doing that!" She looked at the bashed side panel of Quinn's baby, the Town and Country. "I don't want to go back to paint by numbers again." She screamed at the ghost of Michael Devon. She paced and inspected the damage.

She retrieved a hat from the back and then it registered in her mind's eye, she had seen a sign for Homer's Garage a few miles back. The first pickup that drove by driven by a young Marine and another riding shotgun stopped and offered Betty a lift. The drive along a quiet tree lined road, scented with honeysuckle and lilac filled Betty's senses as she sat in the back on her way to Homers.

Once Homer got the Town and Country back to the garage Betty was informed that she would run. “What do you want to do?” Homer asked.

Betty grimaced, “Can you fix that?”

“I can call over to East Side Salvage and see if they have a wreck there. If so I can replace the panel.” Homer offered.

“Yes,” Betty said, “Try that, please. Can you give me a lift to the lodge?”

Quinn woke and dressed. Finding Betty gone and the Town and Country gone he rented a fishing pole and went down to the shore. When Betty found him, he had a Striped Bass and a Red Drum in a bucket.”Good morning,” Quinn waved.

“I’ve been thinking,” he began. “We are being blocked by the attitude we are finding here. Maybe we need to retrace some steps and try to view this as I would a police investigation. We can contact the police here to see if there were any missing person reports. Oh and here is a thought, we can call the south Florida police to see if they have anything on Wik Vlolman. Yes, I like that.”

“Quinn,” Betty swallowed hard. “There has been an accident. “I drove the car into a ditch.”

“Are you OK?” He set down the pole and walked to her. Holding her shoulders, he looked at her and waited for her answer.

“Yes. Yes, thank you for asking. The car is over at Homer’s Garage out on the highway. Here is their number.”

Quinn took the piece of paper and put it in his shirt pocket. He lifted the bucket and pole and they walked together back to the lodge.

Five Days Later

Lt. Cohen sat at the desk of Captain Castillo, "As far as I can tell every man that served with Violman in '56 is dead." He handed two sheets of legal paper with names on it to the Captain. "Also again as far as going through files has turned up, no one named Michael Devon was ever reported missing. Actually no one by that name existed as far as we can tell. There have been a few Devon's through the camp, but the time frame is wrong in each case."

"Well, do a little more checking and if there is nothing to their story just let it go. We have plenty to do." Captain Castillo told him.

"Yes sir," Lt Cohen said rising and leaving the office.

Castillo picked up the phone and called a friend of his at the Pentagon. In his hand was a list of men who served at Camp Lejeune together. At the top of the list was the name Wik Violman. He was alive, as far as anyone here knew, his name was circled.

"Major Benson, Captain Castillo here. Look I need a favor, somewhere in the archives there is a file on a Marine named Wik Violman, can you have someone pull that file and send me a copy? I am checking into a suspected murder. Ok, thank you." The Captain put down the phone and the two sheets of yellow legal paper into the right-hand side desk drawer.

Homer's Garage

"Sorry, this has taken so long. We found the side panel in Beaufort, SC and had it brought in. Big Ed's son drove it down and drove back with his $120.00. There just aren't many of these around these days. If you leave it a few more days, I can get it painted to match." Homer told Quinn.

"We did not expect the delay. I'll paint her when or if we get home. Thanks for all your help." Quinn paid the $247.00 for the bill.

Betty cringed at the expense. She made a mental note to check with her insurance company to see if she had ghost insurance.

The time had not been wasted. Quinn and Betty had made many phone calls. A call to Francesca yielded Violman's service number and now name, rank and serial number were working its way from two directions in the military archives.

It occurred to Betty that their investigation had not gathered one word about the mother. Anthony offered that she was in California, somewhere near the youngest daughter. And another brother the surfer was named Franklin; Frank for short.

Neither Francesca nor Anthony added much about the California branch of the family. Marie Antoinette was now a name they knew and Jewel, the other sister.

Quinn's call to Lt. Cohen's added that Violman's file showed he had two sons, Anthony, Franklin. No daughter's names were in his file as of 1960. There are two entries where MP's showed up to his house on domestic violence calls and he was busted once for some kind of gambling scheme – unclear what that was from the record, Quinn was told.

Quinn told Betty, "The two oldest weren't his and the youngest was born after he left the service."

The Provost Marshal

Colonel Baker and Major Anza walked through the front door of the Provost Marshal Offices at Camp Lejeune and had heels clicking as they passed through to Captain Castillo's office. Lt. Cohen was summoned and both Jr. Officers stood at attention as they were ordered to stand down from the Supply and Logistics Company investigation and water contamination at Camp Lejeune. They were to gather what information they had regarding the Company and water pollution and turn it over to the Colonel immediately. Fifteen minutes later the Major was carrying three files back to the sedan they arrived in. FOR THE GOOD OF THE CORPS, they told themselves.

When they were gone Captain Castillo opened his right-hand side drawer pulled out two yellow legal size pieces of paper and pointed to Violman's name and said to Lt. Cohen, "Find this S.O.B."

He Dreamt of Murder - I Think We Have Him (8)

Both Captain Castillo and Lt. Cohen put in their request to evacuate their camp housing and made plans to move their families out of the Camp. The first either of them had heard the words water contamination was from COLONEL BAKER'S LIPS.

After getting nowhere with asking for assistance from Detective DeLaMonte in Clearview Terrace, Quinn called his old partner at the precinct in the city. After some wrangling and the promise of a visit and delivery of a bottle of Johnny Walker 12-year-old scotch, it was agreed that calls would be made. Quinn requested that any information he found be left with Kate in Clearview Terrace.

The thunder roared around the Town and Country as the highway glowed with the flash of green lighting as Quinn and Betty drove slowly down South-95 heading toward the unknown of Florida. Quinn thought he heard a rattle and was anxious to crawl underneath his baby and tighten her up.

As Betty fiddled with the radio dial looking for a clear station Quinn piped up, "Betty," which made her look up from the radio, "If Violman is getting a retirement check, the Marine Corps is sending it somewhere."

The grin on Betty's face widened, "Quinn," she patted his arm, "I think we have him."

"Thunder, lightening, and rain throughout the early morning hours," blasted from the radio once Betty came upon a station; which made them both laugh as they gazed through the rapidly moving windshield wipers a quarter inch away from the panoramic tempest.

Marie Antoinette

"Buy a lady a drink?" She lifted her near empty glass to the man who sat two seats down at the dimly lit bar. The years of drinking showed in her eyes. Her skin had lost the soft sheen of her youth. The years of just surviving stripped her of her innocence and honed her cunning. Her motto had become, TAKE WHAT YOU CAN GET. At thirty, she had six children and at forty-two she wanted to know where HER pension was. She was alone. She prided herself that only one of her children was in prison. "Hey Mister?" She held up her empty glass. The night wasn't getting any younger, "Do I have to buy my own drink? What kinda place is this?"

A bitter chill gripped her as a memory escaped the black morass that had become her soul and it shocked her core. She lurched to her feet and tottered to the door. There were no eyes on her as she left the bar.

Anthony

Quinn started his morning by giving a call to Kate. He wanted to see if she could see Anthony Violman when he got to work. He had a hunch, but he wanted someone face to face with him. Kate happily agreed.

Kate Moosebroker pulled her green VW Bug out of the Texaco after having an interesting talk with Anthony. She found out that he had a little sister and the little sister was, as far as he knew, the only one in contact with Wik Violman. She found out that the little sister received Wik's pension checks because he moved a lot, and forwarded them to Violman. She found out the telephone number of Jewel, the little sister in California.

Kate was on her way home to make an unofficial call from the USMC to Jewel. In under an hour, if she could reach Jewel, Kate would have a mailing address for Wik Violman.

At home Kate sat in front of the phone, she took a deep breath and lifted the phone and dialed the number. “Hello, yes this is Kate Moosebroker from the Program Service Center I need to speak to Wik Violman. Is he in?” Kate listened for hesitation in the voice.

“Look there is a problem with his pension. It has come to our attention that he has failed to sign the new forms authorizing where the payments are to be sent. If you can give me his address, I can tell you the closest office to him and we can get this mess straightened out quickly. If I get that information today, we can avoid interruption in his pension checks. And believe me they are tough to get restarted afterward.”

“Hold on,” Kate heard her say, “Got a pen?”

“Yes, go ahead.” She wrote down the information. “Thank you very much. We will get him taken care of, don’t you worry.” Kate smiled and put down the phone.

Wik Violman

C/o Oasis Motel

1428 Mayland Ave, #16B

St. Augustine, FL

Michael Devon

At age five, there was quite a bit Michael did not understand. Now that he was freed he wandered - searching both familiar places and foreign. He had spent time in a sandbox watching three children play; children that should have been his nephews and niece. Cathy the youngest seemed to sense he was there. He stood by a young woman teaching in a new school filled with underprivileged kids; the young woman was his baby sister whom he never met. He cheered a young man with sun-bleached hair as he easily swayed atop a wave foaming towards shore. He roamed the sparse rooms of a small mobile home on a sun-soaked lot on the outskirts of a forgotten village and recognized the emptiness of the mind of the owner. He had one more stop to make then he would free himself from the leg restraint and free himself of this world.

He had reached out to Anthony the brother closest to him in age through the dream. Francesca also, but she was very busy with her life. Betty was the big surprise; her connection was so strong. Michael had not known why until he was sought out by a ghost from the legion on the Parade ground of Camp Lejeune.

Pvt Popovich and Pvt Gomez

Pvt Popovich and Pvt Gomez from the Provost Marshal's Office did not mind getting out of the office. Understand that the MOS of Criminal Investigator was one of the nicer jobs a Marine could train for, but when things were slow, the office work really pulled at them. Their investigation at the lost zone sight garnered them a banker's box full of old bones which included one split skull and a scrap of tent seam with two rusted grommets. Their report to Lt. Cohen was completed and they were both sent back to follow up on domestic violence cases.

Lt. Cohen

"Yes that is right Lt. we just received this information and we just knew that you would be interested. We had sketchy information previously, and we are positioning ourselves to be there as early as tomorrow. Does that give you enough time to put something in place?" Quinn listened for the answer. "Sure, I have a pen." Quinn wrote down a number Lt. Cohen read to him. "Yes thank you also." He set the phone down.

Lt. Cohen did not mention the banker's box to Quinn. With the information Quinn had given him, Lt. Cohen was quickly able to track down the whereabouts of Marie Antoinette and had contacted the Butte County Sheriff's Office to pick her up for questioning. He was interested in Wik Violman and equally interested in his ex-wife.

He Dreamt of Murder – Conclusion (9)

Leeward Side Cafe

Betty and Quinn sat at the Leeward Side Café, the ceiling fans whirled to move the air around. Their meals arrived Betty ordered pancakes with two slices of pineapple and a plate with a mushroom omelette was set in front of Quinn. "I am not sure how this is going to go this morning." Quinn began. "I called the number that Lt. Cohen gave me and two MP's will be paying Wik Violman a visit about 1 PM."

"What kind of name is Wik Violman anyway?" Betty said and took a bite of pineapple.

"I am not really sure. Maybe Wik is short for something."

"Yeah, like wicked." Betty smiled at her humor. "Wicked Vile man;

that 's what I think."

Quinn smiled at her humor. "Have you seen Michael? What do you think that connection is?"

"No, I haven't seen him today? Have you?" She smiled, mostly to herself. The thought of seeing a ghost still unnerved her.

"Listen, we haven't really talked about it." Quinn coughed. "What did your George pass away from?"

"Funny question for this morning's conversation. Why do you bring it up now?" She took a sip of coffee and focused her eyes intently on Quinn trying to figure out his point.

"You mentioned at Francesca's house that he was in the Marine Corps. And you have said you don't know much about his time spent there because he did not talk about it. I am just tossing ideas around in my mind that's all."

Betty picked up her napkin and wiped her mouth and set the napkin down. Quinn noticed her glance was more than a glance. "What did he do for a living?"

"He was a printer he learned his trade in the Marine Corps."

"Did he die of cancer?" Quinn just point blank asked her since she did not answer the first time.

"Yes, damn it, he did. Thanks for bringing it up." Betty's mood clearly changed with this line of questioning. "Why are you questioning me about George like this?"

"I sense he has something to do with our case. He passed from cancer that could be a coincidence. He handled chemicals throughout his career. He was a Marine maybe at Camp Lejeune. But, let me change the subject. Here is what I think likely. Violman and his wife were sick to death of Michael and his illness. They received their permanent change of station orders to transfer and tried to make it work to their benefit. In those days it would be nothing to leave one Camp and arrive in another Camp with one less child. Especially a stepchild, if questioned you could just say you left him or her at a relative's for health reasons. The Marine Corps would not blink at this. The Violman's could even have kidnaped a healthy boy and arrived with him as a replacement for the crippled son. There were more kids along that fence in the dream than there were sons of Wik Violman." Quinn lifted his coffee cup and was sorry he brought up George.

"That is just sick." Betty was livid. "I can't wait to see the look on his face."

Oasis Motel

“Come in,” was screamed through the hollow door of the upstairs apartment at the Oasis Motel. Quinn walked through the door. His natural instinct was to reach for the gun in his holster that he had not worn on his belt since his retirement. Sitting there was Wik Violman, his chiseled face furrowed with deep lines. His eyes dark set in dark sockets. The skin on his face browned and weathered from years of working outdoors mostly for the U.S. Marines. He was the same age as Quinn but was not carrying any extra weight. A cigarette was held firmly in his mouth as he gazed at Quinn and Betty, who was standing just to Quinn’s right.

A small screened black and white TV, with a broken horizontal hold made the picture appear to scroll from bottom to top, showed horses making their way around a Gulfstream track. There were newspapers at Wik’s feet turned to the sports pages showing the games that were playing this weekend.

The man staring at Quinn was primitive. The fingers of his right hand were yellow from nicotine. It was clear to Quinn that the teeth were false and also yellowed. He wore khaki pants, an aged and worn tee shirt frayed at the neck, white socks, and black military issue shoes. On his left wrist was an old Timex with illuminated hands.

“Well, what’d yah want? Can’t you see I’m busy?” Wik barked, not understanding why his Saturday was being disturbed.

“We have some information for you. We were doing some inquiries about your unit in Camp Lejeune. We also have some questions about your son Michael.” Quinn said.

"Michael? That scrawny weakling was not my son. What about him? He died of the polio; God that was damn long ago. What's this about?"

"As far as we can tell, every man in your unit from Camp Lejeune has passed. They are dead from kidney cancer; bladder cancer; leukemia and Non-Hodgkin's lymphoma. You remember that duty Wik?"

"Yeah, that was shit duty." He took another deep drag on his cigarette, choked horribly which seemed to distort the shape of his head, and he pushed out the butt into an ashtray piled high.

Betty suppressed a gasp. Standing in line with the black and white TV was Michael. The horizontal bar rolling blended well with the striped tee shirt he wore. The illusion made Betty see Michael's legs and his head and blurred his middle. *If things weren't bad enough*, she thought.

"What happened to Michael?" Quinn asked point blank. "How did you leave one camp and show up at another camp with one less child?"

"You don't know what you are talking about. That was so long ago, who cares?" He coughed that turned into a choke. He glanced at Quinn to size him up. He glanced at his holstered 45 on the coat rack by the door and calculated his odds of reaching it if necessary.

"Anthony told us about a dream he had. In the dream, a young boy was killed by a man in a green hat. We think that man was you." Betty added.

"Anthony – That puke he is just like his mother." Violman spewed the words. The dark eyes in dark sockets narrowed at the thought.

Quinn and Betty still stood, not having been invited to sit. Betty reached over and took Quinn's elbow. "Let's go." She asked Quinn. They had lost Violman's attention as they turned Betty hooked with two fingers the holstered 45 from the coat rack by the utility belt. They heard Wik light another cigarette as he stared at the b&w TV screen. His horse had just lost. They walked from the apartment to seek a breath of air and remove themselves from the pall.

A beastly scream came from the apartment, which caused a smile to appear on Betty's face. She assumed the beast's eyes had finally focused and the ghost of Michael Devon appeared to him. The scream took the two MP's coming up the stairs toward Quinn and Betty by surprise.

Betty held out the holstered 45 to the MP directly in front of her with a smile on her face. The MP took it and said, "Thank You, Ma'am," and draped it over his shoulder.

A few moments later the two MP's walked Wik Violman downstairs in handcuffs. Betty and Quinn leaned against the grill of the 1946 Town and Country and observed. Their only satisfaction would be the knowledge that there would be an investigation and trial.

Quinn walked to the passenger side of the car and opened the door of the Town and Country. Betty got in and slid to the middle of the bench seat. Quinn got in and turned the key. He sensed Betty become tense.

Betty glanced over at Quinn to see if he saw what she saw. The ghost of Michael Devon and the ghost of George Atwood, his father were walking down the stairs hand in hand.

The Radio Players Club Mystery: A Quinn Moosebroker Mystery

The Clean Slate Cafe

Naomi found Jarrod asleep amongst the scattered wooden chessmen at his table at the Clean Slate Café. "Wake up, wake up," she called shaking his arm. "Did you finish the script? It has to be there in an hour and I have to catch the crosstown bus."

"The script?" Jarrod rubbed his eyes. They began to focus on the irritated face of Naomi.

"Yes, the script. You know money for food. Where is it? I have to get over to the station. He'll can us for sure."

Jarrod stood and headed for the bathroom. Naomi reached down and opened the ragged bag that was always near Jarrod's feet. She pulled out frayed sheets of paper and began to read. Some pages had been crumpled and uncrumpled. Many lines scratched through. She went to the last page. A gasp of air escaped her, "It's not finished." She stood by the bathroom door and as it opened, she grabbed Jarrod by the arm. "Let's go, you'll have to finish it on the way."

She glanced at her watch. "We barely have time to make it."

W.A.R.T Radio

Quinn was at the wheel of his 1946 Town and Country heading north on I95. Betty sat by his side and was looking for a station on the radio. Their return journey from North Carolina felt like such a relief from their case to resolve a ghostly mystery.

....ERTS ZST SHRRRRRRR came from the radio. The radio light cast eerie murky ochre across the front seat of the Town and Country on this dark southern night. Betty felt like she could be in a cave during the Stone Age watching the flicking light splashing across the jagged walls. From the radio:

..... IVORY SOAP, IT FLOATS...W.A.R.T RADIO,

AT THE STUDIO, MASSEY DRAGGED A DRUMSTICK ALONG A TIN WASHBOARD....

NOW BACK TO '***A Rose for Opal Ann***"

MASSEY DRAGGED A VIOLIN BOW ON A GUITAR STRING PULLED TAUT ALONG A TWO-BY-FOUR.

NATHAN THE NARRATOR. "DETECTIVE QUENTIN MORSE BRAKED HIS 1946 TOWN AND COUNTRY TO A HALT IN FRONT OF AN ABANDONED APARTMENT BUILDING."

"AROUND BACK. I'LL GO IN THE FRONT."

CLARK HIS PARTNER: "BE CAREFUL, THIS GUY IS DANGEROUS. YOU HEARD THE CALL. HE HAS KILLED TWO PEOPLE TODAY."

MASSEY LET OUT A DEEP BREATH INTO HIS MICROPHONE.

"TWENTY-FOUR, TWENTY-FIVE." Morse began walking up the wooden stairs on the established twenty-five count.

Massey. SOFTLY HIT THE BACK OF THE TWO-BY-FOUR WITH A DRUMSTICK.

Morse. "OPEN UP; THIS IS THE POLICE."

MASSEY TWICE FIRED HIS STARTER PISTOL, AND ROLLED A SACK OF POTATOES ONTO THE FLOOR.

Morse. "Clark! Clark! You alright?"

MASSEY TAPPED SHOES ACROSS A BOARD.

Morse. "I'm coming in."

MASSEY TWISTED TWO ENDS OF A BAMBOO SLIT UP THE SIDES. THE SOUND WAS OF TIMBER SPLITTING. THEN FIRED HIS STARTER PISTOL AND LIFTED AND DROPPED THE SACK OF POTATOES.

"YOU'LL NEVER CATCH ME COPPERS."

MASSEY PLOPPED THE SHOES AGAINST THE PLANK IN A PATTER.

Narrator: THE DARK FIGURE CARRIED THE BODY OF THE KIDNAPED OPAL ANN DOWN THE STAIRS AND DISAPPEARED INTO THE DARK.

....ERTS ZST SHRRRRRRR came from the radio.

Detective Quinn Moosebroker

Quinn gazed out the windshield. A highway sign indicated Highway 83 twelve miles. "Did we ever discuss the night I was shot?" Quinn glanced over to Betty in the darkness barely illuminated by the light of the radio dial.

"You started to once, but we were interrupted by a phone call." Betty adjusted herself in her seat next to Quinn in the front seat. She silently braced herself.

Quinn began, "I don't know quite how to say this. This radio program has described it in a detailed manner; too detailed to be a coincidence to my way of thinking. " Quinn's face was distorting at the thought of the night his partner was killed. After the dark figure fled with Opal Ann Quinn crawled to the back door to find Clark, still. A footprint in a pool of blood oozing from beneath him was the only sign of the killer left as he stepped over the body.

Betty watched in silence as the rage rippled through the muscles in Quinn's face. She could hear his grip on the leather steering wheel tighten.

"Quinn, pull over. I need to drive."

"Take the 83 turnoff when it comes up. We're heading to Allentown."

Betty pulled the car back on the highway as Quinn began again.

"Clark and I responded to a call from a tipster. The kidnapping occurred

48 hours prior and no ransom note had been received. A miss-do-gooder had called the station reporting suspicious activity in an abandoned duplex near the railroad switching yard on the seedy south side. We were not close to the yard, but Clark wanted to rush to the sight.

When we got there, there were no other responders. Clark went around to the back steps and I took the front. At a twenty-five count, we were both to go in. Two shots were fired as I reached the door and I called out and then burst through the door. The gunmen's third bullet caught me on the side taking out a kidney. I heard the footsteps going down the back as I lay there. I crawled to Clark, but he was gone.

They never caught the guy. I lay in a hospital for two months. When I was released, I wore dress blues one last time and they hung a medal around my neck and gave me a small disability pension."

Betty reached over and patted Quinn on the shoulder. Her sideways glance took in the pain and deep loss this sharing with her was causing Quinn. "Who was kidnaped? Which case was not solved the murder or a kidnapping or both?"

Quinn let out a deep sigh, "Neither the murder, attempted murder of me or the kidnapping was solved. The case went cold. Without a ransom demand, the case ended at the bottom of the stairs. The clues we had led nowhere. Without further clues or demands, there was nothing to go on. The Captain felt the guy was scared too badly once he had to shoot his way out of the duplex. Did you notice they used the fictitious name Quentin Morse? That fact alone sets my alarms off. Somebody knows something about this case."

Betty waited patiently for his pause. "Did Clark have family?"

This changed the course of Quinn's thinking. "Yes, his wife is still alive and he had two grown children who live out of state, last I heard. I should call her now that you reminded me."

"The little girl – ah, is that part true?" Betty kept her hands gripped tightly on the wheel for strength.

"Her parents lovingly called her Sapphire Annie because of her eyes, and yes she was taken from in front of her school while waiting for her

Mother to arrive. She was nine at the time. That makes her fifteen now. If I recall, no witnesses came forward."

Betty glanced at Quinn's face to see if she could tell if he believed that or not. She could not tell. "Where are her parents?"

"Still in Allentown as far as I know; this is going to dig at some old wounds." Quinn's face puckered. "I heard they separated shortly after the kidnapping. That's common enough."

A New Partner

"What was that? Did you see that?" Betty asked.

"See what? Not another ghost?" Quinn looked around then at Betty as she slowed the car. "What are you doing?"

"I saw something." She slowed the car to a stop on the shoulder.

Quinn turned his large frame around the best he could and stared into the darkness.

Betty turned to face back, put the Town and Country into reverse and slowly backed the vehicle along the turnpike.

"There, do you see it?" Betty asked.

"No, not yet; what am I looking for?

"A dog, I saw a dog on the shoulder. We can't leave him on the Turnpike." Betty looked over at Quinn hoping to see full approval. She braked to a stop and got out.

"Wait!" Quinn made the full swing back around opening the door to chase after Betty. "Where are you going?" A passing car's headlights illuminated the dog a short distance away then the night faded back to black.

"Here Boy," Betty called as the four legged creature slowly approached. "What is he?" She asked Quinn.

"Some kind of a Terrier I think. I'll be right back." Quinn made his way to the car and rummaged in the ice chest in the back and found two dried at the edges pieces of baloney and grabbed them. He returned to Betty and handed them to her with a wink that went unseen and moved back.

In a moment, they were walking back to the car; the dog was in Betty's arms and eating dried baloney.

The Radio Players Club Mystery, You Can't Go Home Again, (2)

The Town and Country with Quinn at the wheel pulled back onto the turnpike. The turn for Highway 83 was approaching fast. Soon they would have to stop to rest and also get some supplies for their new companion. The baloney was not going to get them far.

"So how are we going to approach this?" Betty asked while tugging at a knot on the dogs back with an old comb she found in the glove compartment.

Betty's voice pulled Quinn back from his thoughts. He had been driving with his subconscious mind and realized that was not too bright. "Approach this?" His mind shifted attention back and forth trying to focus.

"Yes, you said we were going to Allentown. That is the scene of the crime as-it-were. How do you see this going? We don't actually have any new clues. Do we?"

Quinn glanced over at Betty now combing a dog's hair onto his custom upholstered front seat, "We don't have a new clue, but we have new knowledge. I guess it is new knowledge, I wonder how old that radio broadcast is."

Quinn's mind drifted into the past. "The name of the station is W.A.R.T." That is where we will start. Can you get the station tuned back in?"

Betty reached over the dog and moved the dial slowly back and forth. "No, we seem to have lost the signal."

Quinn wondered if he should swing back around on the turnpike to see if he could locate the spot where the radio station received the broadcast, but he kept quiet and kept going.

"Hey, there is a Duncan Waffles, I'm hungry, how about you?" Betty announced. "Hey, we could call the dog Waffles. What do you think?"

Quinn's face did all the talking. "How about we call the dog Duncan instead?" He eased the car up the off ramp heading towards a predawn breakfast.

Allentown

The dome observatory walls that were protection of Quinn's mind began to close as the trio drew near Allentown. The pain was there. The pain of Quinn's deceased wife was there; his deceased partner was there and his deceased career was there. He had driven away those years ago, leaving it all behind to retire. He told himself he would be satisfied being close to his daughter. He told himself he could get lost in art and in books and in the restoration of his Town and Country that he bought out of impound. He had missed the smell of steel that was Allentown. He missed the cold hard riveted structure and his place in it. Hell he missed it all.

He limped into town, with an unpainted right front panel with a shimmy in it, a woman he had known for only a few months, but exciting months and a mutt they agreed to name Duncan by a flip of a coin. He limped into town out of his new life back to the old life.

Betty sat chatting and tending to Duncan's coat. Her words were bouncing off Quinn. Betty noted the shift in the climate of the car and during the years of her marriage became good at recognizing when she was not being listened to. This was one of those times.

The tedious road hours had passed. Quinn was getting tired. Betty was asleep in the seat next to him with Duncan's head resting on her lap. In the distance, Quinn spotted the neon placard of the Bethlehem Motor

Court. He knew the place from the old days. At the time, the cabins had been kept clean so as he approached he pulled in.

The Clean Slate Café

Cass sat across from Jarrod, who was wearing his plaid Oxford Ben Hogan facing backward on his head. Jarrod finished lighting a cigarette and watched the smoke curl skyward. "Conrad wouldn't pay me for the last script. He said we're all getting stale and a group from across town was showing him fresh stuff."

Naomi heard him as she approached carrying two coffees. She set one cup down in front of Cass and sat down with the other. "The rent is due in two weeks."

Belinda sat a cup of coffee down in front of Jarrod and sat her cup on the table. "What did I miss?"

Cass answered, "Conrad at that W.A.R.T. rejected the last story. We aren't going to make rent unless we hustle something from somewhere."

"What does he want at these prices?" Naomi sipped her coffee.

"He wants Sam Spade or Marlowe that is what he wants?" Jarrod took a deep drag from the smoke and let it out. "How short are we?"

Belinda was the accountant, "Right now we are $45.00 short."

Cass reached into her cloth bag. "I got two dollars for a Poster I painted for the dry cleaner." Handing the money to Belinda, she said, "Forty-three. Now we are forty-three dollars short."

Cass and Belinda stood up smoothing their 'paisley granny dresses' and walked toward the door.

Jarrod watched them go. Telling Naomi, "Let me go see what I can find in my Uncle's storage. There must be something." He reached into the crumpled bag at his feet and pulled out several pieces of mauled paper, "This is good stuff. Take a look and see what I am missing." Jarrod stood, emptied his cup and left Naomi to read his submission walking out into the sunlight.

"Where yah 'going?" She called.

There was no reply. The crumpled bag was over his shoulder. His flat cap pulled tightly down, still backward and a jaunty step in his attitude.

Palladium Arena

Jarrod opened the tall double doors of the Palladium Arena. An afternoon of midget wrestling would soon conclude and Lecherous Leprechaun a silent partner sometimes let Jarrod sweep the place out after the matches and slipped him a few dollars for his trouble. His friends called him Nathan.

"So what's with Mr. Timmerson?" Jarrod asked. "He hated my story. That puts us in a fix."

Nathan with his head tilted back looked at him thoughtfully. "You should make an honest woman out of one of those women you live with. That would make your life a little easier. Sid' down kid, you're maken my neck hurt."

"Yeah, I know, I know, but man, well you know. Hey, can you let me sweep out the place? We are all going to be out on the street again because Mr. Timmerson rejected my script."

"He's there to make money. And what I hear is he ain't maken any money. You need to put some 'Pow' into this, its radio not television. He was shown a script from another group; Melody liked it. There was a bigger part for her. She's got pull; watch yourself kid. Ok, get busy. There are more matches tonight. Come see me when you're done."

Sapphire Annie

Stephanie stood behind the sink in the back at Garza's Pizza & Shake Shack and washed her millionth dish. Her eyes were deep morning glory blue, but there was no light shining out of them. There was an echo to her; a pathetic hollowness, her beauty drew no attention. She often envied her shadow which did not know the things she knew.

Garza had bought her from a man who had bought her from a man who had bought her.

Bethlehem Motor Court

Quinn and Betty got the bags into the cabin and Duncan settled in on the bed.

Betty undressed, "I'm going to take a shower."

"While you do that and finish your nap I am going to run an errand and pick up some food for Duncan," Quinn told her.

"Give me ten minutes and I'll go with you." Betty felt awkward just ready to step into the shower.

"I am going to pay a visit to Rittersville Cemetery and pay my respects to Patricia."

Quinn's look tore at Betty who stepped into the shower and let the heated water rush over her to hide her tears for Quinn.

"I won't be long," Quinn called over his shoulder. He gave Duncan a scratch on the head and walked out the door. He did not have a flow of water to hide his tears.

Quinn climbed into the Town and Country steeling himself for a long ride through his history. He would pick up Highway 22 and drop down on Union Street. A tide of memories would flood him as he rushed back through time.

The Radio Players Club Mystery, Gum Shoes (3)

Quinn returned from Rittersville Cemetery having paid his respects and telling Patricia how wonderful a young woman that Kate had become. They had their talk and Quinn tucked that memory away.

Betty opened the door of the cabin at the Bethlehem Motor Court when she heard the Town and Country return. Truth is it was the third time she opened the door as a car approached.

"Hello," Quinn offered. "I picked up a bag of dried food, a collar and a leash for Duncan." He looked around, "where is he?"

"I asked at the desk and there is a groomer in that shopping mall that we passed down the road. We took a walk over and he is there getting a haircut."

"Let's go eat while we wait. We can kick around how to uncover what we want to know over dinner," Quinn offered as he was feeling a bit guilty for leaving her so abruptly.

"Sounds great. Do you want to take a walk over there?" Betty felt much better after a good cry, a hot shower and walk to find a groomer. Betty handed Quinn a piece of paper.

"What's this?" He unfolded the paper and the first smile Betty had seen for hours appeared. The paper said: W.A.R.T. Radio, 395 ½ Lincoln St. There was also a phone number. On the night stand, the white pages were still open.

"Let's go eat." He put his arm around Betty's shoulder. "You might be a better detective than I am."

Now there were smiles on both their faces.

The Clean Slate Café

Jarrod handed Belinda $8.00 of the ten dollars he was paid by Lecherous Leprechaun for the four hours he spent as custodian of the arena. "He gave me two tickets to the wrestling tonight. Where is Naomi?"

"Thirty-seven short still, we have been in worse positions. Naomi and Cass are out looking for some food money." Belinda was hungry but did not want to spend money on food. "Do you think we could scalp the tickets? Give them to me."

They both got up. Belinda headed for the door. Jarrod went behind the counter and poured himself coffee then left a nickel by the cash register. He returned to his seat, took some paper from his bag and began to write. He reached back into the bag and pulled out a photo album with faded boards, and opened it and began reading a newspaper clipping from the Allentown News and Morning Call, Police Officer Dies, then another, Wounded Officer Honored. The album bulged with clippings neatly arranged.

W.A.R.T Radio

After breakfast Quinn, Betty and Duncan climbed into the Town and Country and took a drive to Lincoln. Quinn avoided his old neighborhood skirting well around it on his way. Reaching Lincoln they cruised up and down looking for the right street number, but could not pinpoint it.

"Did the phone book say whether it was east or west Lincoln by any chance?" Quinn asked.

"No, I don't think so?" Betty told him worried that she may have made a mistake.

Quinn pulled the car over and they all got out. Duncan was tugging at his new collar and leash. He found a human but lost some freedom.

Quinn walked around the car looking in all directions. Betty also, but she was not sure what she was looking for.

Quinn called, "There," and pointed to a tall shortwave antenna sticking up from a short distance behind the house.

The three walked down a long drive lined with cypress on one side to find a block building on the rear of the deep lot. Looking at the antenna Quinn was unsure how he ever received a signal from this station.

Betty knocked on the door, but no one answered. She handed the end of the leash to Quinn and stepped behind a bush and peeked into the window.

"I don't see anyone," she said taking the end of the leash back.

The back door of the house opened an elderly lady stood there with her broom. "What do you to want? Are you selling something?"

"Good afternoon." Quinn took his official stance. "We are looking for W.A.R.T. Radio, is this it?"

"There's a group meets here. There is some talk about radio, but none of it makes sense to me. They ain't here now." She shifted her weight on the broom.

Betty broke in, "When do they meet? We heard them last night."

"Last night? They weren't here last night that I know of. Try back on Tuesday. Ask for a fellow named Timmerson, Conrad Timmerson. He's the one who pays the rent, mostly."

"Thank you," Betty added. Duncan barked his thank you, tail wagging.

"Can I drive?" Betty asked as they approached the car.

"Sure," Quinn and Duncan shared the passenger seat. "Where too?"

"To find a phone book. We just got another lead. Now we have a name other than wart." She smiled at her wit.

"Hello. This is Betty over at Knopf Automotive, I want to come and talk to you about buying some airtime. Is this a good time?" Betty listened to the answer.

"We'll be over at three then. Yes, see you then. Oh, we have an address from the phone book. At your office, right?" Betty smiled at Quinn, "Three PM we speak with Conrad Timmerson."

"Let's head over to Tilghmann there's a guy works at a Café use to know everything and we can grab a bite to eat." Quinn scratched Duncan on the head as he climbed in.

Courthouse Café

Maggie stuck her head through the pass through, "Hey, Otto, there' a guy out here asking for you when you have a minute." She turned to Quinn, "We're slow at this hour, and he'll be out in a couple of minutes. Whad'aya have?"

"Two coffees for now." Betty responded.

"QUINN, what are you doing here? Otto's face lit up to see his old pal. "I heard you went down to Florida or somewhere."

Quinn stood and shook hands with is friend. "Good to see you. Got a few minutes?"

"Sure, sure." He looked at Betty. "I'm Otto; I was on the force for awhile same division as Quinn.

Betty slid over so he could sit down across from Quinn.

"We are looking for some information about W.A.R.T. Radio. Ya heard anything about them." Quinn wanted to catch up with Otto, but also wanted to find out if he knew anything.

"Funny name. I think I heard it before. Ya' know there's a midget that comes in here that talks about W.A.R.T radio. I remember cause its a funny name especially com'n from a midget." Otto could see the humor was lost.

"Does he have a name?" Quinn asked.

"There's a small group of them that have gathered in the theater district. But I don't know his name. Something like Colorado Cowboy comes to mind, but that doesn't make sense."

A group of three entered the café. Maggie took their order and came by and touched Otto on the shoulder. "You're up."

Otto looked over and his face excused himself. "Back to work for me. If you're in town awhile stop by we can have a drink. Da both of yah."

Conrad Timmerson

The door said, Conrad Enterprises. Betty opened the door and went in. There was an empty desk where a receptionist may have sat at some point, but the desk was clear with a light layer of dust. There was no receptionist and had not been one for some time. "Hello," she called.

"In here," came a voice from the partially closed door. "Be with you in a minute." The voice turned back to the phone call he was on. "OK, I'll send her over. That's $12.00 for one hour of time. Yes, 6:30 tonight." Conrad hung up, stood and went to greet Knopf Automotive. The sight of Quinn drove the thought out of his head. "Yes, can I help you? I have an appointment that is due any minute."

Betty was silent.

Quinn began, "I think we are the appointment. We are here to investigate a radio performance we heard."

"I have my radio license. What is this about?" Conrad planted his feet firmly on the ground.

"Can we sit down?" Betty asked. "This is not formally official business. Not yet anyway."

Conrad stammered. "Yes help yourselves to chairs."

"Tell us about W.A.R.T. Radio, can you?" Betty began.

"Sure, we are local. I sell time to the local businesses when I can. Times are tough. We play some music from local talent when we get demo tapes from them. All small time and a group perform radio plays. We try for weekly but do not always succeed." He paused.

"A group? Like performers?" Quinn asked.

"Yes, it's a club. Mostly we have fun. If we can get sponsors, the fun pays for itself. We call ourselves The Radio Players Club. I do what I can to cover cost by selling commercials to the local merchants. What is this about?"

Quinn ignored the question and took out a pad from his inside jacket pocket. "What are the names of the members? We'd like to talk to them."

Conrad took a deep breath and said, "Well there is me, and Colorado Cowboy, Melody, and Rosy. If we need more we can find them, the plays usually have four voices. Oh and the sound man, Massey."

"You have addresses for all of these people?" Betty piped up.

"They will all be at the studio tomorrow night. It's over on Lincoln. You can sit in and listen if you like." Conrad offered though he still was unsure of the purpose of the visit. "The address is 395 ½ Lincoln, in the back. We don't usually get visitors."

The Radio Players Club Mystery, The Crib Keeper Caper (4)

Massey stood behind the raised door of his hatchback in the driveway at 395 ½ Lincoln as Quinn, Betty and Duncan-Waffles arrived. He reached in and tugged at a wash bin with his sound tools.

"Here let me give you a hand," offered Quinn.

Massey turned to see the group upon him. "Hi."

"Conrad invited us," Betty added.

"Sure thing, thanks," Massey told Quinn, not wanting to turn down help lugging the basin.

Quinn put out his hand and once Massey extended his, Quinn's hands cupped Massey's hand in friendship. "I'm Quinn, and this is Betty and that is Duncan-Waffles."

"You are early. Come on in, make yourself comfortable while I set up and get things ready."

"Thanks, let us know if there is anything we can do to help," Betty added.

Colorado Cowboy walked through the door. Colorado Cowboy had a beautiful baritone voice. He stood four foot one inch tall and weighed one hundred and seven muscular pounds. His friends called him Nathan.

Massey walked over to him and confided that he thought Quinn and Betty must be potential sponsors. Then he brought him over for introductions. The two Radio Players Club members finished setting up the microphones and went over the radio equipment.

Conrad walked into the studio and greeted everyone. "Where is Melody?" He directed his question to Nathan.

"I didn't hear from her. What about Rosy, have you heard from her?" Nathan asked.

"She's on her way." Conrad looked over at Betty. "Can you read?"

Betty felt an affront. "Sure I can read, what do you mean?"

"I mean if Melody doesn't get here will you read her part?" Then after a pause, "It will be fun. Look this over." He stood and carried a script to her.

The Crib Keeper Caper

For the guest, Conrad propped up the small chalkboard that said. 'On The Air' it was his inside joke.

Colorado Cowboy in his baritone voice announced the presentation.

"Tonight's Radio Player Club mystery performance is titled The Crib Keeper Caper. The voices of Conrad Timmerson, Cowboy Conrad, Melody and a special guest Betty." He turned and pointed at Massey.

Massey picked up a book in each hand and slammed first one against a plank, then two at the same time, then one, one last time and four car doors slammed. Massey dragged the violin bow and tires squealing and shrieked.

Betty as Momma "STEP ON IT MIKEY! LET'S GET OUTTA HERE!"

Massey fired the starter pistol three times.

Colorado as Tony "MOMMA THEY'RE SHOOTING AT US."

"SHOOT BACK, BUT DON'T HIT ANYONE! UNDERSTAND. NOW, MIKEY STEP ON IT, GET OVER TO FOURTH JUST LIKE I SHOWED YOU, THEN INTO THAT BLIND ALLEY."

Conrad as Frankie "I KNOW MOMMA, ONCE THE CAR IS IN THE TURNOUT, I GET OUT WITH THE BAG OF GLASS AND THE BROOM. RIGHT MOMMA?"

"RIGHT FRANKIE, JUST MOVE THE DUMPSTER IN FRONT OF THE ALLEYWAY, POUR THAT BAG A GLASS LIKE I SHOWED YAH AND BE SWEEPING WHEN THE COP CAR COMES BY LIKE NOTHING IS HAPPENING. WITH THAT APRON ON THEY SHOULD DRIVE RIGHT BY. HEY, PUT ON THE APRON, LIKE I TOLD YAH. WHILE YOU'RE DOING THAT WE WIPE THE CAR CLEAN OF PRINTS. THEN THE FOUR OF US WALK RIGHT THROUGH JIMMY CHOO'S RICE BOWL PLACE CARRYING THE FLIGHT BAG WITH THE MONEY AND OUT THE FRONT. FRANKIE, YOU REMEMBERED TO PARK THE CAR OUT FRONT OF JIMMY CHOO'S PLACE, LIKE I TOLD YAH? RIGHT!"

"YES, MOMMA."

Massey dragged the bow across the strings pulled taut along the two-by-four and tires screeched. Massey picked up a book in each hand and slammed first one against a plank, then two at the same time, then one, one last time and four car doors slammed. He grabbed a bag of broken glass and poured it into a cardboard box.

A half hour later the performance was over. Conrad poured the group coffee.

Betty walked over to Quinn. "That was fun. How did I do?"

He took her elbow, "You were great." And he gave her a warm smile and a wink.

Quinn went and sat with Conrad. "Now that script? Can you give me the name of the writer?"

"Melissa and Bradley are the writing team. I bought the script a couple of days ago, thought the script was pretty good. How about you? Betty did great. She is a natural. I am afraid that I don't know where they live. I have a number for them over at the office. I can call you with it. Hey, wait a second." Conrad stood and walked over to the script lying on the sound table and flipped through it. "Here it is on the last page. That girl is smart." He tore the page with the information on it from the rest of the script and handed it to Quinn.

"That's great," Quinn told him. He glanced at the address and noted it was on the south side and that it was just early enough to make it to that side of town. He waited for Betty to finish her visit with Colorado and Massey.

Nathan was telling Betty about the Palladium Arena and the midget wrestling matches that were held on Wednesdays and Saturdays. And he extended an invitation.

Quinn held the door open for Betty to go through and Rosy rushed in.

"I am so late, I am so sorry. Are we still going to do this?" asked Rosy.

Quinn and Betty and Duncan-Waffle glanced over their shoulders as they left down the drive.

Melisa

Melisa sat at her desk. She was wearing a pair of boxer shorts and a wife-beater Tee cut off at her midriff. She was elated; she had been elated for three days. She had sold her script The Crib Keeper Caper and just heard it played on the radio.

She sat in front of her Smith-Corona; her left leg was tucked beneath her and she leaned forward staring at the white paper just itching for the words to flow. The energy was erupting from her when she heard a knock on the door.

"Oh, I thought Bradley had forgotten his key or something." She addressed Quinn and was relieved to see Betty at his side. Betty seemed to take the edge off of Quinn's official side. "Hang-on." She walked back into the room and grabbed her polyester kimono and slipped it on. "What brings you to my door?" Her cheerleader smile was firmly in place.

"We're here to talk about a script you wrote for the Radio Players Club," Betty told her. "We are very curious about the origin of that story and we need you to tell us all you can about it."

"Well, that is very direct. The Crib Keeper Caper, why I made it up. Are you accusing me of stealing that script or sticking up a bank? You listen here…."

Quinn interrupted her, and mid-word she stopped talking. "No, no, not

The Crib Keeper Caper the script titled A Rose for Opal Ann tells us about that. Every detail is important.

Melissa walked over and sat on the edge of the bed. She looked at both Quinn and Betty as a lost child. Her mouth twitched at the corners. "Three days ago I sold my first radio script ever. I didn't write A Rose for Opal Ann." She sat back waiting for the next obvious question and wondered to herself if she should answer.

Quinn looked at this young woman. He dismissed from his mind that she could have had anything to do with the crimes he was sniffing out. He pondered how to get her to tell him what he was sure she knew. "We are on the trail of a man who murdered my partner while on police business, so please consider my question carefully before you answer. Please. Do you know anything about who wrote the script and where to find them?"

The writer in Melisa so very much wanted to get in front of her typewriter and get all of this down. "I know a girl name Cass who I see from time-to-time on the streets. She is with a writer and I think he wrote the script. They are on the south side somewhere, but I don't know where. If it were me I would try the radio station, they must have bought it and have some record. I ran into all four of them a few weeks ago at a Café. That's where I got the idea to sell a script to W.A.R.T. radio. They in trouble?"

Betty answered, "No, no one is in trouble. All four of them?"

"Yes, Cass and, I think the curvy girl is Belinda, were with a handsome chap and a slender girl with cinnamon colored skin. I don't know their names."

"Thank you." Betty turned toward Quinn.

Quinn and Betty walked to the door and let themselves out. Before the door was closed, they could hear the keys of the typewriter blazing.

Clean Slate Café 10 p.m.

Jarrod, Naomi, and Cass were drinking coffee when Belinda came through the door. Belinda grabs a cup and leaves her nickel on the counter. She joined her friends, reached in her bag and showed eight dollars to them. "We are getting closer and closer." She smiled, but her smile was not returned.

Jarrod said, "The landlord caught up with me today. He kicked us out; said he was tired of fighting with us for the rent. Our stuff is behind the counter."

"I just posed in the nude for two hours over at the art school for that eight dollars." Belinda had a scornful look on her face.

"I think I found us a place over in the theater district. They collect by the week. But you are carrying the money for us and I didn't know where you were so we did not make a deal. " Naomi put her hand on Belinda's shoulder. "I know you don't like that particular job. I'll take that gig next time. OK?"

Belinda smiled. "Sure."

"If we hurry we may still get over there and have a place to sleep tonight." Jarrod stood, "Let's go."

The Radio Players Club Mystery, Steel People (5)

Hamilton Street

In the car Betty asked, "Doesn't the FBI handle kidnapping cases? Did they get involved?"

"They do, but getting information from them is tough as nails. They feel they are elite. Why do you ask?" Quinn glanced over at Betty.

"Just the thought crossed my mind. I guess if you are hot on the trail of someone then you can't just hand off the job to someone else." Betty glanced out the window and saw the sign for The Clean Slate Café, 'wanna stop for some coffee before heading back to the room."

"There's a place right up the street called The Music Room, they serve very cold beer or wine and there is usually a musician or two playing soft music. Let's have a drink and a sandwich and see where we are on this case. Cass and Belinda are pretty slim leads."

"OK Moose." Betty flashed her big grin at Quinn. "Do you think they are still at the station, we might catch Conrad and he might have information about Cass?"

Steel People

Betty woke to the sound of Duncan-Waffles scratching at the door of the room. She quietly dressed and with the new leash hooked to the collar she and Duncan-Waffles slipped out. It was the first time she noticed the hard gray of an Allentown morning. She listened for usual morning sounds of birds, but they were not present. The humid air clutched at her and the burnt gray asphalt with faded line markings rippled under her. Her horizon filled with ominous coal black buildings resisting the dawn. Icy fingers took a firm grip of her ankles and the sound of screaming women reached her ears. The cold coiled steel whizzed passed on flatbeds in one direction and a thousand accountants in J.C. Penney suits and Strafford shirts raced toward books that would never balance. The broken street people began to cluster with their pockets full of broken dreams. She picked up Duncan-Waffles and clutched him to ward off the foreboding that crept through her deepest corridors. Duncan-Waffles began to bark, which summoned the sun, the first rays cast them in the spotlight on this gray canvas and the pall was shattered. She stepped free of the rancid mist cast by an army of the damned.

Betty and Duncan-Waffles walked back to the cabin, glancing over their shoulders to make sure there was not a pursuit.

When they returned to the room Quinn was shaving. "We need to solve this case and get out of here." She told Quinn. She walked over to the phone.

"Who are you calling?" Quinn asked.

"Kate," she answered, "we were due back and were sidetracked, she might be worried." Under her breath she said, "I know I am."

The Radio Players Club

Quinn and Betty and Duncan sat in a booth at the Apollo Café down the street from the Cabins and ate a leisurely breakfast. Being on the road, they tended to rise early, too early for the regular folks with regular jobs. The agenda this morning was to reach Conrad and see what he knew about the writer of the script A Rose for Opal Ann. Quinn could not believe that the communication was so flawed. He realized it was his own fault; he got caught up with Betty's role in the performance and just missed a turn when it came to the script writer. He was also sure it was easily corrected.

At nine, the phone finally was picked up at Conrad Enterprises. "Conrad, there was some confusion last night. You gave me the name of the script writer of the radio play that was aired last night. I needed the name of the script writer of A Rose for Opal Ann.

Quinn wrote down the name Lecherous Leprechaun at the Palladium Arena as a friend of Jarrod, the writer. Jarrod had no phone number where he could be reached. Lecherous Leprechaun could be found on Wednesday evenings at the Palladium Arena.

"Say hi to Colorado Cowboy if you see him, he'll be around there somewhere tonight for a grudge match with Dynamite Morgan," Conrad told him.

Once informed of the phone call information Betty felt like they were close to wrapping this case up.

Quinn held the Allentown 'Morning Call' and read about shootings, robberies, kidnapping, extortion and general mayhem.

Reading the back side of the folded paper Betty read about a Catasauqua house fire.

"After breakfast let's head over to the library and see what else has been going on in Allentown since you left," Betty said to the back of the newspaper.

Quinn slowly lowered the paper to reveal a big smile for Betty.

Five hours later Betty had read every word printed in the 'Morning Call' about the case that ended Detective Quinn Moosebroker's official career. She read about the two murders that put Quinn and Clarke into high gear. She read about the shooting; she read about the big car and motorcycle motorcade for Clarke. She silently wept as she read about the medal bestowed by a grateful city and continued to weep when she read the force was not going to let him back in and gave him a disability pension.

For the first time, she looked at Quinn and realized he was a wounded man rather than the strong silent type she believed him to be. There was no hug tight enough, no kiss soft enough to cure him. It was only time and perhaps pulling the rotting nail out of his soul that would allow the wound to heal. She resolved herself. With her help, he was going to solve the case and throw that nail away once and for all.

Quinn left with new information and a sinking feeling in his stomach. A kernel was planted and he hoped it was not true. He wanted more time, he wanted a team to get on this, but there was no one. He wondered what he and Betty were walking into.

Palladium Arena

Quinn and Betty approached the back door of the Palladium Arena. A thick-necked husky guy stood between them and the entrance. Quinn took the lead and walked up the three steps. A look of recognition came over the two men's faces.

"Moosebroker you old son of an old rat; how are you doing? What are you doing back here? You made it out."

"Why you old dog faced scoundrel, what are you doing working the rear entrance of a place like this?" Quinn asked his old friend Lenny Baskins a cop from the old days.

Lenny opened the door and let them through calling, "If you're in town awhile stop by for a drink or two. We'll raise the roof of the Boar's Head, like the old days."

Betty followed Quinn down a dimly lit hallway. Quinn ducked to miss a sign hanging in the corridor and hidden from Betty's view by Quinn. He went through the door and Betty followed.

"Yikes," escaped Betty's mouth before she could catch it. She was backing up.

"Get out of here lady! This ain't no peep show," screamed Lecherous Leprechaun standing there dripping wet quickly reaching for a towel. The two men in the shower simultaneously looked over their shoulders then went back to their showering.

Betty was safely out the door and leaning against the wall with her hand to her chest. She looked up to see the sign that Quinn ducked to miss. It said 'Lo ker R om' and what was left of the lettering was faded. She pushed herself from the wall and walked towards the noise of the arena.

The announcer was speaking into a microphone suspended from the ceiling over the middle of the ring: "For our next match "Crazy Crippler' standing four foot three inches from Cincinnati weighing 107 pounds vs our own Allentown grown 'The Granite Cyclone' undefeated in six matches, weighing in at 109 pounds. He released the microphone and turned the match over to the referee.

Betty watched in amazement as these two athletes twisted and turned, leaped and fell, slammed and were slammed. She heard the names Airplane Spin, Fireman's carry-drop, and double leg flapjack from the announcer now sitting at a table at the side of the ring. She looked over the small crowd some watching many just milling about.

In the locker room, Lecherous Leprechaun dressed in his street clothes answered Quinn's questions. Quinn now had four names Cass, Belinda, Jarrod, and Naomi and learned that these street people who were just getting by had been thrown out of their tenement room and their whereabouts were unknown. He learned one more important bit of information. They often hung out at the Clean Slate Café.

The Radio Players Club Mystery, Chasing Rabbits (6)

Palladium Arena

"I'm telling you," the voice said into the phone, "someone was here asking Lecherous Leprechaun a bunch of questions about your nephew. I thought you might want to know. He looked like trouble." He listened for a moment then stood on his tip toes to hang up the receiver of the pay phone. Then he slipped his finger into the coin return hoping to recover his dime.

The Clean Slate Café

Quinn and Betty ate three meals on Thursday and two meals on Friday at the Clean Slate Café.

After dinner, Friday Betty walked into the kitchen to see a short, stocky man standing over the grill. "We were told a group of writers hung out here and were wondering if you knew who I am talking about."

"Plenty of writers come here. I sell coffee for a nickel. Young or old?" The man asked.

"Why young, three girls and a boy." Betty offered.

"You got to come in after 10 PM to catch them, else it's random, they are street people. They on the street all day working for anything, and anyone earning change for food mostly. Jarrod's the boy, always got a story, always scribbling. Them girls love him, Naomi, Cass and that Belinda, she's a beauty." The man offered.

"After 10 PM, thank you. What time do you close?"

"That door's never locked, people come and go. Come to think of it, don't see them for days now." He flipped something on the grill that was covered in bread crumbs. Betty did not recognize it.

Returning to the table, she told Quinn, "If they show up it is after ten PM, the cook has not seen them for a few days. Now what?"

"Let's go put Duncan to bed and head back over to The Palladium and talk to Lecherous Leprechaun or the Colorado Cowboy. Ah, you wait in the lobby." Quinn smiled at Betty and gave her a wink.

The Prey

The voice said into the phone, "Yeah, I gotta a job for you. Someone has been asking questions. I want some of your boys to chase some rabbits out of town." After a pause the voice said, "How do I know? Get over to The Palladium and get the names from Lecherous Leprechaun. Yeah, that is what I was told. Listen, just scare them off." The phone was returned to its cradle.

Garza's Pizza & Shake Shack

Stephanie opened the back door to the alley at 10 PM carrying a bag of trash to the bin. Leaning on the bin was Jarrod. Stephanie gave a rare smile.

"Hey, Stephanie I got something for you." Jarrod reached into his coat pocket and pulled out a dime bag of marijuana. A clear baggie with one ounce of grass was extended towards her.

She reached into her apron pocket and pulled out a wrinkled ten dollar bill and the exchange was made.

"What time do you get off?" He asked with a gleam in his eye and his Robert Redford smile.

"Off? I never get off. Thanks, man. Come back in a few weeks if you can score some more." She tossed the bag of greasy table waste into the bin and a bag of grass into her apron pocket.

"Come with us Saturday, we are going to head to the park and listen to some music. It will be a blast" Jarrod offered.

"Gotta go man." She returned to the sink and the never-ending dishes and dreamed of her escape.

The Theater District

Quinn at the wheel with Betty and Colorado Cowboy in the Town and Country drove down toward the Theater District. There were rundown secondhand clothes shops and the pizza place. There were second rate antique shops, a three chair barber shop, several decrepit hotels, a tobacco outlet, a couple of cafes and a used bookstore. The Central Movie Theater was on one side of the street and the Emporium Theater on the other.

The street people liked it, mostly because it was so cheap. Small groups hung out in doorways and smoked their cigarettes or pot and laughed. Then they would find cheap food and eat and sit and laugh some more.

Quinn had not seen it this crowded before. Betty had been sheltered from the sights of the city. The street people were both colorful and frightening to most of the older generation.

"Hey," Colorado spoke up, "There, that's Jarrod there; he just stepped out of that alley." He pointed at a boy in his early twenties, bell bottom pants, flat hat pulled backward and loose fitting jacket and a bag flung over his shoulder. "Pretty sure that's him." He said looking around at many young men of similar height and weight.

Quinn jerked the Town and Country over and got out, "Find a place to park this, and then find me," he said to Betty. Quinn walked across the street at a quick pace and began to follow Jarrod.

Jarrod turned into the doorway of Absolom Place a shabby three story hotel on its last legs and made for the stairs.

Behind him, Quinn traced each step reaching the doorway of their room before Jarrod could close the door. Quinn could see Naomi laying on the bed wearing a tee shirt reading.

Jarrod turned to see this hulking man cast a dark shadow over the room. He bolted, leaping over the bed through the window and onto the fire escape platform. He did not wish to be caught with a half ounce of marijuana in his pocket. Having his youth he quickly put distance between himself and the cop. He kept a close eye on him.

Jarrod hit the concrete and split towards the entrance of the alley. Betty and Colorado Cowboy were on the street searching for Quinn when they saw Jarrod fly from the alley. Cowboy saw him make a handoff to a girl walking down the street. Betty missed it. They watched him duck inside the Billet Café and grab a table.

"I'll go watch the back. You watch the front and stay where Quinn can see you when he gets to the street." Colorado Cowboy mosied toward the back entrance of the Billet Café and took up a position to keep an eye on it.

Betty walked into the Café in front of Quinn. They were too close to Jarrod for him to make a repeat of his getaway. Betty took a seat next to him and Quinn sat opposite of him. Jarrod was feeling more comfortable, having handed off the one-half ounce of marijuana to the little honey on the street.

Quinn lifted the bag that Jarrod dropped in his apartment and dumped it on the table.

"Hey man, that is illegal. You can't do that." Jarrod squirmed a little.

Betty reached over and picked up the album and opened it to see news clipping after news clipping of the six-year-old case that had ended Quinn's career. She recognized many of them from her hours in the library. "You comfortable?" She asked Quinn.

"Yeah, why?" Quinn asked. "If he tries to run, I might have to break something."

Betty stood and walked out the back carrying the album. She found Colorado Cowboy and told him they had Jarrod. "Put this in the car. Will you? I don't know how long we will be. Can you get back OK?"

"Sure." He took the book and went off.

Quinn sat across from Jarrod. "You wrote a radio play. We caught it on our way home and turned north to find you."

"Why so interested?" Jarrod asked.

"Give me a minute and I am going to tell you. Then you are not going anywhere until you have told me what I want to know." Quinn looked him directly in the eyes. "Do you understand?" He continued, "If you try and run again I am going to shoot you, tie a bandage on you and then you are going to tell me what you know. You are in serious trouble as far as I am concerned. Your job is to convince me otherwise. This isn't some hippy bullshit thing you can lie your way out of."

It began to sink in that this had nothing to do with one-half ounce of marijuana. He sat quietly and gave his attention to Quinn.

Betty returned inside, saw the exchange taking place at the table and went to the counter and grabbed a seat and ordered coffees; one for her and one for each of the boys.

"Let's start with an explanation of that album."

The waitress placed the coffees down in front of Quinn and Jarrod. Jarrod lifted his cup and judged the distance to the door and decided that even tossing the waitress in Quinn's lap that he could not get to the door fast enough to outrun this old man's bullets.

The Radio Players Club Mystery - Running Foxes (7)

Ten PM rolled around. Quinn was told that the radio play was written based on the news clippings found in the album. When pressed he was told that the album came from storage on his uncle's property. When pressed further and firmer the address of the storage property was disclosed.

Quinn was beginning to like Jarrod. He thought the kid showed some real courage in light of the threat to be shot if he ran. He liked that Jarrod's answers were concise though measured. He liked that the kid was trapped but not necessarily afraid.

Betty bided her time at the counter. She noted with interest that first one young lady, and then a second then a third gathered across the street from the Billet Café and were obviously looking through the door watching over Jarrod.

"Let's go," Quinn said loud enough for Betty to hear. "Come on," he said to Jarrod, "we are almost done."

With Quinn on one side gripping Jarrod's elbow and Betty on the other the three walked to the Town and Country. The three young ladies followed at a distance and witnessed the car pull away with Jarrod in it.

Thirty-five minutes later having crossed under the Lehigh Valley Thruway the three of them turned down a dark and lonely Huckleberry Road. In a flash, Quinn felt like he was being led into a trap.

His mind was eased when Jarrod pointed to a long narrow building, "There."

Quinn stopped and pulled near what he thought was an entrance. When the three reached the door, Jarrod produced a key turning a light fixture and undid the padlock. Once inside he hit the light switch and rows of fluorescent lights came on. Betty gasped.

Jarrod walked toward the east side of the building. Betty's eyes shot back and forth and up and down. The place was like a museum of the history of Allentown.

Jarrod reached what he was looking for. It was a bookcase; on the bookcase were at least three dozen albums like the one that disappeared into Betty's possession. "This is what I told you about. Can we go now?"

"Yes, we are going now. Grab an armful of those; we're taking them all."

Betty loaded up as did Jarrod, under protest. Quinn grabbed the rest.

They each dropped their armfuls in the back of the Town and Country. "I gotta lock it up," Jarrod told them. He walked over to the door, locked it, gauged the distance to the side of the building, the dark and the distance from the car and bolted around the corner and disappeared into the darkness.

Betty started to make chase, but Quinn caught her wrist. "We got more than we could have ever hoped for. It couldn't be better. Jarrod is not just running from us now."

"It's been a long night. Let's go feed Duncan-Waffles. He is probably wondering what he got himself into." And with an odd look on her face she said, "I know I am. Would you have shot that boy?"

He looked at her coolly, "Yes; if I were carrying a gun."

Bethlehem Motor Court

The path of the Town and Country was blocked as they pulled into the gravel drive of the Bethlehem Motor Court. Two rough looking men stepped out of the black Chevy Bel Air. Quinn glanced over his shoulder thinking to back up when a tan 1968 Oldsmobile blocked him in.

Quinn took his foot off the brake and floored it, ramming the Chevy and scattering the two men, then backed up, braked hard and told Betty, "Follow me." He stepped out of the car ran to the back as four men got out of the Olds opened the back and grabbed the bumper jack shaft and the lug wrench. He handed the lug wrench to Betty and said, "Keep those two off my back."

Duncan-Waffles was barking furiously from the cabin a few feet away.

His first lunge with the metal shaft caught the thug directly on the hip bone. The noise of the breaking bone made each of the three left standing take a step back.

Betty stood at Quinn's back taking practice swings with the lug wrench that she was holding like a Lewisville slugger.A big boy of about Quinn's size pushed in hard, his quickness evaded the first cross of the metal shaft, but Quinn's two-fisted back swing with his quarterstaff rang loud across the lad's skull. His hands went to his head as if to catch the blood as he dropped to his knees.

The two men that Betty was facing down charged her. There was the sound of broken glass behind them. She caught the first one solid on the elbow which made him spin-off, but the second one bulldozed her and down she went.

He immediately howled as Duncan-Waffles planted his sharp row of teeth into his calf. The noise spun Quinn around and with two steps forward he planted the quarterstaff like a flag into the man's back.

The two remaining attackers made their retreat gathering their wounded as they went. The two cars pulled out and made their way down the highway at top speed.

Quinn rushed to Betty, who was holding Duncan-Waffles. "That's going to leave a bruise," she said.

"That's it. This place gets no more of my business." Quinn told her while helping her up.

Betty limped into the room and jotted down, 88M-508 and 5E3-534. Then she started putting her clothes quickly into her bag. Quinn followed suit.

Fifteen minutes later Quinn, Betty, and Duncan-Waffles checked out and drove off in search of a well lit Hotel with a bathtub for Betty.

"Let's check in using your name Betty. They seem to know my name."

"Yeah, and next time they won't be so polite," Betty added rubbing Quinn's shoulder while listening to the distinct chatter coming from the front of the Town and Country.

The Phone Call

The hand held the receiver to its ear and listened.

Then the voice said, "You mean to tell me an old man and a woman beat up four of your guys?" Then there was a pause. "What? Why is Lenny in the hospital?" The voice was quiet.

"It gets worse," the caller said reluctantly, "they smashed in the side of the Bel Air."

"Let me get this straight. You brought six guys to chase off some rabbits and the foxes are in the hospital and my Bel Air is smashed up?"

The caller could almost hear the stroke happening as he heard the phone slammed into the cradle.

Howard Johnson Inn

Quinn had gotten Betty fed. She had soaked and Quinn put liniment on her hip, shoulder, and elbow. She was feeling better but bruised and moving slowly. Duncan-Waffles never left her side.

By three, AM Quinn had worked his way through about a third of the albums and compiled an unnerving portfolio.

At seven, AM Betty ordered breakfast and continued as Quinn slept. Betty wept, she wept for the world in general and the enormity of the pain in which she found herself. Looking at the stacks of albums, she could not remain objective.

Reverse the Charges

The phone rang and Kate was there to pick it up. "Hi Kate, Dad. Look at the mail that's arrived. There should be a check. I want you to open it, sign my name to the back and deposit it for me. Use the night teller, there shouldn't be any problems."

"Everything going ok? Betty sounded worried when she called the other day."

"Everything is fine, I just have run into some unexpected expenses. Oh, hey, there is a little money in my sock drawer send that to me. We are at the Howard Johnsons on Hamilton in Allentown. Get a paper I will give you the full address. On second thought, I need you to come to us. My service revolver is in the Quaker Oat Meal box in the kitchen cupboard. Deposit that check, bring the money and the gun. Yes, yes, everything is fine. I will need you to cart some evidence out of here while there is time."

"Allentown? Did you say Allentown? What on earth are you doing in Allentown?"

"I'll try and explain when you get here. Just get here quick."

Howard Johnson Inn

On the third day holed up at the Howard Johnson the portfolio was finished. Betty had begun making trips to the library to make a second copy.

Quinn managed to get the Town and Country to a garage where it would be kept inside while repairs to the grill and fender were made.

Kate arrived delivered everything Quinn had asked for and was introduced to the new family dog. Duncan-Waffles was just the relief they all needed.

The Radio Players Club Mystery, Zip-A-Dee-Doo-Dah' (8)

The hunting of monsters is not for the faint of heart. Nor is it for those who feel bound by such trivial doctrines as law or national borders.

Tess Gerritsen

Pequod

Quinn picked up the phone and called the number from his notepad. "Yes Officer Harcourt, please names and addresses for both numbers. That would be great. How is Eden? Oh, congratulations, you had better slow down son. Let's get together in a couple of weeks and have some cold ones. Yes, thank you." He hung up.

"That was Harcourt on the phone." He told Betty. "Things are in motion now."

"I am getting to know how Captain Ahab felt sizing up his harpoon against his whale." Betty glanced over at Quinn, who was weighing her words.

"I am going to catch the guy who shot Clark and I have plenty enough harpoon for that. The whale, if there is one is just a bonus." Quinn told her. "Everything is just detective work now."

"Then why did you have Kate bring your service revolver?" Betty asked.

Quinn stood with his back straight and addressed her coolly; "Because the next guy who tries to bulldoze you I am going to shoot in the face; that's why," his voice a little louder than he had meant it to be.

Quinn's eyes narrowed to slits and that look told Betty that he meant it and made a note to herself not to let anyone bulldoze her. Duncan-Waffles paced on the bed and listened to the exchange.

The Spout of the Whale

Black fought gray for skyspace. Metallic raindrops crashed cymbals against tin souls. The shadow of the black swan's wings ruffled the heavy air; stilled smokestacks marked industrial graves and the widow maker waltz began. The voice said into the phone, "Find them and kill them."

Kate Arrives

After Kate had settled and had time to rest from her drive. Betty called. "Hey Kate. Let's go for a drive."

"Sure. Where are we going?" Kate asked still a little tired from her trip from Clearview Terrace.

"I'll tell you on the way." Betty had an idea.

They climbed into the green VW Bug and Betty using her newly purchased city map directed Kate towards the Hall of Records. After paying a fee and having Kate bat her eyes at the County Recorder clerk, they were both seated in front of a thick plate book of the city.

In a couple of hours the two detectives, Kate, and Betty had the name and address of the owner of the warehouse on Huckleberry Road.

"Let's go get your father. He is going to want to hear this." Betty told Kate.

Quinn prepares for war

With the girls gone Quinn went to find his friend who worked security at the Palladium Arena. He wanted to have a twelve gauge pump shotgun in his possession after the incidence in the parking lot of the Bethlehem Motor hotel. He was not sure what he was up against and he wanted to level the odds.

Once he acquired the weapons he returned to the hotel and cleaned the arsenal. It occurred to him that he wanted to take another look at the Huckleberry Road warehouse and left the relative comfort of the Howard Johnson's Hotel and took a cab to the warehouse. He wanted to watch the coming and going and if the place remained empty, he planned to reenter and have a slower look around. He remembered where Jarrod found the stashed key.

Aengus Ó Braonáin

Quinn was approaching the warehouse when he saw an old Studebaker pull up to the door. He watched as an elderly man climbed out and with the use of a walker made his way to the door and let himself in.

Quinn stood by the door a few minutes and questioned himself if he should go in. In a moment, he heard music coming from the warehouse. It was a Louie Armstrong song from the 40's.

Quinn pulled the door open and cautiously entered.

The old man was seated directly in front of a stereo record player with the speakers opened like wings. Wearing old shorts and old gray tee shirt his head bobbed with the music; his hands were shaking and if the music were not playing Quinn would have suspected Parkinson's.

"Hello, I heard the music," Quinn announced himself.

"Do you remember this one? It's 'A Kiss to Build a Dream On'" The old man turned back to watch the rotations of the record that carried him back to his times.

When the record finished, he took hold of his walker and moved over to a rack with 45's and returned the record and flipped through and took another.

"I'm Quinn Moosebroker." He held out his hand.

The gentleman putout his hand and smiled as Quinn grasped the hand with both of his. "Aengus Ó Braonáin, I'm seventy-seven." He said in a feeble voice. "Find a chair, should be one here somewhere, we'll listen to some music."

Quinn found a chair and he and Aengus listened to music that Quinn remembered his Mother listened to when he was a young man.

In between listening to 45's Aengus talked to Quinn about his museum of Allentown, but not just any museum he was told, it is a museum of Allentown crime. "No one comes here," Aengus told him. Quinn listened as he talked about his four brothers. He talked about how they made their money as told around a poker table at their regular games over the years. "They would talk and then I would read all the local news and cut out the stories they talked about. Now, me, I was in a band. So much booze and so many women, I'm surprised I got old. The record dropped and 'Who Walks in When I Walk Out' began to play. Aengus' head began to bob and his hands moved as the music entered his mind.

Quinn stood and began glancing around. In a desk drawer, he found an address book written in a strong male hand. In it were notations of a date, a street address, and one, two or three dollar signs. He slipped the book into his coat pocket and returned to his chair as 'Zip-A-Dee-Doo-Dah' dropped into place and began to play.

Risking it, "When was the last time you saw Jarrod?" Quinn asked.

"Jarrod? Jarrod Peter's son? He's a good kid. Does he owe you money?" He asked Quinn.

"Where would he hole up if he had to run?" Quinn asked.

"Probably his Mother's in Wilkes-Barre. He is not in trouble is he? He's a good kid. He's the only nephew that talks to me. He ain't in trouble is he?"

"No, he's not in trouble. I wanted to ask him a couple of questions. That's all." Quinn told him. "You don't happen to know an Opal Ann, do you?"

"Opal Ann?" The old man looked straight at Quinn. "No, nobody named Opal Ann. Jarrod mentioned once a Sapphire Annie with deep blue eyes. You know the kind a man can get lost in. He seemed very interested in her."

"Thank you for allowing me to listen."

Aengus Ó Braonáin's head began to bob, his eyes sunken and cheeks caved in; his hands bounced in time to the music. Quinn turned and walked out the door wondering if Aengus would even remember his visit.

Howard Johnson Hotel

Quinn was sitting in the only chair in the room when the girls returned. He was reading through the address books, all the entries after the date of his shooting interested him.

"Quinn, we found out who owns the warehouse. We spent the afternoon at the Hall of Records. She took a notepad from her purse and flipped to a page, "one Mr. Aengus Ó Braonáin owns it; we have a name."

"Great work," Quinn told her but could see her attention was now fixed on the twelve gauge shotgun and the two pistols lying on the dresser looking freshly oiled.

"You have been busy." She told him, glancing at Kate.

"I've seen guns before," Kate added seeing Betty's concern.

"There's more." Quinn handed Betty the address book. She glanced at a few pages and walked over to the bed and sat crossed legged as she began reading from the beginning. Kate came over and sat next to her and read along with her.

"Quinn, have you studied this?" Betty asked.

"I just started looking at it before you guys arrived." He told her.

"Kate grab that stack of paper over there would you?" Betty pointed.

The stack of papers was the condensed version of the albums found at the warehouse.

Betty and Kate sat and read. Quinn sat in the chair almost dozing off. The ringing of the phone startled him. He said hello and listened and set the phone down.

"The Town and Country is ready. Hey, listen we have to change hotels. No one should know where we are for awhile."

The Radio Players Club Mystery, Leave the Driving to Us (9)

Harcourt's News

Once relocated to their new hotel Quinn called his friend Officer Harcourt of the Clearview Terrace Police Department. When he hung up the phone he told Betty and Kate that the Black Chevrolet Bel Air belonged to none other than Dolan Ó Braonáin of Allentown and the Oldsmobile to one Timmy O'Leary a known associate with an arrest record filled with violent crimes, but no convictions.

Hippie Kate

"So what do we need now?" Betty asked.

"There are just a few links missing before we can make our move." Quinn responded. "I sure would like to talk to Jarrod again. He was coy and I think he has just a little more information he can supply." He turned to look at Kate, "I think you might be helpful in that regard. How would you like to go shopping for some sandals and a granny dress?" He waited for a response.

"A granny dress? I am not the hippie type," she had a puzzled look on her face.

"Jarrod has three women. They are street people; Cass, Belinda, and Naomi. Maybe you can find them if they have not run, and get a lead on Jarrod. But they will never trust you wearing stay press slacks from Montgomery Wards and blouses from that boutique outlet you shop at."

Betty liked the idea and wondered if Quinn was just sending her out of harm's way. "Come on Kate. Let's go shopping. I saw a place in the Theater District that will fill the bill perfectly. And we can get you a clean room down there to make the search more bearable." She liked the idea of placing Kate elsewhere.

Betty lifted her purse and noted the extra weight. She opened it and peeked inside. Quinn had stuffed the smaller of the two pistols there without her seeing it. He did not seem to see her glance at him, but she was sure he saw. She made up her mind then and there and lifted the stack of papers and address book and slipped them into her purse. She wanted to make extra copies.

After finding an ankle length paisley dress in blues and purples with an empire waist and a fresh new pair of sandals, Kate and Betty went and found the Billet Café. They entered and discussed what was next. Kate felt a little odd in her new role. Across the street from the Billet Café was the last place that Naomi, Belinda, and Cass were seen and it was just a block from Absolom Place.

Kate and Betty had coffee and Betty left her there to roam the streets in search of Jarrod's women. The goal was to get information that would lead to Jarrod.

Betty went and found the nearest phone booth. She flipped through the phone book and under the headings of government services found the name and address of the local office of the Federal Bureau of Investigation.

Dropping a dime into the phone, she made the call. "Special Agent Donato," the female voice answered.

"I am going to mail you a package," Betty said into the receiver. "It should make your career."

Special Agent Silvia Donato looked at the phone before she sat it back down and a smile spread over her face.

Betty addressed the package with the copies to Special Agent Donato, FBI Hamilton Street and dropped it into a mailbox on the way back to the hotel. It was getting late, her mind was racing and she had one more task before catching up with Quinn. She returned to the service garage where the Town and Country was ready, and loaded the albums from the back, into Kate's WV bug and went out to Huckleberry Street to return them to the shelves they occupied. She wanted them to be there, as unsoiled evidence when or if the FBI followed up on her information. She kept the one regarding Quinn's case.

Her heart was racing, she knew Quinn might not agree with her decision, she was sure the case was bigger than herself, Quinn and Kate could handle. Quinn's arsenal told her that.

Now she set her mind on a rusty nail. She sat at the Clean Slate Café just as a back up to Kate's prowling the Theater District and went through the album with Quinn's clipping. She stopped and made a note in her notepad when she came to a name; she tapped her finger on the page and said, "Where are you Stephanie Koppel?"

The Public Record

Quinn took his newly harvested information to the Allentown public library and searched through the microfiche archives of the Morning Call. He found that the Ó Braonáin family ran a local Funeral Home, a bar named Lonegan's and a couple of motels, they had come under local authority review on more than one occasion. The notes from Harcourt's call were in his pocket; in the white pages Dolan Ó Braonáin, Aengus Ó Braonáin and Peter Ó Braonáin were listed. News articles made reference to Martin (Spider) Ó Braonáin and Bryan Ó Braonáin but they were not listed.

Making his way to the auto body shop Quinn picked up the Town & Country. He retrieved Duncan-Waffles and made his way across town; he decided to begin his stakeout of Lonegan's Bar.

At dusk, Spider Ó Braonáin entered the bar. Quinn recognized him from a photo in the Morning Call. Quinn and Duncan got out of the car and went into a café and ordered coffee; from the payphone he left a message for Betty back at the hotel.

Back in the car he checked the ammunition in his service revolver and wondered how many Ó Braonáin's were inside Lonegan's. The years of detective work alerted Quinn that Spider Ó Braonáin was a bad guy. His walk and swagger screamed, 'I am dangerous.' The hair on the back of Quinn's neck bristled. Duncan-Waffles paced with restless energy on the front seat by the side of his master.

At 11:30 PM Spider Ó Braonáin came out of Lonegan's climbed into a dark blue Cadillac and drove toward home. He never saw the Town and Country that followed him and parked down the street, but in sight of his driveway. Quinn noted the address on his pad and he and Duncan-Waffles settled down to watch. At three AM, they returned to the Hotel.

There was a note waiting for him under the door 'Decided to stay with Kate. Uncomfortable leaving her there by herself. Betty'

Forty-eight hours of surveillance rotating from the funeral home, motels and Lonegan's produced no new clues. The girls were not having any luck then Betty changed tactics and began watching the local Greyhound Bus station.

In the early morning hours of the third day, Quinn and Duncan-Waffles were sitting in the Town and Country parked at the corner of the cross street facing the home of Spider Ó Braonáin. The arrival of three black four-door Delta 88's pulling up in front of the house and eight FBI agents climbing out and approaching the house with guns drawn made Quinn sit straight up in the seat.

In two hours, Spider Ó Braonáin was in custody and a stream of banker boxes were carried to their waiting vehicles. Unknown to Quinn and Duncan-Waffles, Dolan Ó Braonáin, Peter Ó Braonáin, Bryan Ó Braonáin and Aengus Ó Braonáin were also taken into custody in early morning FBI raids.

Quinn knew it was a waste of time, but he got out of the car and put the leash on Duncan-Waffles and they took a walk right in front of the house under the stern eye of several agents.

Spider Ó Braonáin in handcuffs watched Quinn and Duncan from the back seat of a black Delta 88 and wondered who this stranger was in his neighborhood.

Leave The Driving to Betty

On the morning of the third day while Betty was sitting in the bus station reading a John D. MacDonald's paperback, Jarrod and a girl with cinnamon skin walked in and up to the ticket window. Betty hurried unnoticed towards the window in time to hear them purchase two tickets to Rancho Cucamonga, California leaving at 2 PM.

Betty waited until the couple settled in and went to a payphone and left a message for Quinn at the hotel and called Kate's hotel and left a message for her to get over to the bus station.

At 1:15 PM there was still no sign of Quinn or Kate. Betty surveyed the layout then made her move. She walked over and sat in the seat right in front of Jarrod. "Remember my friend? That big guy leaning against the door pretending to read the paper. And glance to your right, that woman has a 38 stashed in her purse. Do I have your attention?"

Jarrod glanced at the two people Betty spoke of.

Betty secretly hoped both of these people were playing their parts in her charade. "There is a warrant out for your arrest. But I guess because you are here you know that. That's a question for another day."

"What do you want? I told you what I know," he glanced at Naomi, who was anxious about being arrested.

"If you help me, we are going to walk out that door and not another word of your part in this will be spoken. But you have to tell me what your part is and more importantly how and why you picked the name Opal Ann for your radio play. You have information. The price I am willing to pay for that information is your freedom."

Jarrod glanced at the clock on the wall. In thirty minutes, he planned to be on the bus. He glanced at the big man leaning against the wall by the door. He recognized Betty but was not sure about the man. He pinched his nose in thought and wondered if he could trust her.

Naomi starring at Jarrod said, "Tell her what she wants to know. You aren't going to fare very well in prison."

Jarrod took a deep breath. For a moment, Betty thought he was going to call her bluff. "The day I got my driver's license I got a call from my Uncle Bryan. He said he was busy and needed a favor. I was to go to Regal Heights where all the mansions are and pick up a girl and bring her to Garza's Pizza & Shake Shack. I didn't think too much about it until I got there and this little girl with sapphire blue eyes was brought to the back service entrance. Man, I tell you, she looked like she could have been Rosemary's Baby with sunken cheeks and deep-set eyes and weighing almost nothing. She was spooky looking."

Jarrod sat up straight having told his story. "I talked to her on the way over, she did not even know her name or how old she was. I called her Sapphire Annie." The clock on the wall said 1:50 PM.

Betty's heart was racing as first call to board the bus was announced over the intercom system. She wanted to pummel the boy. She wanted to have him arrested. She wanted to have him hurt. Her eyes were full of sorrow.

Jarrod waited for the hammer to drop. Then he said, "She's still there. I just saw her the other day."

Naomi said, "Tell her the rest, it's time to go."

"Later when writing the radio play using the album you took, I figured out she was Stephanie Koppel, who had been kidnaped. There was no one I could tell."

The clock on the wall said 1:55 PM. It was Betty's turn to take a deep breath. She glanced at the door. The large man was gone. The intercom announced last call boarding for Rancho Cucamonga, Ca. Betty stood without speaking and rushed out of the station to find Quinn.

The Radio Players Club Mystery Conclusion 10

Betty found Quinn and Duncan-Waffles, whom she had not seen for three days at the Hotel, she was greeted with doggie kisses. "Hi, I have some interesting news. I think we have found Stephanie Koppel."

"I have some interesting developments also. Do you know anything about the FBI?" Quinn had a solemn look on his face. "Duncan and I were doing early morning surveillance on Martin Ó Braonáin's residence when a caravan of FBI agents showed up. They took him into custody and carried out boxes of evidence from his home."

"Did you hear me? We found Jarrod and he gave us information regarding the whereabouts of Stephanie Koppel. Quinn, she is Opal Ann from the radio play." She paused, "Quinn why are you looking at me like that?"

"Let's check out of this hotel and go and get Kate. We can head home." Quinn opened the top bureau drawer and began putting clothes into his bag.

"Most of my stuff is back in the room Kate and I are sharing. We'll find Kate and get packed." Betty needed to break the ice here and set her mind to it.

Quinn wrapped the twelve gauge in his coat when he brought it to the Town & Country. Duncan-Waffles was so cheerful that Quinn's mood began to improve.

"Someone sent six guys to beat us up. We are outnumbered and outgunned. Yes, I sent the evidence we retrieved to the FBI. Quinn listen to me. It worked. They have taken action. "

The two found Kate talking to three young men on a street corner. They each had long hair and were wearing beads. They made hasty good-byes when they saw Quinn approaching. Quinn had that effect on some people.

"Hi Kate," Betty said. "Listen we are going home."

The odd look on Kate's face demanded an explanation. Betty took her arm and they walked down the street to the Billet Café. Kate was glad to get off her feet. The three ordered coffee.

"The FBI has taken our case." Quinn began. "We were getting close. The evidence trail was becoming clear."

Betty spotted a folded newspaper with the headline:

Morning Call – FBI Breaks White Slave Racket

HANNAH TOWNSEND – FBI sting operation in an early morning raid on the home of Dolan Ó Braonáin on Ruppsville Rd. Allentown, PA Special Agents apprehended the suspected leader in an organized white slave operation operating in Allentown for two decades. In a joint effort with Allentown PD and FBI, the case which has been a top priority has busted wide open.

Lt. Marks of Allentown PD gives credit to investigative police work in conjunction with the resources made available by the local office of the FBI. He stated he believed a small number of people were involved in this tightly knit team of criminal.....

"Look Quinn," she handed the paper to Quinn. "Didn't you say they raided Martin Ó Braonáin's home?" Quinn sat back in his seat and took a drink of coffee. Betty watched his face as he changed his position on the whole FBI issue.

"Well, we could not have raided all their homes at once, that is for sure. Betty you did the right thing. Now tell me about how you caught up with Jarrod."

Betty filled him in on her luck to have found him at the bus station and her ploy to get him to talk. She told him that he abandoned Cass and Belinda or maybe just went on ahead and they would be sent for later. She told him she changed her mind about him, she no longer thought he was a good kid. Then she told him about Sapphire Annie.

Garza's Pizza & Shake Shack

It was only 10:30 AM and the pizza place was not open. Quinn suggested gathering their belongings and getting the cars prepared for their trip home.

There was some discussion about the case.

It was not until 5:30 PM that a white van pulled up to the back door of Garza's Pizza and a short husky balding man with hairy arms climbed out. He went to the side door and opened it and took the young girl roughly by the arm and led her inside.

"Let's prepare for this. We don't know what to expect inside. I'll park the Town & Country in the alley facing the street and Kate you park your bug on the street right outside the alley. Betty you and Kate go in the front door and find her. Just walk right through to the kitchen. I'll go in the back door." Quinn told the girls. "Check your pistols. I doubt you will have to use them, but it is better to be prepared."

Both Betty and Kate patted their purse to remind them of the weight they carried.

"I need a few minutes to get ready," Betty told them and walked down the street. When she arrived back at the front door having signaled Quinn in the alley she and, Kate went in.

They walked right passed the hairy armed man into the kitchen with him on their heels.

"You can't come in here," he screamed. "You hear me lady? Get out." He reached for her just as Quinn opened the back door and stepped in carrying the shotgun.

"Get out!" Hairy man yelled. When Quinn put a round in the chamber, the man stopped making sounds.

Betty turned to Sapphire Annie, who had taken several steps back and was cowering near the baking rakes. Betty extended her arm with the deep red rose she had just purchased, in her hand, "Do you want to come with us?"

Stephanie took the rose. The first she had ever received. Kate approached and took her by the arm. Betty, Kate, and Stephanie walked right passed Quinn and out the door. Kate opened the back door of the Town & Country and Stephanie as she climbed in was greeted with doggie kisses by Duncan-Waffles. Kate walked to the end of the alley and to her car and began her trip home.

As soon as Quinn stepped out the back door, the man with the hairy arms was on the phone. There was no answer at the two numbers that he dialed. Sapphire Annie was free.

In the following days, weeks and months the ALLENTOWN NEWS and MORNING CALL were must reading at Quinn and Betty's breakfast table:

<u>Allentown News</u> – Teenage Girls Released From CAPTORS

FRANCES DUNN – Cold case files on fourteen girls have been officially closed. The return of girls 13 to 19 by police officials marks the start of a new beginning for these families. Statements obtained from each of the young women may lead to more arrest in the scandal that has rocked the city.....

Morning Call – Slave Syndicate Search Widens

HANNAH TOWNSEND – Evidence leading outside the suspected tight family group has surfaced. Corruption charges have been leveled at city officials. Suspected bribery and conspiracy to obstruct justice leveled at local police department. Ongoing investigation.....

Allentown News – FBI Haled as Heroes by Local Law Enforcement

FRANCES DUNN – Lt. Mark... of Allentown PD applauds the FBI in their efforts to rip the lid off the largest scandal to hit the city in four decades. FBI Special Agent Silvia Donato headed up a task force with unrelenting diligence. With full cooperation of the Allentown PD dozens of unsolved cases are being closed. Agent Donato was quoted as saying the FBI has the most highly trained law enforcement agents in the world.....

Morning Call – Slave Trade Trials Begin

HANNAH TOWNSEND – Four Ó Braonáin brothers facing eighty-seven counts of human trafficking begin their trial today in Superior Court. Dolan, Peter, Bryan, and Martin (Spider) Ó Braonáin, face fifteen-years-to-life on each count.

The corruption trials of Judge Collins and Captain Sheryl of the Allentown PD begin in separate cases....

Allentown News – Twelve More Steel Town Indictments Issued

FRANCES DUNN – Indictments have been issued for the former Corporate Executive of the defunct Carson Steel Company. Mr. Paul Monroe is charged with human trafficking including sexual slavery and forced labor at his mansion in Regal Heights. The scope of the investigation has led to all levels of local business and government.

Greg Benton of the District Attorney's office has asked the courts to levy maximum sentences in all cases related to this Syndicate. He wishes to send a message to all those who wish to spread their tentacles into the heart of the operation of our fair city. He further……

Morning Call –Teens Reunited

HANNAH TOWNSEND – Fourteen teens, ages ranging between thirteen and nineteen have been reunited with their families. Six of the teens were listed as missing persons the others were thought to be runaways. The city is hosting a gathering at Rafferty Hall to celebrate the occasion…..

Morning Call – Body of Dolan Ó Braonáin's Brother Found Dead

HANNAH TOWNSEND – Aengus Ó Braonáin, brother of Dolan Ó Braonáin's on trial on White Slavery charges was found dead in his north side duplex. Police have not disclosed the cause of death. Aengus Ó Braonáin was a musician of some acclaim in the 1940's and 1950's…

Morning Call – Slave Trade Evidence

HANNAH TOWNSEND – Police recovered at the home of Martin (Spider) Ó Braonáin a long barreled 38 caliber revolver that is linked to the murder of Gerald Clark detective with Allentown PD who was killed in the line of duty in 1967 answering a call regarding the kidnapping of

Stephanie Koppel. He will stand trial for murder after the conclusion of the trial on White Slavery....

Allentown News – Links to Local Law Enforcement in Slave Trade

FRANCES DUNN – Evidence uncovered in the ongoing investigation of four of the five O'Braondin brothers have led to the arrest of two municipal judges and the suspension of six Allentown police officers ranging in rank from Sergeant to Captain. The judges are being held for accepting bribes and corruption charges.

Arrest warrants have been issued for forty-eight Allentown residents for human trafficking.

Lamb Bor's Linguini

Clearview Terrace

Weeks after the trio returned after getting Stephanie Koppel reunited with her Mother, Quinn and Betty found time to get back to a quieter routine. Quinn suggested a night out even though their budget had taken a hit with the back-to-back cases in North Carolina and Allentown.

THE LAMB BOR'S LINGUINI

When the meal was served and the wine was poured Betty stood and tapped her butter knife against her wine glass to get the patrons' attention.

"I want to propose a toast," she paused for dramatic effect, "to Quinn Moosebroker, Retired."

"Here-here," was heard by the patrons as they returned to their meal.

Betty sat with a smile that expressed her satisfaction.

Quinn winked at her, he stood and tapped his butter knife against his wine glass to the consternation of the patrons. He held up his glass, "I would like to propose……."

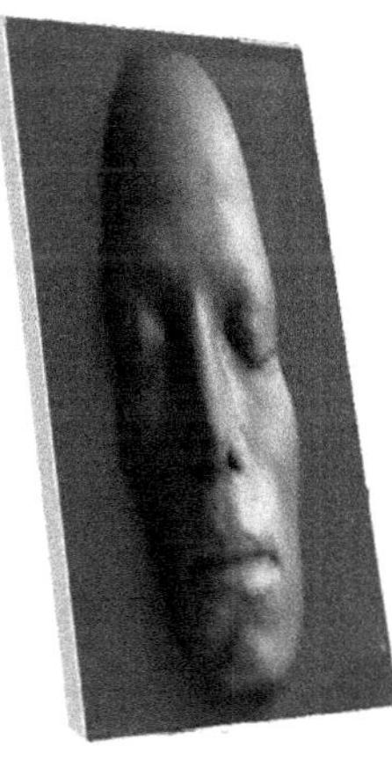

The Case of the Chocolate Girl (1)

Lorcan Bacalao scratched another name from his list. His list had grown since the first call from Dolan Ó Braonáin. Lorcan did contract work and business had seen a spike since the FBI raided the Ó Braonáin businesses. With the four Ó Braonáin brothers in custody, Dolan was exercising a fierce strike at those he felt involved in his capture.

It had taken Lorcan ten days to track the location of Quinn Moosebroker. He first persuaded the proprietor of the Bethlehem Motor Court to give him a copy of the register for the evening that the six assailants fought and lost a battle with Quinn and Betty. Then he scoured every lodge, inn, hotel and motel in the general area. Quinn Moosebroker, Clearview Terrace and Betty Atwood, Clearview Terrace caught his attention, it was just the information he felt he needed.

He still needed to locate Jarrod and his three women. Dolan was sure

Jarrod was involved. There was a line through Aengus Ó Braonáin's name. First he would eliminate a possible witness named Mario Garza then Lecherous Leprechaun.

Clearview Terrace

Betty sat at the kitchen table sipping her coffee as Quinn finished up the dishes after cooking her breakfast on their first Saturday morning after two long back-to-back cases. She reached over to a kitchen drawer and grabbed a pair of scissors and cut a coupon for a discount at a thrift store. "Honey, after we are done here there is a grand opening of a thrift store over on Bastionbury. Want to take a ride over and see?"

"Sure, I'll be done in a minute. What do you need?"

"Need, I just want to look at stuff. You never know – you might find a treasure," she smiled and got up to go get dressed.

Thirty minutes later they arrived at the front door of the thrift store. Betty had the coupon stashed in her purse. The morning was glorious and Betty was very happy they were not chasing down someone or sitting in bus stations.

When the doors opened Betty and Quinn were among the first inside. There was an air of excitement in the store.

Quinn went one way and was amused that Betty went another. He walked to the back and looked at two bookcases filled with old books. Above one book shelf leaning against the wall, was an old painting. He reached up stretching and took slight hold of the lower corner and lifted it and took it down. A man standing close by waited impatiently to see if Quinn would put it back down. The man had spotted it, but could not get to it in time.

Quinn held the painting that was unsuitably framed; he continued to look at the book titles. He spotted a copy of *The Day of the Jackal* by Frederick Forsyth and grabbed it for his bedside table.

Betty arrived at his side, “There is a small table over there. I thought we could refinish it together and use it in an empty corner of your den. It has a drawer you can store your paints in when you are not using them. Come on, I want to show it to you.”

Quinn and Betty got the book, the painting and small table with a drawer in the back of the Town and County. Betty did not forget to use the coupon.

Upon returning home, the table went into the one car garage where the Town & County felt most at home. At the moment, the front right panel lay against the side of the wall while Quinn searched for the shimmy he heard coming from that side ever since the accident in North Carolina.

“Can I treat you to dinner over at The Frosty Mug?” Betty asked. She was again at the kitchen table drinking coffee. “Let’s call Kate and see if she can join us. Maybe see a movie, does that sound OK to you?”

“I am going to stop over and talk to Blake Knightly the owner of the local bookshop, see if I can poke through some of his art books, maybe find out more about the artist. Do you want to join me?” Quinn responded.

Betty lowered the crossword puzzle page of the paper and looked over at Quinn. “Are we on for dinner and a movie? Should I check with Kate?”

“Diner and a movie? Ah, sure. You going to call Kate?”

Betty shook her head and smiled, “Yes, I’ll call Kate.”

Quinn rummaged through the hall closet and found the Polaroid camera. He wanted to carry a couple of snapshots with him. He placed the painting near the window to maximize the light and took his photos.

Quinn left for downtown. Upon entering Knightly Books, he noticed that Blake had rearranged the front of the store. There were new bookcases of what looked to Quinn to be American black walnut. “Where did you get these?” Quinn asked.

“Hello Quinn, they were picked up at an estate sale. It was a ton of work to get them here, but they changed the whole appearance of the place. Just look at them. Of course, the pine shelves are just one step away. How have you been?” Blake asked, not rising from his seat behind the counter.

“Good thanks, where are your new arrivals? And I need a favor. Can I browse through your art books? I found a painting earlier at the new thrift store on Bastionbury. Quinn reached into his pocket and took out the Polaroids and handed them to Blake.

“That’s very nice. It looks like a Dutch painting to me. What do you judge the age to be?”

“To me it looks over a hundred years old. But I am no expert on these things.” Quinn looked around and spotted the art section. He was at a loss as to where to start. “What do you think? Dutch did you say?”

Blake got up and came around to stand next to Quinn in front of a very weak art book section. He reached and took down two volumes. “Try looking through these.”

After an hour of searching through the two volumes Blake handed him and two others, Quinn found nothing to help him identify the painting or the painter. He returned <u>Dutch Painters of the Nineteenth Century and</u>

Painters of the Dutch-Flemish Schools to the shelf where they came from and browsed until he found a nice first printing of Mr. Roberts and purchased it for himself and as a thank you to Blake. He and Blake were the only ones in the store.

Betty had reached Kate and she was able to join them. When Quinn returned home, Kate was sitting in the den with Duncan-Waffles sitting on her lap.

"Hi Dad, I like the painting you found. Did you go and search for information about it at the bookstore?" She glanced over at him; Duncan-Waffles' tail was moving a mile a minute at Quinn's return.

"Blake told me that he thought it might be Dutch, so I spent an hour looking through books about Dutch painters, but I did not find any helpful information," Quinn told her.

"It's beautiful. Though I am not sure, I like the frame." Kate was now standing in front of the painting with Duncan in her arms.

"I thought the same thing." Quinn walked over and stood next to his daughter. They both were absorbed looking at the painting.

At The Frosty Mug, the waitress whose name tag said 'Charlie' placed a schooner of beer in front of Quinn and glasses of beer in front of both Betty and Kate. "Your double burgers and onion blossoms will be right out," she said turning back toward the kitchen.

"That painting really isn't a painting is it?" Kate asked her Dad.

"It is a pastel. It is a very good pastel. I wished I could have found out a little more about it this afternoon." Quinn said.

"I know an adjunct professor over at the college. She teaches art history. Do you want me to see if I can set you up with an appointment, or maybe invite her to the house to see it. What do you think?" Kate said after taking a sip of her beer.

Betty took a sip of beer, "Maybe we should know something about the painting before we invite people to see it. What if it is valuable?"

"Ok, I will call my friend; her name is Paula Joyfelt she's very nice. I'll make an appointment when she is available. Maybe we can meet here."

Charlie came to the table balancing three plates loaded with burgers and sizzling onions.

"What movie are we seeing tonight?" Kate asked as the first onion ring was popped into her mouth.

"It just came out with Al Pacino, a Mafia movie called THE GODFATHER.

"My kind of movie," Quinn said and took a long pull on the cold schooner of beer in front of him.

The Case of the Chocolate Girl (2)

Hit On

The next morning Quinn and Betty made their way to The Food Giant, Betty wanted to cook a roast for Sunday night dinner. Once inside Quinn went in search of a six pack of beer and Betty made her way to the butcher counter. While standing there a tall slender man with a silver goatee approached her.

"I would like to take you to dinner," the man offered.

Betty looked in his eyes, "When I wreck your car, will the first thing you say be, 'Are you all right?' When I say to you, I saw a ghost, will you drive across three states to prove I am right? Are you ready to paint me in the nude on a quiet Sunday afternoon?" Just then, she saw Quinn approaching. When Quinn was within earshot she said, "You might find what you are looking for on aisle three."

Quinn watched the gentlemen walk away. "What was that about?"

"Oh, he was looking for Swedish pastry."

Hit Man, Allentown

Lorcan Bacalao, a hit man who has been paid by Dolan Ó Braonáin to track down Quinn and Betty read the morning Allentown news in the Morning Call., He smiled, a page three a story told of two female street people had been found dead in Canal Park. Their only known identities were Cass and Belinda. What it did not say is they had talked before they died and Lorcan now knew the whereabouts of Jarrod.

Kate contacted her friend the adjunct professor of art history at Hourglass Trinity College. Paula Joyfelt was not the most liked professor; she was tough on her students very tough some would say. She was not that much older than her students. She liked Kate and made an appointment for Quinn and Betty to talk about their question.

Arriving in mid-afternoon Quinn and Betty found that Paula lived in a loft above a garage and walked up the flight of wooden steps that ran along the side of the building. They knocked and Paula quickly came to the door to let them into her one room castle.

This was unlike anything either Quinn or Betty had seen before. The walls were lined with bookshelves that were sagging from the weight of their burden. There were art books of every size and description; some with pages drooping out of their bindings. There were paintings hanging from nails on the bookcase wood. And in Quinn's mind he thought they were excellent paintings.

There was an unmade bed with a bookshelf above it and there was an easel and a second easel with a photo taped to it and the first easel contained a very accurate duplicate of the photo in process. A tabby cat sat on the window sill that let diffused light into the room. A geranium's pink flowers cascaded about its adobe pot on the window sill. Quinn liked the room at once.

"Kate tells me you may have found a treasure. How can I help you?" Paula was hoping to see a parcel in either Quinn or Betty's hands.

"We have only begun our search for details on this," Quinn said, handing a Polaroid to Paula. "One person thought the artist might be Dutch. But we have not confirmed that.

Paula took a long look at the painting. “Not Dutch, I can tell you that right now. This is from a different school of thought altogether. Are you interested in selling it?”

Betty said, “Right now we are just interested in finding a little more about it. I know no one can know everything there is to know in a field. But you come highly recommended. Do you recognize the painting?”

“I am not familiar with this specific painting. The school is from the French, late 1700’s I would say. From the photo, I cannot tell if it is genuine or an offset lithography. I wish you had brought it with you. This is very exciting. Kate said you found it on a thrift store expedition. Can you leave the photograph? I have to get ready for class. When can I see the painting?”

The tabby walked between Betty’s legs brushing against her.

Paula smiled at her aggressive male. “You know who might know more about this is Major Garrity. He is a collector, I’ll see when he is available and we can all go talk to him together. In the meantime I’ll do a search after class of this collection of mine,” she waved at the books “and see if I can find this artist and this painting.” This time she waved the Polaroid.

“We will have Kate call you when we are ready.” Betty offered and we thank you for your time. “We will wait to hear from you.”

Quinn and Betty went down the steps. At the bottom of the steps Betty asked, “I don’t think we know any more now than when we walked in. But it was an interesting room.”

Quinn took Betty by the hand and they walked back to the Town and Country. Quinn’s mind was going fast. The words, ‘Are you interested in selling it?' Grated across his eardrums. She was Kate's friend, but it was unlikely she was going to be Quinn's friend.

They had climbed into the car when they saw Paula Joyfelt rush down the stairs with a large canvas portfolio case carried on a wide strap across her shoulder and a leather satchel in the other hand. She was flying - once again she would be late for class.

Young Anna Künstler sat with her hair piled on top her head in the basement of the Central State Archive in Kiev, Ukraine. She was hired because she worked day and night for her advanced degree in art history. Here she sat cataloging the hundreds of claims from those all over Europe of looted treasures. Treasures looted by the Germans, Russians and British and Americans as their armies swept through wide swaths of Europe on their quest to conquer.

The rows of leather bound books recorded the name of the artwork, what country it was taken from, the name of the owner, the relationship to the owner of the claimant, and if known what army occupied the territory at the time the piece went missing if known.

Young Anna Künstler was not alone in her work. Her contemporaries were at work in basements in Prague, London and Jerusalem and New York. Hundreds of millions of dollars of arts changed hands during the war and the remaining owners and the families of those that did not remain, wanted it back.

A card file contained the name of the artist and then the name of the piece of art and the journal number where the information was recorded. The journals were cataloged by country and city of the claim.

Young Anna Künstler loved the feel of the thick paper of the journals, yet wondered why she needed an advanced degree in art to file the information.

In the second year of her work at the archive, she made a mental note as she began to notice multiple claims for the same items. Everyone wanted the loot.

She often wondered how much of her life she should dedicate to unraveling the work of the Einsatzstab Reichsleiter Rosenberg.

Margaret Singer and her family escaped Germany in 1940 to the safety of London. That was before the bombings started to which she lost her entire family. She wept at the irony. She worked at the London branch of the Central State Archive where her job was to review auction catalogues from America, London, and Paris and cross check objects of art up for auction against Central State Archive records. On occasion, a notification was dispatched to an auction house that a piece they were handling was on file as war loot.

Central State Archive had no authority, but no auction house wanted to be associated with war loot. Not with their rich clients so well rooted in the communities of those looted.

Upon returning from class Paula Joyfelt rummaged through her art book collection. She cursed her lack of organization and found the title she sought. DANS LES COLLECTIONS DES MUSÉES D'ART ET D'HISTOIRE DE GENÈVE in hand, she flipped through the pages and found what she was looking for.

She lifted the phone and dialed a number from memory. When connected she said, ‘Ernest, I think we are onto something. How much money do you have?”

She listened to his stream of questions and said, ‘This could be big.”

Ernest set down the receiver and sat back in his chair in front of a fake Louie XIV desk and smiled. His GALLERY EUROPA was ready for something big.

The Case of the Chocolate Girl (3)

An old Victrola played a scratchy Galli-curci ‘un di felice tito schipa recorded in 1924 in the background as Quinn and Betty were invited to Major Garrity’s private den.

Quinn’s eyes darted from antique to old weapon to astute taxidermy to native shields. Betty gazed at a matching pair of elephant tusks banded at the widest part with a pair of golden bracelets and mounted on marble bases arching the carved desk.

On a side table holding a hand carved chess set, a game was in progress between the Major and a Punjab Colonel. Major Garrity noticed Quinn’s gaze and said, “He is using the Spassky gambit for which I have no defence. In ten moves, the game is his and there is nothing to it. In a week or so a letter will arrive on thin parchment allowing me to resign the game.”

Betty stood looking at the skin of a cheetah draped over a table, on the skin sat a silver tray supporting nineteenth century cut crystal goblets. The voice from the scratchy record filled the room with concert hall quality sound. The sound bounded along the leather books on the strong honey oak shelves. The filtered light gave the room the abeyance of the previous century. She wondered what road it took to reach a room like this.

The Major continued, “I’ll have to have my agent in India dispatch a bottle of Clynelish to the fine Colonel.” As the record ended he walked over and lifted the arm and switched off the set. “I understand you may have found a treasure. Can I offer you two a drink or perhaps tea? How can I help you?”

Quinn accepted a whiskey with the Major and tea was sent for from the kitchen.

Quinn handed a Polaroid to the Major, who walked over and sat at his desk. He picked up a magnifying glass with a carved bone handle and examined the picture. "I had hoped to see the original. What have you found out up until now?"

"Virtually nothing, an art history teacher from Hour Glass Trinity has seen a photograph of it. She did not tell us the name of the artist. She said she would do some research and hinted she would take it off our hands at a small profit." Betty gave the summary.

The Major ran a finger under his moustache. "The art world is a treacherous place. It is so refined and seemingly elegant. But below the surface it is anything but. Do you know anything about this world that you have stepped into?"

Quinn was sitting he took a sip of the excellent whiskey. "I don't." Quinn freely admitted. "The crimes I investigated as a detective were more base in nature."

Betty lifted her tea and took a sip and let herself sink into the settee feeling oddly free and sensual.

"Let me tell you a few examples. There is a Degas; it is hanging in a California museum. It is also hanging in a French museum. It is implied that they are the originals. I happen to know the original is in the penthouse of a Tokyo Insurance Company. That is just one. And the underbelly of the art business gets more and more clever every year."

The Major saw that his guests were listening intently. "There is a profession in these circles called a 'Reliner', this professional takes a painting on wood that has gone rotten and will plane all the wood off, leaving only the crust of paint to which he then sticks a canvas, thus preserving the painting. But is it then still an original? A canvas of proper age and dimension will be used and the uninitiated will be no more the wiser. The same reliner can remove the paint from one damaged canvas and apply it to a fresher undamaged canvas by means of a hot table. Then a competent artist will repair any damaged portion of the painting. I don't suggest you or I try this." He smiled and sipped his whiskey.

"Your artist is one, Etienne Liotard and the painting is The Chocolate Girl painted sometime in the mid-1700's. I can look it up to tell you exactly. His background is Swiss-French and he is collectible though not as sought after as some of the later French painters. Now, I am sure you know that many museums were sacked by not only the Germans and the Russians, but both the British and American armies were not above helping themselves to plunder along the way. Many homes were laid open from inflicted wounds and a finders keepers attitude developed. I refer to this as the autopsy of Europe. She was cut open and every army that passed through looked inside to see the jewels of the disenfranchised spewing forth. There are stories of caravans of trucks making their way to Arles where riches were loaded onto garbage barges and taken across the Mediterranean to sit out the war in Algerian warehouses. Yes, the dealers in the art world are no less hungry for wealth than the local butcher with his thumb on the scale. Not to mention the train loads of art that left Paris and Saint Petersburg for Berlin." He paused to give Quinn or Betty a chance to interject their thoughts. He saw that they were still listening and had not become angered by this piece of information.

“You tell fascinating stories,” Betty offered. “The painting in question, do you have any thoughts.” She looked around the room again with a keener eye wondering how much of this room came from the operating room of European art. Though she thought, more of this looked like it made its way along elephant paths than European rivers leading to Algiers. She imagined Europe differently now, a land swarming with ants gathering without rules - laying waste to the crop of one thousand years of accumulated culture. From this ruble, a tiny speck of this culture made its way to Clearview Terrace. The fate of THE CHOCOLATE GIRL was now in the hands of Quinn and Betty.

“Many, my dear,” said the Major. “If your painting is real it has some value. If it is a fake, but a good fake it has some value but much less. There is a high likelihood that it is stolen. If you are interested in finding out more about that there is an office of the Central State Archives in New York that will be glad to help you. However, if you are interested in selling it, there are dealers all over the world who will handle the sale for you without question for a percentage. There are collectors of art just like collectors of coins or books or other beautiful objects. Every dealer you talk to that makes you an offer is going to tell you you have no provenance. They tell you this to drive down the price.”

He reached into his desk drawer and took a piece of linen paper and wrote down a New York address and handed it to Quinn. “You decide. It would be interesting to find out how it arrived in Clearview Terrace. I’ll give you a spelling of the artist's name so you can do some research.”

The three rose and said their good-byes. “I would like to see the

original if you had any inclinations in that direction.” Looking directly at Betty, he said, “I appreciate the finer things in life.”

"We will call for an appointment," Betty told him. She thought what an interesting dinner guest the Major would make. He seemed to have stepped out of the last century.

Allentown

Lorcan Bacalao behind the wheel of his Cadillac was completely lost in Rancho Cucamonga, California. He could not believe the sunshine or that there were orange groves everywhere, he turned making it even more frustrating for him.

At Gomez's Bar and Grill across from the train stop, Lorcan stopped and began to question people about Jarrod showing a photograph provided by Dolan. Word got back to Jarrod that a man in a sharkskin suit was asking around for him. Hearing that, he and Naomi threw their meager belongings into short duffel bags and climbed aboard the first bus that came through making their way down Highway 395 through avocado groves in quiet valleys and artists' colonies shaded under ancient oaks toward San Diego leaving no clues behind to follow.

Winchell's Donuts

The next morning Quinn got up early and quietly slipped out of the house with Duncan-Waffles. He visited the local donut shop where he ordered coffee and a crumb donut. Some habits are hard to break. He thought about his time during the war and recalled some enlisted men being punished for taking things. He also recalled watching officers ordering items being crated up to ship home through unofficial military channels. He had not given these details of war much thought until now.

He loved the quiet that morning offered, he felt the day take its deep breath in the morning ready to exhale all the day had in store. When done he and Duncan took their stroll home.

A Quinn Moosebroker Mystery

The Case of the Chocolate Girl (4)

"Pawn to queen's knight four," Betty said to the plastic Mattel chess board purchased long ago at a church rummage sale. She laid down the Beginner's Book of Chess by Horowitz and smiled to herself. She looked over at Duncan-Waffles in the other kitchen chair; he was studying the board. She was still held captive by the spell of the Major's den.

Belgium December 1944

In the middle of the night, Corporal Daughtry sat at a table with four other Dog Faces in a rest area near Tenneville. The barn was cold and lit by candles. Cigarette smoke filled the air as he picked up his replacement cards. The third three was a gift. He was having a good run tonight and had all of Sgt Hastings money. One more raise and he could buy the pot.

"I raise you five dollars," Daughtry looked hard at the Sgt. Three other hands folded.

"You know I don't have another five dollars," the squarely faced Sgt puffed at his stub of a cigar. "What say I give you an I.O.U.?"

Daughtry reached toward the pot.

"Wait, wait," the Sgt yelled, he reached for a package near his feet that he had prepared to go out in the mail. "Take this as security it has to be worth at least five dollars." He tore the corner of the package and roughly peeled back a corner so Daughtry could see.

Daughtry nodded and watched the Sgt lay down two pairs, fours, and sixes. Daughtry smiled and tossed his three threes on top of the cash. Still smiling he scooped up the money and reached over and snagged the package.

Later that evening he fixed the corner of the package and affixed his parent's Cumensville, PA address and brought it to his friend in logistics for mailing. A pack of cigarettes insured the proper inspection stamps.

In the morning, the card game forgotten; both Daughtry and Sgt Hastings of the 99th Infantry Division marched into the frozen Ardennes near Bastogne to face their fate stopping the advance of the German 1st Panzer Division.

The mail truck made its way by night through Brussels then waited out the day hidden from Luftwaffe air patrols in some trees. They waited until dark before continuing to Dunkirk where the contents there loaded onto a barge to Margate, England. There the mail moved to a steam train to Brighton where it was moved to the troop ship George W. Goethals for its quiet icy Atlantic voyage bound for New York with mail and wounded.

In the middle of the night, Paula Joyfelt sat in a robe in front of her easel. She had removed the painting she had been working on and pinned the Polaroid that Quinn left to the crown of the easel. A parchment secured and aged by soaking it in tea for the purpose was ready. She was sure she could produce a work that would fool the old couple she met. She was unable to remember the names of Quinn and Betty.

Pastels were not her favorite medium, but she was very confident in her ability to copy any artist's work. She counted her blessings. A gift just floated down and landed in her hands.

Ernest at Gallery Europa was sure he could find a quick buyer that would leave both him and Paula with a very nice payday. All she had to do was get close to the original and do a quick swap. A perfectly good reproduction could adorn the hallway of the old couple.

Quinn sat across from Betty at the kitchen table. “What do you think of this?” Betty said holding up a piece of paper. She read the letter written in long hand to Quinn.

Central State Archive

New York

October 1972

To whom it may concern:

We have come across an old painting. When we sought out information, we were told if it is real, that it is likely stolen.

At the same meeting, we were informed about the work your organization does in tracking the whereabouts of items removed from Europe during the war years. We seek your help to further identify the piece and optimistically find the rightful owner.

We are told the artist is Jean Etienne Liotard, and the painting is The Chocolate Girl, (La Belle Chocolatière) circa 1750.

Looking forward to hearing from you,

Detective Quinn Moosebroker, Retired

Clearview Terrace

USA

“That sounds fine,” Quinn told her. Let’s get this in the mail right away.

Cumesville, PA 1944

Mrs. Margaret Daughtry heard a knock at her door. When she got there, it was old Murray the postman. He held a package posted from an APO address and wondered what her son had sent home for them to store now. She gave her thanks to Murray and as she was about to close the door a Western Union messenger pulled to the curb.

Murray walked to the sidewalk and waited there. The messenger boy came to the door and handed Mrs. Margaret Daughtry, the news of her son’s death. The young boy waited a moment as Margaret hung her head and cried, then hung his head and turned back to his car. Murray hung his head and continued on.

Mrs. Daughtry placed the large package into her son’s room; gripped in pain, she closed the bedroom door for the last time.

Allentown

Lorcan Bacalao sat in front of thick glass quietly taking a verbal beating from Dolan Ó Braonáin. "What do you mean he got away?" The scowl on his face was fierce. Jarrod had escaped his fate.

"California has fields full of orange trees and other groves. Everything looks the same. He must have heard someone was looking for him and high-tailed it out of there." Lorcan said. This killer was not afraid of much, but he felt Ó Braonáin's cold knot of death deep in his gut. Dolan's stare rankled him on a primal level.

"Go to Wilkes-Barre find his Mother's she is bound to hear from him."

"Spider's wife? Couldn't that get messy for you?" Lorcan said.

"Ex-wife and you let me worry about Martin. We are all in here, and that pot smoking hippie had something to do with it." Dolan stood; the meeting was over.

Major Garrity

Quinn trimmed a boxwood shrub near Betty's front porch while Betty placed asters in a planter on the front porch along the rail. She had planned for a few more weeks of color before fall arrived in force. Both stopped what they were doing and watched as a classic yellow Rolls Royce pulled to the curb in front of Betty's home on Maple Street.

"Would you look at that?" Betty told Quinn.

"That is a beauty," Quinn told her putting down the clippers and taking off his gloves.

They both watched Major Garrity climb out from behind the wheel. He had a cigar box size parcel under his arm. He flashed a warm smile and waved.

"Good to find you both home," the Major called to them as he walked up to the front porch. "I am afraid my curiosity has gotten the better of me. I am here to see your treasure if you would be so kind."

"Sure," Quinn told him. "Come on in."

"We sent a letter off to the Central State Archives as you suggested," Betty added. "Come in, please."

The three entered the room where the painting was leaning up against the wall.

"She is a beauty," the Major felt reverent in its presence. "With the understanding that there is no pressure, I want to offer a trade." He opened the box which held rubies, emeralds and sapphires in various sizes. "Any five of these for the painting, each one should bring roughly one thousand dollars."

Betty's jaw went slack. She was momentarily mesmerized.

Quinn looked at the stones, and his instincts gripped him. He waited a moment so as not to step on Betty's toes if she had something to say. He watched her eyes glitter with the reflection of reds, greens, and blues.

"There is a slight gamble for you and slight gamble for me. There are many forgeries in the art world. This piece is so far out of its element here in Clearview Terrace; somewhat like me and perhaps you," he said looking at Quinn.

Betty did not take offense. She felt safe in Clearview Terrace and for the past year found it very exciting. It was painful for her to hold her tongue. She felt the painting belonged to Quinn, and it would be wrong for her to take the lead here.

"Major," Quinn began, "That is an interesting offer. I am afraid I am going to decline for the moment. I would like to find out what the folks at Central State Archives have to say. That is how my curiosity is running at the moment. I would also like to get a good look at that Rolls if you would be so kind."

The Case of the Chocolate Girl (5)

In his line of work, Lorcan Bacalao found that it paid to be patient. He learned the lesson early, and it stuck with him, but watching Spider Ó Braonáin's ex-wife's house was draining. He still had others on his list.

He decided he would take a casual drive to Clearview Terrace and see if he could get a couple of quick kills. Then he would head back to Wilkes-Barre and press Martin Ó Braonáin's wife for information regarding Jarrod.

After a day of watching Lorcan spotted an opening and without hesitation went through Betty's front door where he was assured to find her alone.

Betty had just turned off the kitchen faucet when the whole house chilled. The hair on the back of her neck stood straight up. Her heart slowed, and her eyes became keen. She pulled a butcher knife from the block and clutched it to her chest. Her eyes roamed, and she decided to step into the kitchen pantry closing the door without a sound.

Lorcan Bacalao was not a gambler. He was more like a hungry panther he had caught his prey unaware and would make quick work of her and disappear to strike again. He moved through the living room quickly then checked the bedrooms. He entered the kitchen moving with practiced stealth.

In the pantry, Betty brought the butcher knife up in preparation to strike.

The quiet broke as Quinn came in the front door. "Betty are you ready?" He called as he set down a bag of supplies for their trip.

"QUINN," Betty called stepping out of the pantry. "Quinn, did you see someone? Someone was here. Just now, someone was here."

Quinn rushed by her toward the kitchen and through it out the back door. He ran toward the front of the house but saw no one except a Postman a few houses down. He rushed back to the house and did a room by room search.

When he finished, he calmly walked up to Betty and took the butcher knife from her cold hands and hugged her.

Central States Archive

The letter from Central States Archives lay between Quinn and Betty on the kitchen table. The letter was very courteous and professional. Betty was a little leery. Quinn said he thought the invitation to New York could be above board.

The letter said:

Mr. Quinn Moosebroker,

We are in receipt of your letter. It is not often a private citizen contacts us. We usually are the organization that initiates the contact.

We have forwarded your information to all our locations to see if they had anything on file concerning The Chocolate Girl by Jean Etienne Liotard. While it is not unheard of, it is rare to find that we have two claims on file. One claim is on file in London, and one claim is in the Ukraine Archives but from an elderly Belgian woman living in Italy

since the war.

We ask that you have the painting delivered to us for disposition. We

will have our experts verify that it is what you claim it is and make a determination from there.

Signed

Deborah Bergen

Administrator

Central State Archives

207 Essex Street Market

(Above Schapiro's Kosher Wine)

New York, New York

Quinn convinced Betty that they should drive to the city and see what further they had to say.

Major Garrity picked up his ringing phone, “Ello.”

Quinn identified himself and read him the letter and waited for a response.

“Legally that painting is yours until proven otherwise. I think I know your stance on this. I am just telling you that these people have no authority to take it away from you. I know people who have been able to hang on to their artwork for years while the case made its way through all the court systems of the world. And in many cases the current owners have been awarded the property because the original owners vanished and it was some obscure family member or frauds making the ownership claims. Often two institutions were fighting over ownership.”

He paused, “Let me tell you another secret. Central State Archives

locations work independently, since you discovered where the claims are filed you can contact them individually and request the names and addresses of those making the claims. They are very bureaucratic and may just send you the information in the mail. Include five dollars to cover expenses in each envelope, and you are likely guaranteed a response.”

Quinn liked the Major more and more, though it had occurred to him that he showed up at Betty's home to make the offer of precious gems for the painting. He had wondered if his presence there at the time was a disappointment to the Major.

It was Betty that wrote the two letters out long hand and stuffed a five dollar bill in each of them following the Majors instructions. It was also Betty that called the Central States Archives in New York from with the phone number on their letterhead and asked for and got the addresses of the London Office and the Ukraine Office.

They began packing for a long weekend. They loaded an ice chest with drinks and sandwiches and boloney for Duncan-Waffles as well as dry food. They let Kate know they would be away for a few days.

"I am going to take the picture out of the frame," Quinn told Betty. "I don't want to chance Duncan-Waffles having some accident while he shares the back seat." He lifted the painting and gently rolled it and tied it closed. He lifted the frame and carried it out to the garage and set in leaning against the wall where the front panel of the Town & Country had recently rested.

On their way out of town, Betty, Quinn, and Duncan stood in line at the Post Office to mail their international letters.

Jean Etienne Liotard The Chocolate Girl

Paula Joyfelt put the finishing touches on her copy of The Chocolate Girl she verified the dimensions from her research. She felt sure that it would fool Quinn and Betty and many others. She would get the original out of their possession and then take a nice vacation.

The painting would be brought to New York where Ernest at Gallery Europa would send out discrete inquiries to find the right buyer. The right buyer he defined as the one who offered the highest price. The underground market was hungry for paintings to decorate the homes of those new to wealth.

The midnight hour embraced the small town of Clearview Terrace. With darkness fell a calm that offered Bacalao a concert of rustling leaves. He watched the entrance of Betty's house from a vantage point on the corner of the cross street.

Paula Joyfelt stepped out of her car. Her foot hit the cool asphalt of Maple Street. She crossed the street and walked along in the shadows. She had watched the house for hours and felt sure the house was empty. She did not want to tangle with that Quinn – he was a big guy.

She reached the front of the house the only sound was the rustling of leaves. She took a deep breath and walked into the glow of a street light up to the porch. Reaching the door, she took out a shim from her back pocket and slipped it through the door jamb releasing the catch. She was inside.

She set her rolled up painting down in a corner and taking a small hand size flashlight from her pocket she began to search. First the kitchen, hall, and then bedroom still nothing.

She did not hear the front door swing open or the cat-like footsteps of Lorcan. She did not hear him at all. A fraction of a second before he snapped her neck she felt his steely iciness at the bottom of her spine. The dropped spinning flashlight spun cascading waves of light over her still eyes.

Lorcan left as quietly as he arrived. Back at his motel he scratched Betty Atwood's name from his list. After a drink while he sat on the edge of the motel's bed he wondered why Betty was walking through her house with a flashlight. He found his list and put a question mark by her scratched out name.

The Case of the Chocolate Girl (6)

The drapes of dawn were drawn. The neighborhood early riser while walking his dog noticed the front door of Betty Atwood's home ajar and when he returned home called the police to investigate when no one answered his calls from the front porch.

Detective DeLaMonte responded to the call. He arrived at the home and knocked twice on the front door as he entered calling hello. When he found the body, he called it in as an accident assuming the homeowner had fallen and broken her neck. There were no signs of struggle.

At the station, Detective DeLaMonte wrote up his report of Betty Atwood's death. The local reporter picked up the article, and the Friday afternoon paper reported the passing of Betty Atwood in her home.

The news reached Kate Moosebroker. Her heart pounded furiously as she dialed Betty's house. She set the phone down remembering that her Father and Betty said they were going to New York.

She called their family friend Officer Harcourt. She told him that the report was incorrect as far as she knew and asked who had identified the body.

"Apparently DeLaMonte found the body on the floor of Betty's bedroom. He called the coroner to come and pick up the body. And as he says 'two and two equals" meaning "it is what it is." Do you want to come down and see if you can identify the body?"

"Want is a pretty strong word. Can you meet me there?" Kate asked.

"Sure, see you in thirty minutes." Harcourt hung up and walked over and knocked on DeLaMonte's door. He stuck his head inside, "Just heard that it is not likely Betty Atwood you found dead." He closed the door behind him and smiled.

Thirty minutes later Kate found herself standing next to Officer Harcourt and the coroner's assistant in the basement of the city morgue.

The assistant pulled back the sheet to her shoulders. Kate gasped, "That is Paula Joyfelt. She works at Trinity Hourglass College."

The assistant put the sheet back over her silent eyes.

"Thank you," Officer Harcourt told the assistant.

He and Kate turned to go. Harcourt placed his hand on her shoulder, "You OK?"

"Yeah, thanks. Quinn and Betty just met with her a few days ago. I wonder what she was doing in Betty's house."

At the top of the steps, Harcourt and Kate went their separate ways.

Jean Etienne Liotard The Chocolate Girl

Central States Archive New York

Quinn and Betty took a room on Essex Street. The 1946 Town and Country seemed so out of place in the hustle and bustle of this busy lower east side district. Duncan-Waffle was thrilled with the aroma of Gertle's Bake Shop.

Their appointment with Deborah Bergen of Central States Archives was for ten a.m. Quinn with Betty in agreement decided not to carry in the painting, but rather a couple of new Polaroid's taken the morning before they left.

“So good of you to come,” Deborah began, looking around for the painting.

“Hello Mrs. Bergen,” Betty said extending her hand in greeting.

The two women shook hands. Quinn watched each of them size up the other.

“I thought the letter was specific. You were asked to deliver the painting.” Changing her tone she said, “Can I get you some coffee?” Bergen was perplexed at the couple before her.

“If you can tell us where your expert in located, we would like to bring it to him for his opinion,” Quinn told her.

“I can do that.” Deborah offered. “But does that mean you have changed your mind? I am confused. Your initial letter sounded like you wanted to see the painting returned to its rightful owner.”

“That is still true. We thought we might return the painting ourselves.” Betty paused. She had not spoken to Quinn about this possibility.

"That is not our procedure. I am going to ask you to surrender the painting voluntarily. We have reunited many articles looted during the war to the rightful owners. It appears you have changed your mind. Now that the painting has surfaced, it will be impossible to sell it." Deborah was now perturbed by these goys.

Quinn and Betty smiled. They had shown the painting to two parties and received two invitations to sell.

Deborah Bergen thought for a moment and then excused herself to get the number of Dr. Dieter Levi. She returned handing the card to Quinn. "We have an appointment here at 2 p.m. I did not think you would mind if I at least saw the painting."

"We will see you here," Betty said.

She and Quinn left to get back and take Duncan-Waffles for a walk in the big city.

Walking along Rivington Street Betty saw a sign in a shop window that said Passport photos. She brought Duncan-Waffles to a stop and looked into the window. "Let's get our passport pictures taken," she told Quinn.

Quinn not wanting to question her here agreed and the three of them walked into the shop and had their photos taken. They left the shop with their photos and their application.

They were back at Central States Archive at 2 p.m. painting in hand. Quinn and Betty were introduced to Dr. Levi.

He unrolled the painting on a table normally reserved for lunch sandwiches and began to examine it with a magnifying glass. "This is most unusual. I must be given more time for my assessments."

Quinn observed the doctor. The collar rim of his white shirt had yellowed with age. His suit jacket was from another era. His shoes were shined but well worn. His thick rimmed glasses magnified his eyes. Something was out of place, but Quinn held his tongue.

Betty watched as he so very slowly moved his magnifying glass back and forth over the surface of the painting.

"It's impossible; I need more time." The doctor straightened putting the magnifying glass in his jacket pocket. "Leave it with us. We will take proper care of it."

"Do you think it is the real thing?" Quinn asked reaching over and beginning to re-roll the painting.

The corner of his mouth twitched, his clasped hands tightened noticeably. "I am afraid sir, that I cannot give you my expert opinion with so little time."

Quinn picked the painting up, and Betty clutched her purse under her arm.

"Thank you for your time Dr. Levi and you Mrs. Bergen. We will try and keep you informed of our progress." Quinn told them as he and Betty walked out the door.

Once back on the street Quinn asked, "Did you see the doctor's face when I asked him if it was real? He practically choked. I could not get a good read on him. He is so very old world."

"Quinn, what are we doing?" Betty's hand linked with Quinn's elbow.

"Well, we seem to be heading off for adventure," his smile reassured her.

They stopped at a delicatessen for pastrami on rye sandwiches. It was Duncan's first pastrami experience. They ate their sandwiches, and soft drinks, and people watched.

Once back at the hotel Betty went down to use the phone. "Hello Kate, it's Betty. Just checking in to let you know we are OK and may be headed home in the morning."

Kate blurted out, "Betty, I am so glad you called. Something terrible has happened. In the morning paper, you are reported as dead; that your body was found on the floor of your bedroom. This is just terrible. A neighbor noticed your door ajar when he was walking his dog about dawn. He called the police. I am so glad you are all right."

"I… I don't understand. There was a body found. Ah, your father is upstairs. Let me get a breath." She took a deep breath.

The operator broke into the call, "Please deposit $0.35 for three more minutes."

"Betty there is more. I…."

Kate was interrupted by the sound of coins being deposited.

"I identified the body. It was Paula Joyfelt. You guys need to come home." Kate said.

"We will leave for home in the morning. Listen stay away from my house until we get there. Listen is there someplace you can stay for a couple of days?"

Betty felt flushed. She slowly walked up the staircase to relay Kate's news to Quinn and Duncan-Waffles.

With the car loaded they left the sights, sounds and smells of lower Manhattan. Duncan sat in the back seat staring out the window as they rolled down the turnpike. He was anxious to get home. Betty sat at Quinn's side in the front seat. "What do you make of this so far? Everyone that has heard of the painting has wanted to take it away from us. And now this news from Kate has me unnerved. Quinn my head is just …just in a whirl."

"We are going to have to find a reasonable explanation as to why Paula was in your home. As far as I can figure there is no explanation for her death. None of the details that I am aware of equals – Paula Joyfelt dead." Quinn took a deep breath, "The only people that knew about the painting are Paula and the Major."

The Case of the Chocolate Girl (7)

They reached Quinn's home in the early AM after long hours on the road. They woke Kate when they arrived, and the family rehashed the events that happened both in New York and Clearview Terrace.

Then they all got some much-needed rest. The next morning Quinn and Betty reported to the Clearview Terrace police station and asked to talk to Detective DeLaMonte. Once seated in the office DeLaMonte began, "Moosebroker since you arrived in Clearview Terrace our crime rate is starting to rival that of New Jersey." He sat down his coffee. Looking at Betty, he said, "Glad you ain't dead – can you prove your whereabouts on Thursday evening?"

"Why we were both in New York, and we can prove it, if necessary," Betty told him, asserting her very alive spirit.

"Do you have any leads on this DeLaMonte, because, so far you are just doing your usual huffing and puffing?" DeLaMonte bored Quinn. Quinn felt he was lazy in his work and took lots of shortcuts.

After a few more questions, he spoke up; "Don't leave town," he stood to show them out of his office.

Betty smiled knowing the passport photos were in her purse and today the applications would be sent off.

"Shoot," Betty explained as they were driving towards home.

"What is it?" Quinn puzzled looking over at Betty; she had swiveled around to face Quinn directly.

"I don't know how to say this. We have to go over to Paula Joyfelt's place. That tabby cat is likely locked in and hungry." She swallowed hoping Quinn would not think her nuts.

Quinn checked the rear view mirror and once safe, made a wide u-turn in the right direction.

Paula lived on a quiet tree lined street. Quinn pulled to the curb, and they both made their way up the stairs. As yet, there was no police tape. At the top of the stairs, Quinn put his shoulder into the door and in a moment they were inside.

Quinn looked around while Betty picked up the cat and put the geranium pot on the front porch. Quinn spotted the painting that was on the easel a few days back leaning against the wall. Then he noticed his Polaroid and a color page from a book of the Chocolate Girl pinned to the corners of the second easel.

"We should get going in case someone saw us," Quinn told Betty.

"I think Mrs. Jones, my neighbor will appreciate this," Betty said stroking his head. "Listen – Quinn I am not going to be able to sleep at my house. Let's go pick up some things and then figure out what is next. There are so many memories there, yet Paula's death has cast such a pall over me."

Quinn put his hand on her knee. "Sure, let's grab some clothes and whatever you need. We can figure it all out."

They reached Betty's house. There was no police tape which Quinn found odd. Betty walked over and knocked on Mrs. Jones door. In a few moments Mrs. Jones had a new tabby, and Betty felt strong enough to enter her home.

They were not greeted with the usual warmth that Betty's simple home had provided them. There was a haunting chill left by the ghastly intrusion. Quinn followed her into the master bedroom and watched as Betty put her things into a suitcase. There would be three staying at Kate's place. Quinn knew that had to be temporary.

Weeks went by, and Betty found a realtor to list her house. There was so much to think about.

Once their passport applications were mailed Quinn brought up the subject of travel money. "It is not like loading up the back of the car and spending time together while driving and seeing the countryside. There are some real expenses involved," he told Betty. He was quietly concerned that the funds were going more quickly than arriving.

"I have been thinking about that travel money situation, and I know there is so much going on. I found a solution. I sold George's 1960 MG. He loved that car, but he's gone now. In fact, I talked to the Major, and he gave me a number of a friend of his. The Major told me to ask for $1,800 and settle for $1,600 and told me he felt that was a fair price." Betty walked to a kitchen drawer and took out an envelope with the money. "Surprised?"

"Yes, that is the least that I am surprised." Quinn did not like where his mind led him. "So, that takes care of travel money? Now, we need to hear back from Central States Archives."

Betty walked over to him and embraced him, “This will all workout. I have a good feeling about it. Will you go with me over to the house? I don’t like being there alone after what happened.”

“Sure after lunch, let’s grab a sandwich at the Frosty Mug and then we can spend the afternoon getting what you need and maybe start boxing things up for the move.”

They were not at the house long when Betty noticed something rolled up leaning on the arm of the sofa and the wall of the living room. “What on earth?” She said loud enough to bring Quinn to the living room.

“What is it?” Quinn asked coming into the room.

Betty took the roll and brought it to the kitchen table. With Quinn by her side, she unrolled The Chocolate Girl. She looked at Quinn.

His eyes gazed at the painting, “It’s a copy. The one we bought is sitting in the corner of the bedroom closet in our room. I am sure of it.”

“So, this is what Paula was doing here?” Betty’s heart was racing again. She had not dissolved the feelings associated with Paula's death in her home.

Quinn was quiet and still. Finally, he walked to a kitchen drawer and rummaged around and found a pencil. He took it and marked three xxx on the back side of the parchment before them. “This may explain why Paula was here. She came to swap the paintings. ” He took a deep breath, “It does not explain her death. It is so unlikely she fell and broke her neck. Nothing could convince me the death was accidental.”

“You are telling me that her death was meant for me?” Betty rolled the painting and secured it with twine. “Let’s gather what we came to gather and talk about this somewhere else."

Lorcan Bacalao knew he had to stay away from Clearview Terrace, so he went back to California. He had little hope of getting a lead on Jarrod; the hippie lifestyle did not leave much of a paper trail. Dolan's impatience worried Lorcan, and he worried about the wrath of his boss.

Lorcan hired a small timer from Allentown to quietly keep track of the Moosebroker's in case they decided to run.

Kate, Betty, and Quinn sat at the kitchen table having dinner. Betty made a meatloaf and opened a can of corn. Quinn pitched in with potato peeling duty and mashed them once boiled.

"Replies have arrived from both locations of Central States Archives," Betty said talking to Kate. "Your father and I are planning a trip. There is some uncertainty, because they provided us with two names of claimants'; one of them in London and one near Lake Como, Italy. We will have to fly from London to Verona and then rent a car. That is if I read the maps right. We have their addresses and one at a time we will make an appointment to see each of them once we arrive. I am heavily relying on Quinn's instinct on this."

They sat at the table and chatted for an hour. Then Kate got up and began to clean up after the meal prepared for her by Betty and her Dad. Her place was more crowded than she liked but understood Betty's reluctance to spend time at her home.

Her Dad had mentioned gathering boxes for an eventual move once the house sold. She was happy for her father but at the same time this reminded her of her mother and there was sadness swirling with the happiness she felt with the lifted spirits of her Dad.

Quinn and Betty said goodnight to Kate and went to their room. Betty changed into her pajamas while Quinn took a quick shower. She turned down his side of the bed. He climbed into bed and switched off the light on the table.

In the dark room Quinn heard Betty say, “Hey Mister, did you propose to me or not?”

The Case of the Chocolate Girl (8)

Mr. Small-time Allentown said into the phone, "It is just like you thought I saw her coming out of a travel agents office. They are going somewhere."

Lorcan responded, "Well find out where. Sweet talk the travel agent or use muscle I don't care. I want to get this contract done. I'll be back there in three days time. I am sick of California and for that matter Clearview Terrace. Damn." He hung up the phone.

London Calling

Quinn and Betty and planned out their trip. They would visit London first. That had been the easiest travel plans to make. Betty told Quinn that something told her to, of course, take the original that he had found, but also to take Paula's copy with them. Quinn did not understand, but Betty's instincts had proven themselves. So, he rolled them together and slid them into a corrugated tube and laid the tube cater-cornered in his suitcase. Their trip departure date was arriving quickly and when the time came they wanted to pick up the bags and go without drama.

When the time arrived Kate agreed she could drive the Town and Country back from the airport, but asked that her Dad drive them to the airport. At the airport they said their goodbyes to Kate and Duncan-Waffles, who was confused by the whole thing. He yelped his dissenting vote as they left, and he and Kate began to wrestle the Town & Country down the highway.

Quinn and Betty approached the check-in line. He found himself reaching for a sidearm that no longer resided on his hip. He looked around at the people in line and scanned the crowded terminal. He told himself he was just nervous about the trip.

"What's wrong?" Betty looked around to see.

"Just an odd feeling. It's nothing." He gave Betty his best smile. "Let's get checked in."

An hour later they were in the air and once the seat belts signs were off Betty excused herself for the restroom. When she returned, she grabbed Quinn's arm and said, "When you go use the restroom check out the man in 38C he looks just like Clemenza in that 'Godfather' movie we saw, thin tie and all." She pushed her nose to one side, smiled at herself and her conspiratorial whimsy. "Let's take a nap."

The man in 38C was a big guy. Easily matching Quinn's size; with him sitting Quinn didn't get a good fix on his weight. The man had trouble written all over him. Quinn returned to his seat thinking he would not want to tangle with that guy in the close quarters of an airplane at thirty-five thousand feet.

The plane landed without incident. Quinn and Betty walked off the plane and saw signs that said 'Customs' they both turned to look at each other at the same time with the same thought.

Once Quinn's suitcase was open, the customs agent asked what was in the corrugated tube.

"It's a painting. We are showing it to a woman here in London. She is very interested in it." Betty told him.

The customs man called over his supervisor. "Would you look at this?" He told his boss.

The inspector looked at the two identical pieces. He looked at Betty. He looked at Quinn. He looked again slowly at the paintings. "They are obviously reproductions otherwise there would not be two of them. Stamp their customs papers and let them go." He turned to Quinn and Betty. "Enjoy your visit to our country."

They found a cab and gave him the address of the hotel the travel agent had booked for them. Lorcan Bacalao checked in the same hotel from the information taken from the travel agent. He would have to take care of them here.

In the morning Quinn and Betty were jet lagged and still sluggish. They took a walk looking for a place serving breakfast.

Mr. Henry Good rushed from his hotel and to the corner where a row of Beardmore cabs waited for customers. He climbed in throwing his one bag in before him. "The Airport and there is an extra twenty pounds in it for you if you can get me there in thirty minutes."

The driver gave his fare the once over, decided he could pay and gave it the petrol. He wove in and out of traffic, expertly avoiding other drivers making their way through the streets of London in route to their various destinations.

The driver was going fast, but not insanely fast. His eyes measured distance; all his moves were planned seconds in advance. He cut over to the shoulder lane to make a turn. Everything calculated out, and the twenty pounds would be his for certain.

Then a man in a well-made suit looked to his left for traffic and stepped off the curb in front of Nigel Allgood's hack. The sound of Nigel's brakes echoed through the corridor of buildings. The crumpled man, in a well-made suit, passed with the screaming of a fellow pedestrian in his ears and a life of mayhem flashing before his eyes. The cold seething hands of his many victims waited his imminent arrival in hell.

Nigel Allgood sat on the curb muttering 'bloody Americans' while waiting for the Bobbies to arrive.

Mr. Henry Good missed his flight.

The Bobby, Cecil Best reached into the breast pocket of the man lying in a heap on his beat looking for identification. The passport confirmed Nigel's assertions that Lorcan Bacalao was an American. Good, Allgood and Best had undone Dolan Ó Braonáin's notorious hit man.

From a short distance away, Quinn and Betty heard the screeching of brakes. "I hope no one was hurt," Betty said stepping into a café.

The Wraysbury Hall

Wilhelmine Gurlitte lived quite well in her Central London flat occupying the top floor of her four-story building. At seventy-eight, she had things all figured out. The big war left its mark on her, and she felt it was now her duty to take whatever there was to be taken. The world of art had been good to her. She took what she had learned about art and art value and combined that with the knowledge that many valuable pieces were cast to the winds.

Her time at the hands of the Germans left her with knowledge of who had what, and who no longer had a voice to claim what was taken from them. She had many claims filed with the Central State Archives in Kiev, Prague, London, Jerusalem and New York, and many pieces had been wrongfully returned to her.

Quinn and Betty had an appointment to visit Wilhelmine Gurlitte. They decided not to bring the painting with them at the first meeting, just as they did at the Central States Archive in New York. They wanted to survey the surroundings prior to carrying in something they now felt sure was valuable.

They arrived at the appointed time. Ms. Gurlitte greeted them and invited them to sit in her parlor. She remained silent when she saw they were not carrying the painting. She knew how to handle this class of people.

The walls decorated with Matisse, Chagall, Picasso, Otto Dix, Max Beckmann and others beckoned the eyes. The furnishings were French provincial. A small Auguste Rodin sculpture sat on a marble table in the foyer. A manservant brought in tea on a silver platter.

"You have a beautiful home," Betty made her impression of the room known.

"Thank you, Dear. I see you forgot my painting." Wilhelmina's eyes did not shine. Her frail hands took a sip of her tea.

Quinn let his tea sit on the table in front of him. Here he felt penned in this room with no place to roam. He drew an instant conclusion of the room, the manservant and his host.

"You haven't touched your tea Mr. Mooseblanket." Wilhelmina thought, *how very American.*

"I am not much of a tea drinker. And the name is Moosebroker, you said Mooseblanket." He shifted in his seat to face Betty. "When you are done with your tea, let's get this lady her painting and be on our way."

“Can my man, provide you with transportation back to your hotel?” Ms. Gurlitte did not want them out of her sight, not with a small fortune so very close to being delivered.

“That will be fine.” The three of them stood and shook hands.

“Fergus, bring the car around and drive Mr. Moosebroker wherever he wants to go.”

Back in their room Betty asked, “Well what do you think of her?”

“I think I am not turning over another painting to her. Did you see the walls of her apartment? Those are masterpieces.” He unrolled the two paintings from the corrugated tube. He checked the back and placed one into the tube. The one with three pencil xxx on the back he rolled to deliver to Fergus to deliver to Ms. Gurlitte.

The Case of the Chocolate Girl (9)

Betty would remember for the rest of her life the train trip from Paris to Verona. She was enthralled with the beauty of the Lake Como area of Italy. Her eyes saw colors that were new and fresh and crisp, her senses sharpened with her every step.

Quinn who had always worn his mental armor in public found he allowed the artist in him to explore the bold warmth of adobe rooflines, tall vibrant artichoke green cypresses and periwinkle blue sky reflected in the crystal mirrored lake.

Their first evening in Italy they learned that the dinner required three hours as their Ligurian seafood stew with bread and Monferrato Freista wine filled their stomachs. The trellised loggia with bougainvillea trimmings looked upon a castle built on an island in the middle of the lake. Music and laughter filled their souls. Betty's eyes sang Cinderella songs.

Quinn put his hand on Betty's, "Let's get married here. We can find the woman. Then we can stay an extra day and find someone to marry us. What do you think?"

"I think, YES!" They stood and kissed. The water sparkled on the lake.

They drove up and down the street where they thought the address of their appointment was and could not locate it. Betty insisted they backtrack and ask for some directions.

They reached a tavern with the words Alba Osteria above the door. The two walked inside and took seats at the bar. The bartender came over and put two napkins on the bar in front of them. "Cosa possofare?" He waited for an answer.

Quinn tapped the handle of the name of an Italian beer he recognized and held up two fingers.

When he returned with the beer, Betty held out a piece of paper with an address on it. The bartender took it and looked carefully. The woman behind the bar came over and looked at the paper. The two looked at the paper and each other. The lady nodded.

"La scuola di musica." She came around the end of the bar and tapped Betty on the shoulder to beckon her to follow. She walked to the front door and onto the gravel parking area. She pointed to a white building at the top of the next hill. "Music. Musica, si," she said, looking for understanding in Betty's face, and then turned to go inside.

Quinn and Betty sat in the relaxing atmosphere of the old tavern and finished their beer.

The hand carved worn wooden sign said ‘Pianoforte Coppens’ next to it another sign said, ‘Immobili in Vendita’ (for sale).

Quinn turned up the lane and guided the vehicle up the smoothed dirt path into the courtyard. He parked under the gray elm whose branches swayed in a light breeze. The shadowy leaves skipped like fairies across a white washed stucco wall.

The sound of the car brought Alayna out to see. A very young girl stood at her side. “Ciao,” Alayna said. The school was her favorite place on earth. “There is a line of these gray elms by the Damascus Gate along the Prophets Road in Jerusalem,” she offered pointing to the tree putting on the fiery show against the backdrop of the wall.

“Hello,” Betty said hoping this would be easy.

“Hello,” Alayna said. “Can I help you?”

“We are the ones that called. We are here to see Lotte Coppens. Is that you?” Quinn addressed this middle-aged woman in a sunny courtyard in this warm country.

“Please come in. She is just finishing a lesson. I will let her know youare here. It will be just a few minutes. Follow me, please.” The little girl came over and took Betty's hand and led her through the door. Quinn followed Alayna.

They were guided along an old wooden covered floor to an alcove shaded by an olive tree and bordered with dazzling flowers. A tide of music swept through the hall escorting them to their chairs. They had only been seated for a moment when a young girl carried in a tray with three glasses and a pitcher of lemonade. "Mrs. Coppens will be here shortly," the girl said in a sweet accented English.

The music stopped. A chorus of young girls echoing laughter followed. Lotte Coppens entered the alcove. She was elderly. For some reason, Quinn thought she would be younger. She had a reassuring smile. She put out her hand in welcome.

Quinn and Betty stood and greeted her. They all sat down, and Quinn poured lemonade.

"So nice to meet you Mrs. Coppens," Betty told her.

"Oh, please call me Lotte. It is so nice to meet the two of you," Lotte was charming. "Can I show you the school? The children are taking a break. I am afraid it will be impossible to get them back to their lessons on this sunny afternoon. We were almost done."

"Show us the school, sure – we called about a painting, remember?" Betty smiled her best smile.

"Oh, I was confused. I thought you were a couple that may have some interest in buying the school. There just isn't money to keep it going any longer," her heart sighed.

"We would like to see the school if you have time." Betty offered and stood up. Quinn followed.

Lotte stood and walked back down the hall the way they had just come. She entered a wide open room with a long mirror down one side and a rail along the wall. "We used to offer ballet, but I got too old and we stopped." A large old polished piano sat in one corner. "The acoustics in this room are wonderful. It comes alive with music."

"We listened to you playing while sitting in your beautiful alcove." Betty chimed.

"Me? No dear, that was not me; one of my students has become a maestro."

The tour ended with the three of them standing on a terrace filled with the scent of a nearby lemon tree. The adobe pots spilled over their colorful contents. "Let's go finish our lemonade," Lotte told them.

At the table, Betty took the picture from the corrugated tube and unrolled it.

"Why that looks like my Grandfather's painting. We lived in Belgium at the time. Those were sad times." Lotte's eyes shined with tears. Her heart was racing. "Alayna," she called. When she arrived in the doorway, she said, "Call Mario and tell him to come and get his sign off my driveway. We don't have to sell." She stood and kissed Quinn on both cheeks and went to Betty cupped her hands around hers and did the same.

Alayna left the room, in a very few minutes a half dozen girls rushed into the alcove and gave hugs to Lotte, Quinn, and Betty. Alayna leaned in the doorway smiling.

"Lotte, maybe you could help us. We want to get married in Italy. Can you direct us to someone that can accomplish that? We are only here for a short period of time." Betty felt she and Quinn had accomplished the original mission.

In the excitement of the moment, Lotto said, "My friends, you should get married here. We will invite the whole village."

Quinn looked with amazement at the three women at his side.

"Sunday, is two days away. Let's do this Sunday. Alayna, can we be ready by Sunday?" Lotte said with some apprehension.

"It will depend on the Mayor, but yes, I think so."

Quinn walked out to the front drive and leaned on the rented vehicle, pulled his pipe from his jacket pocket and filled it. The women remained in the alcove and planned a hasty wedding.

The Case of the Chocolate Girl (10) Final Episode

Betty and Quinn lay side by side in bed; they would be wed in the morning.

"I don't have a lot to offer you," Quinn told her.

"Before I was introduced to you I stayed home alone for two years after George passed. And now I am here with you in Italy. Our wedding is planned for the morning. Together we have done so many exciting things. So, in reply to you, I say, let's fix that thinking, starting now." She moved closer and kissed him, then put her head on his chest and listened to his heartbeat.

Quinn began: "Did you know I was the one you were waiting for? You remember, you were wearing an emerald green dress opening the door? I was wearing the same suit I am going to wear tomorrow. You made my heart roar. By the end of the evening, you had crawled through a window and were sprawled on the floor." He smiled at the thought and continued, "It was clear from the start that you would not be a bore. This will make a great chapter in the family folklore. I don't care if we are rich or we are poor," Quinn stopped talking and with Betty's head on his chest he gazed at the ceiling and listened to her snore.

Lotte Coppens and Alayna had handled the arrangements. The wedding would proceed right after church let out. The Mayor would preside over the proceedings per Quinn's wishes. The local priest would also be in attendance. The entire village was welcome. The plaza would be used for the reception. Lotte Coppens and Alayna felt Quinn and Betty were the benefactors of the school from the day they arrived carrying the painting.

Quinn stood as the church bell tolled. He and Betty just needed to walk across the plaza. The Mayor would perform the ceremony. They church goers would be served a meal from the Alba Osteria. Lotte called in favors and her musician friends setup to play music for the price of a meal.

With the lingering sounds of the bells hanging in the scented air, the Mayor began. Betty smiled to herself as it had not occurred to her that the ceremony would be in Italian. Everyone in attendance but her and Quinn would understand the words. The priest stood a few feet away from the Mayor adding the needed reverence to the service. Quinn and Betty were quietly prompted by Lotte as their parts arrived.

After the rings were exchanged Betty lifted her veil and the newlyweds kissed and the plaza rang with applause. The band started playing and the wine started flowing. Hours passed as the village shared in the celebration.

Betty was asked to dance by the Mayor. While they were on the dance floor, Lotte came over and sat next to Quinn, who was alone at the table. “We knew the Germans were coming and were making preparations to leave. We never dreamed they would arrive so quickly. My grandfather was a clever man and was hiding the family fortune and had plans to get it to safety. The painting you found was stolen by a cousin from the shipment of goods headed for England. We never heard from him again. The shipment to England never arrived. That the painting arrived into your hands proves to me that he did not benefit from the theft."

She took another drink of wine, "The painting is a treasure. It will keep the school running for years to come; many more years than I have left. You are a great hero to me and this party is to celebrate you and

Betty's wedding but also to celebrate who you are as people." She patted him on the knee and stood. She turned to him and said, "Too bad you did not find the frame," she winked, picked up her glass of wine and walked with a slight wobble over to Alayna and embraced her with joy.

In the morning, a glow of happiness still surrounded Quinn and Betty as they gathered their things and said heartfelt goodbyes to their gracious hostess. They climbed into their rented car and made their way back towards the main road. They would grab train tickets to Milan and would fly home from there. The two of them were completely worn out from the trip. They had, unknown to them avoided danger and had avoided fraud from the woman in London. They sat in their seats in somewhat of a daze at all that had happened to them recently.

After hours in the air the engines roared to a stop as the plane came to a stop at the terminal. Quinn and Betty limped off the plane, shaking off their aches and pains. It was good to be home. Quinn retrieved their bags. Kate was not there to meet them. The delay in Italy had thrown off the schedule. The two took a shuttle and caught a bus into Clearview Terrace arriving in the early hours of the morning. They grabbed a cab home.

Duncan-Waffles welcomed them with enough joy and happiness for ten return trips. He was happy to see them. Kate woke and greeted them with sleepy eyes and went back to bed as Duncan bounced and danced at their arrival.

"I am going to take a shower and get some sleep," Betty announced. "Come to bed, you look tired."

"In a while, I'll get cleaned up after you and be in shortly."

Duncan was pulled Betty went one way and Quinn another. He followed Quinn. Quinn walked out into the garage and found the string to turn on the light. "Hello," he said to his Town & Country. There against the wall was the frame that had been placed there when the painting was removed.

He brought it over to the bench under better light to take a good look at it. It was the same gaudy terrible looking frame that he remembered. He turned it and examined the back. He decided to take the ends apart at the seams. He grabbed a cloth and wrapped it around the edge and put that in a vise and tightened it. He rummaged around and found a rubber mallet. He tapped the side apart and did the same until the four pieces were lying on the bench.

He picked up one of the longer pieces and examined it carefully. Getting his nose close, he spotted a seam running along the back. Someone had done a nice bit of cabinetry on this frame. He found a wood chisel and started separating the wooden fitted cap from the frame. In a few minutes, four metal cigar cylinders with metal caps lay on the bench, one from each pane edge.

Just as Quinn sat down the mallet Betty walked in wearing a nightie. "Come here," Quinn said to her. "I was just about to go and get you." He lifted one of the cylinders and opened the top. He looked inside and spilled a stream of diamonds onto the workbench.

“Oh, my holy hannah,” Betty said as she reached over and opened another of the cylinders. More diamonds tumbled amongst the others. The glittering stones spelled a comfortable future for the newlyweds. Quinn turned his attention to Betty; he reached up and turned off the light. He guided her to the Town & Country and opened the back door lowering her in and climbed in embracing her.

Duncan-Waffles stood guard. In the morning, Betty opened the third cigar cylinder and there were more quality stones. Quinn took the fourth and last. To his surprise there were no diamonds, but instead inside the cigar tube he found a note string-tied to an old key written in Yiddish, the words, Dy r‘şt

The End

A Quinn & Betty Moosebroker Mystery (1)

Dy r'șt

Quinn and Betty Moosebroker returned home from Italy. Their recent case had brought them there in the quest to return 'The Chocolate Girl' painting that was stolen from Lotte Coppens' family during World War II. To show her appreciation, Lotte Coppens hosted the couple's wedding and the village celebrated. Lotte hinted to Quinn that the frame the painting traveled in contained something of value and it was a shame he did not find the frame also.

The tired travels found that they were generously rewarded for their honesty when they found three old metal cigar cylinders filled with diamonds hidden in the recesses of the carved out ornate frame. There was a fourth cylinder that contained an old key with a note attached that said, 'Dy rst.'

Duncan-Waffles, their rescued dog, sat at Quinn's feet as they stood by the stove; one frying bacon the other hoping for bacon. "Good morning sleepyhead," he said to Betty as her nose led her from the bedroom to the kitchen where a hot cup of coffee was placed in front of her. When the sunny-side up eggs were done, Quinn brought two plates to the table and sat down with them with Duncan-Waffles not far behind.

"You look beautiful this morning."

Betty's eyes smiled. "Moose, I am never going to let you forget that."

"We don't have to wait until your house is sold now before we start looking for something," he told her.

"House, yes, we can contact a realtor and get that started. But I am so curious about that key and the note. Are you ready for another adventure?" She put a fork full of eggs into her mouth and wiped up some yolk from her plate with the edge of her toast.

"That will likely mean returning to Europe. We should wait and see if we can find any clue at all? We sure do not have much to go on." He drank his coffee. "I don't want to leave Duncan-Waffles behind. I'll call the airlines and see what it requires to bring him with us."

"I know you have some misgivings about Major Garrity, but I am going to call him. I think we need his advice. I am sure he will be happy to see us." She looked across the table at Quinn and winked. She got up and refilled both their coffee cups. "In the meantime, we should find a place for us to stay. There is no real reason to impose on Kate now, is there?"

"No, I guess not. We can find something close by and temporary while the realtor does his work." Quinn stood and brought his plate to the sink. "Go ahead and call the Major. Maybe he can help us."

Early Tuesday Morning

Betty sat at the linoleum-topped kitchen table spinning an eight-karat diamond like a top. The tile of the floor was cold against her feet and her eyes gazed at the glittering shiny spinning stone and she tried to see into the future.

Quinn walked into the kitchen and Betty stood and gave him a quick kiss and poured him a cup of coffee. "You want some breakfast?" She asked as the stone twirled to a stop sending fiery light scattering against the walls.

"What time is the appointment with the Major?" Quinn looked at Betty and glanced at the stone on the table. "Are we going to show him the diamonds?"

"Just this one, this might be the biggest diamond in Clearview Terrace. Outside this house," she added and took a deep breath. "I made an appointment for ten a.m. That gives us plenty of time for breakfast."

Major Garrity

The Major greeted them at the door and Quinn and Betty followed him to his den.

Betty again stood looking at the skin of a cheetah draped over a table, and a silver tray supporting nineteenth-century cut crystal goblets. Being surrounded by leather books on strong honey oak shelves did something to her. Filtered light gave the room the abeyance of the previous century. The combination of antiques, stuffed animals, African spears all carried the senses to another time.

"What brings you two to my door? Betty, I was both surprised and happy to get your call." He waved his arm in invitation to find a seat.

"When you offered to purchase the painting we found, you brought a box of gemstones with you to barter with. You told us that each gem was worth at least $1,000. That leads us to believe you know something about the business end of... shall we call it the jewelry business." Quinn began.

The Major pulled a cord on the wall and a manservant entered the room. "Bring in a tray of tea."

Quinn sat up straight, wondering why everyone was offering him tea. And he wondered if it meant anything. "Like I was saying..."

Betty interrupted; she stood and crossed the room to the Majors desk, "We located this." She dropped the eight-karat diamond on the desk while carefully watching his dark brown eyes and wondered what stories they held.

"We located this," Quinn said mockingly to Betty's back, smiling to himself. He stood and placed the key on the desk in front of the Major.

The manservant took that moment to enter with a tray of tea. He sat it on the desk, glanced at the diamond and turned and left the room.

Quinn made a note that someone else now knew about at least one of the diamonds.

"Can I pour your tea?" Betty asked the Major.

"Please." He opened his top desk drawer and pulled a jeweler's loop out and examined the diamond.

Betty handed Quinn a cup of tea. Quinn always felt uncomfortable with balancing a cup and saucer. These items were much too delicate for his large hands.

"Do you two know anything about the diamond business? I suspect not. It is a very tightly controlled cartel; at the top of that cartel is De Beers. From the mine to the jewelry store, the price may increase as much as tenfold as it passes along towards the display window and finally to the finger of some blushing bride, starlet or other peacock. This is a beautiful stone. I can go and fetch my karat scale and tell you exactly what it weighs and then estimate what said blushing bride would be asked to pay at a high-end store in the city. And the funny thing is that a couple of miles away in the diamond district she would pay half for the stone and get to select the setting of her choice." He handed the rock and the loop to Betty, "Take a look at the clarity. I am not a professional diamond grader, but that looks to me like a VVS2, which means with a 10x loop like the one you are holding any small inclusions are visible from the crown."

After taking a look, Betty handed the loop and the diamond to Quinn and he maneuvered for some light and peered into the glacial realm of the diamond in his hand. He felt deeply drawn into a world that he knew nothing about and wondered if this was what Alice felt like falling down the rabbit hole. He set the loop and diamond back down in front of the Major. "You mentioned a karat scale."

The Major stood and went to the bookshelf with two doors at the bottom. He opened them and returned with a weather-beaten wooden box and took his seat. He opened the box, lifted the arm of the scale. He placed the diamond on one side of the scale and set weight stamped coppers into the other side until there was a near perfect balance. "Looks like an eight-karat stone."

Betty smiled. She was not a student of diamond karats, weights, clarity, but as a young girl, she had spent time looking through the windows of jewelry stores and dreaming.

"I know it is just a little after ten in the morning, but Quinn can I offer you a drink? You did not touch your tea."

Betty reached into the cup of the scale and retrieved the diamond and held it.

Quinn set the cup and saucer down. "Yes, that would be fine."
The Major stood again and went and lifted a bottle, returning and announcing, "God's Elixir" and poured two glasses with two fingers. He handed Quinn a glass and took his, "Cheers" and took a sip. He twirled the remaining elixir in his glass and stared at the key.

A Quinn & Betty Moosebroker Mystery (2)

The Major got up and refilled his glass, and topped off the glass Quinn was holding. "Are you a student of history? Do you know the stories of the Knight Templars? What about the Rothschild's or Oppenheimers'? Oh, no matter. Do you have time for a story? I will make it short as possible.

The world does not run like we are told it runs. Money runs all things and those that control the money make all the decisions. It is quite simple really. We all go about our daily life, we eat and drink and make love and some of us vote and we feel we are doing our part. But we are governed by forces that are mostly unseen.

It is said the Knight Templars discovered the treasures of King Solomon. The fortune made its way back to Europe and is reported as the seed money for the greatest banking houses in the world. These Knight Templars and their offspring became the most rich and powerful in the world. They are in control of banking and industry, railroads and mining on many levels. You will have to read up on it at the local library.

The point I am trying to reach is that amongst their highest priorities are privacy. Their banking activities are private, but there are always prying eyes. Once a member of their group is identified they are watched by journalist and novelist and even government do-gooders. Over the years, and especially the war years, a system was put in place just to protect and hide stashes of wealth. It was a minor subset of their banking activities. Used by members to hide wealth and to have easy access to funds in cities all over the world. No reporting required. Think of it as your cookie jar at home, but more sophisticated.

I see you sitting there thinking what does this have to do with a small diamond that you placed on my desk before me. And the answer is nothing at all. I am a storyteller by nature. Are you two hungry?"

The Major reached over and pulled the cord that brought the manservant. When he arrived, he was instructed to serve lunch.

"Where was I? Oh, yes the money lenders. Mind you I have limited personal experience with this. I heard the tale told in a club in Bombay when I was an aid for an old Colonel. One evening he was feeling no pain and said a letter from a dead man made it into his hand. With the letter was a key and that is where this story may have easily begun. The letter identified the whereabouts of a shop in the back streets of Calcutta a nothing of a shop that sold tobacco located down a dangerous alley.

Reaching the shop, the Colonel looked around at the dinginess and drew in the aroma of exotic tobaccos and wondered how the story and the key connected to this dimly lit confinement. He thought to leave but instead took the key in his hand and tapped in loudly against the wooden counter which brought the proprietor.

A man of many years arrived staring cautiously at the Colonel and then took a look at the key in his hand and according to the Colonel stood straight up like he went to military attention and put his hand out for the key and disappeared into the back of his shop where he had first appeared.

A few moments later a wooden box was placed before him on the counter and the old man again disappeared.

The Colonel loved his story. Standing now in the dinginess of the shop where there were footprints in the dust on the floor from his arrival he slowly opened the box. It contained gemstones of rubies and emeralds and sapphires. You may recall seeing some of them a few months ago when I tried to buy your painting.

When the Colonel suddenly died of a heart attack, I was instructed to clean out his quarters. The gemstones…well, the gemstones found their way into my hands along with many of these artifacts. He had outlived his family - the climate in Bombay is not for everyone. Over my years of service, I had become his family."

The manservant arrived and announced that lunch was served. The Major stood and lifted the key and held it up where Quinn could see it. Betty took the diamond from the desk.

Both Quinn and Betty followed the Major into a dining room where lunch waited.

"I hope I am not boring you," the Major said as the two began to eat. Neither Quinn nor Betty was used to having someone serve them.

"You are wondering why I am telling you this story," he took a bite of his food. "It is simply this," he held up the key that had been placed before him an hour ago. "This key is just like the key that the Colonel described to me."

Betty's fork halted midway from her plate to her mouth and she lowered it slowly.

"It is antique with an ornate bow, and there will be numbers inscribed across the shank. But without my glasses, I cannot see them." He paused to watch their reaction. "Unless you have just not shared with me a letter identifying the location you have your work cut out for you." With his fingertips, he rubbed above his right eye.

"Now this is some fact, and some speculation. I think because I have heard other stories that hints of such things as these are very private people who want as little as possible known about their comings and goings and they have wealth stashed in many areas of the world. There is no need for paperwork or signatures or documentation. A person shows up with a key to a particular location and no questions asked they were given the contents of a vault. Understand I am just speculating that all these things go together. One searing night in a den of pleasure in the alleys of Balasore, India, an upper-class gent, while lying in an opium induced stupor confessed that he was escaping murder in Bangladesh. Well, that night I heard for the first time the term *Rothschild Vaults*.

When the three finished lunch and the Major's story seemingly over, Quinn and Betty said goodbye. At the door, the Major said, "Shop that diamond around and then bring it to me, I'll give you twenty-five percent more than your top offer."

When he saw Quinn and Betty climb into the Town & Country, he closed the door, walked to his den, returned the karat scale to its place and picked up the phone to make a call. His manservant anticipated the call and was alert to listen in on an extension.

Back in the car, Quinn asked, "You have the diamond right?"

Betty asked, "You have the key right?"

They both smiled at each other leaving the winding driveway. "What did you make of that story?"

"Before I answer that, how did you happen to pick that diamond?" Quinn asked her.

"Oh, I just picked one of the small ones. I did not want all the alarms to go off in the Major's head. Seems the key did that anyway," she replied.

"Oh, ok. The story, yes that is such a string of wild events I think if I had a suspect in custody and he started telling a yarn such as that I would have to get his thinking straight in a hurry. What were all those names? Knight Templars? The Rothschild's? The Oppenheimers? I'll have to put on metal chainmail armor and you a gossamer gown before we are done with this."

They both laughed at the thought.

Next morning Betty found herself at the Clearview Terrace library flipping through the pages of a history of The Knights Templars and the capture of Al-Aqsa Mosque and thinking of desert caravans and harems. When her mind wandered to violet-blue tanzanite crystals, she knew she had gone from research to day-dreaming and put all the books she had gathered back on their shelves.

A Quinn & Betty Moosebroker Mystery(3)

Quinn sat at the kitchen table in the middle of the night thinking about the questions in front of them.

Betty arrived tying her robe and took her place at the table. "I rolled over and you were not there," she said. "What's wrong?"

"You know, that Major is a natural born storyteller. He and I must be near the same age, yet he tells a story about a man fleeing up the Budhabalanga River across the Bay of Bengal to escape murder in Bangladesh, into the back streets of Balasore." He looked at his hands. "And what has any of that have to do with us now. I'll be right back." He left the table and walked out to the garage.

"You want some coffee?" She asked as he reached the kitchen door. "No, no, none for me thanks."

She got up and went to the refrigerator, grabbed the glass milk bottle and set it on the table. She got two glasses and poured each of them a glass. The sound of the refrigerator brought Duncan-Waffles to her feet. "Hello, boy, can I get you something?" she scratched his head. Quinn returned and set four sides of an old picture frame down and four old metal cigar containers down in front of the. "Whatever clues we have are right here."

"Do you think that the painting itself hold any clues?" She asked and took a drink of milk. "We are going to have to consider that."

"I never thought of that. What gives you such insights?"

"Just an overactive imagination, I guess." She inwardly smiled that her contribution was accepted so readily.

Duncan-Waffles wagged his tale and wondered why they all did not go back to bed.

"Let's stare at these things in the morning," Betty offered as if reading Duncan-Waffles mind.

Kate said goodbye to Quinn, Betty and Duncan-Waffles as she left for work in the morning. Quinn had cleaned up after the four of them had finished their pancakes and sausage breakfast. Duncan-Waffles had grown partial towards sausage for breakfast.

Quinn gathered the evidence from the counter and brought it back to the table. That included four sides to an ornate frame with hollowed out spaces. It included four old metal cigar tubes with lids. He went and found the Polaroid pictures of the painting titled, 'The Chocolate Girl' all these things lay on the kitchen table as Quinn, Betty, and Duncan-Waffles sitting in a chair stared at them. The diamonds had been removed from the cylinders and put into a purple velvet bag that a bottle of Crown Royal whiskey had been packaged in and stashed away from possible prying eyes.

"I went to the library as you know and read a little about Knight Templars and The Rothschild's and The Oppenheimers. I even browsed some pages regarding, The Lost Valley of Precious Stones and The Lost Magato Trail in Africa, then closed that book. I have determined that once we settle down to spend more time at the library." She went and retrieved a journal and brought it to the table.

"What is that for?" Quinn asked.

"Are you kidding this is good stuff. I am going to write some of our adventures down. Maybe write about them someday." Duncan-Waffles tail wagged at the sound of Betty's voice.

"Well, write this down; Joseph Pierret, Semois Valley, Vieux Semois. Quinn read what was printed on the side of the first cigar tube he had picked up. He looked at the second and the third that had the same thing written on them. The fourth cylinder varied in that it said Royal Semois rather than Vieux Semois. "This one says Royal Semois," he told Betty. "This ties in well with the fact of where Lotte Coppens' family came from. Don't you think?"

"I don't know. Where is Semois Valley?" She asked.

"Oh, sorry it is in Belgium, near the Ardennes. The area was made famous as the location of the Battle of the Bulge." Quinn shivered at the thought of an American army pinned down in an ice storm from hell in the midst of battle, sent without the right winter clothing, or enough food or munitions.

“Anything else,” she asked.

“I guess if we did enough research we would trace the frame back to some famous frame maker, but I don’t see how that information aids us,” Quinn told her while looking at one piece of the frame.

That night under the cover of darkness, a shadowy figure broke a back window of Betty’s house on Maple Ave. He rummaged through all the kitchen cupboards, the drawers in the living room and he did not stop until he reached the bedroom closets which were near empty, he then realized that no one was living at the house. He climbed back out into the night empty handed.

Five Days later

Betty was waiting for Quinn at the door when he arrived home from an errand. “Look what the Postman brought today.” She handed him a letter with postage paid in Lira on it. “It’s from Lotte. It is amusing in a way, once it all sinks in.”

The letter was written by Alayna, Lotte’s assistant at her Music School, announced they needed money. She assured Quinn and Betty, as the letter was addressed to both of them that it was temporary. Lotte had paid for the couple’s marriage ceremony on credit knowing she would soon sell the painting, ‘The Chocolate Girl’ at auction in Milan run by Sotheby’s.

There was a slight problem, and that was that a Ms. Wilelmine Gurlitte in London had at the same time put up for auction a painting by the artist, Jean-Etienne Liotard, The Chocolate Girl through Christies in London. A buyer in Brussels spotted the item in both catalogs and both items were pulled as a shockwave roared through the art world. There was a newspaper clipping included inside the envelope, but it was printed in Italy in Italian and of little use.

Lotte had asked Alayna, not to write, but the need for money was desperate.

Betty took the letter from Quinn when he was done with it and returned it to the envelope. "What do you think is the easiest way to get that woman some money?" Betty asked Quinn.

Quinn had not liked Wilelmine Gurlitte on his one visit to her London apartment while trying to find the rightful owner of the painting "The Chocolate Girl' and smiled at the likely repercussions about to visit the woman. The impending investigation would undoubtedly turn up the fact that artworks looted by Nazis, during World War II, were returned to her through false claims. She had made her money, successfully soliciting the Central States Archives in London, Tel Aviv, Kiev, and New York, using information garnered from her time in the camps. She did not know that she would soon be stripped of her Picasso, Matisse, Chagall, her Otto Dix and her Max Beckman.

"I think the first thing to do would be to get some money. I am going to get the Town and Country serviced and then we can go back to the city and find a *diamantaire.* Maybe we can stay at the same place on Essex Street where we stayed the last time we were in the city. You remember above Gertle's Bake Shop. And then I think you will agree we are going to need a lawyer."

A Quinn & Betty Moosebroker Mystery (4)

Betty set the phone down and said to Quinn, "That was the Realtor's office she said the house on Maple has been broken into. A window is broken and someone searched through everything. She said she called her guy to come fix the window. What do you make of that?"

Quinn sighed, "Not sure what to make of that. It could be kids. They could have noticed no one was going and coming from the house. Or it could be something else. Let's worry about it when we get back from the city. Did you select a couple of diamonds to bring with us?"

"Yes, I wish I knew more about this," Betty told him. They were both aware that they were out of their depth here. "We could see if the Major had something he could tell us. Though that comment, about paying us twenty-five percent more than our top offer, tells me that he knows what kind of offers we are going to receive."

"Are you comfortable with the hiding place for our diamonds?" Quinn asked. Not fully knowing he asked the question out loud.

"Are you comfortable with the hiding place for the key?" She asked patting her chest where the key hung from a chain tucked under her shirt. She gave Quinn her coy smile.

Quinn loaded the Town & Country, Betty checked the luggage and Duncan-Waffle supervised the goings on. "We are not getting the early start we had planned on," she told Duncan-Waffles. "What do you say we stop at the Frosty Mug and get an early lunch before we start?" Duncan's tale wagged in a fury.

"Are we about set?" Quinn asked entering their room.

"I promised Duncan lunch at the Frosty Mug. That OK with you?"

"Sure, our early start has already come and gone." Quinn scratched Duncan's head. "I'll leave a note for Kate. I called an old friend of mine. He is younger and a disabled Vet but still one of the meanest bobcats around. His name is William, but he answers to Recoil. A nickname he got in Army. I asked him to stay at your place on Maple. With us out of town, I want Kate to have someone to call if need be. Now, with the news of the break-in, I am really glad I did this. He is a scrawny guy, but the first time I arrested him he was beating on two much bigger guys."

Betty did not like the sound of this but did like the precautions Quinn was taking for Kate's safety. She told herself this was not a vacation and steeled herself for things to come.

With the Town and Country serviced and their steak sandwiches and cold beer finished, Quinn, Betty, and Duncan-Waffles, caught I295 to the big city and into the unknown. They reached their destination in the early evening and got checked into the Essex Hotel. The clerk remembered Duncan-Waffles and Duncan greeted her accordingly. The trio was tired they walked down to the nearby deli and ate then returned to the room to sleep.

Quinn and Betty finished their pastry and coffee and drove into the Jewelry District. They looked in one window, then another and another. Both were apprehensive. After peering through the third window, Quinn gently took Betty's elbow and guided her through the door of Fabian's Diamonds. He could not see much difference from one shop's offering to the next.

"Hello," Quinn heard as he stepped inside with Betty, "How can I help you?" The man with pe'ot (side-curls) and beard set down a jeweler's loupe and returned a tray of sparkly rings to the display case turning the key in the lock without looking, just from habit.

"We are interested in selling a diamond." Quinn started, "We are looking for a legitimate offer."

"We share that in common, an interest in selling diamonds," he said with a practiced rhythm and innate smile.

Betty took the diamond out of her purse and set it on the counter. Betty watched the man's eyes. What she saw placed there were boredom and disinterest; that made her feel bad.

Simon Fabian had been buying and selling diamonds his entire adult life. It was a good living and once you had reached a certain level of inventory the diamonds seemed to walk in the door. The whole block was filled with diamond wholesalers and they all made money. Simon knew to let no expression cross his face when offered a diamond.

Simon picked up the brilliant cut white diamond and looked at it with his loupe. He knew from the feel it was eight karats, knew it had a value of about $8,000, and knew Saul would give him $4,000 in less than an hour. He put the diamond down and said, "I'll give you $2,000 for it." Then he waited.

Betty took the lead, "Why, I have already been offered $2,500 for it. I thought this was an honest shop." She picked up the diamond and said, "Let's go." She took Quinn gently by the elbow and guided him towards the door.

When they reached the door, they heard, "Wait."

They both turned and looked at Simon, "I'll go $2600, but that is my final offer."

A few moments later Quinn and Betty left the shop with a nice folded stack of $100.00 bills.

When the door was shut behind them, Simon picked up the store phone and called Sauly. He had a beautiful rock that Sauly could sell this afternoon to his stone-setter for a quick $1,000 profit. The stone-setter, in turn, would select a setting and then consign it to an uptown retailer netting his full investment back plus $500 and then receive a commission when sold. Everyone in the food chain would eat today.

"Oh, wow, that was fun," Betty told Quinn. "Should we sell the other one now or go find a lawyer and get some advice about money transfer?"

"We have enough money to pay Lotte for the wedding and another trip to Europe. Let's find a New York lawyer and talk it over with him." Quinn offered.

“Or her,” Betty smiled and hugged Quinn’s arm.

Duncan-Waffle wagged his tail as they all walked along the active N.Y. street back to the parking lot.

After checking a phone book and making an appointment, Quinn and Betty made their way, with Duncan-Waffles and relayed their story to Adina Meyers, Attorney at Law.

“And you said, you did not receive any compensation from Ms. Wilelmine Gurlitte in London? In that case, you cannot be held liable for selling or trying to defraud Gurlitte. Though she will certainly attempt to come at you for the prank or even perhaps damages though she likely will find herself in enough trouble to worry about you.” She looked at the two sitting before her. “About Lotte Coppens, you can wire transfer her money if she has an account at a major bank in Italy but if it were me, I think I would go there and hand her the money. Italy is always worth it and she sounds like a beautiful soul.” Adina Meyers bit her lip. “You are here in the city to sell diamonds. You used the plural when you were telling me what lead you here to my door. It so happens I have a nephew looking for a wedding ring. Would you be interested in selling a diamond to us? It will keep us from the hands of the ganef.

In another hour Quinn, Betty, and Duncan-Waffle had sold their second diamond for $4,000 to the nephew who in his head calculated the cost of the setting his soon-to-be bride coveted and the diamond and the price he would have had to pay retail and thanked his aunt who just saved her brother, his father, and himself $2,600. It was a good day.

A Quinn & Betty Moosebroker Mystery (5)

Back at the Essex Hotel Betty told Quinn, “It’s a shame to have to drive back to Clearview Terrace. We could pick up some things here in the city and the three of us could get on an airplane and continue our trip. What do you think?”

“I hate to leave the car parked in the city,” Quinn told her. “As a matter of fact, I hate the thought of putting Duncan in the hold of a plane for twelve hours.”

“Oh, I had not thought about the car. I have been fretting over putting Duncan in a cage. But he will be alright. Don’t you think?” Both were worried about Duncan’s travel arrangements. “Are you a tough guy?” Betty asked Duncan scratching his head.

Duncan’s tail wagged acknowledging he was a tough guy.

“I’ll tell you what, we can find an Army surplus and find a cover for the car, then park her in some long term parking and cover her up while we are away. Maybe we could also find something to line the container that will hold Duncan to make him more comfortable.” Quinn was thinking out loud, and Betty was listening.

They agreed and after a nap, the three of them went shopping for their trip.

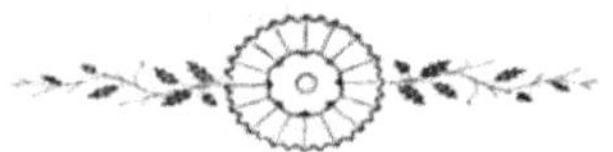

The Road From Milan

Quinn was behind the wheel of the rented car driving out their past. The landscape of a thousand years assaulted their senses. Duncan-Waffles stuck his nose out the window, again enjoying his freedom from the hole of the plane.

Betty's eyes played the cinema of the scenery and her mind drifted to the past as she thought of her deceased husband and the life they lived. It was a nine to five life with no time off for good behavior. She was not sitting staring out the window regretting; rather she was thankful for her second chance. The scent in the air of sunflower fields bathed her in a glory she had not known before.

A Simon and Garfunkel song came on the radio, and Betty was freed from the restraints of the car and was flying over fields of sunflowers and vineyards; her soul danced.

As Betty's body quietly swayed, Quinn felt the car fill with her energy and his inner smile beamed. Her sense of well-being was not lost on him. The road required his attention as both Betty's presence and the Italian sunset distracted him. He was unaware of the black sedan that was following them since the car rental station.

Sir Walter Raleigh

The three reached a village about dinner time and stopped and had a meal. "Let's stop for the night. We can get an early start in the morning. What do you think?" Betty asked

They found a room for the evening. "I am going to take Duncan for a walk. Why don't you shower." Quinn told Betty as he walked Duncan out the door.

The two men with nutmeg colored skin watched from a vantage point of their car.

Betty was thankful to get clean as she stood in the shower washing off the hours of the plane flight and the drive. She did not hear the door of the room open or the two men who were quietly gathering all their processions and just as quietly slipped out of the room with their loot. Back in the car, they searched for diamonds and cash that they were told would be there.

Betty stepped out of the shower and leisurely dried herself. She wrapped a towel around her and stepped back into the room. She gasped when she saw, both bags were gone, and her purse and even the dirty clothes she took off. She grabbed the phone but did not know who to call.

When Quinn returned about twenty minutes later, he found Betty sitting on the bed wearing a towel. At first, he smiled, but when the smile was not returned, his disappeared. "What's wrong?"

"We have been robbed! They took everything we had with us."

"Are you OK?" Quinn said while unbuttoning his shirt. He removed his shirt and then his trousers.

Betty lifted her eyebrows. "What are you doing?" She asked with an amused smile.

"I am loaning you my clothes. There are shops open two blocks from here, turn right at the corner with the cafe. And here is money for the shopping spree."

Betty dropped the towel and donned the shirt and pants. Quinn kneeled and rolled up the pants legs and thought how beautiful Betty looked. The shirt tails worn on the outside hide the pants bunched up at her waist.

Betty stepped out the door feeling both a tiny bit odd and very sexy. She walked through the streets carefully trying to remember the last time she walked barefooted. She wondered about a man who could trust enough to be left in a room wearing only his boxer shorts in a foreign country. She patted the key that still hung around her neck. An hour later she returned with shopping bags filled with Italian clothes. She set the bags down, stepped out of her new white linen dress with embroidered collar and climbed into bed next to Quinn, who was sleeping.

The Next Morning

"I am so glad you were carrying the money," Betty told Quinn as they stepped into the shop where she replaced much of her wardrobe the night before, "we would be in such a bad way otherwise."

"That's for sure, lucky the passports were in a pouch around my neck also." Quinn looked around at the Italian men's wear and took a deep breath.

"Come on, it will be fun," Betty told him feeling free in her new outfit and Italian sandals.

“Are we going to report the break-in to the police?” Betty asked at the counter while placing three pairs of Poplin pants and three Seersucker Shirts for Quinn.

Quinn was quiet regarding the suggested clothing. “The police? Yes, I guess we should report it.”

Leaving the Police Station

“That went pretty much like I thought it would. Their report will say a couple of tourists left the door of their room unlocked and their luggage was stolen.”

“Not much satisfaction from them,” Betty said.

“Yeah, but it gives them something to do.” Quinn smiled at his own humor.

“Let’s get a cappuccino,” Betty said before we get on the road again.

Betty was beginning to feel very continental. She had a new preliminary wardrobe, new sandals, and a pair of fancy sunglasses. The midriff of the dress she was wearing was Venice lace and made her feel special. Duncan-Waffles wagged his tail.

At least, I was not asked to wear a beret. Quinn thought and tipped his Alpine Oktoberfest hat back on his head.

An hour into their drive, Betty spotted two hot air balloons, one in the air, and one on the ground near a field of sunflowers. “Go over there,” she pointed toward the stationary one, “let’s stop and see, maybe we can go for a ride.”

A ride into blue skies and cumulus clouds would be a treat and a brief escape from the Italian sun, so Quinn pulled off the road and followed the tire tracks through the field.

They parked their car next to the cars that were there and both got out and walked over to a man that Quinn judged to be about ten years his junior. The woman with him was perhaps five years younger than the man.

"Hello, we saw the balloons and I'm afraid our curiosity got the best of us." Quinn put out his hand, "I am Quinn Moosebroker and this is my wife, Betty." He was still getting used to that.

"Hi," Betty said to the man extending her hand.

The man took her hand, bowed and kissed it. "I am Baron Aldous Fulco," and pointing to the young lady smiling as she walked towards them, "and that is my wife Avice, and the pouty little girl is Sophie. Please don't call me Al."

Betty smiled as Avice reached them, she again extended her hand, "I am Betty."

"And I am Avice, pleased to meet you."

After some negotiations, Quinn and Betty took a ride in the Hot Air balloon while a smiling girl named Sophie played with Duncan-Waffles.

A Quinn & Betty Moosebroker Mystery (6)

Cool Crystal Air

Betty, Avice, Aldous and Quinn standing in the basket were quickly lifted into the sky. The cone of the hot air balloon in red, yellow and black pushed through to a magical height. In the distance, spires from an old fortress accented cypresses and vineyards. People dotted the shoreline of a nearby lake. The road they were traveling became a black ribbon dragged along the ground by the sensuous mistress that is the Italian landscape.

"We are on holiday," Aldous said looking at Betty. "What brings you here to this beautiful country?"

"We meet an incredible woman the last time we were here and are we are going to pay her a visit, then do some sightseeing. This ride is such an excellent opportunity for us. Don't you agree Quinn?"

"Yes, this is amazing. It is no wonder that every tourist has a camera hanging from their neck. I would not know what to take a picture of, there is so much."

Avice added, "You don't look like tourist and that is a compliment. Listen, you said you were going to go exploring after you visited your friend. Well, Aldous and I are hosting a gala at our place and I want to invite the two of you. I have invitations in the car don't let me forget to give you one. It has the details. It is not for a few weeks. We have to get back and get busy."

"That is so nice," Quinn told her. "If we are in the area, that sounds like it could be a memorable occasion."

Aldous pulled the lever that released a blast to heat the air in the bubble that was carrying them. In the distance, the first balloon was making its way back to where the cars were parked. "Sadly we are losing the sunlight. We should make our way back."

"We can certainly be of help getting all this gear packed once we land." Betty offered. The air was deliciously cool. Betty scanned the panoramic vista and thought: *This is better than ruby slippers.*

Sophia and Duncan-Waffles were asleep on a blanket in the shade of her parent's car when the two couples set down.

It took two hours to get the gear packed and loaded on the top carriers. Aldous appreciated the help Quinn and Betty offered.

The group said their goodbyes and Duncan-Waffles was torn to have to leave Sophie, his new friend. "We will see you soon," Betty told Sophie.

Quinn, Betty, and Duncan drove back up to the road and continued on toward their destination. The black sedan followed at a distance.

Pianoforte Coppen's

Two days later the trio turned into the lane and followed the smoothed dirt path that led into the courtyard in front of Lotte's school. Quinn parked under the gray elm, the shadows of leaves skipped along a whitewashed stucco wall in this timeless haven.

Alayna hearing the unfamiliar sound of an automobile in the drive walked out to investigate.

Quinn, Betty, and Duncan climbed out of the car and stretched. Seeing Betty, she rushed toward her and hugged her. Betty said, "Hello Alayna, we received your letter. Is Lotte here?"

"Yes, she will be so eager to see you."

Betty stooped and clipped a lease on Duncan's collar and they all walked towards the house.

As they entered, Betty was engulfed by the noticeable silence. "Where are the students?" Betty looked inquiringly at Alayna.

"How do you say...? Things are a mess. Our door has been darkened....Is that how you say? The students do not come."

Lotte walked in the room. "I heard voices. Quinn, Betty how lovely to see you. Do you need to freshen up?"

Once everyone was settled, Alayna brought in fresh squeezed lemonade and the four sat and talked over the situation.

“We will get this taken care of,” Quinn told Lotte. “We can go right now if you want to. At least, we will get the creditor off your back.”

Lotte rose at the invitation. “Please, let’s go see them and they will stop talking so poorly of us.”

Quinn stood and followed Lotte to the front door.

Betty and Duncan were offered a bed to take a nap. They accepted.

In two hours time, Lotte and Quinn returned having appeased the creditors in the village. It was the first time Betty saw Lotte smiling on this trip.

Pianoforte Coppen’s Dinner on the Veranda

Lotte, Alayna, and Betty carried food to the table while Quinn filled the wine glasses. Once again, Lotte’s heart was light because Quinn and Betty graciously returned her gift of paying for their wedding.

With a bowl of pasta on the table, breadsticks and a fresh salad both host and guests were happy.

Quinn began, “Lotte, what can you tell us of your family’s wealth before it was lost during the war? Was your family originally from Belgium?”

“My grandparents were very well off. My grandfather made his money selling to the government before World War One. When he passed on my mother inherited and my father tried to run the business, but he preferred to drink. There were even rumors of infidelity. Then the Germans came roaring back and the wealth was stolen and scattered to the winds as far as I know. Because of you and Betty, that is no longer an issue.”

Alayna raised her glass of wine and offered a toast, “To Quinn and Betty.”

Duncan wagged his tail. The four clinked their wine glasses and took a sip to friendship.

“Is there any family left in Belgium?” Quinn inquired.

"I have a cousin, my mother's brother's youngest son. He calls himself a Viscount, but he is just bourgeois. He lives in Ghent, in what was my grandfather's summer house. One of the few things the family could prove was theirs after the war." She put a fork full of spaghetti in her mouth and slowly chewed.

"This is so good," Betty offered after taking a bite of spaghetti.

"Are you taking a trip to Belgium?" Lotte asked. "Have you become filled with wanderlust?"

"We rushed back here to get you out of trouble in the quickest way possible. We may take our time going back home. With Duncan-Waffles here with us, most everything we need is with us." Quinn told her.

There was knocking at the door and with a confused look on her face, Alayna got up to see what it was.

At the door was a young, handsome Italian youth. He handed Alayna an envelope, tipped his hat and climbed back on his bicycle.

Alayna returned to the table, "There is a telegram for you." She handed the envelope to Betty.

Quinn sat straight up and took a gulp from his wine glass and reached over and refilled his glass.

Betty opened it and read. When done, she reached across the table and handed it to Quinn.

He read, 'You are in danger. Beware an Indian gang is following your scent. They are after diamonds.' Signed *Major*

Quinn emptied his glass and reached over and refilled it. He looked across the table and wondered how the Major knew we would be here.

Later that evening, after things were cleaned and put away and coffee, was served with more conversation the group said goodnight.

Once in bed together Quinn asked Betty what was on his mind. "How did the Major know we were here?"

"He may have sent that telegram to be here when we got here. He did not necessarily know we were here. But that is not what you are asking is it?" Betty paused to see if Quinn wanted to add anything. After a moment of silence, she continued, "We told him the story of our wedding day. He could have remembered the name of the school and chanced that we would pass this way again. He had nothing to lose. Quinn, I did call him from New York and let him know we sold the diamond that we showed to him so not to expect it. And I did mention we were leaving. Quinn, I think he is our friend. I know you have misgivings."

"You mean misgivings like an Indian gang following us?" Quinn sighed and thought of Kate by herself. He rolled to his side and kissed Betty good night.

"Good night," Betty said, her feelings hurt, with a tear running down her cheek.

A Quinn & Betty Moosebroker Mystery (7)

In the morning after coffee and a shared plate of Italian cookies Quinn, Betty, and Duncan climbed into the car and rolled out of the drive with the gray elm and left Pianoforte Coppen's behind them. Near the border, the car entered a long tunnel heading toward Highway SS340. When they exited the tunnel, they headed north out of the sun quenched burnt sienna of the Italian landscape into the cobalt blue of Switzerland.

"I am going to need a sweater," Betty said suddenly chilled.

"Tonight when we stop I need to contact Kate and Recoil. I want to alert him." Quinn replied.

"Did you hear me?" Betty reached over and touched his arm. "When you have a chance pull over, I want a sweater from the truck."

Quinn glanced in the review mirror, pulled to the side of the highway and stepped out into the noticeably cooler air. He lifted the trunk lid and retrieved both Betty's and his sweater. Climbing back in he handed Betty her sweater and watched as a black sedan passed driving slower than all the other traffic.

When he pulled back onto the Highway Betty said, "Stop at the first place you think will have a phone. You can call Kate and Recoil. And I can get The Major's number from Kate and call him. I want to get this idea that he is somehow behind this out of the way."

"You don't have the Major's number?" Quinn said, unthinking.

"Everything I had was stolen, down to my underwear," Betty said, still trying to dissolve that somehow Quinn felt she was responsible.

Quinn spotted a sign that said Via Luigi Cardona two kilometers and pulled off when he arrived. He spotted a place to purchase gasoline and some food to carry in the car and pulled in. When the car was serviced, the three made their way to the phones.

Kate was not home to receive the call. Quinn reached Recoil. "Listen, I want you to be on higher alert. We have heard that an Indian gang may be interested in us but do not know any facts. If you have to, sleep in your car outside her place of work and outside her house at night." Quinn told him.

"OK," Recoil told him.

"Hang on," Betty wants to talk to you.

"Hi, ah, Recoil? In the kitchen drawer nearest the phone is an address book. Look at it under Major Garrity. Yes, M. And give me the number, please. Yes, I have a pencil." There was a pause while he found the address book and Betty wrote the number. "Thank you." She hung up and made the call.

"Hello Major, this is Betty Atwood, I mean Moosebroker, Betty Moosebroker. Quinn wants to talk to you." She turned abruptly and handed Quinn the phone.

"Hi Quinn, I take it you got my telegram? Listen, old boy, I don't want to unnecessarily alarm you but, I caught my manservant, former manservant that is, on a phone extension. He was telling someone about some precious diamonds that might be easily obtained. Money is so scarce in India that what seems like a small sum to us may very well feed a family there for years. These can be nasty fellows. Quinn are you there?" The Major uncharacteristically paused.

"Yes, I am here. Can you tell me anything about this gang?" Quinn asked.

"From what I heard, they don't like to lose. But I cannot tell you anything specific. Listen, I have connections all over the world, so if you run into more trouble than you feel you can handle call me. Let me talk to Betty, if you don't mind." The Major asked. Quinn handed Betty the phone.

"Hello Betty, I think he understands now. Sorry, if the message caused any harm. Be well and I will see the two of you when you return home." The Major hung up and went back to sleep wishing he was out on an adventure.

Betty hung the phone up and turned to Quinn. "There were some shops we passed on the way here. I have to buy warmer clothes this crisp air cuts right through these summer dresses I picked out."

Once their wardrobes were supplemented, they returned to SS340 and climbed towards Berne.

The two men with cinnamon skin serviced their black sedan at the same station where Quinn had filled up. They also used the phone to make an International call.

Quinn felt a little hot under the collar. The Seersucker Shirt, all of a sudden, chafed his neck. “My cop nose is irritated. Have you noticed a black sedan that keeps appearing and seemingly out of place?”

Betty looked around, “No, no, I have not.” She strained her neck to the rear window. “I’ll keep an eye out. Do you want me to drive for awhile?”

Hours later they arrived in Berne and found a hotel for the night. Both Quinn and Betty walked Duncan-Waffle together at Betty’s insistence. When they returned to the room, Betty showered with Quinn on guard.

Once all were clean and fed and again back in the room Betty was rummaging around in her new purse. She spotted Avice’s invitation and saw that the gala was in two days time in Stuttgart. She unfolded her pocket map that she had bought to try and keep things straight in her mind and saw that Stuttgart was not that far from Berne. “Quinn, let’s take a little detour, to Stuttgart. Remember Avice’s invitation to the party. I’d like to go.” Betty handed the invitation to Quinn, who never actually took a good look at it.

“You know all the aristocratic types are not going to be as friendly as Avice, Aldous, and Sophie?” Quinn said as Duncan wagged his tail at the mention of Sophie. “It could be boring.”

“How many chances are we every going to get to go to a party at a castle?” Betty walked over and kissed him. “Please.” She playfully batted her eyelids.

Quinn reached over and turned out the lights.

In the morning, Quinn put their bags in the car and then with Betty at his side walked Duncan-Waffles before they started out. Quinn made mental notes of the cars parked nearby. The two felt good wearing their new leather jackets. Quinn climbed behind the wheel and they navigated their way toward Highway A81.

Betty studying the map said, “We have to have lunch in Zurich. Don’t you think?”

After a four-hour drive, on which the couple had passed two castles, they reached Zurich. Betty and Quinn got out and stretched their legs. Betty turned in a circle. Standing on the cobblestone street, she felt she could have been transported back hundreds of years. There were shops in every direction and even better than that there were restaurants and cafes on every corner.

“Let’s get Duncan walked and then grab something to eat.” Betty offered as she closed and locked the car door.

“Take a close look around; see if you can spot anything out of place, and also to remember where we parked.” He twisted his waist left and right trying to get his blood circulating after the long drive. His legs were asleep and he used caution as he took his first few steps.

“We should switch off on the driving so you don’t get so worn out. Starting in the morning, I’ll take a two-hour shift then we will change back and forth. What do you say?” Betty sneezed.

“Gesundheit.”

A Quinn & Betty Moosebroker Mystery (8)

Stuttgart

"Would you look at this driveway," Betty said while Quinn was driving up it and feeling apprehensive.

"Yes, I am glad I do not have to maintain this place. This is much more than I was expecting." Quinn added as he parked to the side of the entrance.

Heath was responsible for greeting the guests at the door. He opened the door as Quinn and Betty approached with Duncan near her feet. "Yes, can I help you?" Heath asked trying to conceal his thoughts.

"We're here at the invitation of Avice," Betty handed him their invitation.

"Oh my. Will you wait here a moment?" He said, leaving the door open.

"At least, he did not slam the door in our faces," Quinn winked at Betty and glanced at the manicured lawns.

In a moment or two, Avice appeared. "Oh, Betty, you made it. Sophie will be so happy to see Duncan. Come in. You two are early?"

"I mistakenly thought we could be of some help," Betty told her.

"I think everything is under control." Avice made a face. "Where are your costumes?"

Quinn raised an eyebrow and an odd look came over Betty's face. "Costumes?" She asked.

Avice turned to Heath, who was hoping to show these two to the door and said, "Show Mr. Moosebroker to the room were some older costumes are waiting, maybe he can find something." She turned to Betty, "Come with me, I am sure I can find something for you, we are about the same size." She put her hand out and Betty took it as she watched Quinn follow the butler.

Betty and Avice climbed two flights of stairs and they entered a room as large as her house. Avice walked to a room-sized closet as Betty followed. “Get out of that dress and try this on, I think it will fit. It might be a little snug at the top, but we will see.”

Betty lowered the zipper and stepped out of her dress looking for a hanger.

“Oh, here,” Avice said. Betty’s necklace held her attention.

Betty feeling just a touch conscious smiled and took the hanger and put it up. Then she took the gossamer gown and pulled it over her head with Avice’s help.

“How does that feel?” Avice asked. “You look beautiful. You did not let on you were an aristocrat.”

She caught her next words. Then began, “We were not sure you were going to attend. I’m sorry most of the rooms here are reserved. I can offer you space in the dungeon, or there is a bed in the belfry.”

“I’ll speak to Quinn and see what he thinks. I am sure he does not expect to spend the night.” Betty told her feeling suddenly like Cinderella. She had no shoes that would go with this gown, but the gown was long enough she thought it would work out. She was not one for glass slippers. “Why do you say I am an aristocrat?” Betty ventured.

“You didn’t strike me as one. You are so friendly. Most aristocrats feel antediluvian which is to say their families were here before the great flood of Bible times. Listen, I could not help but notice you are wearing a crowned key around your neck. Ah,” she stopped. “Listen, we are going to have to talk later. Can you find your way back downstairs?”

“Yes, thank you,” Betty said watching her hostess rush out. She found a brush in her purse and stood looking at herself in a full-length mirror. She brushed her hair while wondering who this woman in the mirror was.

Heath stood behind Quinn adjusting the chainmail vest over an itchy undergarment. He begrudgingly wore the tight, dusty gray pants and the baldrics which supported his sword. He struck a menacing figure when he adorned the cowl. “Will that be all Sir?” Heath asked and headed for the door without waiting for the answer.

"Yes, thank you," Quinn squirmed.

There was a tap on the door of the room where Betty stood. She turned as a short man, wearing wire-rimmed glasses and a court jester costume walked in carrying his hat under his arm. "I understand you to have a crowned key. Can we meet later tonight about it?"

"Yes, I suppose so." Betty answered and the man left the room beaming his best smile.

Betty walked to the door and followed him out. She turned and walked down the corridor toward the stairs. She quietly hoped that Quinn would be at the bottom of the stairs to watch her walk in her borrowed gown.

Betty found Quinn, and Heath directed them to a room where drinks were being served to some other guests who had arrived early.

Quinn and Betty sat at a table at the far end of the room with drinks in front of them. As Quinn looked over the federative group before him, he wondered what Betty and he were doing there.

"Listen, Quinn, while I was changing Avice noticed the key around my neck. She was cautious at first then she asked about it. Then only a few moments after she left me a man entered the room and inquired about the key and asked that we talk to him about it later this evening." After a pause, she said, "Quinn she thinks we are aristocrats."

A man who was at the wet bar walked over and said to Betty, "Hello, I am Duke Jeffery Conrad of Muscovy. I don't remember seeing you at one of these. Perhaps we can get together later."

"And perhaps, not," Quinn interjected.

The man straightened and walked back to the bar just as Aldus entered the room. Upon seeing Quinn and Betty, he walked over and greeted them. "Avice told me you were here," he told Betty. "Hello, Quinn, sorry about the confusion regarding the invitation. At least, we do not have to wear these silly things too often. I have to go talk to some of the other guests, let's try and catch up later."

Heath was greeting more guests as Avice walked into the room where Quinn and Betty sat. She walked over to Betty and asked Quinn if she could steal her for a minute or two. Betty stood and the two walked a few feet away from Quinn and the others. “Have you decided if you are staying or not? I have to tell you that this group feels entitled like no other. The corridors will be very busy in the early morning hours as they all attend their liaisons. They will all assume you are participating if you stay. It can get very intense. Do you understand?”

Betty acknowledged that she understood and Avice drew closer and kissed her on the cheek.

Betty’s heart rate had increased as she walked back to Quinn. She picked up a drink that had been sat in front of her and took a sip. The blush had left her cheeks. She got close to Quinn’s ear. “I think we have been invited to an orgy.” She swallowed hard, “I think I accepted an invitation for later.” She moved back and laughed to herself and Quinn. “Where is Duncan-Waffles?” She asked.

“Last I saw of him he was with Sophie. Whose offer did you accept for a suitor? Was it a Count, Duke, Prince, perhaps an Earl? There is plenty of good hunting here.” He smiled at her.

“You silly. Only you.” Betty resolved to be more cautious with her listening skills this evening.

A Quinn & Betty Moosebroker Mystery (9)

The sounds of the kettle drums shivered along the walls. The last of the guest paraded up the drive and filled the large room. Quinn and Betty watched the promenade, the costumes ranged from regal to humorous. “We should mingle,” Betty told Quinn. “Watch yourself,” she told him with a wink and she went in search of the little man that may offer some information about the crowned key.

Quinn watched her walk away. He was left wearing chainmail and this sword supported over his shoulder, and the shirt itched. He went and found the table where there was plenty of finger food and watched the who-is-who, and what-is-what of the gathering.

Two men about the size of Quinn and wearing tunics with a large red cross from the sternum to mid femur approached him. Their Norman helmets looked very uncomfortable to Quinn. “Follow us,” the man who approached from his right said.

Quinn glanced from his right to his left looking for Betty to make sure she was alright. Quinn followed the first man as the second one followed. “We are from The House of Savoy. I am Count Alberto and the chap following you is Count Rivera.” After climbing a flight of stairs, the Alberto turned down a corridor and opened a door.

Rivera took off his helmet and opened a suitcase. The man smiled finding what he was looking for. He picked up a cotton tunic and handed it to Quinn. “That Heath character has a nasty streak in him. I bet that shirt itches terribly, it has a coarse weave. Try this on it should fit.”

“I am not sure I can get this chainmail and collars off by myself,” Quinn told him.

Count Alberto walked over and undid the fastener of the chainmail shoulder harness then he took the shirt by the tail and raised it over Quinn’s head. “You haven’t told us your name,” Alberto said.

“Quinn, Quinn Moosebroker from America,” he said.

Alberto glanced at Rivera, “Is that a bullet hole scar on your back?”

"Yes, I was shot in the line of duty. I was a police officer," Quinn told him.

Rivera sat on the bed. "How do you happen to be here at this party?" His intentions evaporating with the words police officer.

Quinn turned toward Alberto, "It went right through." Pointing to the entry wound. And to Rivera, "We were fortunate to meet Avice and Aldus in Italy a couple of weeks ago and they were kind enough to offer an invitation. Avice really took to my wife, Betty."

"Put your arms up, we'll get this tunic on you, the cloth is much softer." Alberto helped Quinn into the awkward garment.

Rivera sighed and reached for his helmet and put it back on. "Let's get back down to the party."

At the bottom of the stairs, Quinn again thanked them for the loan of the tunic. He was much more comfortable. "I am going to go and find Betty."
"Enjoy your evening Quinn," Count Alberto said parting ways. And to Rivera, he said, "Pity."

Clearview Terrace

Kate Moosebroker sat at her kitchen table enjoying the quiet misty morning hours. The car carrying six nutmeg skin colored men that were responsible for twenty-five percent of the crime in Clearview Terrace pulled to the curb in front of the house and got out. The leader, the former manservant of Major Garrity, checked a piece of paper to make sure they were at the right address. They intended to search the house for the hidden diamonds.

The sound of a car door closing roused Recoil from his slumber sitting at the wheel of Quinn's 1946 wood-paneled Town and Country, which was his mobile home while serving as unseen bodyguard to Kate at Quinn's request.

Recoil rubbed his eyes, and as they cleared, he saw one of the men's feet take a step onto Kate's property. In an instant, his combat boot clad feet hit the pavement. A vale of darkness drew around him as he rushed soundlessly toward this small band of men.

There was a pall of confusion as the first boy went down with a blow to his spleen that left him crying. The second turning quickly at hearing the gasp of his cousin was met with a boot to the knee. The sound of the snap brought the other four down on him.

Kate jumped to her feet and looked out the window. First she thought to get her dad's service revolver, but instead grabbed a black rot iron skillet and went to the door.

Recoil's two rotations in Vietnam had honed his skills at hurting people. An open palmed jab to the nose of the third assailant demonstrated how Recoil received his nickname, as the jab lifted the man off his feet and he fell flat on the ground.

The manservant produced a knife.

Seeing this Kate rushed up behind him and smashed the knife-wielding man over the back of the head.

Blue-red orbs filled the twilight hour with surreal shadow and light as Officer Harcourt pulled his police cruiser in front of the car the last two assailants seeing the rout were making haste to reach. Kate's neighbor had reported a disturbance.

Kate realized she was standing barefoot on the lawn wearing her night slip and holding a frying pan and went in and donned her robe and returned to the yard.

Officer Harcourt escorted five of the men and crammed them into the back of his cruiser and called an ambulance for the one with the broken leg.

Once Officer Harcourt got them loaded into the car, he walked over to Recoil. The two men sized each other up. Recoil extended his hand, "5th Special Forces Group."

Harcourt paused a moment, then put his hand out, "101st Airborne Division." Recoil was asked a few questions and seeing Quinn's car, Harcourt felt Recoil's story was collaborated and let him go. Then he walked over to talk to Kate.

Stuttgart

Betty and Quinn danced together in a large room filled with guests of Avice and Aldus. After three dances, Quinn begged for a break and went and found a seat to rest his feet. He was only there a moment when a plump Duchess spotted him and made a beeline towards him.

Betty did not make it off the dance floor before she was approached for a dance. The 'Prince Charming' holding her a bit too closely was tall with a well-groomed white beard trimmed close to his face. Just as he finished whispering in her ear causing a slight flush to rush to her cheeks Avice appeared by her side followed closely by the Court Jester wearing red and black tights that were too tight. "Hi," Betty said. "I am feeling a little flustered," she told Avice.

Avice took her left hand and elbow and took a step away, "He can be a bit much I'm afraid. I'm told he is a good lover."

The Court Jester said to Betty, "Can we go somewhere?"

Betty looked at Avice, who said, "I'll go with you. I can sneak away for a few moments." The three made their way out of the room unseen by Quinn.

Avice lead Betty up to the room where she had helped Betty into her gown and where Betty had first seen the Court Jester and had her sit on the bed. Then she sat down next to her. The Court Jester sat on the other side of Betty and too close.

"Can I see it?" Jester asked.

Betty could not reach the chain with the dress buttoned up the back and started to reach around to unbutton a couple of buttons. Avice reached back and undid several buttons making the front of the dress droop. Betty became self-conscious with the Jester sitting there staring at her, her back exposed. She reached the chain and brought out the key.

The Jester, unthinking, reached for it and balanced it in his palm; further encroaching Betty's space. "This is a replica of the crown of Leopold III, King of the Belgians." He stifled the question, 'are you part of the Royal family of Belgium?' He put his other hand on Betty's leg as he brought his face close to the key.

The slap was quick and hard and as Betty stood her dress dropped further. Avice was on her feet with her hand on Betty's bareback trying to recover the bodice to its proper place.

The Jester rubbed his face. Not the first time he had been slapped, but never quite so hard. "Perhaps you should take the chain off for me to take a look at that key," he said still rubbing the side of his face. He saw Betty hesitate. "If I can see the numbers on the shank, perhaps I can tell you what city you are going to find your treasure. I don't wish to be slapped again, so if you could hand it to me. Avice will protect you." He smiled, but it was not a charming smile.

Betty was regaining her composure, yet still did not like being in a bedroom with this man wearing black and red tights, costume party or not. She handed Jester the key.

He brought it close to his face to read the numbers. "You are to search the city of Ghent in Belgium. It will be a small shop. One a sole proprietor would operate. A tobacco shop, or perhaps a woodworker's shop, something of that nature. It will not be on any main street. Present the key and you will be handed a box of some kind. Jester took a deep breath, took the offending slapping hand and placed the key into it. He closed the key in her hand and held her hand in both his hands then leaned in and kissed Betty and stepped away saying, 'for services rendered," walking toward the door.

"I have two hands you know," Betty told him.

"Yes, I know," He said as the door closed behind him.

"I have to get back to my guests, are you going to be OK?" She started to button Betty's dress.

"Don't, I think I am going to change. Avice, thank you so much for the invitation, I am going to gather up Quinn." She reached over and gave Avice a hug and kiss on the cheek. Betty changed, putting the key back in the safe.

Downstairs back in her Italian clothes and new leather jacket she searched for Quinn. He was hiding in the bar having escaped the Duchess. "What do you say if we call it a night?" She told Quinn, who wondered why she had changed.

"Fine by me. Let me get out of this Crusader's outfit and I will be right down." He walked away.

"Scotch and soda," she said to the bartender.

Ten minutes later Quinn returned and took Betty by the arm and led her to the front door. They opened it and went through. The couple took two steps outside and Betty stopped. She put two fingers to her lips and whistled. Then took two steps back and again opened the door to the castle.

Duncan-Waffles leaped off of Sophie's bed and raced down the hall to the amusement of many of the guests and raced to the call of his momma. Once outside and into the car with Quinn behind the wheel with their baby on momma's lap, Quinn asked, "Where to?"

Betty said, "Kind sir," throwing an imaginary shawl over her shoulder, "straight on 'til morning."

A Quinn & Betty Moosebroker Mystery (10)

The quiet hours weighed on Quinn as Betty slept at his side in the front seat of the car traveling to Ghent. He spotted a rest area near Luxembourg City and pulled in to give himself and Duncan-Waffles a walk. He pulled the car near some benches and he and Duncan took a stroll then returned to the car to sleep.

Betty woke to the sound of a car door in the distance and spied the black sedan that Quinn had mentioned. She watched as two men climbed out and stretched. They seemed to consult each other then walked over to the facility that said 'Showers.'

Betty watched as the two men paid the matronly attendant for the rental of towels and then go inside. Duncan sat up when Betty silently opened the car door then he went back to sleep. She went to the attendant and after a minute of negotiation and exchange of a few dollars, the attendant went off for a smoke.

Betty now wearing the attendant's smock pushed an empty mop bucket inside using the handle of the loaned mop. She could hear the two in the stalls showering. She spotted their stacked clothes and the towels sitting on top of them and grabbed them and stuffed them in the mop bucket. She quietly left them to their showers.

She went to their car and with a bobby pin let the air from their tires. She checked all the doors and finding one open reached inside and grabbed two small bags that contained the rest of the two cinnamon-skinned men's clothing. She then locked the doors of the car.

Moving quickly back to Quinn and Duncan she put the stuff in the back seat and woke Quinn. "Trade places with me, I feel like driving," she told him.

Without question, Quinn climbed out and swapped places. Betty took the wheel feeling jubilant and thought, *turnaround is fair play.* Miles later, notified by the entertained rest stop attendant, who enjoyed her shift, Luxembourg City Police were making an arrest of two angry young men for indecent exposure as Betty pulled off the road and tossed their belongings in a ditch.

Ghent

Lying across the bed Betty flipped the pages of the travel brochure she had picked up in the lobby when the three checked in. “It says here that a Godfrey of Bouillon came from around here and he was one of the leaders of the First Crusade. Quinn, you may have been dressed as the first ruler of Jerusalem last night.” She rolled over and smiled at him. “It also says that Duke Philip of Good is the one that captured Joan of Arc and turned her over to the Bishop of Beauvais. Did you know that?”

Quinn put on his Alpine hat. “No. No, I didn’t. I do know that the courtyard we walked through last night looks like a nice place to have a cup of coffee and maybe a pastry; after we walk Duncan, of course. Come on now, get up.”

After their morning refreshment, the two began their search. Betty found a phone book and wrote down the addresses of the tobacco shops. She remembered the Major relaying the story of the Colonel and thought it a good place to start based on the Jester’s information.

In the third shop, after the crowned-key was shown with merely a flicker of interest the man in the shop asked Quinn, “If you were looking for something special I have just received a supply that a man of your standing may be interested in.”

“Please, what is it?” Quinn said.

Betty watched with interest as the crowned-key seemed to transmit something to Europeans that was missing in America.

The man stepped into the back of his shop and brought back a small brick wrapped in gold paper stamped *Pur Semois* and set it in front of Quinn. “It is expensive, but you will find it most satisfying. It is Belgium tobacco, prepared by hand near here in the Semois Valley. You won’t find it anywhere else.”

Quinn reached into his jacket pocket and drew his pipe and filled it from the brick. A mixture both rich and savory filled his mouth. The smoke was husky and earthen and floral all at once. Quinn was elevated to fantasy and asked to purchase a second brick. He was brought a second from the back, this one stamped *Reserve du Patron* and was assured he would be as pleased with this as the first.

"Sir," began the shopkeeper, he paused and thought a moment. "At the end of this street is a bicycle rental shop." Handing Quinn a card he continued, "Tell the proprietor I sent you, and tell him you are looking for the Violin Maker. He and I have been friends for thirty years. It is about two-mile ride down a path that follows the canal."

Betty's heart raced as they stepped out the door of the shop. "Quinn, this could be it."

Quinn put his arm around Betty and with Duncan-Waffles clearly in the lead the three walked to the bicycle shop.

With the bikes rented and the directions obtained the three rode along the tree covered path along the canal. Quinn's senses were inundated with the Viridian, mantis, and mint of the leaves lapping into the Brandeis blue, sapphire and shades of cyan of the water. The cool air was crisp and the pathway was smooth. Duncan was sitting comfortably in a basket on the front of Betty's bike; they passed houseboats moored to the banks. They waved at the young hippies and the hippies waved back.

"Quinn?" Betty called ahead the few feet he was in front of her. She stopped the bike and leaned on one leg as she waited for Quinn to respond.

When Quinn felt she was no longer right near him, he stopped and circled around. "What is it?"

"Let's not go on. If we go on our adventure will be all over." Betty said as Duncan watched wondering why they stopped.

Quinn stepped off the bike and walked it by Betty's side. "Isn't this why we came all this way?"

"Moose, we have had a wonderful time. Ever since we met, there has been one adventure after another. Why, we have hardly been home at all. I can hardly remember the last time I watched TV." She looked at him trying to see if she was reaching him.

"To my thinking the adventure can be over right here, or a mile from here." He got back on his bike. "Let's go see what that key is all about." He pushed off.

Betty was quiet the last mile. She pulled to a stop right behind Quinn and they both stepped off their bikes at the same time. She took Duncan from the basket and he ran in circles getting his circulation restored. When Duncan returned to her side, she took a leash and put it on him. She took the key from its resting place all these weeks and handed it back to Quinn.

Quinn hesitated but took the key and knocked at the door of the little cottage overgrown with vines.

The door opened slowly and there before them was a stooped man with gray hair and gray beard. Quinn peered passed him into a dim workshop.

The man backed up and invited them inside. Quinn and Betty were immediately taken with the aroma of maple wood shavings, and spruce. There were blocks of wood resting in trays leaning against the wall to air dry. There were sharp knives and calipers everywhere. There were bending irons and peg shavers on benches and tables. There were purfling scribes and purfling picks standing in beer mugs.

Betty stared along the edges of the ceiling were violins hung. The glimmer of wood russet color and rust sent waves along copper and Sienna and bronze of these artistic creations. There were bowls filled with bridges and tuning pegs. Betty felt reverent and silently forgave Quinn for insisting on coming. She would never forget this room.

“Have you come to buy a violin?” The old man asked.

Quinn responded by showing the old man the crowned-key.

The knurled fingers of the old man took the key and walked through a door to another room as Quinn and Betty waited patiently.

A few moments later the gentleman returned and walked close to Quinn and whispered. Then he turned and Quinn followed him. Betty and Duncan waited.

Quinn was led to the room and he saw a pry bar lying on the floor. The old man got down on his knees and invited Quinn to follow. The old man no longer had the strength to pry up the wooden planks hiding their treasure.

He pointed to the slat that needed Quinn's strength. A moment later both men were standing. Quinn lifted a small heavy hand polished box with a carving of a violin on the lid. They both returned to the workshop where Betty and Duncan anxiously awaited.

"Open it," Betty said.

Quinn again hesitated. But set the box down and looked at the lid not seeing how the box opened.

The old man stepped closer and peered at the box. He turned it up on its side and then reached over and pushed at a dark corner which swiveled releasing the lid.

Quinn stepped back and turned up the lid and the three of them watched as handfuls of Belgium 20 Francs Gold pieces spilled onto the table. Quinn picked up one and found it dated 1914.

Quinn thanked the man. Betty started returning the coins to the box and learned the catch mechanism.

"How much for that violin?" Betty asked. "And that one?" She said pointing.

Quinn was amused and remained silent.

In a few moments, Quinn was on his bike and held Duncan's leash. Betty was on her bike with a basket holding violins. They were back on a quiet path along a canal in Belgium as the sun twisted and tossed through the leaves as Duncan happily trotted by their sides.

The end

www.ingramcontent.com/pod-product-compliance
Lightning Source LLC
LaVergne TN
LVHW020655110826
845149LV00012B/2008

* 9 7 8 0 9 8 6 0 1 1 4 3 6 *